Praise for the *Steel Girls* series:

'A riveting saga about love, courage and, above all, female friendship'
Best

'A lovely read'
Bella

'Rich, evocative and spellbinding . . . prepare to be swept back in time'
Kate Thompson

'A heart-warming story perfect for saga lovers'
Nancy Revell

'A heart-warming tale of the brave women who stepped up to become the backbone of Sheffield's steel industry during the Second World War'
Yours

'A sweeping tale of friendship and hope against the odds'
My Weekly

'A heartwarming, yet moving and poignant tale, of courage, friendship and hope'
Milly Johnson

'A tale of friendship, hope and love. I couldn't put it down'
Alexandra Walsh

'This is storytelling at its most vibrant and closely researched . . . if you love sagas, you'll love the Steel Girls!'
Betty Walker

Michelle Rawlins is an award-winning freelance journalist with over twenty-five years' experience working in print and digital media. After learning her trade, Michelle began her freelance career writing for national newspapers and women's magazines concentrating on real-life stories – living by the mantra: 'It's always the most ordinary people who have the most extraordinary stories.' Michelle currently teaches journalism at the University of Sheffield.

She is the author of *Women of Steel* and *The Steel Girls* was her debut novel. You can follow Michelle on X @ Mrawlins1974 and on Facebook/MichelleRawlinsAuthor.

The Steel Girls series:
The Steel Girls
Christmas Hope for the Steel Girls
Steel Girls on the Home Front
Steel Girls at War
Steel Girls in the Blitz
Joy for the Steel Girls

Joy for the
Steel Girls

Michelle Rawlins

ONE PLACE. MANY STORIES

HQ
An imprint of HarperCollins*Publishers* Ltd
1 London Bridge Street
London SE1 9GF

www.harpercollins.co.uk

HarperCollins*Publishers*
Macken House, 39/40 Mayor Street Upper
Dublin 1, D01 C9W8, Ireland

This edition 2025

1
First published in Great Britain by HQ,
an imprint of HarperCollins*Publishers* Ltd 2025

Copyright © Michelle Rawlins 2025

Michelle Rawlins asserts the moral right to be identified as the author of this work.
A catalogue record for this book is available from the British Library.

ISBN: 9780008598563

Typeset in Sabon by HarperCollins*Publishers* India

This novel is entirely a work of fiction. The names, characters and incidents portrayed in it are the work of the author's imagination. Any resemblance to actual persons, living or dead, events or localities is entirely coincidental.

All rights reserved. No part of this publication may be reproduced, stored in a retrieval system, or transmitted, in any form or by any means, electronic, mechanical, photocopying, recording or otherwise, without the prior written permission of the publishers.

Without limiting the author's and publisher's exclusive rights, any unauthorised use of this publication to train generative artificial intelligence (AI) technologies is expressly prohibited. HarperCollins also exercise their rights under Article 4(3) of the Digital Single Market Directive 2019/790 and expressly reserve this publication from the text and data mining exception.

Printed and bound in the UK using 100% Renewable
Electricity by CPI Group (UK) Ltd

This book contains FSC™ certified paper and other controlled sources to ensure responsible forest management.

For more information visit: www.harpercollins.co.uk/green

*To my wonderful children, Archie & Tilly,
who fill my heart with joy.*

Chapter 1

Friday, 7 February 1941

'I hope m' tea's ready.'

Hattie and her mum tensed as the drunken demand travelled from the back door into the kitchen.

'Here we go again,' Hattie muttered, silently sighing, instinctively knowing the peaceful evening she had hoped to share with her mum would be ruined.

'It's just in the pan,' Diane said, already on her feet, failing to disguise the anxiety she was feeling.

'It better be hot,' Vinny grunted as he dropped into one of the kitchen chairs, the stench of alcohol emanating throughout the small room.

'I've kept it warm,' Diane affirmed, as she scooped a ladleful of chicken broth from the pan into a bowl before tentatively placing it on the table in front of Vinny.

'What's this slop?' He snarled in disgust. Diane had bought as much meat as she could with the rations and money she had, but she'd known it wouldn't be enough to satisfy her husband. Nothing ever was.

'It's tasty, Dad,' Hattie said, jumping to the defence of her worn-out mum.

'It's tasty, Dad,' Vinny whined, mocking and glaring at his daughter, not even attempting to disguise the look of contempt in his eyes, which were glassy and bloodshot due to the amount of alcohol he'd consumed. 'I might have known you would stick your two pence worth in.'

Hattie bit her tongue, knowing whatever she said next would just enrage her dad further. Neither she nor her mum were strangers to Vinny's drunken rants. She had lost count of the number of times her dad had come home drunk from the local boozer, shouting his demands and spurting out a tirade of insults.

'I've cut you up some fresh bread too,' Diane said, trying to avert another row, as she put down a chipped saucer holding the heel of a loaf she'd made the night before.

'No butter?' Vinny barked, spit spraying across the table. 'What does a man have to do to get a bloody decent meal in this house?'

Hattie frowned, wishing she had the courage to stand up to her dad. She hated seeing how he treated her mum. His selfish, self-centred attitude was the very reason her poor mum scrimped together every penny she could to pay the bills. For years Diane had robbed Peter to pay Paul. The only reason Vinny had allowed his wife to take a job in the canteen at Vickers, where Hattie worked as a turner, was because she would bring more money home than her previous jobs as a cleaner.

'Did yer get paid today?' Vinny demanded as he noisily slurped a mouthful of his tea.

'I did.' She nodded, knowing there wouldn't be much left after Vinny took what he wanted, with little regard to the bills that needed paying.

'And I hope you have tipped up yer keep,' Vinny growled, glaring at Hattie, who was sat across the table.

'Of course,' Hattie replied, forcing a smile, hiding the disgust she felt at her dad's greed.

'I should think so too. You have an easy ride here.'

Hattie bit her lip. Her anger turning to hurt. *How had her dad become so hostile?* He hadn't always been so nasty. For years he had been the perfect doting father, but it had been quite some time since he resembled the man that would read her bedtime stories as she curled up on his knee. Over recent years, her dad's drinking had got to the point where he wouldn't get through a single day without seeing the bottom of an empty glass. Diane had explained it was his way of blocking out what he'd seen in the Great War.

Initially Hattie had felt sorry for her dad, but it was hard to remain sympathetic when he was so cruel. What she really wanted to do was stand up to his barrage of abuse, but no matter how many times she vowed to tell her dad he was being selfish, she could never muster up the courage.

Instead, it was her mum who tried, as gently as possible, to appease him.

'Leave her be, Vinny,' Diane interjected, right on cue, feeling more protective than ever since she had discovered Hattie was pregnant. They hadn't told Vinny yet. Hattie was adamant the next person to know should be her husband, John, but like so many other young men, he had signed up to the war effort and was currently posted on Salisbury Plain.

'Are you telling me what I can and can't do in my own house?' Vinny stormed, his unpredictable temper erupting.

'No, luv . . .'

But it was too late. Before Diane could calm her red-faced husband, he was on his feet. Slamming his clenched fists on the table, Vinny glared at Diane.

'You are always protecting that girl,' he ranted. 'I have every bloody right to ask her about her rent.'

'Dad, it's fine,' Hattie said, just wanting to stop the row from escalating.

'Oh, here we go,' Vinny shouted, the blood vessels in his eyes ready to pop. 'I might have known the two of yer would stick together and gang up against me.'

'We're not,' Diane said gently.

But her attempts at reconciliation were ignored.

'Stop yer backtracking,' Vinny snorted, pushing his chair so forcefully it toppled backwards onto the stone floor.

Hattie momentarily clenched her eyes shut. How on

earth could she bring a child into the world and risk her baby being exposed to her father's unpredictable mood swings?

'Where's yer chuffin' wages? I'm going somewhere where I can get a decent bit of scran and not have to be lectured.'

Hattie glanced at her mum. They both knew there was no point in protesting. The more they objected to Vinny spending their hard-earned wages, the angrier he would get.

'On the mantelpiece,' Diane whispered, resigned to the fact she would now have even less money to pay the bills and buy food for the week.

'It better all be there,' Vinny warned, pushing his barely eaten bowl of chicken broth across the table. As Diane went to stop it, before the meal ended up all over the kitchen floor, Vinny barged into her, his thick elbow catching the side of his wife's slender body.

'Ow,' Diane gasped, the heavy knock sending her sideways.

'Oh, give over,' Vinny grunted, 'I barely touched yer.'

And he stormed out of the room, not once stopping to look back at his wife who was now keeled over in agony.

'Mum,' Hattie cried, rushing to Diane's side. 'Are you okay?'

'It's nothing, luv. I'll be okay in a second.'

But guilt pierced through Hattie for not standing up to her dad. Despite her mum's insistence she was all right,

Hattie knew she was once again putting on a brave face in a bid to protect her.

'Come and sit down,' Hattie said, gently ushering her mum to one of the still-standing chairs, just as the front door opened and then was slammed shut.

'I doubt Dad will be back for a while.'

'Thanks, luv,' Diane whispered, catching her breath, acutely aware, by the pain she was in, that she would end up with a nasty bruise on her ribs. The only saving grace was that it wouldn't be visible and she wouldn't have to answer any awkward questions at work.

Chapter 2

Friday, 14 February 1941

'Are you all right, duck?' Dolly asked Hattie, as she handed over her traditional Friday fayre of mince and onion pie and mash. 'Yer mum says you have been more tired than usual the last few weeks.'

'I think it's the time of year,' Hattie replied, not convinced Dolly believed her white lie, the lack of conviction in her voice a mirror image of her depleted energy levels. She had barely slept since her dad's outburst a week ago. 'It's dark when I get up and dark when I get home,' Hattie added, hoping her explanation was convincing. 'It makes you feel tired, doesn't it?'

'It does that,' Dolly agreed. 'But just you take it steady. You have your work cut out on the factory floor. You need yer wits about yer.'

'Thanks, Dolly. I will,' Hattie promised, but as she walked over to the table where she and her friends all gathered for dinner, she was grateful she wouldn't have to keep her secret for much longer. Not only had she been on tenterhooks since her dad's drunken explosion, but she also still hadn't told anyone, apart from her mum, that she was pregnant. Her husband, John, had been granted forty-eight hours' weekend leave and it was only a matter of hours before she could clap eyes on him for the first time since they'd married four months earlier. Ever since she had realized she was expecting, Hattie had been desperate to tell John their news, but she was waiting to see him in person, so she could watch his reaction. Hattie was also hoping her husband would calm her nerves and placate her ever-increasing fears. It wasn't that she wasn't excited, far from it, but life at home had become unbearable with her drunk of a father, and Hattie was terrified she and her unborn baby would end up on the receiving end of his volatile temper. As the previous week's explosion had revealed, Vinny's mood swings had become increasingly erratic, his drinking now a daily occurrence, and when he didn't collapse through the door, he wasn't shy in reminding Hattie and her mum that he could use his fists to let them know he was still *the master of the house*. Not only that, when the war had first broken out, Hattie, like all her friends, had hoped that it would be short-lived and that John would be back in Sheffield soon enough. Her hopes, like those of so many others, had been quickly dashed. And now, after the barrage of bombs that Hitler's Luftwaffe had rained down on the city, alongside the rest of the country at the end of last year, Hattie had resigned herself to the fact that the assault playing out across Europe and North Africa was far from over.

'Hattie. I've saved you a chair,' Patty called out, pulling her friend out of her melancholy state and back to the moment.

'Thank you. How's your morning been?'

'Oh. Same as ever,' Patty sighed. 'Non-stop. I barely came up for breath. How about you?'

'It's certainly been full-on. I'm happy for a cup of tea and a break.'

'I'll second that,' Daisy interjected. 'I thought dinner time would never come.'

'How's your mum doing since she came back?' Patty asked Daisy. 'Has she been okay this week?'

'Actually, I think it's helping. She's still in a state of shock but having some routine is good for her.'

'That's good,' Hattie commented. 'You have all had so much to cope with.'

'We have, but we're not alone and we have to keep going. We can't do anything but.'

'You are all doing remarkably well,' Betty, who was sat next to her friend, commented.

'Thanks to all of you, and Ivy.'

After Daisy's dad, Alf, had been killed during the Sheffield Blitz two months earlier and their home severely damaged, Ivy and Frank had insisted that Daisy, her two younger sisters and their mum move in with them. Ivy had fussed around Annie and Polly alongside Frank, keeping them entertained, giving Josie the time she needed to grieve. Christmas had been hard, Alf's absence leaving a gaping hole in all their hearts, but Daisy and her mum had made the best of the day for her little sisters. Then, four days into the new year, Frank and Ivy had got married, after Frank had proposed on Christmas Day. Once again, they had ensured Annie and Polly were a special part of their day by asking them to be flower girls, spoiling them with yet another new outfit. Now, in between shifts at the Women's Voluntary Service, Ivy made sure that Daisy, Josie and the girls always had a hot meal every night, as well as time to be alone and heal as a family.

'I'm just glad we have been able to help,' Betty replied, patting Daisy's arm. 'We all need to stick together.'

'Speaking of which,' Patty chirped up, 'does anyone fancy a quick one in The Welly tonight after work?'

'What do you think?' Betty asked Daisy. She had become increasingly protective of her friend over the last six weeks. She was the first to grip her friend's hand when she woke up in the night, tears rolling down her cheeks, or when Daisy spotted a man who resembled her father from behind, stopping her in her tracks.

'I'll just check with Mum if that's okay. She might be tired after coming back to work this week and need a hand with Annie and Polly when I get home.'

'Now, don't you be worrying about that, duck,' said Frank, who was sat at the other end of the table. He had one ear on the conversation the women were having, while he and Archie discussed what orders needed to be finalized before the end of the day. Hitler's raids across

Sheffield might have quietened down, but the war was far from over. Fighting was still carrying on in Europe and across North Africa.

'Oh, Frank. You have done enough, I can't expect you to look after the girls tonight,' Daisy protested.

'Now, now,' Frank said, in a mockingly stern voice. 'Annie and Polly have challenged me to another draughts competition. After the beating they gave me last night, in which they took great joy in trapping me in a corner, I need to at least try and regain my dignity.'

'Don't let him fool you,' Daisy smiled at the rest of the table, as the image of her sisters whooping with joy flashed before her, 'Frank gave them a run for their money until the last few moves.'

'Well, it would have been a bit mean of me to beat them.'

'Is that your excuse?' Archie said, giving his gaffer a friendly nudge.

'Of course!' Frank said, unable to keep a straight face for more than a couple of seconds. 'Anyway,' he added, turning to Daisy, 'it will do you good to go and relax for an hour or so. I will spend some time with the girls, and I'll let Ivy know you will have some tea a little bit later.'

'Thank you,' Daisy replied in appreciation. 'In that case, as long as Mum is feeling okay, I'd love to come to the pub.'

'Good!' Patty beamed. 'How about you, Hattie?'

'I'm sorry, I can't. John is due home, so I need to get back. I'm not quite sure when he will arrive, but he said he would come round as soon as he could.'

'You kept that quiet!' Patty exclaimed, before lifting another mouthful of pie to her lips.

'Sorry. I didn't want to tempt fate. He wrote last week and said he was hoping to get back, but he only confirmed it in his letter that arrived yesterday.' After her dad's recent drunken outburst, Hattie had felt so relieved that her husband would soon be by her side, even if it was only for a couple of days.

'That's wonderful news.' Betty grinned, delighted for her friend. Her own fiancé, William, had surprised her by turning up at Frank and Ivy's wedding, and she'd been overtly aware that Hattie would have loved to see her husband too.

'Thank you. Have you heard from William much since he went back?'

'I have.' Betty smiled. 'He writes at least once a week, which I'm grateful for.'

'I hope it's not too long until he gets leave again,' Hattie said, knowing that letters were a comfort but nothing beat having your loved one by your side. She and Betty frequently chatted about how they longed for those visits.

'Me too, but I got to see my William last month. You haven't seen your John for months. It will be lovely for you to have a weekend together.'

'I am really pleased,' Hattie said, putting down her cutlery next to her barely touched meal. 'I just hope my dad doesn't start on one of his drunken escapades and ruin it all.'

'Does he normally behave himself in front of John?' Betty asked.

'He does, but his drinking has got so much worse, I don't think he cares what anyone thinks of him anymore. It's like he's lost all self-respect and is completely oblivious to how horrible he is.'

'Don't let him ruin your special weekend,' Patty said, squeezing her friend's hand. 'You and John haven't seen each other for ages.'

'I'm certainly going to try my best,' Hattie replied, secretly trying to envisage John's reaction to her news that they will soon become parents. The last thing she wanted was for her dad to tarnish the moment.

'Have you got anything nice planned?' Nancy asked, sitting back down after chatting to a couple of women at the Swap Box.

'I haven't really, as I know John will want to see his parents too, but we might go out for a bite to eat or to watch a picture.'

'Well, you just enjoy it, luv,' Nancy said. 'You deserve a nice weekend.'

'Right, ladies. I'm sorry to break up your conversation, but I'm afraid it's time to get back to it,' Frank said apologetically as he stood up.

'Dinner time always goes far too fast,' Patty sighed, rolling her eyes in jest.

'Aye but think about your little soiree at the pub later.'

Patty's eyes lit up at the thought. 'Okay!'

As the group dispersed, all heading to their own sections of the factory, Daisy and Hattie went towards the turner's yard.

'I'm so glad your mum is doing as well as can be,' Hattie said as they made their way into the huge, noisy workshop.

'Me too, I'm sure work will do her good. She needs a routine again.' Daisy turned to Hattie. 'And how are you doing? You still look peaky.'

'I'm just a bit tired.' Hattie yawned, lifting her hands to her mouth. 'I'm not sleeping that well.'

As her eyes momentarily closed, Hattie didn't notice the pile of steel shavings in front of her. Before Daisy could warn her, Hattie lost her footing and stumbled backwards.

'Hattie!' Daisy yelped as her friend landed in a heavy heap on the floor.

The bump knocked the wind out of Hattie, and for a few seconds her vision blurred.

'Oh my goodness, are you okay?' Daisy asked, bending down to see if she could help.

Instinctively, Hattie's hands clasped her stomach, a feeling of nausea flooding through her and all colour draining from her face.

'Hattie,' Daisy repeated, 'are you hurt?'

Hattie's eyes flitted between Daisy and her own stomach. *Please let my baby be all right*, she silently prayed, berating herself for being so absent-minded.

'Let me help you,' Daisy said, putting one of her arms around Hattie's back and gently encouraging her to stand up.

In a daze, Hattie allowed Daisy to guide her, all the time not letting go of her tummy, as she tried to work out if she felt sick due to the shock of the fall or if something awful had happened.

'I think I need to go to the toilet,' Hattie whispered, her eyes averting to her belly.

'Okay,' Daisy replied. 'Do you need me to get you anything? Some water, maybe?'

'I don't know,' Hattie muttered.

'What's happened here?'

Daisy and Hattie instantly recognized their foreman's brusque voice.

'Hattie's had a bit of a fall,' Daisy explained. 'She's not feeling so good.'

'You don't look so clever, luv,' the stern but kindly old man said.

'I'm sorry,' Hattie said, annoyed at herself for making such a fuss, but simultaneously desperate to get to the loo.

'Don't be sorry,' Mick said. 'Go and take a breather, then come back when you are ready.' Turning to Daisy, he added, 'Go with her, luv, and make sure she is okay. In fact, take her up to the canteen and get her a hot drink. I think she needs it.'

'Okay.' Daisy nodded, ushering Hattie back out the giant archway of the shop floor.

'Come on, let's go and get you a cuppa.'

'I really do need to go to the toilet first,' Hattie insisted, gripping her jittery tummy even tighter.

'Okay. Let's get you there,' Daisy replied, assuming the fall had left her friend feeling sick.

But when they got to the loos, as opposed to vomiting, Hattie sat on the toilet, her fears dissipating when she realized she hadn't started bleeding. 'Thank you,' she whispered to an invisible God, momentarily forgetting Daisy was stood outside the door.

'You okay, Hattie?' her friend asked, on cue.

'Yes. Sorry. I think so.'

But when Hattie emerged from the cubicle, the relief was replaced by tears, her emotions a whirl.

Daisy gasped. 'Hattie! What is it?'

'I'm sorry. I think the fall and how tired I'm feeling have just made me a bit weepy.' As much as she wanted to tell Daisy the real reason she was crying, this wasn't how she envisaged sharing her happy news, besides which, she was adamant John should know first.

'You poor thing,' Daisy said in sympathy, giving Hattie a hug. 'You're probably exhausted and ready for a day off. Let's go and get you that drink. I bet Dolly will pop a bit of sugar in for you. You could certainly do with it.'

As soon as the two women walked into the canteen, Diane spotted them from where she was stood serving a long queue of hungry workers. Hattie attempted to reassure her mum by throwing her a weak smile, but she knew from the concerned look on Diane's face that she had done little to extinguish her fears.

'You sit down,' Daisy prompted. 'I'll go and get you a hot brew.'

'Thank you,' Hattie said, as she made her way to an empty table.

As soon as she sat down, Dolly was by her side.

'What are you doing here, duck?' Then taking a second glance at Hattie's flushed and blotchy face, she added, 'Goodness me. What's happened?'

'It's nothing,' Hattie lied, hating herself for being so secretive. 'I just had a bit of a fall, and it left me feeling a little winded.'

'Okay,' Dolly said, in as convincing a manner as possible, but she wasn't daft. Hattie was gripping her stomach, and Dolly had had her suspicions for a while about why Hattie had been off her food and looking so pale, but she was also astute enough to know that you couldn't force anyone to disclose something they weren't ready to talk about.

'Would you like a hot drink?'

'Daisy has just gone to get me one, thank you.'

'Good. Would you like me send you mum over?'

'I don't want to disturb her, it looks like you are pretty busy. But would you just mind letting her know that I'm okay? I know she'll worry otherwise.'

'Don't you be fretting about how busy we are. I'll go and relieve her, so she can come and see you.'

'Thank you.'

'And listen, duck, you take care of yourself. This

factory can be a tough old place, especially on the shop floors. Your health must come first.'

Hattie nodded, grateful it was Dolly who was talking to her, an unspoken understanding passing between them.

'Here we go,' Daisy said, returning to the table nursing a steaming mug of tea. 'There was still some in the urn at the share table, and I managed to find a bit of sugar too.'

'Reyt. You get that down yer, duck, and I'll send your mum over,' Dolly said, gently rubbing her shoulder. 'Please remember what I said and be careful. You've had a bit of a scare.'

'Thank you,' Hattie repeated, Dolly's words feeling more pertinent than ever.

A minute later, Diane was at her daughter's side. 'Are you okay, luv? Dolly said you had a fall.'

'I did, but I'm okay, I promise.'

'Are you sure?' Diane couldn't hide the concern in her voice, but she also knew she couldn't break her daughter's confidence.

'It was just a bit of a shock, but this cuppa is sorting me out,' Hattie said, hoping to reassure her mum. The last thing she wanted to do was add to her worries. She had enough on, navigating her dad's drunken episodes, but Hattie knew she'd had a lucky escape and the fall was a wake-up call.

Chapter 3

By the time Hattie got home that evening she was exhausted. Although she hadn't suffered any injuries, the fall had knocked her for six. As usual her dad had already gone out, and for once she was relieved. As much as Hattie dreaded what state he would return home in later, she was grateful for the peace and quiet. After a quick soak in the tin bath in front of the fire, Hattie had spent twenty minutes doing her hair and applying a dab of rouge and a slick of lippy. Now all she could do was wait until her John finally arrived.

She didn't have long to sit before the kitchen door swung open.

'John!' Hattie gasped, as her red-cheeked husband appeared in the doorway.

'Hello.' He grinned, crossing the warm kitchen in a couple of steps and lifting his wife into his arms. 'I have missed you so much,' he said, before tenderly kissing Hattie on the lips.

'I have missed you so much, too,' she replied after their

lips parted, nestling her head on John's shoulder, instantly comforted by the familiar feeling. 'I can't tell you how long I have waited for this moment.'

'For as long as I have, I should imagine,' John replied, squeezing his arms a little tighter around Hattie's back.

But instead of enjoying the affectionate gesture, Hattie winced, pulling away. And it wasn't just how tender she felt after her earlier fall that caused her to take a step back.

'Hattie?' John quizzed, alarmed by the reaction.

She instantly apologized, silently chastising herself.

'What is it?' John asked, lifting Hattie's chin with his hand.

Blast, Hattie thought. This wasn't how she'd hoped the evening would go.

'Why don't you take your coat off and come and sit down. I've just made a fresh pot of tea.'

'Okay,' John replied, not sure what to think about Hattie's uncharacteristic behaviour.

'I'm sorry,' Hattie said as she poured two mugs of tea. 'We haven't got anything stronger. It never lasts more than two minutes.'

John eyed his wife, suspecting her strange behaviour must be somehow linked to her dad's ongoing drinking habit. Maybe she was worried he would walk through the door at any moment and catch them in each other's arms. John knew her dad could be a bit of a tyrant and assumed Hattie didn't want to do anything to aggravate his volatile temper.

'It's okay,' he said, doing his best to reassure his wife. 'A good strong cuppa is exactly what I need. It's been a long day.'

'Mum has made some vegetable broth. Would you like some? She's baked some bread too.'

'I wouldn't say no. Mum offered me some tea when I dropped my bags off, but I politely refused. I just wanted to get here and see you.'

A pang of guilt coursed through Hattie. She knew John must be wondering why she was acting strangely.

'Have you eaten yet?' John asked, as Hattie took a bowl from the cupboard.

'No. I haven't had much of an appetite.'

John eyed his wife with concern. 'Have you been poorly?'

'No. Not really. Well, maybe just a little bit off.'

'Hattie?' John probed, knowing something was bothering his wife. 'Why don't you come and sit down and tell me what's bothering you.'

Hattie metaphorically gave herself a kick. She was making a pig's ear of this!

'Okay,' she answered, carefully placing the two bowls of steaming soup on the table, before carrying over a side plate of sliced wholemeal bread. John brought over the two mugs of tea.

As the couple sat down, adjacent to each other, John touched Hattie's arm. 'Has something happened?' he asked. 'Is it your dad? Speaking of which, where are your parents?'

'No. No. It's nothing like that,' Hattie said, shaking her head. 'Dad's drinking is worse than ever. Nothing Mum or I say makes any difference. He's been in the pub since he finished his shift, and Mum is just in the front room. I think she's a bit tired after work, and I suspect she is probably giving us a little bit of privacy too.'

'If it's not your dad . . .' John said, ripping up a piece of bread and dipping it in his stodgy broth, 'Although, I have to say that sounds bad enough, what is it, Hattie?'

'Oh dear,' she answered, shaking her head.

Feeling more than a little baffled, John bit into his bread, before adding, 'If it wasn't for the fact you are being so nice to me, I would be worried you were about to tell me you had gone off me. But maybe that is a guise?' he teased, hoping Hattie would relax a little. He was unable to recall the last time she had acted so oddly, it really wasn't like her.

'No!' Hattie exclaimed. 'I promise it's nothing like that.'

'I was only joking, but clearly something is on your mind, so why don't you just spit it out before you get yourself in an even bigger muddle.'

'Okay.' Hattie put her spoon back on the table and instinctively placed her hand on her tummy.

John threw her a curious glance. 'Are you poorly?'

'Not really. Well, I have been but I'm starting to pick up a bit now.'

'Why didn't you tell me?' John asked, the concern in his voice evident. 'How long have you been poorly for? Have you had a bug? Is that why you pulled away from me? Is your tummy tender?'

'Well, yes, but no, it's not a bug. It's something a little more permanent.'

'Hattie?' John's mind was working ten to the dozen, but he really couldn't make head nor tail of what his wife was telling him.

'Sorry! I've made a right pig's ear of this, John. This is not how I imagined telling you.'

'Telling me what?'

Hattie took a deep breath.

'I'm pregnant! We're having a baby.'

For a split second, John didn't say a word, as his mind took a moment to digest the news. Then, just as quickly, a huge smile appeared on his face, his confused expression changing to one of utter delight.

'Hattie!' he gasped. 'That's amazing. I can't believe it.' And then he was on his feet and wrapping his arms around Hattie again – only this time a little less tightly, fully aware now of why his wife had winced. 'This really is the best news.'

'It is, isn't it?' Hattie replied, relief flooding through her that she had finally been able to reveal the secret that she and her mum had been carrying around for weeks.

'Yes!' John exclaimed, sitting back down but taking both of his wife's hands in his own. 'I'm so happy. This really is wonderful. The most perfect coming-home present and Valentine's surprise.'

'Oh goodness, I nearly forgot.' Hattie grinned, picking up an envelope from the worktop. 'This is for you.'

John grinned as he opened the card and read the note inside.

To the only Valentine we could ever want.
Lots of love,
Your wife and your baby.
xx

'I don't think this day can get any better,' John said, beaming.

'I've been desperate to tell you.'

'Then what on earth took you so long, you daft thing?'

'I didn't want to put it in a letter. I wanted to tell you in person. It just felt more special, but then when you hugged me so tightly, I got a bit paranoid that we'd hurt the baby. I fell over at work today and I guess I'm just feeling a little bit protective.'

'What do you mean you fell over? Are you okay?'

'Yes, I'm fine. It just knocked the stuffing out of me for a few minutes and I got scared the baby would be hurt, but my bottom took the brunt of it.'

'Are you sure?'

'Yes, but it did make me think that working on the shop floor probably isn't the safest place for me at the moment.'

'I was just about to say exactly the same. You need to be careful, Hattie.'

'I know. I'm going to speak to my foreman on Monday, but I didn't want anyone at work to know that I was pregnant before you. Mum guessed when I felt so sick at Frank and Ivy's wedding. You don't mind, do you?'

'Of course I don't. In fact, I'm pleased your mum knows. It makes me feel better that there's someone who has been able to look out for you. But, beyond all of this, your safety must come first. I think you need to tell your foreman.'

'I know. I just wanted to tell you first. It felt wrong telling anyone else before you knew you were going to become a daddy.'

'Oh, Hattie. You really are the best wife, and I know you are going to be the best mummy too.'

With that, tears flooded Hattie's eyes.

'Hattie, I'm sorry. I didn't mean to make you cry.'

'It's okay. I'm not sad. I just haven't used the word mummy yet in relation to me. It sounds so lovely, if a little surreal. I've felt so sick and out of sorts, I've not really had time to imagine myself as a mum.'

'Well, you better get used to it, Mrs Harrison. Now tell me, when is this baby going to make his or her appearance?'

'If I've worked it out properly, I think in July.'

'That's going to be here before we know it!'

'I know. Can you believe it?'

'It's still sinking in.' John laughed, leaning across the table and kissing his wife's crown of dark glossy hair.

'Oh, and I nearly forgot. Here's your card,' John said.

Hattie smiled as she opened the missive.

To the only Valentine I would ever want.
Yours forever & always,
John

'Thank you,' Hattie said, reaching over and squeezing her husband's hand.

'You have made me the happiest man alive.'

'I'm so pleased you are as happy as I am.' Hattie smiled.

'Of course I am. I'm just sorry I have to go back to Salisbury on Monday. I want to be here with you every step of the way. I feel terrible that I haven't been around to look after you while you have felt so rotten.'

Hattie reached over for John's hand. 'Don't be,' she reassured him. 'It can't be helped and if the truth be known, I haven't been much fun. I'm sure Patty is wondering what on earth is wrong with me. I've turned into a boring old maid! I've not had much energy for going out and having fun.'

'You poor thing,' John said. 'I still can't believe you managed to keep it a secret, especially from Patty.'

'I do feel quite guilty, but I know she'll understand when I explain.'

'She will. Now why don't you go and ask your mum to join us. I'm sure she must be desperate to celebrate the thought of becoming a nannan.'

'Are you sure?' Hattie asked.

'Absolutely! Why don't you fetch her, and I'll pour these bowls of broth back into the pan to heat up. I think they've gone cold.'

'Sorry! I should have got to the point a bit quicker.'

'Don't you be worrying about that.' John smiled. 'I think it was worth my soup going cold for. Now go and get your mum. She should definitely be part of our little celebration.'

The nerves Hattie had been feeling were now replaced with a fizz of excitement as the reality of her situation began to sink in. *She was having a baby!*

A couple of minutes later, Diane, John and Hattie were sat around the kitchen table. 'It really is lovely to see you,' Diane said, looking at her son-in-law. 'You must be so pleased to have a weekend's leave. Your parents must be over the moon to see you.'

'I am and they are,' John replied. 'Although they have barely seen me yet. I literally dropped my bag off and came here. I did promise them, though, that Hattie and I would have a roast with them on Sunday. You would be very welcome too, Mrs Johnson.'

'Diane! I think you have known me long enough.'

'Sorry.'

'That would have been lovely, but I probably need to catch up with some jobs here.' What Diane didn't say was Vinny would hit the roof if she didn't put a Sunday dinner on the table, and she really didn't want John to invite her husband, knowing there was every chance he would refuse or have a drink and humiliate Hattie.

'Well, if you change your mind, the offer stands,' John reiterated.

'Thank you, luv, but I think your mum deserves to have a bit of time with you both. So, what other plans have you got for the weekend?'

'Actually, Mum,' Hattie interjected, 'we called you in because I've told John about the baby.'

'Oh,' Diane responded, her eyes instantly glistening. 'Of course you have, and here's me waffling on.'

'Not at all,' John said kindly. 'I'm glad Hattie had someone to look out for her.'

Emotions flooding Diane, she wrapped her arms around her daughter. 'I am so happy for you, luv.' Then looking at John, she added, 'For both of you.'

'Thanks, Mum.' Hattie grinned. 'We are really happy too.'

'It is the most special time,' Diane said, sitting back down, her cheeks now a bright flush. 'You should cherish every minute.'

'I'm trying,' Hattie answered, placing a hand on her tummy. 'I'm just hoping I start to feel better soon.'

'You will, luv. The first trimester is the hardest, but then you enter the lovely stage and can just enjoy being pregnant and feeling your baby grow.'

'I'm looking forward to that.' Hattie smiled.

'Did you really not realize until Frank and Ivy's wedding?' John asked.

'No!' Hattie laughed. 'It seems so daft now. I'd been

off my food for a while, but just thought I had a bug. I'm such a klutz for not putting it together. Mum had to point out the obvious.'

'It took me a while to realize when I was pregnant with you too,' Diane explained. 'Then, when I did work it out, your dad was the first person I told.'

Hattie reached across and touched her mum's arm, wishing – as she was sure her mum did – that the closeness and love her parents had once shared hadn't been slowly eroded by her dad's drunken behaviour.

'No time for maudlin thoughts,' Diane asserted, reading her daughter's mind. 'Now, tell me, still no twinges?'

'I keep thinking I've felt something, but it's so faint, I don't know whether I'm just imagining it.'

'That's lovely. And a summer baby too. How perfect. I can't believe I am going to be a nannan, and that my little girl is going to be a mummy.'

Chapter 4

Sunday, 16 February 1941

'Your mother told me yer news last night, while you were off out gallivanting,' Vinny barked, as he took a noisy slurp of his tepid tea.

Hattie wasn't sure how to respond. Far from *gallivanting,* she and John had been to the pictures, a rare treat. But now the excitement that had been fizzing inside her all weekend quickly evaporated. Part of her had naively hoped her dad might have also been pleased for her, but at his unimpressed tone, Hattie's wishes vanished, and she accepted they had been nothing more than wishful thinking.

Using his daughter's silence to further fuel his heartless venom, Vinny added, 'You better not be thinking I'm going to support that bloody bairn of yours. I work hard enough having to keep a roof over yours and yer mum's head. Don't be expecting me to provide for another little blighter.'

Hattie recoiled. The fact Vinny didn't provide for Hattie and barely contributed to the running of the house, spending most of his wages in the local boozer, was almost by the by. What stung more was Vinny's vitriolic resentment towards his first grandchild.

'I won't' was all Hattie could whisper, as she swallowed back the pain that was threatening to consume her, feeling stupid for even daring to think a baby might see her once-loving father, the one Hattie recalled from her childhood, re-emerge. Knowing there was no point trying to persuade her dad that he could be a loving grandfather, Hattie carried on drying up the breakfast pots, washing away her fears about how she would cope financially after her baby arrived. Not only that, how was she going to keep her unborn child safe in a house so full of anger and resentment? Every feeling of happiness had now been replaced by fear and frustration at herself for assuming she would be able to bring a baby into the world. Her mind a whirl of suffocating worries, Hattie didn't notice her dad rise from his chair and stomp from the room, spilling the remains of his tea across the table as he knocked his half-full chipped mug out of the way.

'Penny for them?' Diane asked a couple of minutes later, interrupting her daughter's thoughts.

'Oh!' Hattie whispered, turning round. 'I didn't see you there.'

'I could tell. You were in a world of your own. Thinking about the baby?'

'Yes,' Hattie replied, forcing a smile. She didn't want to worry her mum, knowing if she told her the truth, then

Diane would once again be riddled with guilt about not protecting her daughter.

'I know I keep saying it, but I can't tell you how happy you and John have made me,' Diane added, inadvertently reinforcing what Hattie was thinking.

'And as I keep telling you, you will make a wonderful nannan. This baby is very lucky to have you.'

'Aw, luv. That's lovely of you to say. I must admit, your news has given me a real boost. There's nothing like a newborn baby to make you smile.'

'I hope so, Mum.'

But before Diane could ask Hattie what she meant, there was a knock at the back door.

'And speak of the devil, is that your John now?'

'I suspect so,' Hattie said as the back door opened and John walked into the kitchen, rubbing his hands, the heat a welcome retreat from the bitter cold air outside.

'Good morning.' John beamed, giving Hattie a kiss on the cheek. 'How are you and our tiny little bean today?'

'Is that what we're going to call our baby?' Hattie grinned, her mood suddenly lifting. John always made her feel better.

'Why not? I'm assuming that's about the size of our baby right now. Mind you, I'm only guessing. You will know better than me.'

'What do you think, Mum?' Hattie asked. 'Is John right?'

'He won't be far off, but that little baby will be growing

fast. I was always amazed when I thought about how quickly they grow. It really is quite miraculous.'

Right on cue, John proudly placed his hand on Hattie's tummy, which still looked as flat as ever, disguising the fact she was around four months pregnant.

'Are you off to your parents for a roast?' Diane asked.

'Yes. Are you sure we can't tempt you?' John offered. 'Mum said you would be very welcome. There will be plenty to go round.'

'Maybe next time, luv. I've got quite a few jobs to get done and I've already bought a little joint to cook for myself and Vinny.'

Hattie knew her mum wasn't being entirely honest. There was every chance her dad would spend most of the day in the pub or inebriated. The real reason Diane had politely declined the offer was she was frightened Vinny would make a show of himself, and the last thing she would want was to cause Hattie embarrassment.

'I'll hold you to that,' John replied, playing along with the game. Hattie was pretty sure he knew the real reason too.

'Thank you and please send my regards to your mum and dad,' Diane replied. 'Hopefully I will see them soon.'

'I will, and I think Mum has been baking, so I'll make sure we bring some treats back with us.'

'Well, I'll never say no to that. Now you two go and have a lovely day. I'm going to go and get some housework done and I will see you later.'

'Thanks, Mum,' Hattie said, as Diane picked up a cloth and a bottle of vinegar to start cleaning the windows.

After Diane left the room, John wrapped his arms around Hattie.

'I've missed you,' he whispered, nuzzling his face into Hattie's neck. 'I wish we could have spent the night together.'

'Me too.' Hattie could have spent the night before at John's house – they were a married couple, after all – but she'd worried about leaving her mum alone with her dad.

'Well, once this blasted war is over, we will have the rest of our lives to be together,' John said, giving Hattie a gentle squeeze. 'And hopefully this is just the start.'

'Let's see how we get on looking after one baby first.' Hattie grinned.

'Oh, I think we are going to be brilliant! I would love a house full of kids. What could be more magical than the sound of playing and laughing.'

Hattie allowed herself to be carried away with the moment, envisioning a home full of happiness and love.

'I'd like that.' She smiled.

'We can have fun trying to make it happen.'

'John!' Hattie exclaimed, her cheeks reddening.

'I'm sorry, but it really is the thought of what our future holds that keeps me going. The last few months have been so hard and it's only going to get harder. I just want us to be together and never have to be apart again.'

'Me too. It's been hard without you here. My dad . . . Well, you know what he's like.' Hattie whispered the last sentence, fearful Vinny would walk in at any moment and overhear their conversation.

Sensing his wife's trepidation, John gripped her hands, a surge of guilt coursing through him at the news he would have to break to Hattie before the day was out.

'Shall we go for a walk before heading over to my mum and dad's?'

'That would be lovely.'

Ten minutes later, the couple, wrapped up in gloves, hats and scarves to protect them against the lingering frost that hadn't shifted all morning, passed hand in hand through the entrance of High Hazels Park.

'So, would you like to chat to me about what's worrying you about your dad? We didn't get a chance to talk about him yesterday, but I assume his drinking isn't getting any better?'

Hattie bit down on her bottom lip. She really hadn't wanted to dampen the mood of the weekend, especially after telling John they were going to have their first baby.

'Come on,' John insisted, gently pulling Hattie round to face him. 'It's me, remember. You can tell me.'

'I know. It's just—'

'No excuses,' John broke her off. 'There's a bench just up here. Shall we sit down?'

'It might be a bit cold?'

John whipped his scarf off from around his neck. 'Your seat, madam,' he proffered, folding the knitted garment in two.

'You are quite the gentleman,' Hattie conceded, as John led her to the bench and laid the makeshift cushion, which was covered in what looked like a fine layer of perfect white lace, on the seat.

As they sat down, John placed one arm across Hattie's shoulders and held on to her with his other.

'I'm assuming things are getting harder with your dad. Is there anything I can do?'

Hattie shook her head. 'I don't think so. It's just hard. Dad is drinking every day, and his temper is getting worse.'

'Has he hurt you?' John asked, the lilt in his voice changing from gentle to firm.

'No. Well, not really. It's Mum that bears the brunt of his outbursts.'

'What do you mean?' John quizzed.

Hattie took a deep breath and repeated how Vinny's behaviour now frequently resulted in him stumbling through the door, shouting obscenities and, more often than not, pushing her mum about, his shoves increasingly becoming more forceful.

'And he refuses to go to the public shelter. Mum gets frightened something will happen to him, so we end up taking cover under the stairs while he carries on drinking at the kitchen table.'

'Hattie, why haven't you told me this before now?'

'You have enough to worry about, exposed to the elements on Salisbury Plain.'

John took a sharp intake of breath. How could he tell

Hattie the news he had been trying to tell her all weekend? It felt so much harder now. It was his job to protect his wife and baby, but he felt like he was letting them both down when they needed him more than ever.

'I'm sorry,' Hattie said, mistaking John's apprehension.

'Don't be silly. You have nothing to be sorry for. It's me that should be apologizing.'

'What do you mean? You can't be held responsible for my dad's actions. He is the one who should be ashamed of himself. I just wish he'd realize how much he has pushed me and Mum away. I can't even stand being in the same room with him, and I know Mum is terrified.'

Then putting her free hand on her tummy, Hattie added, 'And I must admit, I'm quite scared of him too.'

Feeling a mixture of anger and uselessness, John racked his mind on how he could try and protect his wife, their unborn baby and his mother-in-law against the tyrant Vinny had obviously become.

'I don't suppose you would consider moving in with my parents until the war is over?'

Hattie appreciated the offer but shook her head.

'I can't. I couldn't leave Mum. I wouldn't be able to live with myself if something happened to her.'

'My parents have plenty of space. Your mum could move in too.'

'That's a lovely thought, John, but there will always be a part of my mum that loves my dad and wants to try and fix him. And even if she found the courage to leave him, and I really wish she would, he would come after her. There's no way he would just let Mum go. He would hunt her down, and I dread to think how that would end.'

'This godforsaken war,' John cursed. 'I hate the fact I'm not here to protect you.'

'I'm just worried Dad will . . .' But Hattie couldn't finish her sentence, scared she would be tempting fate if she dared voice her fears.

'Please don't,' John sighed. 'Surely your dad wouldn't be that cruel?'

'I don't know. Half the time he has no idea what he's doing. I really don't think he can remember how violent he's been the day after one of his outbursts. At least when he's sober it's only his words that are hurtful.'

'And there's no one that can talk any sense into him?'

'I wish there was, but he doesn't have any family nearby. At least, none he's in touch with. Mum used to be able to make him realize how horrible he was being, but since his drinking has got out of hand, she's too scared to even broach the subject.'

'I can ask my dad to pop round every now and again, just to let your dad know there is someone watching him.'

'Oh, John. It's a nice thought but honestly if my dad thought he was being watched, he would only take it out on Mum. She would end up suffering even more. I think we have just got to hope that dad's behaviour doesn't get any worse.'

John wasn't daft. He might have grown up in a family

where alcohol was only drunk in moderation and on special occasions, but he had heard enough tales about how booze could soon take over a person and change them beyond all recognition. And now, he was going to be even further away from Hattie, unable to be the protective husband he should be. This blasted war had so much to answer for. If Hattie wouldn't move in with his parents, and he couldn't ask his dad to keep an eye on his wife, he had no idea how he was going to keep her and their baby safe. Taking a deep breath in, John pulled Hattie closer to him.

'Please don't fret,' Hattie said, sensing how worried her husband was. 'Mum and I will be okay, I promise,' she added, almost on autopilot, far from convinced by her own words.

Then, trying to boost John's spirits, she said, 'Besides which, you are only a few hours away, so hopefully you will get some more leave soon. Next time you are home, our baby will have grown, and you might even get a chance to feel him or her kick about.'

Despite her efforts, the sudden drop in her husband's mood was palpable as his broad shoulders slumped and his eyes clenched.

'John. I'm sorry,' Hattie said, feeling guilty, assuming he was upset that he wasn't able to be in Sheffield constantly. 'That wasn't very tactful of me.'

'No,' John interjected. 'You haven't said anything wrong. It's me who should be saying sorry.'

'What do you mean?'

'Oh Hattie, I've been trying to find a way to tell you all weekend.'

'Tell me what?' Hattie released herself from John's arm and sat bolt upright, turning to face her now very anguished-looking husband, confused by his cryptic announcement. Surely he hadn't fallen out of love with her. John had been so attentive and kind since he'd arrived at her house on Friday evening.

'You do want our baby, don't you?' The desperation in Hattie's voice was visceral.

'Of course I do,' John gasped, taking hold of his wife's hands. 'I want our baby more than anything else in the world. You have made me the happiest man alive this weekend. I can't wait for us to become a family.'

'Then what is it?' Hattie's voice softened, seeing how visibly distressed her husband was.

John momentarily closed his eyes as he bit down on his lip. Training soldiers how to handle bombs in the pitch black felt like a walk in the park compared with the news he had no choice but to tell his wife now.

'Please, whatever it is, tell me,' Hattie pleaded, her heart racing in apprehension.

'Okay.' John nodded. 'One of the reasons my commanding officer granted me leave this weekend is because it might be the last time I can come home for quite a while.'

Hattie forced herself to be strong. 'That's okay,' she

said, hoping her tone was upbeat and not betraying the sadness she really felt. 'As long as you get home for when our baby arrives, that's all that matters.'

Another heavy pang of guilt coursed through John. 'That's just it,' he sighed. 'I'm being sent to North Africa.'

It took a few seconds for the news to register. North Africa. She recognized the name from geography lessons at school.

'Isn't that the other side of the world?'

Hattie wasn't entirely surely whereabouts it was exactly, but she knew it was thousands of miles away, and certainly further away than France, where John had previously been posted. She'd seen mention of the battles going on in North Africa in Frank's *Daily Mirror* and heard on the wireless about how Mussolini was trying to take over part of the land, after Italy had invaded Egypt the previous October.

'When?' was all Hattie could whisper, her mind a whirl of conflicting thoughts. She needed to be brave for John, but the thought of him being so far away at what should have been one of the happiest times of their lives was just devastating.

'I'm not sure exactly, but I think in the next few months,' John replied, his voice breaking. 'They are moving us out in sections.'

Hattie gulped back the lump in her throat. 'Do you know how long you will be away?'

John slowly shook his head, his fingers gripping around

Hattie's a little tighter. What he didn't say was that he was worried, too, about Britain's decision to try and defend the Suez Canal and the oil fields, when the Allied forces were already doing everything they could to stave off the Luftwaffe's air raids across England.

'They have said they can't tell us. I don't think anyone really knows.'

The reality of what John was telling Hattie felt like a punch to the heart. He couldn't voice it outright, but she knew what her husband was trying to say was that there was every chance he wouldn't be home to see their baby enter the world.

'Oh, John.' Hattie finally broke, tears erupting from her eyes as she buried her head in her husband's chest. *How had this weekend gone so wrong?*

'I'm so sorry,' he replied, his arms now enveloping his wife's shaking body. 'Please believe me, I would do anything to stay here with you.'

Unable to stop the flow of tears, Hattie felt consumed by the enormity of John's announcement, mixed with how nasty her dad had been that morning and the fear of what was still to come. She had been so elated on Friday night, but now it felt as though her whole world was tumbling down around her.

All John could do was hold Hattie in his arms as the emotion poured from her. He felt awful for destroying what should have been such a wonderfully happy occasion. He hated Hitler, and now the Italian dictator,

Mussolini, for the untold misery they were causing across the world. And to make matters worse, there was no end in sight. Although Sheffield hadn't fallen victim to another one of Hitler's catastrophic bombardments, coastal towns up and down England were still being targeted and cities destroyed.

It was several minutes before Hattie could stem her flood of tears and sit herself up again, her cheeks now red and blotchy.

'I'm sorry, John. That was very selfish of me,' Hattie said, using her woollen gloves to dry her eyes.

'It wasn't at all,' John asserted. 'None of this is your fault.'

'And it's not yours either,' confirmed Hattie, her voice a little less shaky. 'I think these pregnancy hormones must have got on top of me.'

'Hattie,' John said, gently lifting his wife's chin, 'you don't have to be brave and strong. I don't particularly feel stoic myself, and I would really rather be here with you.'

'I know you would.' Hattie knew she had to try and make John feel better. As much as she would prefer he wasn't being posted in some far-off place, Hattie appreciated John had no choice but to obey orders and do as he was told. And despite how much she hated this blasted war, she knew John, like tens of thousands of others, was just doing his bit to defend the country against Hitler.

'I will write as often as I can,' John promised. 'But it might be a little while before I go.'

'And I will keep you fully updated on how this little one is getting on,' Hattie replied, placing one of her gloved hands on her tummy.

'I will be home the first chance I get,' John added, doing his best to keep his voice from faltering.

With that, Hattie nestled her head into John's chest, thoughts swirling around her mind. Excitement was replaced by overwhelming fear, as she desperately hung on to the delicate thread of hope that she was sure was on the verge of snapping.

Chapter 5

Monday, 17 February 1941

'Hattie!' Patty gasped, taking one look at her best friend's forlorn face and sensing something was terribly wrong. 'What's happened? I was worried when I didn't see you clocking in this morning. Is everything okay?'

'Sorry. I got here at the last minute,' Hattie answered, as she and Daisy sat down, having walked together from the shop floor to the canteen.

Patty glanced at Daisy, who quickly but discreetly shook her head, indicating she had no idea why Hattie looked so down in the dumps either.

'Did John not come home?' Patty asked tentatively, assuming that must be why her oldest friend looked so utterly crestfallen.

'Oh no. He did,' Hattie confirmed, taking her pack-up from her bag.

Betty now looked across the table, recognizing Hattie's weary expression of concern and exhaustion from her own experience.

'You don't have to tell us,' she started, 'but we are happy to listen if you think it will help.'

'I'm sorry,' Hattie sighed. 'I should be over the moon, but after what John told me yesterday, I feel like I'm going to burst into tears every ten minutes.'

It's not her dad then, for a change, Pattie quietly thought to herself.

'Do you feel up to talking about it?' Betty asked, standing up. 'Let me go and get you and Daisy a tea. A cuppa always helps.'

'Thank you,' Hattie replied gratefully. After John had told her he was due to fly off to North Africa at some point in the not-too-distant future, the rest of the day had felt like there was a shadow cast over it. Hattie had forced herself to smile through the family Sunday lunch John's mum had prepared, refusing to ruin the special occasion, knowing her husband's parents must have felt as anxious as she did. Only after John had taken Hattie home and kissed her for the final time, had she rushed up to her bedroom, sat on the edge of her bed and allowed her tears to fall unbidden once again.

'Here we go,' Betty said, carefully placing the two mugs of steaming liquid down on the table in front of Hattie and Daisy.

'You are kind,' Hattie said, thanking her. 'And I'm sorry for bringing the mood down. I didn't mean to.'

'Not at all,' Betty insisted. 'Can we help?'

'Oh dear,' Hattie said, letting out a deep breath. 'I'm

not entirely sure, but I think I am going to need you all more than ever.'

'Hatts!' Patty interjected. 'You're really worrying me now. Please tell us what's happened.'

'Sorry,' Hattie said again, lifting the hot mug and encasing it into her hands. 'It's John. He's being posted to North Africa.'

'Oh, luv,' Nancy said, holding her sandwich in mid-air, immediately understanding why Hattie looked so sad. She wanted to tell her it would all be okay, and John would be back before Hattie knew it, but Nancy knew the words wouldn't ring true after her friends had supported her through the agonizing wait for her husband, Bert, to come home.

'I just feel so worried,' Hattie admitted. 'It's such a long way away.'

'I'm sure,' Nancy replied. 'I know exactly how hard it feels, and no matter what we say, it won't change things, but we will be here for you.'

'I'll second that,' Betty interjected. She too knew how Hattie felt, after her William was posted to Canada as part of his RAF pilot training. 'Remember how you all rallied around me?' she added.

'We'll all be here for you,' Patty confirmed. 'We'll do everything we can to help.'

'Thank you.' Hattie nodded. 'I know I'm no different to lots of people. It just somehow feels worse now.'

'What do you mean, luv?' Nancy asked.

Hattie inwardly reproached herself. After the enormity of the weekend, it had almost slipped Hattie's mind that her friends didn't know she was pregnant.

Instinctively Hattie glanced down at her tummy, hidden underneath her mucky khaki overalls.

For once Patty didn't miss a trick. 'Hatts!' she exclaimed. 'You're not, are you?'

Betty, Nancy and Daisy all swapped a quick glance, praying Patty hadn't done her usual and put two and two together and got five.

'I am,' Hattie confirmed, the smallest hint of a smile appearing across her very pale face.

In a split second, Patty was on her feet and dashing around the table to her friend.

'This is the best news,' she squealed excitedly, throwing her arms around Hattie. 'When did you find out and when is this baby due to arrive?'

'Patty!' Archie, who had been sat at the other end of the table with Frank, half laughed and half berated. 'Give poor Hattie a chance.'

Patty apologized, releasing Hattie from her grip. 'I'm just so excited.'

'Thank you,' Hattie answered. 'I am pleased, even if I don't look it. It's just, well, with everything with my dad and now John having to go away, it's put a bit of a dampener on everything.'

'Oh. I'm such a klutz,' Pattie acknowledged, realizing she had been a little premature in her reaction.

'Not at all,' Hattie commented, taking a sip from her mug of tea. 'I have felt excited too. I suppose I just wanted everything to be perfect.'

'Of course you do,' Nancy interjected. 'That's completely normal. You wouldn't be human if you thought any different. I know it's no compensation, and it isn't the same at all, but you really can count on us all to be here for you. You don't have to do this alone.'

'Nancy's right,' Betty said. 'We will all be here for you every step of the way. And congratulations. This really is lovely news.'

'You are all so kind. Thank you. I didn't mean to sound like such a misery guts.'

'You haven't at all,' Daisy said, touching her friend's arm. 'And you have been here for all of us when we have needed it. The very least we can do is be here for you.'

'You have such a lot on already,' Hattie replied. 'I don't want to add to your worries. Listen to me, harping on. How is your mum? Are you all coping as well as can be?'

'Don't be worrying about us right now,' Daisy said, kindly diverting the conversation back to Hattie. 'Today is about you. We should be celebrating your happy news.'

'What's this?' asked Dolly, who had sauntered over to the table to check the tea urn.

'It's—' Patty began.

'Patty!' Before she could finish her sentence, Archie cut her off.

'Sorry!' Patty said again, quickly checking herself, her cheeks blushing.

'It's okay,' Hattie said. 'I know she's just happy for me.'

'Have I missed something?' Dolly said, somewhat baffled by the exchange of words.

'Hattie has some news,' Betty said tactfully.

Dolly eyed Hattie, who still looked pale and yet again in need of a good night's sleep. She'd had her suspicions for weeks about why the ashen-faced lass looked so exhausted.

'Am I allowed to ask what it is?' Dolly ventured carefully.

'Of course. I'm sure my mum will be pleased that she can talk about it with someone.'

'Talk about what?'

'I'm pregnant,' Hattie said, repeating her news.

'Oh, duck!' Dolly beamed. 'This is wonderful news. You must be over the moon.'

'Yes. Yes, I am,' Hattie said, even if she didn't feel quite as jubilant as her words indicated.

Dolly wasn't daft and noted the slight lilt of worry in Hattie's voice.

'Is something wrong?' she asked gently.

'Sorry! I really am delighted. It's just John, he's being posted to somewhere in North Africa in the next few months and he doesn't know when he will be back. I guess it's just taken the shine off it a little.'

'Ah, luv. Of course it has, but as I'm sure everyone else

here has told you, we will be here every step of the way for you. We might not be John, but we won't let you go through this alone.'

'Thank you,' Hattie said, feeling incredibly grateful. Never did she imagine when she joined Vickers, one of the biggest steel factories in Sheffield, that she would quickly be taken into the arms of these wonderfully supportive women.

'And don't forget,' Nancy interjected, 'you are never alone when you are pregnant. Your tiny little baby means there is someone with you constantly.'

'Aw, that's lovely. I hadn't thought about it like that,' Hattie said, reaching for her stomach.

'Nancy's right,' Dolly added. 'When I was carrying both my boys, I felt blessed that I had this precious little baby inside me, and already we had an unbreakable bond. I know it feels a little daunting without your John by your side but try and cherish every moment if you can. It is a very special time.'

'Gosh. You will have me in tears again,' Hattie whispered, her voice faltering. 'You're right. I am very lucky. And after this war is over, John and I will have the rest of our lives to be a family.'

'That's the spirit,' Dolly said, squeezing Hattie's shoulder. 'Now, on a very practical note, do you think you need to have a word with the gaffers? I'm not sure working in the turner's yard is a suitable place right now for you and the little one.'

'My goodness!' Betty interrupted. 'Dolly is right. I know your fall the other day wasn't while you were operating any machinery, but you don't want to be putting yourself at risk of getting hurt.'

'I must admit, I did wonder what I was supposed to do. I was just worried that they might let me go and I really can't afford to lose my wages.'

At this, Frank, who had been quietly smiling as the women all clucked around Hattie like the protective mother hens they were, said, 'Don't you be worrying about that, duck. We can't afford to let a single pair of hands go. But Betty and Dolly are right, you shouldn't be on the shop floor. We need to move you somewhere a little less dangerous.'

'I don't want to let any of my colleagues down, though,' Hattie said, quickly turning her head towards Daisy.

'Don't you be worrying about me,' Daisy replied. 'You and your baby are far more important.'

'Daisy's right,' Frank reiterated. 'There are plenty of other places in the factory you can be more than useful. And safer.'

Hattie nodded, a surge of guilt soaring through her that she could have inadvertently already put her unborn child at risk. When she'd slipped three days earlier, the first thing she'd thought about was her baby, yet she'd carried on working with red-hot steel rods that had left countless women with nasty burns and dodging lethal sparks.

Sensing her concern as she gathered up the empty

mugs, Dolly added, 'You've had a lot on yer mind, duck. Don't beat yourself up, but maybe have a word with your foreman this afternoon.'

'Okay.' Hattie nodded.

'Promise yer will,' Patty parroted protectively, paranoid her best friend could end up hurt. She'd heard enough horror stories of severed limbs and near-fatal accidents to know it was a very realistic possibility.

'I will,' Hattie vowed, a pang of maternal instinct telling her that from now on her sole job was to protect her baby.

Chapter 6

Saturday, 22 February 1941

'Josie,' Ivy called, opening the door into the kitchen, where her lodger was showing her two daughters how to knead dough until it was springy enough to be placed in the brown pancheon to rise.

'Are you after me?' Josie asked.

'Not me exactly, but you do have a visitor.'

'Me? Who is it? I'm not expecting anyone.'

'Why don't I take over here,' Ivy suggested, 'and you nip into the front room? I'll bring you and your guest a pot of tea.'

Perplexed by how cryptic Ivy was being, Josie followed her out into the hallway. Only once the kitchen door was shut did Ivy explain that the woman who was sat in the front room was the mother of the baby Alf had saved on the night he had died.

'Oh!' Josie gasped, her eyes widening as she lifted her flour-dusted hands to her lips. Although the family had crossed her mind intermittently in the last two months, Josie had pushed the thoughts away in a bid to stop herself feeling angry and jealous that they had survived but her husband hadn't. On more than one occasion, her thoughts had disappeared down a complicated rabbit warren, wondering if Alf hadn't insisted on saving the family of the woman who was now sat just a few yards away, whether he would still be here for his own grief-stricken daughters.

'Would you like to see her?' Ivy whispered, sensing how anxious Josie was feeling.

'I don't know . . .' Josie muttered.

'I understand,' Ivy whispered kindly, sharing Josie's understandable trepidation. But she was conscious the woman who had knocked on her door a couple of minutes earlier was not only within earshot, but probably also feeling nervous about meeting Josie.

'If you would rather I tell her you aren't available, I will.'

Josie shook her head, wiping her hands on her apron.

'No. It's okay,' Josie said, mustering up every reserve of courage she had, but simultaneously unsure how much braver she could be. Her ability to keep painting a smile on her face for the sake of Daisy, Annie and Polly had been tested to a point Josie hadn't realized was possible since they'd lost Alf.

'It's not fair to turn her away when she's made the effort to come here. I'm just not sure I'll be able to hold myself together.'

'I'll only be in the next room if you need me, or if it all gets too much.'

'Thank you. Could you keep the girls with you? I don't think they would be able to take it all in and I don't want them to see me get tearful.'

'Of course. If Daisy comes back from the WVS, would you like me to keep her in the kitchen too?'

Josie took a couple of seconds to ponder the question. She knew Daisy would be cross if she thought she was hiding anything from her.

'Maybe let her decide. I just don't want her getting upset.'

'Okay,' Ivy agreed, rubbing Josie's arm.

Josie took a deep breath. *I can do this*, she thought, more to convince herself, as she took the couple of steps to the front room and pushed down on the door handle.

As the door opened, the woman, still dressed in her dark brown winter coat, looked up, holding a baby close to her chest and revealing an expression Josie couldn't quite read on her face.

'Hello,' the quietly spoken woman said, holding her baby a little tighter as she went to stand up.

'Please. Don't get up,' Josie insisted, as she stood nailed to the spot, despite how lightheaded she was beginning to feel.

'I'm Margaret,' the tired-looking woman offered.

'Josie.'

'Thank you for agreeing to see me. I hope I haven't caused you any inconvenience.'

'No. Not at all.'

'I just wanted to let you know how grateful I was. Sorry, I mean I am, to your husband. But I can see how painful this is for you, so I can go.'

Again, Margaret went to stand up, this time using her hand to cup the back of her baby's head so the child didn't fall backwards.

'Please,' Josie said, taking a step towards the brown leather Chesterfield sofa that Margaret was perched upon. 'Please stay. I'm sorry. I just wasn't expecting you.'

'I didn't mean to upset you, but maybe I should have written instead. It just didn't feel personal enough somehow, but I realize me just appearing here wasn't very thoughtful.'

'It's okay,' Josie insisted. 'I don't mean to appear rude. It's just. Well. Oh, what I'm trying to say is I still haven't got used to Alf not being here. I'm not sure I ever will.'

Margaret nodded empathetically.

'Oh, luv. I know exactly what you mean.'

'You do?'

Margaret nodded, biting down on her bottom lip as she pulled her sleepy baby a little closer to her chest.

'My Peter. He died in North Africa fighting the Italians.'

'Oh. I'm sorry,' Josie gasped. She had heard Allied troops had been sent to the region in the last eight months, after Mussolini had ordered an attack on Egypt in a bid to expand his Empire.

Josie's mind was a whirl of emotions. She'd naively assumed this woman would be coming here to posthumously thank Alf, and announce her family were now able to carry on as normal, or as normal as anybody could at the moment. And wasn't North Africa where Daisy had told her Hattie's John was being sent to?

'It's not your fault. This flaming war has a lot to answer for,' Margaret finally said.

'I won't argue with you there.'

Before either woman could say anything else, the front room door slowly edged open.

'Sorry to interrupt you both,' Ivy said as she placed a tray loaded with a pot of tea, cups, a milk jug and biscuits on the table.

'Thank you,' Josie said, once again feeling very appreciative of the kindness Ivy and Frank had shown her.

'Just call me if you need a top-up,' Ivy said. 'I'll only be in the kitchen with Annie and Polly.'

After Ivy left as quietly as she'd arrived, Josie stood up and poured two cups of tea, realizing the poor woman sat opposite her was finding this meeting as hard as she was.

'How old is your little one?' she asked, placing a steaming cup of tea on the table nearest to Margaret.

'Johnny here. He's two months old.'

'Still so little,' Josie mused, fond memories of her own daughters at the same age flashing through her mind.

'Aye,' Margaret agreed, stroking the back of her son's head. 'I wouldn't mind being a baby again right now, with not a care in the world or any clue on what's going on.'

'It must be nice,' Josie agreed, sitting back down as she nursed her own hot cuppa.

'I just wish—' Margaret stopped mid-sentence.

Josie looked across at the woman, noting the corners of her eyes were now starting to glisten, her fortitude faltering. Josie didn't need to ask why. Despite her own anguish and initial hesitancy about the unexpected visit, Josie couldn't watch this woman suffer. Putting her china cup and saucer back down on the coffee table, she stood up and went and sat next to Margaret on the sofa.

'I'm sorry,' Margaret whispered, her voice cracking. 'I came here to say thank you, not get myself in another tizz.'

'You don't have to apologize to me,' Josie kindly insisted, placing her own hand on Margaret's knee, which was still covered up with her winter coat. 'I don't think there's many of us who haven't been affected by Hitler's, and now Mussolini's, senseless tirades.'

'I know.' Margaret nodded, an isolated tear escaping from the corner of her right eye. 'I just feel so sad that this little one will never meet his daddy. It doesn't feel fair.'

'Oh, luv,' Josie said quietly. 'You're right. It's not fair. Nothing about this rotten war is, but I'm sure you will find a way to keep your husband's name alive for your little boy.'

Despite the fact the bombs had ceased, for the time being at least, Josie knew that most people across Sheffield were still reeling from the aftermath of the Blitz. People were terrified of being outside after the tea-time blackout curfew, frightened Hitler would strike again and further destroy their broken city.

'Thank you. I'll certainly try my best,' Margaret answered. 'I know this sounds odd, but in a way it's easier for him than his brothers and sisters. Telling them their daddy wasn't coming home was just awful.' The words acted as a catalyst for Margaret's tears, which now flowed unbidden down her cheeks. As Margaret's shoulders shuddered, Josie could see the baby was at risk of waking, sensing how distraught his mum was.

'Here, let me,' Josie offered, opening her arms.

'Sorry,' Margaret cried, hesitating for a second before allowing Josie to take her son from her arms as she tried to recover herself.

'It's okay,' Josie insisted. 'I've cried more than my fair share of tears over the last two months. You let it all out, luv. Nothing good comes of us locking it in.'

Margaret managed a small nod as she pulled a crumpled, used tissue from her pocket. As the woman blew her nose and used her sleeve to wipe away her tears, Josie allowed the tiny baby to nestle himself into the crook of her arm.

'I really didn't come here to cry on your shoulder,' Margaret sighed as her tears began to recede. 'I've been building up to today for weeks. I really thought I was finally brave enough.'

'I'm sure, but there's no rules when it comes to grief. I burst into tears at work this week after the smell of the pie

I was serving up reminded me of my Alf. He always loved pie and mash.'

'I can understand that,' Margaret agreed. 'Everywhere I turn I seem to see memories of Peter. Even kissing the kids before they go to bed sets me off. Their dad loved kisses and cuddles with them before bedtime. And the other day my mum treated us all to fish and chips, and all I could think about was Peter saying, "Make sure you ask for extra scraps."'

'Maybe, one day, we will find a way to smile at these memories, instead of cry,' Josie offered.

'Do you think we will? It seems so painful right now.'

'I think I'm hoping that will be the case,' Josie admitted. 'It's too hard to think that this awful pain will last forever. Was it recently that you received the news?'

'I suppose it depends on what you describe as recent. In some ways it feels like yesterday, but in other ways it feels like Peter has been gone forever already.'

Josie didn't say anything, worried she had been too intrusive.

'It was Christmas Eve,' Margaret whispered, taking a deep intake of breath, the words physically assaulting her. 'We knew he was missing, but I suppose we were just praying for good news.'

Josie flinched at the revelation. This war was beyond cruel.

'Not long after our house was destroyed, Peter's mum got one of those awful telegrams. As soon as she saw the brown envelope, she knew it was bad news. The messenger had taken it to her when he didn't know how to find me. Me, my own mum and the kids were still in a rest centre. It said Peter was missing in action. I tried to stay hopeful, telling myself missing didn't mean he wasn't alive. And I know it sounds daft, but I was sure God couldn't be cruel enough to make us deal with any more bad news, not after our house had been destroyed and our Patricia had been so badly hurt, with her leg being broken, but I realize now it doesn't work like that, does it?'

'No,' Josie whispered. 'I don't think it does.'

'They say God only deals you as much as you can handle, but I don't think I'm as strong as him upstairs thinks I am,' Margaret said softly. 'Another telegram arrived on Christmas Eve. This time, there was no uncertainty. Peter, well, he'd been killed. He wasn't coming home.'

'Oh, Margaret,' Josie said. 'I'm so sorry. That's awful.'

'It's not your fault. There are too many power-hungry dictators in this world, and I suspect their greed is going to cause a lot more pain before this war comes to an end.'

'I think you're right. How are you all doing now? Have you found somewhere to live?'

'We are all cramped in with Peter's mum. It's a bit of a squash, but I think Maureen, my mother-in-law, quite likes having us all there.'

'I'm sure. How many little ones have you got?'

'Four. Our Johnny,' Margaret glanced at the little

bundle wrapped up in Josie's arms, 'then there's our Patricia who got hurt, Irene and Charlotte.'

'How have they all been?'

'Irene is only two and Charlotte three. They keep asking when their daddy is coming home. It breaks my heart to tell them he's in heaven. We nip into the backyard most nights and point to the shiniest star, and I tell them that's their daddy looking down at us. I don't think they really understand, though. But our Patricia isn't doing so well. She's that bit older and keeps asking questions about how Peter died and why he didn't just hide from the horrible people.'

'That's hard,' Josie empathized. Her own two girls had asked a myriad of questions that she had found almost impossible to answer. All she could do was keep reminding Annie and Polly how much Alf loved them, and that he would always live on in their hearts.

'It is. There's so much advice about how to bring a child into the world but no manual on how to help them when they lose a parent.'

'You're right, luv,' Josie agreed. 'How old is your Patricia?'

'Eight.'

'Aw, she's only a couple of years younger than our Polly. Maybe, when her leg is on the mend, we could introduce them. You never know, it might help them both. And if your Patricia is anything like Polly, she loves having a new friend to play with.'

'That would be lovely. Thank you. She could certainly do with something to cheer her up and look forward to. Maureen is doing her best to help keep Patricia's spirits up, but she's struggling too. It's the wrong order of things, isn't it – your kids going first.'

'It certainly is. As a parent, losing a child is your biggest fear, no matter how old they are.' Josie was almost grateful Alf's parents were no longer here to cope with the pain of losing their son. 'The offer is there if you ever fancy another visit. Frank and Ivy, who insisted we come and live here, are absolute godsends. As well as looking after me and keeping me upright, they have taken Annie and Polly into their arms and looked after them as if they are their own. I really don't know what I would have done without them.'

'That's lovely. Maybe when things have settled down a little, I would love to, but I wouldn't want to cause you all any more pain. I realize me and my kids are only here because . . .'

Josie lifted her free hand. 'It's okay. My Alf was the kindest soul you could ever meet and would do anything to help someone else. I'm sure he would be smiling, knowing our girls had become friends after he helped save you all.'

'Life throws us some horrible curveballs, but if we could do something to try and make it a little easier, maybe something good can come out of all of this.'

'I hope so.'

As if he knew that now was the right time to add to

the conversation, Johnny started to stir in Josie's arms, his eyes opening.

'Hello there,' Josie said quietly, looking down. 'He really is beautiful.'

'Thank you.'

As Josie smiled at the youngster, she marvelled at the idea that new lives were beginning, despite the tragedy of the world around them. Hitler might be doing his best to cause unbearable pain and anguish, but seeing Johnny in her arms gave Josie the first feeling of hope she'd felt since Alf had been so cruelly taken from her.

'He hasn't beaten us yet,' Josie said.

'What's that?' Margaret asked.

Josie looked up, realizing she had said the words out loud.

'Seeing your little one. It makes me realize there's hope. I don't know, I suppose with every life lost, there's another just beginning. I know it doesn't take away the pain, but it does make me think that there's still a future.'

'I know what you mean. I've found it hard to even think about tomorrow, but you're right. I was so angry that my Peter had been killed, I couldn't see any light in the whole horrible mess, but I need to try and concentrate on the future and, at the moment, it's the kids who give me a reason to get up each day and carry on. I mean, we don't have any choice, do we?'

'No, we really don't. Don't get me wrong, I've spent more hours than I can recall sobbing into my pillow, but when I look at my girls, and holding this little one, it makes me realize that while there's innocence, there's hope.'

'Thank you,' Margaret replied.

'What for? I haven't done anything.'

'You have. I came here today terrified I would cause you more pain, or that I'd fall apart. Every day has just been so hard, but your words have helped me so much.'

Josie placed her free hand on one of Margaret's arms. 'We all need to help each other where we can.' But even as she said the words, Josie amazed herself at her own fortitude. She knew there was still a long way to go, and no doubt there would still be many more moments when life felt too much, but meeting Margaret and holding her son had made Josie see there was some light at the end of this very dark tunnel.

Chapter 7

'Mum,' Daisy said, peering around the living room door. 'Are you all right?'

Josie looked up. Since Margaret had left half an hour earlier, she had barely moved, unable to stop thinking of the terrible sadness this war had inflicted.

'Ivy said you'd had a visitor,' Daisy added as she and Betty walked across the front room and sat down in the armchairs opposite Josie.

'I did, luv.' Josie hadn't really thought how she would tell her daughters about Margaret. She might be able to skirt around the details when it came to Annie and Polly, but Josie knew she couldn't hide much from Daisy.

'Can you say who it was?' Daisy prompted. She guessed by how worn-out her mum looked, that whoever it was had taken quite the toll on her.

'I can, yes, but it might upset you.'

Betty glanced from Josie to her friend.

'Would you like a bit of privacy?' she asked. 'I can go and make a cuppa and spend some time with Annie and Polly.'

'No. No,' Josie insisted. Betty had always been a huge support to Daisy, and her daughter might want her friend to be close by when she explained how she had spent the last couple of hours.

'Mum. You're starting to worry me,' Daisy said as calmly as she could, not wanting to add to her mum's distress but beginning to feel quite anxious.

'Oh, luv. I'm sorry,' Josie said. 'I didn't mean to. I think the last couple of hours have slightly knocked the stuffing out of me.'

'Was it bad news?' Daisy quickly asked, the panic inside her rising.

'No. It was just a bit of a shock,' Josie reassured her daughter. 'I wasn't expecting it.'

'Are you sure you wouldn't like me to make a pot of tea?' Betty offered.

'Thank you, but honestly I'm all right,' Josie replied with a smile.

'Why don't you just start at the beginning?' Daisy prompted.

Josie looked at her daughter, feeling blessed by her kind and patient nature.

'Okay.' Josie knew no matter how she retold the events of the afternoon, it would undoubtedly leave her daughter feeling a little fragile. But she also knew she couldn't hide the visit from Daisy.

Taking a deep breath, she started, choosing her words carefully.

'You remember the night that we lost your dad, he had very bravely saved a little girl who had been injured when her family home took a direct hit?'

'Yes,' Daisy tentatively replied.

'Well, it was her mum who came to see me today.'

'Really?' Daisy responded, unable to disguise her surprise.

'I assume that you didn't know she was coming?' Betty interjected, realizing what a shock that must have been for Josie.

'I can't lie. It was the last thing I was expecting, and it was hard to listen to what she's had to endure.'

'But her daughter was all right, wasn't she?' Daisy asked, slightly confused. 'Dad got her to an ambulance?'

'Yes, he did and she's on the mend, but they didn't just lose their home . . .' Josie stopped, knowing her next words would upset Daisy and Betty.

'What happened?' Daisy asked.

'Margaret's husband, he had been in Africa.'

Betty felt herself stiffen, sensing what Josie was about to say was only going to compound the underlying angst that never left her.

'Go on,' Daisy gently encouraged.

'He didn't come home. They found out on Christmas Eve that he had been killed.'

'Oh gosh.' Betty gulped, unable to stop herself, the reality of the war once again thundering down. Another family destroyed. More needless pain. Her heart instantly went out to the poor woman as what Josie had said sank in. Losing her home, and then her husband. Betty couldn't imagine how Margaret had picked herself up again. But then again, what choice did she have? And isn't that exactly what Josie and Daisy had been forced to do? Alf killed and their home left inhabitable.

'I'm sorry,' Betty whispered. 'It must have been very hard to listen to.'

'It really was,' Josie acknowledged. 'It made me realize how many lives this blasted war is ruining.'

Betty nodded, then despite her best intentions, her thoughts turned to William. Wasn't this exactly what she had dreaded from the moment her fiancé had signed up to train as a pilot for the RAF? She had always been painfully aware that William was putting his life at risk to serve King and Country, but hearing about Margaret's husband had brought home the reality of how precarious his life was. The idea of him being killed in action was too much to bear, but Betty knew it was a very real possibility, and her life could fall apart in a heartbeat too. She clenched her eyes shut, desperately trying to block out the thoughts. But no matter how hard she tried, the terrifying thoughts cruelly danced across her mind.

Only when Josie spoke again did Betty manage to blink away her fears.

'It was like listening to my own life,' Josie said. 'I know it's not exactly the same, but we've both lost our husbands and homes.' Then looking at Daisy, her voice cracked. 'And you and your sisters have lost your lovely dad.'

'Oh, Mum,' Daisy gasped, getting up from the chair to be next to Josie.

'I'm sorry, luv, I didn't mean to upset you. I shouldn't have said anything.'

'Of course you should,' Daisy responded, putting her arm around her mum's shoulders. 'I'm not a little girl anymore and we're a team, remember.'

Neither woman could control the tears that had collated in the corner of her eyes. Margaret's story was as painful as their own – virtually a mirror image. And in that moment, the huge weight of sadness Daisy had felt since her dad had died consumed her. Alf had been her constant protector, her hero, and the one man she knew would never let her down.

Daisy buried herself in her mum's arms, unable to stop the heavy sobs that left her whole body shaking.

'I'll get us a pot of tea,' Betty said, quietly standing up, conscious Josie and Daisy would appreciate a bit of time to themselves. Her own mind was a whirlwind. The fear of losing her fiancé, watching her friend suffer and the future looking so uncertain. Betty knew she also needed a few moments to steady herself, not wanting Josie and Daisy to see her falter while they were coping with so much.

Betty took her time to make the tea, letting it brew for an extra few minutes, giving her friends the time they needed, as well as repeatedly telling herself that, more than ever, she needed to be strong. By the time she returned to the front room, carrying a tray holding a teapot, a milk jug, and three cups and saucers, both mum and daughter looked slightly more composed.

'How many children does Margaret have?' Daisy asked.

'Four. The little girl your dad helped, then two younger daughters and a baby.'

'That's a lot to cope with. How's she managing?'

'The same as us, really,' Josie replied, gratefully taking the fresh cup of tea Betty had poured. 'They have moved in with her husband's mum. I think they are trying their best to rebuild their lives.'

'We are lucky to have such good friends,' Daisy said, turning to smile at Betty.

'We all are.' Betty smiled, returning the sentiment.

'I guess it shows, we just have to make the most of what we have,' Daisy said.

'We do, luv. None of us could have predicted our lives would be shattered into a million pieces, but your dad wouldn't want us to just give up.'

'No, he wouldn't,' Daisy affirmed. 'But I still miss him so much. There isn't an hour that goes by when I don't think of him.'

'That's normal. I'm the same. I keep telling myself, though, the sadness I feel will hopefully be replaced one day with cherishing the special moments we all shared as a family.'

'That would be nice,' Daisy mused. Hearing about the

family of the little girl her dad had rescued had reopened the wounds that were still so tender. She had loved her dad with all her heart and still found it hard to believe how much their lives had changed in the space of two months. If it wasn't for Betty, Ivy and Frank, Daisy couldn't imagine how her family would have survived.

Her mind a jumble of emotions, Daisy turned her thoughts to Hattie.

'I hope Hattie's John will be okay,' she said. 'He's going to North Africa too.'

'I was thinking exactly the same,' Betty answered. Like William, John was going into the unknown.

'Oh, girls,' Josie said, her maternal instinct kicking in. 'We are all facing so much, but we will get through it. We don't know what the future holds. We just have to find a way to get through today.'

Daisy knew it had taken all the strength her mum could pluck up to be so positive.

'Thank you,' she whispered.

'What for?' Josie asked.

'For being the best mum me, Polly and Annie could ask for.'

Chapter 8

Monday, 24 February 1941

'How was it?' Patty beamed, as Hattie, dressed in a neat navy-and-cream skirt, sat down at the canteen table.

'Well, it's certainly different from the turner's yard,' Hattie said. 'I'm not covered in dust and filth, for starters.'

'Don't rub it in.' Patty laughed as she looked down in disgust at her own mucky overalls.

'Sorry!' Hattie replied.

'Don't be. I was only joking, but tell us, what's it like working in the office?'

It had been a week since Hattie had told her foreman she was pregnant. Just as Frank had assured her, Hattie's boss had been kind, insisting that working on the shop floor was too dangerous. He had arranged a transfer to the accounts office by the end of the week.

'I think I'm starting to get the hang of it. It helped that I did a typing course when I finished at school. I'm a bit rusty, though. All the women can type so fast.'

'I'm sure it will soon come back,' Betty reassured.

'So, do you get to read all about the secrets of Vickers?' Patty interjected.

'No!' Hattie laughed, not in the least bit surprised by her friend's amusing question. She wouldn't have expected anything less.

'That's a shame. I was hoping you would have some gossip for us.'

'I'm sure they won't trust me with the country's biggest war secrets yet.'

'Do you think the gaffers know what's happening with the war?'

'I'm not sure anyone really knows,' Frank tactfully interjected. 'We are all just hoping and praying that someone can make Hitler see sense.'

Betty knew in her heart of hearts it didn't seem likely. She'd heard on the wireless that the Luftwaffe had bombed Iceland, and a British submarine had been lost in the Bay of Biscay. Churchill had also appealed to the United States for support, and terrible rumours were seeping through about how Hitler's troops were treating Jewish people.

But Betty was keenly aware that Hattie was anxious enough about the future with John away. 'We just have to remain hopeful and positive that the powers-that-be are doing everything they can to put an end to it all.' Betty may not have been convinced that was the case, but for her own sanity she had to believe someone knew what they were doing, acutely aware that William's training would soon be over, and he would be qualified to be sent on operations. Betty knew the moment she had been dreading ever since William announced he wanted to be 'the best pilot the country had ever seen' was getting closer and closer. She'd just about managed to keep her nerves under control so far, even after her conversation with Josie, but she would need all the strength she could muster to keep herself galvanized for William flying over the skies of Europe.

'Have you heard from your William lately?' Hattie asked, almost reading her friend's mind.

'I have actually,' Betty answered, keeping her tone as upbeat as possible. 'He's still training but seems to be getting through his exams at a rate of knots.'

'Is he still in England?' Hattie asked tentatively, hoping her friend didn't have to cope with the anguish she was feeling, but also fully aware Betty knew exactly how that felt.

'He is,' Betty replied. And quickly trying to move the conversation on, she added, 'He seems to have got pally with someone called Oliver and they are training together.'

'That's good,' Hattie said, knowing how much Betty worried about her fiancé and what the war had in store for him as an RAF pilot.

'What are the other women in the office like?' Patty now asked, aware that changing the subject would be a helpful distraction. 'Obviously, they can't be as nice as us!'

'Obviously.' Hattie laughed, also relieved to keep the

conversation light. She was missing John so much and her dad's drunken spates had become part of the norm. 'In fairness,' she added, 'they are all lovely. They have helped me settle in and been ever so patient with all my questions.'

'I'd be chuffin' useless.' Patty laughed. 'I'd be ripping more pieces of paper out of the typewriter than the number of letters I was actually writing. I doubt I'd last more than a morning!'

'I wouldn't be so sure,' Nancy encouraged. 'You manage to operate a crane. There are not many people who can say that.'

'I suppose, but you have seen my attempts at knitting!'

'Mmmm.' Nancy grinned and the rest of the table all chuckled and raised their eyes in amusement as they remembered Patty's less than skilful attempts at contributing to the ongoing winter woollies collection for those in need and the Allied troops. 'You do have a point there.'

'Anyway, I'm glad you are settling in,' Betty added. 'You must feel a little less anxious too?'

'Yes.' Hattie smiled, looking down at her tummy, where only the keenest eye would have spotted the tiny swelling of a bump. 'As much as I miss working with everyone, I'm not worrying as much that I could accidentally harm the baby.'

'And that's all that matters,' Nancy commented as she finished her ham sandwich. 'You and your little one must come first now.'

'Thank you.'

'Have you felt any movements yet?' Patty asked, before taking a slurp from her mug of tea.

'I don't think any proper ones. I've had the odd twinge but nothing I could really call a kick.'

'It's still early days,' Nancy said, recalling her own pregnancies. 'And you will definitely know when that baby starts moving. Our Billy had a habit of waking me up in the middle of the night with all his kicking. I swear he timed his little jigs until I was asleep. It was as though he was reminding me he was still there.'

'I'll look forward to that then,' Hattie said as she opened her pack lunch, which consisted of a flask of homemade broth and a slice of bread.

'Do you know, despite the lack of sleep, I loved every minute of carrying both our Billy and Linda. Saying that, I didn't have the awful morning sickness you've had. Are you beginning to feel better?'

'I am. I'm still not eating as much as I used to. Little and often seems to be the key, but at least I don't feel nauseous every time I put something in my mouth.'

'That's good, luv,' Nancy replied. 'No strange cravings yet, then? I went through a few months with our Billy when all I wanted were sticks of liquorice.'

'Really.' Hattie stated more than asked. 'But no, not yet. I just like anything warm – hence the soup. It feels quite comforting.'

'Especially in this chuffin' weather, I'm sure,' Patty

chirped up. 'It's flaming miserable out there. I either freeze or get soaked through every time I leave the house.'

'It has been nippy,' Daisy interjected. 'But hopefully we are nearly over the worst of the winter and all the snow we've had. And, Hattie,' she added, turning to her friend, 'it will be lovely having a baby in the summer, when you can go for lots of walks in the sunshine.'

'Yes.' Hattie nodded, trying to remain positive. 'I'm trying to stay upbeat. I know I've got to. It's just hard but I'm sure I'll get stronger.'

'You will,' Betty promised. 'I know we aren't a substitute for John, but you aren't alone. We are all here for you.'

'I might need some of your tips on how to stop myself from falling to bits.'

'Well, I'm not always as strong on the inside as I am on the outside, but I suppose, like the rest of us, I just have to keep thinking all this will pass one day and life will eventually return to normal. When I feel myself drifting towards the ifs and maybes, this is what I remind myself of,' Betty replied.

'That's a good reminder,' Hattie said. 'I will do my best to think that too.'

For a few seconds, no one said anything, the words resonating with everyone around the table. Daisy was still working her way through the indescribable grief she and her family had suffered, while Archie was struggling to escape the memories of the night he'd seen Alf lose his life and Patty didn't know how to pull him out of the dark mood that was engulfing him. Nancy was acutely aware that her own worries had nearly broken her while Bert was away, and she couldn't help but take on board the emotions of all her friends.

Resilient to the core, Betty was the one who broke the silence. 'So, what are we all doing this weekend?'

'I think if the temperature goes up a notch or two, I'll be out in the garden, clearing away any stray weeds,' Frank commented, also aware he needed to do his bit to keep up the morale of his workers.

'Oh yes, Ivy will have us all planting up seedlings again soon,' Betty commented. 'I'm sure I can spare an hour or two. Daisy and I are just nipping to the WVS on Saturday afternoon.'

'How about you, Archie? Have you got any plans?' Frank asked, noticing how quiet his young friend was.

'I'm on patrol tonight and tomorrow night, but I think we are taking Patty's sisters skating on Sunday.'

'We are!' Patty confirmed. She was determined to get Archie doing something apart from work, hoping it would be a distraction to the demons in his mind.

'That will be fun,' Nancy encouraged. 'Our Linda loves it.'

'Why don't we take her?' Patty suggested.

'I didn't mean it as a hint!'

'I know, but it's no bother. The more the merrier.' Patty quietly thought it would mean Archie would have to help her and skate too if there was a few of them, as opposed to sitting it out on the benches.

'Well, if you don't mind, that would be wonderful. Why don't I return the favour by cooking you both some dinner? I'll be doing a roast anyway.'

'You don't have to,' Archie replied politely, unsure if he was up to socializing all afternoon.

'I insist,' Nancy said, waving her hand to indicate it wasn't a problem.

Perfect, Patty thought to herself, before saying out loud, 'That would be lovely. Thank you so much.'

'That's that, then,' Nancy said. 'Just let me know what time you are heading out and I'll make sure Linda is ready for you.'

Chapter 9

Sunday, 2 March 1941

'Here you all are,' Nancy said, as the herd of children piled in through the back door, with Patty and Archie at the rear. 'Have you had fun?'

'Yes!' came the chorus of replies.

Patty had offered to take her sisters, Sally and Emily, along with Nancy's daughter, Linda. And she didn't hesitate to say yes when her little friend from next door, Alice, asked if she could come to the skates too. She had hoped it would also help lift Archie's spirits. He was still struggling to come to term with losing Alf, and no matter how many times friends tried to reassure him that he couldn't have done anything to save him, the images of the building collapsing haunted him.

'Thank you again,' Nancy said. 'It sounds like they have all had a blast.'

'It was a lot of fun.' Patty grinned. 'And they should all be worn-out, the number of times we've been round that hall.'

'Give me a minute and I'll make us a cuppa. I'll just get

some biscuits out for the girls. I'm sure they could all do with a snack.'

'Yes please, Mummy!' Linda chirped up.

'Why don't you all sit round the table, and I'll make up some juice too.'

Five minutes later, after treats and drinks had been served up, Nancy poured water from the boiling kettle into a teapot.

'Archie, I think Bert was hoping he might be able to tempt you to go for a quick pint, if you have time?'

'Er. Okay. You don't mind, do you, Patts?' he called to his girlfriend, who had nipped into the pantry to fetch the milk jug from the cold stone.

'No. Not at all. You go,' she encouraged, grateful Archie couldn't see her face, convinced she would give the game away. She and Nancy had secretly planned the little excursion after Patty had explained how much Archie was struggling.

'Okay. I'll see you soon then,' Archie said, pecking Patty on the cheek as she remerged. Bert already had his coat on, grey cap perched on his head, and his gas mask hanging loosely from his arm. 'I shouldn't imagine we will be long.'

'No rush,' Patty replied. 'It will give me and Nancy a chance to have a good natter.'

'Because you hardly ever see each other!'

Patty threw Nancy a conspiratorial glance, silently reproaching herself for not thinking of a better line.

'See you in an hour or so, luv. And kids – be good,' Bert added cheerfully as he ushered Archie out of the back door.

'We will,' Linda replied, always keen to show her daddy what a good girl she was.

'That was close,' Patty sighed, after the two men had had left the house.

'Don't worry! Bert will be subtle. Don't forget it wasn't that long ago he was in a pretty dark place himself. If it wasn't for Frank, I'm not sure where Bert would be now.'

'Is he back to normal?'

Nancy glanced over to the table, double-checking the girls weren't listening, keen to ensure Linda didn't overhear anything she shouldn't. The little girl had found Bert being away at war so hard, and then when he'd returned from Dunkirk a shadow of his former self, she had continually asked Nancy if her daddy would ever be happy again.

'I'm not sure he will ever fully recover, if I'm honest,' she replied, lowering her voice. 'He still won't talk about what happened in France and more often than not he wakes up through the night shaking and sweating, but during the day you would never know, apart from his slight limp, that something had happened. Working for the Home Guard has been a godsend. I'm grateful that the kids have no inclination that he's still struggling, but part of me wishes he would open up.'

'Do you think he ever will?' Patty asked, simultaneously

thinking about Archie, who had spent the last two months avoiding talking about the night Alf died.

'I'm not sure, but he knows I'm here to listen if he ever feels he can. I'm just grateful he has found a way to smile again. The Home Guard has given him a purpose.'

Hearing Nancy gave Patty hope. Archie had been saved from witnessing the atrocities the Allied troops had to endure, due to his heart condition, but his work as an air raid warden during the Blitz had taken its toll. More than anything, Patty just wanted Archie to stop beating himself up for something that he couldn't possibly have prevented.

'What are you having?' Bert asked as he and Archie approached the bar at The Welly.

'I can get them,' Archie instantly volunteered.

'I wouldn't hear of it,' Bert insisted. 'You have just looked after our Linda for the best part of the afternoon. Call it a thank you.'

'It was no bother, but if you're sure, a pint of ale would be great. Thank you.'

The barmaid, who had overheard the exchange, looked towards Bert.

'Make that two, then,' he said, propping his crutch against the barstool as he reached inside his pocket to find his wallet.

After they had both been served their drinks, and Bert had taken a long sip of the dark liquid, he turned to Archie.

'How are you doing, pal?' Bert didn't see the point in beating around the bush.

'How do yer mean?' Archie asked, his barriers instinctively rising.

'Sorry. That was a bit blunt, wasn't it? Our Nancy told me you hadn't been yourself.'

Archie took a gulp of his pint, giving him a few seconds' reprieve.

Bert sensed Archie's apprehension. 'I don't want to put you on the spot, son, and you can tell me to mind my own business. I won't be offended. I just wanted to make sure you were all right.'

Archie placed his glass on the wooden bar. He was used to Patty and his mum continually quizzing him, but hadn't prepared himself for a Spanish inquisition from Bert too.

'Oh, I don't know,' Archie finally replied, aware of the gaping silence between him and Bert.

'Are you sleeping?'

'Not brilliantly.'

Bert nodded knowingly. He wanted to say that things would get easier, but he knew he would be lying. He couldn't remember the last time he'd managed a full night's sleep without flashbacks of his fellow soldiers being shot invading his dreams, causing him to sit bolt upright in bed, his heart racing. If it wasn't for Nancy holding him in her arms, Bert was sure he would struggle to close his eyes.

'I think that's the hardest part,' Archie added. 'I keep reliving that night over and over again.'

'The human brain can be a hindrance,' Bert stated.

'You're not wrong there. I just wish I'd stopped Alf. He shouldn't have even been there, but I let him out of the shelter.'

Bert understood. Thoughts of how he could have saved the men who had become his closest friends during the attacks in France had played havoc with his mind and nearly sent him crazy in the days and weeks after he'd finally been rescued.

'From what I've heard, you couldn't have stopped him.'

'Maybe, but I should have tried harder.'

Bert took a mouthful of his pint, before adding, 'Take it from me. This life is full of ifs and maybes. If I allowed myself to think about every decision I made in France, I would have sent myself half mad.'

'But you can't be blamed for what happened in France,' Archie protested.

'I know that now, but far too many people I fought alongside weren't as lucky as me. I came home, which is more than most.'

Even as he said the words, flashbacks of his fellow soldiers being indiscriminately shot, falling helplessly to the ground and staining the grass crimson red made Bert flinch.

'How did you learn to cope again?' Archie asked.

'It took a while. Don't tell Nancy this, but when I first got back to England, there were days when I was lying in that hospital bed wishing I'd been killed too.'

'Really? But what about Nancy and the kids?'

A surge of guilt shot through Bert as he recalled those initial days, when he hated himself for surviving.

'I'm sorry,' Archie said. 'That was insensitive of me.'

'No. No, it wasn't. In fact, you have hit the nail on the head. It was the thought of seeing my family again that eventually pulled me through. Don't get me wrong, I felt utterly wretched knowing there were countless wives and kids out there that wouldn't see their husbands and dads again, and I continually questioned why I had been spared. But in the end, I realized no matter how awful I felt, I couldn't change anything. As you can imagine, it wasn't as straightforward as that. I was angry that the shot I'd taken to my leg meant I couldn't go back and fight. I wasn't much fun to live with for a while.'

Archie recalled seeing how pained Nancy had been when she couldn't make her husband feel better in the weeks after he'd finally come home from Dunkirk.

'I don't think I'm great company at the moment either,' he confessed. 'Patty is being very patient and hasn't said anything, but I can tell she feels as though she is banging her head against a brick wall at times.'

'She will also know you are struggling, son,' Bert said. 'It's only natural after what you have been through.'

'I just don't want to drive her away.'

'From what our Nancy tells me, Patty adores the bones of you. If she's anything like my wife, Patty will just want to help you find a way to feel better.'

'I wouldn't mind that myself,' Archie sighed, bringing his glass to his lips. Then after taking a gulp, he added, 'I do have moments when I feel okay, but then I see that building crumbling and it's as if everything closes in on me again.'

'Have you tried explaining that to Patty?'

'In dribs and drabs, but most of the time I avoid talking about it. To be honest, I think I've told you more than anyone else.'

'Sometimes it's easier to chat to someone who is a little further removed from the situation. I'm not great at talking about what's going on inside my own head, son, but I've found I can chat to one of the old boys at the Home Guard.'

'I'm pleased for you,' Archie replied.

'Can I give you a couple of bits of advice?' Bert asked.

When Archie nodded, Bert added, 'If this last year or so has taught me anything, it's that life is precious and none of us know what's around the corner.'

'True enough,' Archie conceded. The war aside, his own heart condition had shown him life could be precarious. As a child, his parents had been warned several times that Archie might not survive another winter.

Interrupting Archie's thoughts, Bert said, 'And there comes a time when we have to make the decision to put away the things we can't control and concentrate on the things we can.'

Archie took a few seconds to think about the sentiment

behind the words. He knew Bert was right. There was nothing he could do to bring Alf or the other air raid wardens back. No matter how much he questioned his own actions, or wished he'd stopped Alf leaving the public shelter, it wasn't going to change what had happened.

'But what can I do now?' Archie asked, with a hint of desperation.

'You keep doing what you are doing,' Bert answered authoritatively.

When Archie didn't answer, his eyes clouded with confusion, Bert explained: 'We don't know what Hitler has in store next, but what we do know is the work you do at Vickers is vital in keeping our Allied troops safe. Without munitions and military vehicles, we don't stand a chance in winning this war. And there's one other thing.'

'What's that?'

'I reckon Hitler thought he could break the country's spirit and walk all over us, especially when his air raids first started. And don't get me wrong, there was a time when I thought he'd destroyed mine. It wouldn't have taken much more for me to give in, but what the luxury of time has taught me is that I need to keep going to do my bit to make sure that bloody man doesn't win this war.'

Archie let the words settle in his mind. He knew Bert was right. It wasn't just about bombs and bullets. He could hear his nannan's voice too. *We can't let this chuffin' man destroy our morale.*

'Thanks, Bert,' Archie said.

'What for?'

'Giving me a pep talk. I reckon I needed it.'

'We all need one occasionally, son. I know I certainly did. It was your gaffer, Frank, who helped me find a way through the chaos in my head.'

'I think's he probably given up on mine!' Archie said with half a chuckle, the hint of a smile emerging.

'I find that hard to believe. He's a good bloke. I reckon he will probably have just been giving you the space you needed.'

Archie knew Bert was right. Frank was like a second father and had always looked out for him, choosing his times carefully to offer any words of wisdom.

'I needed this,' Archie added.

'Happy to oblige,' Bert responded, tilting his glass towards Archie's.

'Cheers,' Archie said. 'Here's to tomorrow.'

'That's the spirit. Now, let's get another quick half in before Nancy sends out a search party.'

Chapter 10

Friday, 7 March 1941

'Hiya, luv.' Diane smiled as Hattie walked into the kitchen, hanging her gas mask and coat on the hook by the back door.

'Hi, Mum. Have you been home long?'

Diane normally finished at Vickers mid-afternoon after all the dinners had been served up, the dishes washed and the preparation for the next day's snap had been completed.

'Not long, maybe half an hour. Work doesn't seem to get any quieter. Quite the opposite, in fact. Not that I mind, the extra money comes in handy.'

'I take it Dad hasn't found your new hiding spot yet?' Hattie said, lowering her voice to a whisper.

'No. And don't worry. He's in the pub, so we are safe for a little while at least.'

'Okay.' As much as Hattie had agreed her mum shouldn't hand over all her wages to her dad, knowing he would squander most of it on booze, she had also worried that he would find her latest spot under a floorboard in the front room. The consequences didn't bear thinking about.

'Try not to fret,' Diane said, reading her daughter's mind. 'The fact I'm contributing more than I ever have to the weekly pot is hopefully enough to stop him getting suspicious. Anyway, I want to be able to treat my first grandchild when he or she enters the world.'

'You should be treating yourself,' Hattie protested. 'When was the last time you bought yourself anything?'

'I don't need anything, luv. Besides which, I'll get more joy out of treating your little one. It's not every day you become a nannan.'

'I know, Mum, but you are allowed to get yourself things you need too.' But even as Hattie said the words, she knew they would fall on deaf ears. Her mum had spent most of her adult life trying to ensure everyone else had what they needed, never giving a second thought to herself.

'Don't you be worrying about me. Why don't you sit down, and I'll serve up dinner.'

'Can I do anything to help?'

'No. It's just leftovers from the casserole we had last night, but if you don't fancy it I've got some homemade bread, and some leftover soup.'

'Actually, that would be lovely, Mum. I don't think I can face anything heavy, but I promise I did have a small portion of Dolly's mince and onion pie at dinnertime today.'

'Good!' Diane enthused. 'You need all the energy you can get, especially now you are eating for two.'

Hattie couldn't help but smile. No matter how much she tried to get used to the idea, she still couldn't quite believe a tiny baby was growing inside her.

'It still feels surreal,' she qualified.

'I know what you mean. When I was pregnant with you, I couldn't imagine what you would actually be like. It didn't feel real, even as my tummy got bigger and bigger.'

'I think that's how I feel too,' Hattie agreed, as her mum handed her a mug of steaming tea. 'I can't really believe I am going to be a mum.'

'It will be wonderful, luv. I promise you,' Diane said, rubbing her daughter's still very bony shoulder.

'I hope so.'

'Now, enough of that,' Diane insisted, as she placed a pan of vegetable soup on the hob. 'We'd all rather this war wasn't going on, but think about how much happiness and joy having a baby around will bring. My own mum used to say every house needs a newborn baby to make them smile.'

'Did she? That's lovely.'

'It is, isn't it? And she was right. No matter how hard life feels, when you see your baby gazing up at you as if you are the only person in the world, it fills your heart. Nothing else compares.'

'Thanks, Mum. I am really excited. I suppose I just wish John was here, that's all.'

'Of course you do. That's perfectly understandable. And my goodness, I nearly forgot,' Diane said, shaking her head.

'Forgot what? Is everything okay?'

'Yes, yes. It's me just being dopey,' Diane answered, making her way out of the kitchen into the hallway, before returning a few seconds later holding an airmail envelope.

Hattie's eyes lit up. 'A letter?'

'Yes. Sorry, luv. I meant to give you it as soon as you walked in.'

'It's okay,' Hattie replied as Diane handed her the letter. She instantly recognized her husband's handwriting, her name and address written in his usual block capitals.

'Shall I give you a chance to read it before your soup?'

'Would that be okay?'

'Absolutely. In fact, I just need to nip upstairs and double-check all the blackout blinds. Take your time.'

Hattie knew her mum was just making an excuse to give her a bit of privacy, something she was grateful for, as she felt tears welling in her eyes before she'd even opened the envelope. Taking a deep breath, her hands ever so slightly trembling, Hattie carefully peeled open the seal.

My dearest Hattie,

I hope you and that tiny little baby of ours are well. Words can't express how much I wish I was there with you both. I am so sorry I had to spoil our wonderful weekend together with the news that I was being posted abroad. Please believe me when I say, I would take Sheffield over ▮▮▮▮▮▮▮ any day of the week.

The sensors had obviously read the letter and crossed through John's exact destination in the name of security.

I am still in England, but I've been moved about a bit, and this is the first chance I've had to write to you. You and our baby are all I have been able to think about. When you get a chance to write back, do tell me if you have felt any little kicks yet, and how you are feeling? I hope with each day you are starting to feel a little better. Please make sure you look after yourself and eat as and when you can. I'm sure your mum and all your friends are telling you exactly the same too. I promise we aren't nagging, it's just because we care and love you so much.

At that, the tears that had been collecting leaked from the corner of Hattie's eyes and dripped down her now flushed cheeks.

'I love you too,' Hattie whispered, 'so much.'

I do hope you have requested a move to a safer part of the factory. I promise I'm not telling you what to do, I just don't want you to get hurt. I realize you know Vickers better than me, though, so I'm sure you will have already thought about what the best options are.

I was thinking as well, when the baby comes, I don't want you to worry about money. I've been putting a bit aside every week for years, and I've built up a bit of a pot. I want you to use it to take some time off work. You should take all the time you need to spend time with our baby.

Hattie gulped back the lump in her throat. John had always been the kindest man she had known – a sharp contrast to her own father, who had made it crystal clear he would not abide her 'freeloading'.

I don't want you to worry about me either. I'm with a good group of men. Some of them were in France too. It's good to be surrounded by people who I already know and trust. I can't say what we will be doing eventually, otherwise I should imagine this letter won't even get to you, but I promise you don't need to worry. I'm in safe hands and every one of us will be working hard to make sure we can get home as soon as possible.

Hattie knew John was just doing what he always did and putting a positive spin on things. He wouldn't dream of telling her anything negative, even though she had told him countless times that she was happy to understand what he was doing, so she could try and offer some comfort.

It's getting late now and the other blokes in my section are desperate for some sleep, so I better turn off my torch before they start cursing me.

Please take good care of yourself and our baby, and write as soon as you can.

I love you both with all my heart and you are in my thoughts every single minute of the day.

All my love, now and forever,
Your husband,
John xx

As Hattie held the letter in her hand, she saw small dark circles expanding, some of the words leaking into the next, as her tears dropped onto the thin paper.

'Oh, John,' she cried, her voice breaking and her heart aching. 'I miss you so much.'

Wiping her eyes with the sleeves of her navy woollen cardigan, Hattie felt her lips quivering and she struggled to contain her emotions.

'Please come home safely. Me and our baby need you.'

With that, Hattie dropped the letter onto the table, lifted her hands to her face and sobbed. Her chest was physically heaving, a mixture of sadness and love. Hattie didn't hear her mum quietly re-enter the kitchen, only noting Diane's presence as she sat down on the next chair over and wrapped her arms tightly around her. Hattie allowed herself to be enveloped in her mum's protective embrace.

'One day all of this will be over,' Diane soothed. 'I promise John will come home, and you will be a family.'

'I hope so.' Hattie sniffled into Diane's chest.

'It will.' Diane knew, in her heart of hearts, she had no right to promise her daughter something she had no way of knowing, but now more than ever, she had to keep Hattie buoyed. It wouldn't do Hattie or her unborn child any good to become so overwrought with emotion.

'Everything comes to an end eventually,' Diane added. Of that she could be sure. 'And this war will pass.'

Gradually Hattie's tears receded and her breathing returned to normal. She slowly managed to gain some level of composure.

'I'm sorry,' Hattie said when she finally released herself from her mum's arms. 'I didn't mean to get myself in such a state.'

'There's nothing to apologize for. You wouldn't be human if you didn't feel any emotions.'

'I can't be falling to bits every time a letter arrives, though.'

'I think you can be forgiven if you do. I was exactly the same when your dad was away in the Great War. I prayed every day for a letter, and then when one did eventually arrive my emotions took over, and I would fall to pieces. We aren't made of stone, luv.'

'Thanks, Mum.'

'Nothing to thank me for. I'm your mum. That's what I'm here for.'

'I don't know what I'd do without you.'

'Well, you don't have to worry about that. I'm not going anywhere.'

In that moment, as she got an insight into what it was like to be a parent, Hattie's admiration of her long-suffering mum intensified. The complete devotion to your child, to shoulder their pain, ease their angst and find a way to make everything feel better when their world was crumbling around them. This would soon be her job. She would have to find the strength her mum mustered.

'I hope I can be as good a mum as you,' Hattie commented, her voice still shaky.

'Oh, luv. You will be a million times better than me. I have no doubt.'

'Don't say that. You are amazing. You are always here for me. What more could I ask for?'

Diane bit the inside of her cheek, guilt once again consuming her for not protecting Hattie against Vinny's sinister side. When she'd been pregnant with Hattie, Diane had such dreams and hopes of the family the three of them would become. Those were the days when Vinny hadn't succumbed to the escapism alcohol provided. He had been so excited when Diane had announced she was expecting, lifting her up into the air and tenderly kissing her. He said he couldn't have wished for happier news after the

Great War, proclaiming it was just the tonic to give him something to smile about. 'A new start,' he'd exclaimed, his eyes glistening. Vinny had been the perfect, attentive father-to-be, insisting that Diane took it easy after she'd got home from her cleaning jobs. He'd bring her cups of tea in bed before he left for the pit, and would surprise her with flowers every couple of weeks. Slowly, though, the flashbacks that cruelly haunted Vinny in the dead of night interceded his waking hours too. Diane would watch with worry as a vacant look came over him. She'd see him try and blink away whatever had intruded his thoughts, an internal battle playing out in his mind. So, initially, the odd drink to release the demons that were haunting him didn't seem like anything to worry about. *If it helps*, Diane had reasoned with herself, on the nights he insisted he needed a pint. Only now with the power of hindsight did she realize what a slippery slope that had been.

'Mum?' Hattie whispered, interrupting Diane's thoughts.

'Sorry, luv,' Diane replied, with a little shake of her head, knowing no good would come from reminiscing. No matter how much she wished she could, Diane knew she couldn't change the past, or the path that had led them to the monster Vinny had become.

'None of this is your fault,' Hattie reiterated, reading her mum's mind.

'I just wish I'd tried to find a different way to help your dad. I never stopped him going to the pub.'

'There's no way you could have. No one could.'

'Maybe I should have forced him to talk more.'

'You can't make anyone talk about something they want to bury away.'

'I suppose you're right.' Diane nodded with more conviction than she felt. But right now, the last thing she wanted to do was add to Hattie's upset. She knew how much her daughter worried about her. She might not be able to change Vinny, but she could try and do what she'd always endeavoured to, and protect Hattie and her unborn child.

'Okay,' Diane added, once again bolstering herself. 'Shall I get you that bowl of soup and a fresh cup of tea?'

'That would be lovely.' Hattie smiled, also galvanizing herself. Life was throwing her some difficult challenges, but she knew she had to try and keep herself strong – it was the least she could do for John and their baby.

Chapter 11

Sunday, 30 March 1941

'Right, girls, are you ready?' Frank asked, pulling on his jacket.

'Yes,' Annie and Polly replied in a cheery unison.

'Before I forget, I've got these for you. You will need them,' Frank said, pulling gardening gloves from his pockets and handing a pair to each girl. 'We have a lot of digging to do today.'

'Thank you,' Annie said, quickly followed by Polly.

'It's no bother. They will be better than getting your good mittens ruined.'

'Thank you for this,' Josie said.

'It's me that should be thanking these two,' Frank said. 'Having a pair of helpers means we will get all the jobs done in half the time.'

'And when you are finished, I'll have a nice roast waiting for you,' Ivy added.

'She's good to us, isn't she?' Frank added, looking at Josie's youngest daughters.

'And I've managed to make an apple pie for after,' Ivy said, causing the two little girls to smile at each other in delight at the thought of the sweet treat.

Once the trio of workers had headed out of the back door and into the garden, Ivy turned to Josie. 'Right, dear. Let's have a cuppa, or would you rather have some time to yourself?'

'A cup of tea would be lovely. I think I'm probably better off being with people today. If I go upstairs, it will take all my willpower to stop me hiding in bed and staying there until tomorrow.'

'No one would mind, luv. It's a tough day to get through.'

'It is, but I think the build-up has almost been harder. I never imagined not spending our twenty-second wedding anniversary together.'

'I'm sure, dear,' Ivy said sympathetically, as she poured boiling water into her rose-printed teapot. 'Those days that are supposed to be special can feel incredibly cruel.'

'I won't argue with you there,' Josie sighed, as she carried the milk jug and two china cups and saucers over to the table. 'Alf would always make a big deal of the day.'

'What would he do?' Ivy asked, hoping the question would help Josie recall some of the happy memories she and Alf shared together, as opposed to making her feel worse.

'Oh, he was an old romantic. Every year, he would write a new message in the same card that he bought me for our first anniversary.'

'Really?' Ivy asked, warmed by the story.

'Yes. And every year, he would always find something new to say. He was far more imaginative than me like that.'

'How thoughtful of him.' Ivy smiled, stirring the tea, which was now nicely brewing in the pot.

'It is. I'm so glad I managed to find it at the house. It was in Alf's bedside drawer.'

'Oh, I am pleased, dear. Have you felt brave enough to look at it today?'

'Sort of. It's in here,' Josie replied, patting her gingham apron. 'I held it close to my chest this morning when I first woke up, and it feels nice having it with me, but I haven't quite mustered up the courage to open it.'

'That's understandable.' Ivy nodded, recalling how after she'd lost her Lewin in the Great War, it took her months and months before she found the strength to read his old letters. 'You will know when the time is right.'

'It's not that I don't want to. I really would like to. I've been trying to find the right moment all morning.'

'Is now a good time?' Ivy asked, as she poured her and Josie a steaming cup of tea each, letting the hot liquid run through the strainer. 'I can give you some space, and I have no doubt Frank will keep the girls busy for a couple of hours at least.'

'Actually,' Josie started, her hands reaching into the wide apron pocket, 'would you be happy to have a look at the card with me?'

'My dear. Of course I would,' Ivy responded.

'I warn you, I might have a little weep,' Josie said, as she carefully lifted out the card and placed it on the table.

'Well, we have tea and handkerchiefs, and I am told I give a good hug when needed.'

Josie nodded gratefully as she placed her hand on the front of the card, which was adorned with a painting of a bouquet of pink roses and the words 'Happy Anniversary' printed in silver across the top. The corners were a little worn and the card slightly yellowing, but considering how old the missive was, Ivy couldn't help but note what good shape it was in.

Handled with so much love, Ivy quietly thought to herself, as she gave Josie the minute she needed to feel strong enough to open the card.

Taking a deep breath and sitting upright, Josie anxiously rubbed the fingers on her right hand against her thumb, as she momentarily closed her eyes.

'It's not like I don't know what every message says,' she finally whispered, breaking the silence. 'I've memorized them all.'

'Take your time,' Ivy comforted.

Josie nodded, her face showing the first signs of crumpling as she bit down on her bottom lip.

'No. I want to do this,' she said. Then after a few more seconds, and before her courage escaped her once and for all, Josie opened the card, revealing an array of neatly written messages at different angles and sizes, covering nearly all the white space available. Again, Josie closed her eyes, this time squeezing her lips firmly together. When she opened them, her eyes were glistening.

'This one was on our first anniversary,' she said, her voice ever so slightly cracking as she gently fingered the heartfelt words.

Ivy looked at where Josie was pointing and read the message, which after over two decades was beginning to fade.

Dear Josie,
Happy first anniversary.
You have made me the happiest man alive.
I love you with all my heart.
Your husband, Alf
xxx

'It was such a special day,' Josie whispered. 'Our Daisy was only a couple of months old, and I remember thinking life couldn't have felt any happier. We didn't have much, but we had each other, and we were so in awe of Daisy and that she was actually ours. We were still in that honeymoon period when you have to keep pinching yourself.'

Ivy had never been blessed with children, but she perfectly understood the all-consuming feeling that life would never be happier, knowing how fortunate she was to have been given a second chance with Frank.

'Very precious memories,' Ivy confirmed.

'They were.' Josie dabbed her eyes as the memories of that special day came flooding back. Their neighbour at the time had offered to watch Daisy so she and Alf could go out for a drink, but they had politely declined, neither one of them wanting to leave their tiny daughter. Instead, Alf had nipped out and brought back a fish and chip supper, which they'd enjoyed with a glass of shandy each while Daisy napped.

'It was the simplest but most wonderful of times,' Josie added, wondering how the years had slipped by, but at the same time it felt like just a split second ago.

'Our memories should be bottled,' Ivy commented.

Josie nodded. 'They definitely should. As much as they sometimes hurt to think about, I'm so glad I have them.'

'If it helps, one day those memories will make you smile.'

'I hope so. They are special and I hate the fact that right now they all make me cry. I'm sure Alf would be devastated too.'

'He would understand. And I know it's a cliché, but time really does become the greatest healer.'

'That and the support of good friends like you. Thank you, Ivy.'

'Aw well,' Ivy said, touching Josie's arm, 'we are all here for you.'

Josie managed a weak smile in appreciation before looking down at the card again. 'This was last year's.'

Dear Josie,
Can you believe we are celebrating 21 years together?
I am the luckiest man alive.
Here's to another wonderful year.
I love you with all my heart.
Your husband, Alf.
xxx

'Oh, Ivy!' Josie cried, unable to utter another word, emotions finally overtaking her.

Ivy pulled her chair closer to Josie's and wrapped an arm around her friend's shoulder, which was shuddering as pain flooded her. Ivy knew there was nothing she could do to ease the agony Josie was enduring, knowing it would take months and months, if ever, for Josie to come to terms with her earth-shattering loss. Instead, she let Josie do what she needed to do, and weep until she had exhausted all her tears and her gasps came to an end.

'I was so scared of falling to bits in front of the girls and them seeing me a mess,' Josie finally said. 'They have had to cope with so much already.'

'They are good girls,' Ivy commented.

'I'm very lucky,' Josie agreed. 'But I don't think any

of us would have coped so well if it hadn't been for you and Frank. Just being here in your lovely home has been such a help. I know it sounds odd, but I think we might have found life a lot harder if we had gone straight back to the house. As much as I want to feel Alf close to me, not seeing him in the house that we shared would have been so painful. I'd keep expecting him to walk through the door at any time, and I don't think I could bear to sleep in our bedroom.'

'I'm happy we could help,' Ivy insisted. 'And it's been such a pleasure having the girls here. They have brought the house to life. It's too big for just me, Frank and Betty.'

'But you have only just got married. Wouldn't you rather have a little more privacy?'

'Not at all!' Ivy said firmly. 'I really do mean it when I say we love having you all here. The girls keep us young, it's nice for Betty and Daisy to have one another, and I enjoy our natters. This house needs to be lived in, so I don't want you to worry about it. You are all welcome to stay as long as you want to.'

'Thank you. I'm not sure when our house will be repaired, so I am ever so grateful.' The authorities had arranged for Josie's furniture to be stored securely, and over the last three months Frank, Ivy and Betty had gradually rescued all their personal belongings, leaving Josie's family home little more than a shell.

'As I've said, there's no rush. I don't want you to give it another thought.'

'Thank you. I haven't said anything to the girls yet, but I'm not sure if going back to our old house is a good idea. I've been thinking we should maybe look for somewhere else entirely.'

Ivy looked at Josie and thought very carefully about what she said next, knowing Josie would never want to be treated as a charity case.

'You don't have to give me an answer yet, but you and the girls are welcome to make your stay here a little more permanent. I'm sure we could come to some sort of arrangement we are all happy with.'

'I didn't say it as a hint!' Josie responded, horrified that her comments might have been misinterpreted.

'I know you didn't, but as I say, we like having you here. The house would feel very empty without you all.'

'You really are a very good person,' Josie affirmed, touching her friend's arm.

'Takes one to know one,' Ivy answered, never one to bask in compliments. 'Now,' she added, 'what would you like to do? I'm happy to do whatever it takes to help you get through the day, but I better start peeling the vegetables, otherwise we will never eat.'

'Actually, if I won't be in the way, can I give you a hand?'

'You most certainly can.'

'Where shall I start?' Josie asked, standing up from table.

'If you do the carrots and swede, I'll start on the potatoes and cabbage.'

'Perfect.' And with that, Josie took a deep breath and felt as though she could tackle the next few hours at least. It might have been the toughest of days, but for the time being, Josie felt strengthened by the love and support she was surrounded by.

Chapter 12

Thursday, 3 April 1941

Stifling a yawn, Hattie was relieved to get home, make a cuppa and have ten minutes before helping her mum with tea. Although her secretarial work wasn't physically tiring, it didn't take much to wear her out these days. Being in the family way seemed to zap any spare energy she might have had. But as Hattie stepped into the house, the familiar sound of her dad's angry bellows became clearer.

'Why isn't there any money left?' came Vinny's furious demand. Hattie quickened her step, desperate to get into the kitchen to protect her mum, even though there was a part of her that wanted to turn around and run as fast as she could in the opposite direction.

Hattie took a deep breath, silently praying she could help defuse the situation quickly. It was times like this she wished more than anything John was here, knowing her dad wouldn't dare behave in such a bullish manner in front of him.

'Oh, look who it is,' Vinny snarled as Hattie made her way into the kitchen, where her red-faced dad was pacing the kitchen, the blood vessels in his neck bulging. 'Lady Muck hersen.'

Hattie quickly glanced at her mum, who was clearly worn-out and terrified about what the night ahead would bring, despite desperately trying to keep her face neutral.

'Don't be looking at yer mother like that,' Vinny growled. 'Don't think I don't know how the pair of yer are plotting against me.'

'Nobody's working against you, Vin,' Diane countered as gently as she could, knowing how much her husband hated to be contradicted.

'Don't lie to me!' Vinny yelled, spinning round to face his wife, causing her to physically flinch. He slammed his clenched fist on the already heavily dented wooden table; another consequence of his constant outbursts.

'You two think I was bloody born yesterday,' he added, making sure he looked at Hattie too. 'Well, I wasn't, and I know one of yer must have some money left over from yer wages. It's not like we've been living like royalty, is it? I mean, look at the state of this bleedin' place. Half the bloody plates are chipped, and we live on stews that have never even seen a joint of meat, or god-awful watery broths. What the bloody hell are you doing with all the money I bring into this house?'

Once again, Hattie bit her lip, knowing no good would come of telling her obnoxious father that if he didn't spend every spare penny they had on booze, then they could eat better and afford to give the house some much-needed tender love and care.

'I do my best, Vin,' Diane offered, any confidence she'd garnered from working at Vickers suddenly dissolved.

'Yer best! If this is yer bloody best, I would hate to see what yer worst is.'

Hattie could feel the resolve that normally stopped her from arguing with her dad extinguishing. Her mum worked herself into the ground to try and keep the wolves from the door, barely ate so her dad could selfishly indulge in every spare morsel they could afford at the butcher's, and when she wasn't at work, was scrubbing the house clean.

'Yer don't know how bloody lucky yer are.' Vinny took two steps across the kitchen, so he was only an inch from Diane's face, splatters of spit from his rancid breath hitting her cheeks. 'I don't know any other bloke that would keep a roof over yer head, when yer can't even cook a half-decent tea after I've slaved away in the pit for hours on end. What sort of bloody wife are yer?'

'I'm sorry,' Diane said, her courage long gone after years of being belittled and humiliated.

'Sorry?' Vinny stormed, his tirade of abuse fuelled. 'Sorry! Is that all yer can say, yer useless bitch.'

'Dad!' Hattie gasped before she could stop herself.

'What?' he barked, turning to face his daughter.

Hattie stared back at her dad, knowing how unkindly he took to being called out.

'Come on then,' he said. 'What is it yer wanted to say?'

Hattie instantly regretted opening her mouth. As much as she would defend her mum to the end of the earth, she also knew no good ever came of arguing with her dad.

'Cat got yer tongue all of a sudden, has it?'

'No,' Hattie whispered, hating herself for being so visibly feeble.

'Well, come on then, say what you wanna say.'

Vinny was so close to his daughter, she could smell the stale alcohol on his breath. He'd either been to the pub on his way home from work, or the alcohol from the night before was still emanating through his pores.

'It's nothing,' Hattie whispered, her free hand automatically spanning across her tummy. 'I didn't mean anything.'

'Don't you lie to me too, yer uppity little cow.'

Hattie clenched her eyes shut. This wasn't the first time her dad had cursed at her, but it still pierced her, the venom in his voice a far cry from the tender tone he'd used with her when she was a little girl.

'Come on. Tell me what's going through that stuck-up bloody mind.'

Vinny had never approved of John – he hated the fact Hattie had found someone whose family had done better in life than he had. Instead of being pleased for his daughter, he resented the fact John's parents were able to afford a house of their own and holidays on the south coast, and that his dad wore a suit to work as opposed to donning a pair of grubby overalls.

'Honestly. I didn't mean to say anything.'

'Don't give me that,' Vinny retaliated, his ruddy cheeks turning from pink to crimson. 'You've clearly got summat to say, so yer may as well just get it off yer chest.'

Hattie knew she was fighting a losing battle. Experience told her that Vinny wouldn't let up until she had at least given him some sort of response, even though Hattie also knew whatever she said next wouldn't satisfy his desire to pursue an argument.

Thinking about the least inflammatory reply, Hattie acquiesced. 'Mum wouldn't lie to you.'

But as soon as she'd said the words, Hattie regretted them.

'Oh really?' Vinny laughed manically, his eyes widening as he shoved Hattie – the heel of his calloused, dirty hand pushing against her shoulder. It wasn't hard enough to knock Hattie off her feet, but there was enough power in his deliberately aggressive action to make her stumble back a step or two. Spurred on by his own sadistic power, Vinny hissed, 'Then tell me this. Where has all this week's bloody money gone, because there ain't much to show for it?'

Stunned, Hattie reached out to one of the chairs to stop her falling backwards. She regained her balance, but it didn't stop her heart racing, her thoughts instantly going to her unborn baby. *What if I'd fallen?* The thought didn't bear thinking about. Hattie wished more than anything that she had the strength to stand up to her dad and point out the obvious, that it was him who had squandered most of the housekeeping money down the pub. But Hattie knew that would only turn an already explosive fight into a full-scale eruption.

'There's been bills and the rent to pay,' Diane interjected, her voice trembling.

'Of course there has! Don't take me for a fool. But where's the rest of it?'

Hattie prayed her mum wouldn't cave and admit where she had been hiding any spare money she could every week. If her dad found out they had been squirrelling away cash, she dreaded to imagine how he would react. One thing was for sure, their lives wouldn't be worth living.

'I swear, Vinny, I haven't bought anything different,' Diane pleaded.

'And what about you?' Vinny turned back to Hattie. 'Have you tipped up yer keep yet?'

'Yes.' Hattie nodded. 'Of course.'

'Don't get wise with me.'

Hattie knew there was no point in arguing. He spat out the same accusatory question most weeks. It wouldn't matter what she said, her dad would twist it to suit his own agenda.

'Where's yer purse?' Vinny demanded, glaring at his wife. 'You must have summat left.'

'I really haven't got anything.'

'Do I have to say it again? Don't bloody well lie to me,' Vinny screamed, his voice reverberating around the kitchen. Then, without waiting for a response, he stretched his arm out and grabbed his wife's tiny wrist.

'Argh!' Diane cried.

Enjoying seeing his wife squirm, Vinny smirked as he squeezed her wrist tighter, taking a perverse pleasure in watching his wife reel in pain.

'I promise I'm telling you the truth,' she whispered through the tears that were now escaping the corners of her eyes.

'Dad!' Hattie cried. 'Let go. You're hurting her.'

'I want some bloody money,' he retaliated, squeezing Diane's wrist so tight her fingers went numb as the blood drained from them.

'Please stop. Let me see if I've got anything left,' Hattie said, horrified.

'No, luv. It's okay,' she muttered, shaking her head.

'Oh really? I can press even harder if it's okay,' Vinny threatened.

'Please,' Hattie pleaded. 'Just let me look.'

Vinny didn't relent. He had money in his sight and he wasn't going to stop until he got exactly what he wanted. Desperate to end her dad's latest violent onslaught of abuse, Hattie hastily rummaged in her bag until she found her little leather pouch and unfastened the clip. She pulled out what coins were left inside and expeditiously threw them on the table.

'There. Take it. But please, just let Mum go.'

Seeing the loose change, his eyes widened. But unable to

just put an end to his cruel act, Vinny pushed his fingers in a little deeper, forcing Diane to drop to her knees in agony.

'You've got what you want. Get off her,' Hattie cried, as she rushed to her mum's side.

'Oh, aren't you the bloody hero,' Vinny said contemptuously.

'Just let go of my mum,' Hattie repeated, instinctively reaching out to knock her dad's arm away.

'You wanna go, do yer?' Vinny unleashed Diane from his grip. Spinning round to face his daughter, he roughly shoved her shoulder, knocking her backwards.

'Argh!' Hattie yelped as her lower back hit the corner of the wooden table, the sharp, agonizing pain causing her to fall to the stone floor.

'Hattie!' Diane gasped, as she scrambled to her daughter.

'Where yer both belong.' Vinny laughed sardonically, his dominance over his wife and daughter giving him a sadistic pleasure.

'Take that,' he jibed, kicking out his steel-toe-capped boot, which sharply connected with Hattie's hip and his wife's hand. 'Yer both bloody useless.'

And with that, he marched out of the kitchen and through the back door, satisfied his cruelty would show Diane and his snooty daughter exactly who was the boss.

As the door slammed shut, the deafening bang reverberated through the house; Vinny's parting shot.

Diane threw her arms around Hattie. 'Are you okay? Has he hurt you?'

'I don't know,' Hattie whispered, pulling herself into a sitting position. 'It's my back.'

'Can you stand up?'

'Yes. I think so.'

'Let me help you onto a chair.' Diane used the hand that Vinny hadn't left throbbing to help support her daughter into a standing position.

'Ouch.' Hattie quivered as she straightened up, a red-hot searing pain taking her breath away.

'I'm so sorry. This is all my fault.'

'No, Mum. It's not.' Despite the agony she was in, Hattie's voice was firm.

Shuffling herself onto a chair, Hattie took a deep breath in a bid to manage the sickening pain that was threatening to consume her.

'This is no one's fault but Dad's. You didn't turn him into the cruel brute he has become.'

Diane knew this wasn't the time to analyze her disastrous marriage, but the guilt she felt at seeing her precious daughter writhing in pain was unbearable.

'Your tummy. The baby,' was all Diane could say to her stricken-looking daughter.

'My back took the brunt of it.' Hattie winced.

'Where does it hurt, luv?'

'My lower back mainly and my hip. But what about you, Mum? Let me see your wrist.'

'It's fine,' Diane insisted, brushing away her daughter's concerns. Her arm was in agony, but she'd survived much worse. What terrified her more was the thought of Hattie and her unborn child being hurt.

'Shall I call for Mrs Taylor? She could come and check you over,' Diane suggested.

Hattie considered the thought. The woman who lived halfway down the street had been delivering babies and laying out the dead for decades.

'Let me see how I feel in half an hour or so.'

'Are you sure, luv? I can nip and get her. It might be best.'

Hattie shook her head. If the truth be known, if it was bad news she didn't think she could cope hearing it. Not now. Not after what had just happened. How on earth would she ever recover, knowing her own dad had . . . Hattie shook her head, pushing away the unthinkable thoughts. *Stay positive*, she silently told herself, trying to channel her friend Betty's formidable attitude.

'Why don't we have a hot cup of tea first?' Hattie suggested, trying to remain calm, knowing if she showed the first sign of panic there was every chance her mum would well and truly crumble.

'Okay,' Diane said, but the concern etched across her tired face didn't fade. 'Let me put the kettle on,' she added, giving her daughter's arm a rub before moving towards the hob.

Hattie momentarily closed her eyes, trying to work out how she and her mum could ever recover from what had just happened. Her dad's cruel and violent behaviour wasn't anything new, although he'd never attacked Hattie as viciously before. Nor had she ever succumbed to giving him money specifically to fund his out-of-control drinking habit. She knew most of the money she tipped up out of her wages every week for housekeeping was probably squandered in one of the many local public houses her dad frequented, but this was a new low. Now she'd done it once, Hattie was in no doubt he would use his bullying tactics to coerce cash out of her again. How many more times would she and her mum have to suffer, and when would this heinous spiral of behaviour end? There was no ignoring the fact Vinny's outbursts were becoming increasingly violent. As the reality of the situation pierced her consciousness, Hattie reached for her tummy. 'Please be okay,' she whispered, barely audible to avoid catching her mum's attention.

But Diane didn't need to be reminded. As she filled the kettle, she too was praying Hattie's baby had survived. She had already failed her daughter; she could never live with herself if she couldn't protect her grandchild. Even worse, she wouldn't blame Hattie if her daughter couldn't forgive her either. Her mind went round in a terrified flux of never-ending circles, wondering how she would ever be able to protect her daughter and grandchild from Vinny. God knows she'd thought about leaving her husband a million times, but where would she go? Apart from the small amount of money Diane had managed, by some miracle, to keep hidden under the floorboards in the living room, she had nothing to fall back on. Besides which, she knew Vinny would hunt her down and the reprisals would be far worse than what she had already endured. It wasn't like the police would protect her. She knew they wouldn't be interested in what they deemed a private affair. And, over the years, Vinny had cut Diane off from all her friends, and she had no family to turn to. But maybe, if nothing else, she could persuade Hattie to go and live with John's parents. At least that way her daughter would be safe, and that's all that mattered.

'Mum,' Hattie said, punctuating Diane's thoughts. 'The kettle.'

'Sorry, luv.' Diane hadn't noticed the water boiling out of the spout. 'I'm being a klutz,' she added. Wasn't that one of the milder insults Vinny often threw at her? Maybe he was right, after all. Feeling utterly hopeless, Diane lifted the steaming kettle from the hob, taking care not to let the bubbling water hit her hand.

'Would you like a bowl of soup too?' she meekly asked her daughter, whose cheeks had been stripped of colour.

Hattie shook her head. Any feelings of hunger had vanished. She was trying hard to concentrate on her tummy or any indicator that might reveal whether something was wrong.

'Actually, I'll just nip to the loo.' Hattie knew if something serious was wrong, then there could be a very obvious physical sign. As much as she'd rather not know, just like when she had fallen in the factory, the instinct to find out was greater. Pushing her hands into the chair, she lifted herself up, grimacing as the pain in her lower back coursed through her.

'Let me help you, luv,' Diane insisted, and within a couple of seconds she was by her daughter's side.

'It's okay, Mum. I'll be okay.' If the truth be known, she needed a minute to try and compose herself, in case the unthinkable had happened.

'Okay. I'll have a cuppa waiting for you when you get back.'

'Thank you.' Hattie smiled appreciatively as she hobbled out of the kitchen and into the yard, the cold, dark air pinching at her cheeks and piquing her senses further. As she reached the door for the outside lavatory, Hattie gripped the freezing-cold handle. 'Please let everything be okay,' she said, her tummy now churning, either out of fear or something more unbearable.

Once inside the draughty stone outhouse, Hattie took a deep breath and tentatively checked for signs of any blood. Thankfully there was no evidence any harm had come to her precious baby. Tears of relief burnt Hattie's eyes. 'Please let it stay this way,' she whispered.

Composing herself, she stood up and slowly made her way back into the kitchen, where two mugs of tea were waiting on the table. Diane looked up.

'All okay?' she asked tentatively, instinctively sensing why her daughter had nipped to the loo.

'Yes.' Hattie nodded as she eased herself back into one of the wooden kitchen chairs.

'Thank goodness,' Diane replied, placing her own trembling hand onto her daughter's.

'It's okay, Mum.' No more words were needed right now, Hattie and Diane each understanding exactly what the other was thinking.

'How's your hand?' Hattie asked, diverting the conversation.

'I'll survive, luv. Nothing for you to worry about.'

Hattie looked at her mum. Maybe for the time being, the next few hours at least, there was nothing to worry about, but they both knew there was plenty to be concerned – no, not concerned – downright terrified of, but after the last hour, neither of them had the energy left to try and work out how they would survive. One thing was for sure, though, Vinny's unrelenting need for money and alcohol meant his indominable behaviour was putting all their lives at risk.

Chapter 13

Friday, 4 April 1941

'Have you got a minute, duck?' Dolly asked Hattie, as she paid for her heavily subsidized hot dinner.

'Okay, but just let me put this down. I'm likely to drop it otherwise. I seem to have adopted Patty's clumsy ways,' Hattie replied, hoping her white lie would disguise the truth that her back was throbbing and just lifting the tray felt uncomfortable.

'Here, let me take it for you.' Before Hattie could resist, Dolly took the tray and popped it down on a free table near the cash desk, just out of sight of the serving counter. 'Have a sit down for a minute,' she added.

Hattie didn't argue. She sensed what was coming. As much as she felt drained after her dad's drunken attack the night before, she also appreciated having someone to talk to about it.

'I don't want to pry, duck,' Dolly started. 'It's just I caught sight of your mum's wrist and I'm guessing something happened at home last night. She hasn't said anything, but you don't end up with bruising that colour for no reason.'

Hattie momentarily closed her eyes. She knew Dolly wasn't daft and Hattie would have been more shocked if the eagle-eyed canteen manager hadn't spotted her mum's injury.

'Listen, duck. You know I'm not judging, don't you? I'm just worried.'

'I know.'

'Would you like a cuppa?' Dolly offered.

'Please, but only if you have time. I don't want to pull you away from your work. I should imagine you are run off your feet.'

'I can always spare ten minutes, duck. Stay here. I'll be back in a jiffy.'

Hattie nodded gratefully, and a couple of minutes later Dolly was back, holding a steaming brew.

'Right,' she said, eyeing Hattie's plate, noticing she hadn't eaten a single morsel. 'Make sure you have some snap and get this down yer. There's not much a cuppa can't cure, and you need your strength.'

Hattie nodded, picking up her knife and fork. She knew Dolly was correct and right now, when life seemed like a never-ending battle, it was her unborn baby that was giving Hattie the determination to carry on.

'So, do you feel up to telling me what happened? I'm guessing yer dad was responsible.'

'As always.' Hattie sighed as she lifted a forkful of mince and onion pie to her mouth. 'He's getting worse, Dolly.'

The canteen manager listened as Hattie hurriedly recalled the harrowing events of the previous evening, keeping one eye on the serving counter, ensuring her mum hadn't spotted them talking.

'Dear God,' Dolly sighed when Hattie had finished. 'No wonder yer mum has barely said a word today and is as white as a sheet.'

'I know. I doubt she slept a wink, worrying he would come back and start again.'

'And did he?'

'He came back, but he was conked out on the front room sofa when we got up. Mum had to wake him, otherwise he would have been late for his shift at the pit.'

'Maybe a bloody good rollicking off his boss is just what he needs,' Dolly replied, trying to stay calm.

'I'd agree with you, apart from the fact it would be Mum that suffered for letting him sleep in.'

'Sorry, duck. I didn't mean to speak out of turn. It just makes me so angry to see you and yer mum suffering like this. Speaking of which, how did you fare in all of this?'

Hattie looked down at her plate, moving her fork around her food as a distraction.

'Oh, I'm okay,' Hattie lied, somewhat unconvincingly.

'You can tell me to mind my own business, duck, but no good will come of keeping yer dad's hideous actions to yerself.'

'I know, but I'm more concerned about Mum. I don't think he would hurt me in the same way.'

'If you don't mind me saying, you don't look so clever yourself today.'

'Honestly, I'll be all right. Mum ended up taking the brunt of it. Once I gave him what money I had, he disappeared again.'

The look on Dolly's face betrayed what she was thinking. She didn't believe Hattie, sensing there was a fair amount she hadn't revealed.

'I know I don't need to remind you, but you're pregnant, duck. There's nothing more precious than that baby of yours.'

Hattie's eyes watered as she looked at Dolly. She was desperately trying to stay composed, knowing she didn't have the energy to break down at work, especially while she was still learning the ropes in the secretaries' office. The thought of Dolly and her friends enveloping her in love and sympathy was bound to break the dam in the back of her eyes and leave her in a flood of tears.

'I'll be okay,' was all she could muster. 'I just need to try and keep Dad from losing his temper.'

To Dolly, the words were all too familiar. It was like listening to herself all those years ago when her husband used her as a punchbag. For years she had tried to come up with ways to prevent his cruel and brutal actions. *If only she could stop him*. Wasn't that what she had told herself over and over again? Never once thinking he shouldn't be carrying out the vicious acts in the first place. Like Diane, Dolly had become the submissive victim, and now it looked like Hattie was going the same way. Dolly knew it wasn't her fault, but she also knew Hattie and her mum would never escape Vinny's reign of power if they constantly bowed down to his every demand. There would be no end to his bullying behaviour.

'Hattie, duck. Can I say something?' Dolly said, unable to let the moment pass.

'Of course.'

'I might sound a bit harsh but what I'm about to say is with the kindest intentions and comes from a good place.'

'Okay.' Slightly discombobulated, Hattie placed her cutlery down on the table, a cold shiver coursing through her. It wasn't like Dolly to pre-empt what she was about to say.

'I don't want to worry yer, duck, but you're beginning to sound like I did before I had the courage to stand up to my late husband. And you are mirroring the words your mum has probably told herself for a long time.'

'What do you mean?'

Dolly rubbed the thumb and finger of her left hand together, as she thought carefully about what she was about to say next.

'I'm worried you are losing your fight in standing up to your dad.'

Hattie let her friend's words sink in. She didn't have to think too long or hard about them. She knew Dolly's evaluation of the situation was spot on, but what other choice did she have? If she stood up to her dad, it would only provoke him further, and Hattie dreaded to think what the consequences would be. Last night had felt like a close escape, and one that was far too close for comfort. She'd been terrified her baby had been hurt – or even worse – and had gone to the loo several times through the night, just to check there was no sign she'd miscarried.

'What else can I do, Dolly? He's a damn sight stronger than me and even if he didn't take it out on me, there's no way he would spare Mum. I can't deliberately let her get hurt. She's already had to cope with so much.'

'I know, duck. And I wouldn't want yer mum to suffer any more than she already has, but I don't want you to become controlled by him either.'

'I'm scared, Dolly. Not just for me and Mum, but for my baby too.' And with that, a solitary tear escaped from the corner of Hattie's eye and crept down her cheek, leaving a straight line through her carefully applied blush.

'Oh, duck,' Dolly said kindly, reaching her hand across the table and placing it on Hattie's arm. 'I'm sorry, I didn't mean to upset you. I should have held my tongue. You have had a hard enough time of it already, without me harping on at yer.'

'No. It's okay. It's not like you have said anything I don't know already. Last night was the first time I caved and gave my dad the extra money. I've always refused in the past, but I couldn't just stand by and let him carry on twisting and squeezing Mum's wrist. I don't think he'd have stopped until he'd broken it. You should have seen the look in his eyes. It was pure evil, as if he was enjoying it. I really think he was getting some sort of twisted and sick pleasure out of seeing her in pain.'

Dolly could just envisage the sick, sadistic smirk on Vinny's face. She'd lost count of how many times she'd seen a mirror image of that face on her ex-husband. Like Diane, and now Hattie, she would agree to anything to prevent their boys hearing or seeing what their pathetic excuse of a father was doing.

'I don't know how to make him realize how cruel he is being,' Hattie said, pulling Dolly back to the present moment. 'I know he isn't a good man anymore, but he never used to be like this. I'm sure underneath it all he must still have a good heart.'

'Maybe, duck, and I hate to tell you this, but unless yer dad stops drinking you may never see that side of him again. The booze does a flamin' good job of putting a brick wall between the person someone used to be and the person they have turned out to be after one too many.'

'I suspect you're right,' Hattie said, tired of trying to fathom if the dad she adored as a little girl would ever return. 'But what do we do? I know I could go and live with John's family until the war is over, but I could never leave Mum, and she's far too scared to walk away from Dad. And to be honest, I don't blame her, he would come after her, and what he would do to her then doesn't bear thinking about.'

Dolly gently shook her head in resignation. As much as she wanted Diane and Hattie to escape Vinny's tyrannical behaviour and leave, she knew it was wishful thinking. Her own husband would have beaten her to within an inch of her life if she had even looked at him sideways, let alone attempted to escape. And she knew there was no point in going to the police. Dolly had tried once, naive enough to believe they would help her, but was told the same as countless other abused wives: *It's a domestic, luv. Nowt to do with us. We can't interfere in what goes on in a marriage. It ain't our place.*

Dolly thought to herself, *What sort of flamin' society did they live in where it was acceptable for women to be subjected to continual physical – let alone verbal – abuse and it be deemed as a private matter?*

'This chuffin' world isn't fair at times, duck. I wish I had a magic wand and could make this all better for you both. Is there anything at all I can do?'

'Just being here to listen, and giving Mum a job, is more than enough,' Hattie replied. And she meant it. Her mum now at least had friends, and a life away from her dad, for six hours a day, and Hattie couldn't be more grateful to be able to talk about what was going on at home. She was sure she would have driven herself half mad if she'd had no one to confide in.

'Is your mum still managing to put a bit of money away every week?' Dolly asked.

'She is, but it's no king's ransom. Hardly enough to

disappear and make a new life for herself. And I'm terrified Dad will find it one day.'

'Is it well hidden?'

'As well as it can be. He hasn't found it so far and he's a dab hand at sniffing out money, especially when he's desperate for a drink, although that's all the time now.'

'The offer is still there if you want me to look after it. I hope I don't have to say this, but I swear on my boys' lives you can trust me, duck.'

'I know that!' Hattie gasped in confirmation. 'You don't have to swear on anyone's life. I did mention it to Mum a while ago, but she finds it hard to involve other people; another consequence of being controlled by my dad for years. He cut off all her friends and made her feel as though no one would want to have anything to do with her. I guess it takes a long time to recover from that, if ever.'

'You don't have to tell me, duck. Sadly, I've been there, but if it gives you any sort of hope I am living proof that you can recover and lead a normal life again. Don't get me wrong, it takes a while, but it is possible.'

'Thank you, Dolly. And I'm so sorry you suffered too. No one deserves to be treated this badly.'

'No, they don't, duck, and that's why I want you and your mum to know you can always count on me. If there is anything you need at all, you only have to say.'

'Thank you. I really am so grateful, and I know Mum is too. It means so much.'

'Don't mention it. I just don't want you and your mum suffering alone. We are all here for you. Don't ever forget that.'

'I won't.' Hattie nodded, once again grateful to be surrounded by such kind friends. They might not be able to cure her dad's demon addiction to the bottle, but they could certainly keep her and her mum propped up when they needed it the most.

Chapter 14

Saturday, 12 April 1941

'What are these for?' Patty asked, a grin spreading across her face, as she accepted the bunch of pretty pink chrysanthemums tied neatly with a white ribbon.

'To say thank you and sorry.'

'Yer big dafty,' Patty exclaimed, throwing her arms around Archie.

'Watch the flowers.' Archie laughed, quickly lifting them in the air before they got completely squashed in between their bodies.

'Oops,' Patty said, before plonking a kiss on Archie's lips. 'They are very pretty.'

'You deserve it. I haven't been much fun lately.'

'No, but you have had good reason,' Patty responded, her tone now serious. 'It's been a tough time.'

'It has, but I didn't mean to take it out on you.'

'We're a team, remember?' Patty said.

'Thank you. I do appreciate how patient you have been.'

'It's okay. Now don't give it another thought.'

'Any chance of a cuppa, then?' Archie asked. 'I don't think I've warmed up all day. It's still pretty nippy out there.'

'Sorry! Of course. Take yer coat off and once I've put these flowers in water, I'll pop the kettle on.'

'Thank you. M'nannan isn't 'alf a slavedriver when she gets started. I've been at the allotment since we finished at the factory at lunchtime.'

'Oh. You poor thing. Have you eaten anything?'

'My nannan isn't daft. She took me a flask of soup, mainly because she didn't want me sneaking off for a break!'

Patty couldn't help but giggle. Archie adored his nannan and would move heaven and earth for her, so she knew his gripes were light-hearted and contained no bad will.

'How's the allotment looking?' she asked, carefully arranging the flowers in a jam jar, tying the silky white ribbon in a neat bow around the rim.

'Tidier. I got rid of all the old foliage and cleared away a stack of weeds. I've popped some potatoes in but have held off everything else. M'nannan is adamant we haven't escaped the last of the frost yet.'

'Don't say that. I was hoping now April was here that the cold weather might finally come to an end. I'm fed up with walking to work in the freezing cold. I swear to God, it's a miracle I haven't come out with chilblains.'

Archie broke into a laugh. 'You are a case. Think of those poor blokes outside in the yard all year round. They're the ones you should feel sorry for.'

'I suppose,' Patty conceded. 'Anyway, can I ask what's happened to make you feel better?'

Patty hoped her question wouldn't set Archie back. Despite how much she tried to pull him out of his dark mood, he'd spent the last three months barely communicating. He was constantly blaming himself for Alf's death and was devasted by the loss of so many air raid wardens, many of whom he'd classed as friends.

'I'm not sure really. A few things, I suppose. I keep seeing Josie and Daisy at work and they are managing so well. At first it made me feel even worse. Every time I looked at them, I felt responsible for their pain, even if they were putting on a brave face. But I started to realize, if they could cope, then I should be able to. But it's not like flicking a switch, is it?'

'No.' Patty quietly poured Archie a steaming mug of tea from the freshly brewed pot, not wanting to disturb him, sensing he needed to voice his feelings.

'Anyway, I was at the allotment this afternoon, and there was a woman working away in the plot next to us and we got chatting.'

'Oh right. What was she saying?' Patty had now sat down at the kitchen table next to Archie.

'It was really sad, actually. Her sister was at The Marples the night it got hit.'

'Gosh,' Patty gasped. Over sixty people had been crushed to death after the city-centre hotel took a direct hit during the Sheffield Blitz.

'This woman – Lily, she was called – was supposed to be there too but didn't go at the last minute, as she had a bit of a cold and fancied an early night.'

'I don't know what to say,' Patty confessed. 'I mean, I'm glad she didn't die too, but she must miss her sister terribly.'

'Yes, she was saying there was only a year between them, so they were best friends. Anyway, she said she had been plagued with guilt for not going out that night. She'd convinced herself that if she had gone, her sister might somehow have survived.'

'But she could never know that,' Patty reasoned.

'No and I think she knows that now, but she also said that she had felt guilty for being alive when her sister wasn't.'

'Dear God,' Patty whispered, putting her mug of steaming tea down and placing one of her hands on her sweetheart's, knowing the very same thoughts had haunted him.

'It's okay. When I told her I felt the same, she said something that really made me think about things.'

'Can I ask what it was?'

'Yes. She said her sister would be cross at her if she wasted the life she still had, and that she had to try and do something good so her sister's death wouldn't be in vain.'

Patty clenched her lips together in a bid to stop herself from getting upset. How cruel this world was, so many needless deaths for a war that made no sense.

'What a brave woman,' Patty finally said, working hard to stop her voice breaking.

'I agree. It hit a real chord with me.'

'It did?' Patty asked.

Archie looked up at Patty and nodded solemnly.

'It made me think how my gaffers at the ARP were doing their jobs to help others and would want me to carry on. And Alf, he was always helping other people. Losing them is the hardest thing I've ever had to cope with, but hearing Lily today made me realize I still have a life. I nearly died so many times as a kid due to my dicky ticker.'

Archie lifted his free hand to his heart.

'Anyway, it was like a light had finally come back on, and I realized not only how lucky I was to be alive, but that I had to keep on doing what I could to save other people.'

'You do that every day, just working at Vickers.'

'I haven't volunteered for as many shifts as I could have done at the ARP.'

'That's understandable.'

'I know, but I'm going to start pulling my weight again.'

Patty forced an encouraging smile, the thought of Archie protecting the streets of Sheffield was bittersweet. On the one hand, she couldn't be prouder of him and was delighted to see his mood lifted, but the other part of her was terrified she could lose the man she loved with all her heart to this nonsensical war.

'And the other thing is,' Archie added, a smile emerging, 'I know how lucky I am to have so many people around me who love me, including you.'

Then leaning across the table, he tenderly kissed Patty, sending goose pimples down her spine.

'I love you, Patty,' Archie said when they finally parted.

'And I love you too.'

'I really am so sorry for being a misery guts the last few months.'

'You don't have to keep saying sorry. It's been a really horrible time.'

'I know, but I shouldn't have taken it out on the people who care for me the most. My mum and nannan have been at their wits' end too with me.'

'Maybe today was your nannan's way of trying to help you,' Patty suggested.

'Possibly, but I don't think even she could have realized exactly how well it would turn out.'

'No!' Patty agreed. 'I'm just glad you are feeling better. I hated seeing you so down in the dumps.'

'Me too, but I am determined to make it up to you.'

'Really?' Patty asked, a glint appearing in her eye; never one to turn down a bit of attention.

'Yes.' Archie grinned, knowing how much Patty loved to be made to feel special. 'Starting with a trip to the

Pavilion tonight. I'll even buy you a bag of your favourite toffees.'

'Oooh! You do know how to spoil a girl,' Patty cooed.

'We could go dancing if you prefer. I might have to go home and get changed, though,' Archie suggested, looking down at his comfy cable-knit jumper.

'Maybe next week.' Patty smiled, looking at her own outfit, consisting of a pair of wide-leg trousers and a pale-blue long-sleeved blouse. 'I'm hardly dressed up to the nines. Besides which, I heard *The Philadelphia Story* is on.'

'Trust you to know,' Archie mock-teased, knowing Patty would never turn down the chance to see Cary Grant on the big screen.

'But,' Patty added righteously, 'I quite fancy a night snuggled up with you.'

'Well, I won't argue with that,' Archie replied, squeezing Patty's knee under the table. 'I really am a lucky man.'

'I know!' And with that the pair grinned at each other, all the tension between them over the last few months disappearing.

'Hello, you two,' Bill greeted, as he bound through the back door, his arms laden with newspaper packages from which were emanating the most mouthwatering of aromas.

'Thank chuff for that!' Patty exclaimed. 'I'm starving.'

'You're always hungry.' Bill laughed, rolling his eyes.

'I'm a hard-working girl, I'll have you know.'

'No need to convince me, luv.' He winked at his daughter, then turned to Archie. 'You will join us, won't yer, son?'

'I don't want to put you out.'

'Not at all. There's plenty. You must stay.'

'What's that?' Angie asked, joining Patty, Bill and Archie in the kitchen.

'I was just saying Archie should stay and have fish and chips with us.'

'Of course!' Angie reiterated. 'It's lovely to see yer, luv.'

'Shall I get some plates?' Patty suggested.

'Nah,' Bill replied. 'No need for the Sunday best. Archie won't mind. We can eat out of the wrappers. They taste better that way.'

The smell of a chippy dinner, mixed with salt and vinegar, quickly wafted through the house, causing an onslaught of footsteps to enter the kitchen.

'Food!' Tom Tom screeched excitedly.

He ran towards Archie, who scooped him up onto his knee.

'Would you like to sit with me?'

'Yeeeees,' Tom Tom squealed, wrapping his arms around Archie, whom he had always adored.

Within a couple of minutes, Angie had divided out the Saturday-night treat amongst her family and Archie, abandoning cutlery for the little wooden forks that came with the takeaway tea, while Patty had busied herself getting them all a drink.

As Patty glanced around the busy table, taking in the several conversations that were all going on at once, she couldn't help but smile. Archie and Tom Tom were laughing as they playfully fought over a chip, and for the first time since the Blitz, the love of her life looked genuinely happy, all the worry lines that had been commonplace on his face over the last four months now vanished.

Chapter 15

Monday, 14 April 1941

'Vinny?' Diane called by habit as she and Hattie came through the back door, the noise of something being dropped loudly stopping them in their tracks.

But as the pair peered into the kitchen, they realized the sound was coming from the front room, and a fissure of dread coursed through Diane.

'Oh luv,' Diane whispered, gripping her daughter's arm, her voice revealing the terror she felt.

Hattie's eyes widened as it dawned on her too what her dad was doing.

'Let me sort this,' Hattie offered. 'I can say it's my savings.'

'No! I am not putting you and my grandchild at risk. None of this is your doing.'

'Why don't we just go back out?' Hattie said as quietly as possible. 'By the time he comes back he will be so drunk, he'll not be fit for anything.'

But even as Hattie said the words, she knew her dad was as evil in drink as he was sober.

'If only I'd not gone to the butcher's after work, I'd have been home before him.'

'He might just go straight out,' Hattie replied hopefully.

'Is that you pair of conniving bitches?' came Vinny's thunderous voice, as his heavy footsteps indicated he was making his way to the kitchen.

Diane clenched her eyes shut, forcing back the tears that were desperately trying to force their way out. Trying to galvanize herself, Hattie took a deep breath and reached for her mum's hand.

He's got what he wanted. Hopefully he will just go straight to the pub, she silently prayed.

But as her dad stampeded into the kitchen, the look of sheer fury on his face told Hattie that her hopes were little more than wishful thinking.

'Did you really think I wouldn't find your sneaky little lies out?' Vinny was waving the paper bag of money in the air.

'It's mine,' Hattie lied before her mum could say a word. 'It's for when me and John get a house of our own.'

Vinny eyed his daughter, considering if she was telling the truth.

'Really?' he spat, taking a step forward so he was just centimetres away from her and Diane's faces, the stench of stale alcohol from the night before emanating from his breath.

'Yes,' Hattie muttered. 'I've been putting a bit aside every week.'

Vinny stared at his daughter, his eyes ever so slightly narrowing, unsure what to believe. Then as if a shard of clarity had pierced his thoughts, they widened again.

'You're lying,' he accused.

'I'm not. I just wanted to have a bit put aside to help with the baby too.'

'And that's how I know yer lying, yer little bitch,' Vinny stormed, pointing a finger into her chest.

'Leave her alone,' Diane said instinctively, temporarily overriding her fear.

'You can shut that stupid mouth of yours too.'

'Vinny,' Diane answered, in a desperate bid to reason with her husband.

'I said shut up,' he roared, his cheeks turning red as his temper flared. 'Here's how I know the pair of yer are lying.' Turning his attention back to Hattie, he added, 'You must think I was born yesterday. There's no bloody way you would move that heavy couch. Not in your state. You wouldn't risk harming that chuffin' baby of yours.'

Hattie bit the inside of her cheek, quietly berating herself for not thinking her lie through. Her stunned silence was all the conformation Vinny needed.

'I knew it,' he roared, then spinning round to confront Diane head-on, he grabbed her wrist.

'You thought you could hide money away from me, did you?'

'It was just to help pay the bills.'

'I asked you time and time again and you swore blind

we had no money. I knew you were lying to me. Well, I'm going to show you what happens to women who lie to their husbands.'

'Dad,' Hattie pleaded as Vinny scrunched the money into his pocket, then, using both hands, grabbed his wife's coat collar.

'I'm sick to death of you, yer useless cow,' he snarled, his grip tightening and lifting Diane off the ground.

'Let go of her,' Hattie repeated. 'You're going to really hurt her.'

'That's exactly my intention.' Vinny laughed sardonically. 'The pair of yer have been pushing yer luck for months now.'

'I'm sorry,' Diane whimpered, barely able to catch her breath as Vinny pulled the collar tighter and tighter around her neck.

'I'm sure yer sorry now. Now that I've caught yer red-handed. But how many other lies have yer told me? What other secrets have you kept from me? How many?' Vinny's nose flared and his eyes betrayed the burning anger bubbling inside him.

'None,' Diane mouthed, unable to voice the word as Vinny constricted the air in her throat.

'Dad. Please let her go. You're going to kill her,' Hattie warned, now terrified. She'd seen her dad attack her mum more times that she could count, but this new level of violence was a step above his usual heavy-handed punches and shoves.

'At least that way, I wouldn't be lied to. I could find m'sen a decent woman.'

The colour was draining from Diane's face as she tried to pull her husband's hands away from her, but he was far too strong. As well as pulling Diane's collar tighter around her neck, he was digging his thick knuckles into her throat.

Gasping for air, Diane opened and closed her mouth, but her body was beginning to go limp. Instead of deterring him, seeing his wife so weak encouraged Vinny; a sadistic and satisfied look appeared across his face.

Petrified, Hattie desperately grabbed at her dad's arm.

'Let go,' she cried. 'Please. Don't do this, Dad. You can have every penny I bring home, but let Mum go.'

'Shut up!' Vinny yelled, kicking his right leg out, sharply catching Hattie's shin with his steel-toe-capped boot.

A piercing pain shot through Hattie, but she ignored it, only able to focus on her mum who looked as though she was about to pass out. Frantic thoughts passed through Hattie's mind. She could run next door, scream for help, pray someone would come to her mum's rescue, but she knew her mum could be dead in the time it took to raise the alarm. There was no doubt in her mind that if she didn't act fast her dad was going to kill her mum. Hattie's eyes darted around the kitchen, looking for anything to put a stop to Vinny's brutality, but as always everything was neatly put away in cupboards; the worktops cleared of clutter.

In that moment, she wished her mum hadn't always been so house proud. But then she saw it – her dad's gas mask, sat idly in the corner of the room, no longer in its cloth bag. Vinny had dumped it there weeks earlier, nine times out of ten refusing to use it. Hattie reached for it, knowing this could be her only chance to save her mum. Grabbing one of the rough straps, Hattie pulled it back behind her shoulder and swung it with all her might at her dad's head.

The impact was instant. The shock caused Vinny to let go of Diane, who dropped straight to the floor like a sack of potatoes.

'What the bloody hell!' Vinny screamed, one of his hands grabbing the side of his head. 'You stupid little bitch. You're going to pay for that,' he retorted, immediately going to attack his daughter.

Hattie used one arm to cover her now slightly rounded tummy and the other to protect her face, knowing her dad wouldn't let her get away with what she'd just done.

'You're right to cower, yer useless little cow!' he shouted, his arms flaying. 'Yer gonna pay for that little trick.'

Hattie steeled herself, but just as Vinny was about to swing a punch at his now frozen daughter, Diane was in front of him, a bread knife in her hand.

'Don't you dare lay a hand on her,' she croaked, her voice hoarse but her determination to protect Hattie undeniable.

Vinny smirked, as if seeing Diane threatening him was nothing more than an irritating hindrance.

'You wouldn't dare,' he said, laughing. 'And even if you did, I'd make sure you paid for it for the rest of yer life. Now put it down, yer stupid bloody woman.'

'I won't let you lay another hand on Hattie,' Diane reiterated defiantly.

'Really?' Vinny stormed, as he went to knock the knife from his wife's trembling hands, temporarily forgetting about the aching pain the blow to his head had caused.

A rage like never before was fizzing inside Diane. Instead of letting the knife fall from her hand, she gripped it more tightly, and the sharp serrated blade caught the top of Vinny's hand. The dragging motion pierced Vinny, crimson spots of blood accumulating on his mottled skin.

'Look what you have done!' Vinny roared incredulously.

Stunned, Diane looked at her husband's hand with a mixture of shock and terror, knowing she would pay for her defiance.

Vinny grabbed his wife's fragile wrist. This time her fingers splayed open, and the knife fell to the floor, clattering loudly against the stone.

But before Vinny could attack his wife again, Hattie quickly bent down and grabbed the wooden handle of the knife.

'You go . . . gonna have another go?' Vinny snarled, turning to his daughter. But his words were beginning to slur.

'Just leave it, Dad. You have got what you wanted.'

'Don't you bloody tell . . .' Vinny paused, swaying ever so slightly. 'Don't you tell me what to do,' he managed the second time, gripping the back of a kitchen chair with his untouched hand. 'The pair of yer are not worth the ground yer walk on.'

Diane looked at her husband. His nasty words were still pouring out of him like venom, but something in his physical stance was wavering.

'I can't be arsed with either of yer,' he spat, stumbling towards the back door, wiping the blood from his cut hand on the back of his filthy work pants. 'Yer not worth it. I'm going out.'

Diane took a quiet intake of breath. *Thank God.*

But as Vinny reached the back door, he glared back at his wife and daughter. 'Don't think you've got away with this,' he spat. 'I'll sort yer both when I get back.'

Chapter 16

'Luv, are you okay?' Diane asked, rushing to her daughter's side as soon as Vinny had staggered out, the door slamming shut behind him.

'It's only my shin. Don't worry about me. Let me see your neck, Mum.'

'It's nothing.' Old habits die hard, and Diane was more than used to playing down the heinous injuries her husband had inflicted.

'Mum. Let me see,' Hattie insisted.

'Oh, luv.' After the events of the past half an hour, Diane was unable to hold back her tears as she sat down on a chair, her fingers gently touching her tender throat.

'Let's see,' Hattie said kindly.

Carefully Diane undid the buttons of her coat, revealing the extent of her injuries. An angry purple bruise had formed a collar around Diane's neck, deeper in colour where Vinny's fingers had pressed harder.

'Oh, Mum,' Hattie gasped, horrified her own dad could be capable of such sickening violence.

'Is it bad?' Diane whispered.

It was. There was no point denying it, but Hattie knew what her mum needed right now was hope.

'It will pass, and a scarf will cover it. Don't worry. Let me see if we have got some witch hazel in the cupboard.'

'I can go,' Diane sighed as she went to get up.

'It's fine, Mum. I'll get it and then I'll put the kettle on. I think we could both do with a cuppa.'

Ten minutes later, Diane was holding an ointment-soaked handkerchief to her neck, as Hattie poured them both a comforting cuppa.

'Does it hurt?'

'It's not bad,' Diane said, but Hattie knew her mum was trying to protect her. Every time she moved the white handkerchief to a new spot, she visibly winced.

'Mum—' Hattie started, taking a sip of her own steaming cup of tea.

'I know what you are going to say,' Diane interrupted.

Hattie looked at her mum, her eyes full of compassion.

'I just don't know how I can leave your dad.' Diane looked physically and emotionally exhausted. 'Where would I go? And you know he would come after me. I'd never escape him, and then I dread to think what he would do to me. I just need to try and keep the peace.'

'We could go to the police?' But even as Hattie said the words, she knew it was a hopeless venture.

Hattie momentarily closed her eyes. *How could this be allowed to happen?* It was a miracle her dad hadn't killed her mum. *Was that what it would take for anyone to do something?*

'I don't suppose I can persuade you to come and stay at John's parents. We could go together?'

Her face revealing the sadness she felt, Diane slowly shook her head.

'He'll just come after me, luv, and I can't bear the thought of everyone knowing what he's done. I couldn't face the humiliation. I know that's not very strong of me. I just haven't got it in me, luv.'

Hattie nodded. She would have been shocked if her mum had said anything else. Her dad had destroyed every ounce of confidence her mum had once possessed. Hattie wasn't cross at her mum, but she was very worried.

As if reading her daughter's mind, Diane said, 'Do you think he will still be angry when he gets home?'

Truth be told, Hattie didn't know, but if years of experience was anything to go by then her dad wouldn't just be angry, he would be apoplectic, fuelled by even more booze. That is when his fists really would fly and there would be no reasoning with him.

'Maybe we just need to do something to protect ourselves from him?'

'Like what?'

Hattie bit down on her lip, a flurry of thoughts speeding around her mind. *Could they lock her dad out, or barricade themselves into her bedroom?* But she knew the reality was this would incense him further.

And if she asked John's dad to come and stay with them, she knew it would only be a temporary solution. As soon as he left, Vinny would explode and they would really pay for it.

'Oh, Mum. I just don't know,' Hattie sighed. Then placing a hand on her tummy, she felt a course of fear flood her. She had to think of a way to protect her unborn child. The thought of her baby coming to any harm didn't bear thinking about.

The next hour passed in a blur as Diane nursed her neck, which was now throbbing, and Hattie tried to think of a way to placate her dad when he finally returned home full of fury and resentment. She went through every scenario she could think of, from hiding at a neighbour's house, to taking her mum to Patty's or Betty's house. But all of them led back to the same thing – when Vinny finally had them on his own again, which he invariably would, all hell would let loose.

'Maybe I can try and reason with him?' Hattie said half-heartedly, now exhausted.

'No!' Diane replied staunchly. 'You are not putting you or your baby at risk. I won't allow it. I'm your mum, it's my job to protect you.'

'We just need to look after one another,' Hattie commented. More than ever, she wished John was nearby. He would know exactly what to do.

But before Diane could respond, a racket from outside brought the conversation to an abrupt halt.

'Diane!' Vinny's bellowing voice penetrated the walls of the family home.

'Oh God,' Diane gasped, her eyes widening as a new fissure of terror soared through her.

Hattie clasped her mum's hands, her fear replicated. Her naive hopes that her dad might have gone into a more docile mood after so much alcohol quickly evaporated.

'Let's just stay calm,' she whispered. 'Maybe if we agree with everything he says, he will calm down.'

'Wait until I get inside that house!' Vinny yelled, his threat rapidly dissipating Hattie's hopes.

'What are we going to do . . .' Diane stated, more than asked.

'I don't know,' Hattie said, panicked, utterly terrified. Her dad was clearly in a rage, which could only mean one thing.

'Maybe we should hide under the stairs,' Diane suggested, already on her feet.

'I'm not sure.' Hattie knew any act of defence would only inflame her dad, but they couldn't just wait like a pair of docile sitting ducks, although she wasn't sure how much protection the cupboard, which they had used as a shelter against the Luftwaffe, would offer against her incandescent dad.

'You're right,' Diane said, reading her daughter's mind.

'Let me in my own bloody house,' Vinny yelled from outside the front door.

'He never takes that key with him,' Diane whispered.

'Leave him out there,' Hattie said. 'Maybe the fresh air will do him good.' But even as she said the words, Hattie knew he would only break the door down if he couldn't get in.

Terrified of enraging Vinny further – let alone what the neighbours would think – Diane rushed to the front door.

'No, Mum,' Hattie protested.

But Diane was already turning the key.

'You're going to pay for it this time,' Vinny shouted from the other side of the door, his sinister words not leaving anything to the imagination.

'Mum,' Hattie gasped, grabbing a heavy-based frying pan from the worktop and dashing towards the door.

'Diane!' came another roar from Vinny as the front door flew open.

His face red with fury, Vinny lurched towards his terrified wife.

'No,' Hattie bellowed, a fury like never before coming over her. She wasn't going to let her dad lay another finger on her mum.

Vinny's eyes darted towards his daughter, as she lifted the frying pan above her head.

'You going to try and attack me again,' he snorted.

Despite her own fears, Hattie refused to be threatened by the taunt.

'You can't keep doing this,' she cried.

'And how are you gonna stop me?' Vinny half laughed, half snarled, taking a step closer to her and Diane.

Dread coursed through Hattie. She knew if her dad got hold of her or her mum, his rage would hold no boundaries.

'Just go,' Hattie retorted, positioning herself between her parents.

'Luv, no,' Diane pleaded, gripping her daughter's arm.

But Hattie knew if she backed down now, her dad would forever reign over them. With all the courage she could muster, she inched another step forwards.

'Yer really think I'm going to be thrown out of m' own house by you,' Vinny spat.

'Just go and sober up,' Hattie responded.

'Don't yer tell me what to do, yer hard-faced little cow,' Vinny exploded. But as he tried to grab Hattie, she swung the frying pan. Vinny stepped sideways to avoid being hit, but as he did, he lost his balance and stumbled backwards out of the front door.

Hattie knew this was her only chance. Before her mum could argue, she quickly slammed the door shut and locked it.

'Oh, luv,' Diane sighed, her cheeks sodden with tears. 'He's going to be so angry.'

'I know,' Hattie said, her voice now revealing how scared she was. 'But he can't keep bullying us like this. He's going to really hurt one of us.'

The two women looked at each other, knowing this was far from over.

'The back door,' Hattie whispered, aware her dad could storm through it any second. 'Is it locked?'

'I don't know,' Diane replied.

Both women rushed into the kitchen. Hattie checked the handle. Realizing the door was unlocked, she immediately turned the key.

'Let's just have a minute,' Diane said, sitting down at the table. Hattie joined her, knowing she needed to try and calm down. Placing her hands on her stomach, she knew the stress couldn't be good for her baby.

'I'll make us a drink,' Diane said, on her feet again.

But just as she went to fill the kettle, a loud screech of brakes stopped Diane in her tracks.

Chapter 17

'What was that?' Diane gasped.

'A car, I think.'

But before either women could speak, a voice they had never heard before penetrated the silence. It was so muffled they couldn't make out what was being said.

Then, all of a sudden, there was a scream.

'Help! Someone. I need help here.'

'What's happened?' Diane whispered.

'I don't know,' Hattie replied. But as the words escaped her, she knew something was very wrong. Her dad's threats had stopped and, judging by the desperate screams for help, something serious had happened.

'I'll go and see.'

'No!' Diane protested, grabbing her daughter's arm. 'Your dad! I don't want you to get hurt.'

'He's gone quiet,' Hattie stated.

The two women went into the hallway. Tentatively Hattie opened the front door. Further down the road, people were calling for help and doors up and down the street were opening and closing.

Then came the ominous words, which cemented Hattie's thoughts.

'It's Vinny,' a voice she recognized as one of their neighbour's said.

'Mum,' Hattie breathed hard, gripping the door handle, too scared to open it, 'something's not right.'

Diane stared at her daughter, the same sense of dread coursing through her, as the kerfuffle from outside seemed to get louder.

'Someone get an ambulance,' a woman instructed, 'and quick.'

Hattie and her mum exchanged a terrified look.

'It's your dad!' Diane finally gasped.

On autopilot, Hattie stepped onto the dimly lit street.

'Diane,' one of their neighbours gasped as Hattie and her mum looked down the road. 'It's your Vinny.'

Diane's eyes locked on the scene ten or so yards away. A taxi had stopped at an awkward angle and a group of people had gathered at the other side of the vehicle.

'What's happened?' was all Diane could manage.

'Mum,' Hattie started, putting her hand on Diane's arm. 'I think . . . I think Dad has been hit.'

'No. No . . . It can't be.'

'Luv. Don't look,' said the woman who had first suggested Vinny was involved.

'Mrs Wilson,' Hattie asked. 'Has my dad been hit?'

The kindly-looking woman, with her hair in rollers and a coat tightly wrapped around her, slowly nodded.

'No,' Diane gasped again.

Before Hattie could stop her, she ran to the parked vehicle.

'Vinny!' she cried, her screams parting the group. On the ground, the dim glow of the taxi's headlights lit up her husband, his lifeless body twisted into an unnatural position.

'I'm sorry, luv,' a man announced. 'He just ran out in front of me. He seemed to come from nowhere. I tried to stop.'

'Is that blood?' Diane whispered, dropping to her knees next to her husband, as she stared at the pool of crimson liquid pooling around Vinny's head.

'Mum,' Hattie choked, taking in the sight of her dad. But as the enormity of the situation hit her, Hattie's legs began to give way. *This is all my fault. I threw him out of the house.*

'Hey. I've got yer,' Mrs Wilson said, putting her arms around Hattie's waist in the nick of time.

'Dad,' Hattie mouthed. 'I'm sorry.'

'Ralf,' Mrs Wilson beckoned. 'Help Diane up. We need to get them indoors.'

'C'mon, duck,' Ralf said, doing as his wife instructed. 'Let me get you up. It will do you no good looking at your Vinny like this.'

'Is he . . .' But Diane couldn't say the words.

Ralf looked from Diane to the distraught taxi driver.

'I couldn't find a pulse,' he said by way of explanation.

'Oh God,' Diane sobbed, placing a hand on her husband's cheek. As her eyes adjusted to the dimmed light, Diane realized all signs of life from Vinny had vanished. He was terrifyingly still, no breath leaving his nose or mouth, and his eyes had rolled backwards.

'Oh, Vinny,' she sobbed, tears rolling down her own cheeks.

'What have I done?' Hattie cried.

Diane looked up at her daughter, who was only managing to say upright thanks to their kindly neighbour.

'What are we going to do?' Hattie said, her whole body shaking.

'Why don't I take you both inside?' Ralf said again.

'I can't leave him. He's my husband.'

'The ambulance will be here soon,' Mrs Wilson said gently.

'I'm staying with him,' Diane stated with an insistence that revealed she wouldn't be persuaded.

Hattie was too shell-shocked to argue. 'I'll stay too.' Then releasing herself from Mrs Wilson's protective arms, she lowered herself down onto the cold road next to her mum.

'How has it come to this?' Diane asked, her eyes bestowing the horror and shock that was rippling through her.

'I shouldn't have forced him to leave,' Hattie murmured, guilt soaring through her.

She was desperately trying to comprehend how just a few minutes earlier she and her mum were terrified her dad was going to attack them. But now he was lying on the ground, dead.

'I'm so sorry,' the taxi driver, who was as white as a sheet, repeated. 'I didn't mean to hit him.'

'C'mon, pal,' Ralf said, seeing the state the poor bloke was in. 'Let's sit you down.' Ralf led the taxi driver to the kerb. Another neighbour had arrived with a tray, holding mugs of steaming tea.

'Give him one of these,' she instructed Ralf. 'I've put some sugar in.'

Ralf accepted a mug on the driver's behalf. 'Here you go, pal. Take this.'

A crowd had now gathered on the street, but neither Diane nor Hattie noticed as they sat next to Vinny, unable to really take in what had happened.

'Why did you have to get so angry?' Diane whispered, talking to the body of her motionless husband.

Hattie put her now trembling hand on her mum's arm.

'I always thought it would be me that ended up dead,' Diane said, barely audible, but Hattie was close enough to hear.

'Mum,' Hattie said, her voice breaking, unable to think of anything else to say.

'Here's the ambulance,' one of the bystanders announced.

Hattie looked up. Coming down the road was an old van that had been converted into an emergency vehicle.

'Maybe we should give them some space,' Mrs Wilson suggested as she bent down next to Diane and Hattie.

'She's right,' Hattie said, looking at her mum.

The tears in Diane's eyes welled. 'Okay,' she accepted. But first she leant in closer to her husband. 'I loved you,' she whispered, placing a gentle kiss on his cheek. 'I never stopped loving you.'

Then she allowed Mrs Wilson to help her stand up, just as the ambulance pulled up behind the stranded taxi and the driver jumped out.

'What's happened here?' she asked.

The words were too much for Diane. 'Oh,' she inhaled.

'Come on, duck,' Mrs Wilson said. 'Ralf can talk to them. Let me get you inside.'

But Diane couldn't move. She froze. They would take her husband away. *I might never see him again.*

'Please be gentle with him,' she whispered, pleading with the ambulance driver, who was quickly surveying the scene.

'Of course,' the woman, who couldn't have been any older than Hattie, replied.

Bending down, she expertly placed her finger and thumb on Vinny's neck, if only to confirm what she had already ascertained.

'Is this your husband?' she asked.

Diane nodded, a fresh cascade of tears erupting from her now puffy eyes.

'I'll look after him,' she assured Diane, her voice gentle and kind. Aware her next task wasn't one any relative of a dead person would want to see, she added, 'I'll need a bit of space to get your husband on a stretcher. Why don't you go inside? A policeman will come and talk to you soon.'

'A policeman?'

'It's just so we can understand what happened.'

Hattie gasped. *Was she responsible for her dad's death?*

'Let's do what she's suggested,' Mrs Wilson interjected. She didn't want Diane or Hattie to see the extent of Vinny's injuries when he was lifted.

Diane looked down at her husband for the final time. 'You're at peace now,' she pronounced, before allowing Mrs Wilson to lead her away and back through the front door they had run out of minutes earlier.

Hattie took one last glance at her dad. 'I never wanted it to end like this,' she whispered, her voice breaking.

Twenty minutes later, a bobby dressed in his navy uniform sat opposite Diane and Hattie at the kitchen table.

'I'm sorry to have to ask you this,' he said gravely, 'but do you think you can tell me what happened?'

Diane didn't even blink. Instead, she looked straight ahead into the middle distance, unable to digest what the policeman had asked.

'Maybe I can explain?' Hattie offered hesitantly. She had to tell the truth. No matter how hard it was, she had to tell the officer how she had forced her dad out of the house.

'Take yer time, duck,' the kindly-faced officer replied.

Still shaking, Hattie took a sip of the mug of tea Mrs Wilson had made for her, before taking a few seconds to compose herself.

'My dad. Well, he was not in a good way,' she started, almost on autopilot.

'In what way?'

Hattie momentarily closed her eyes and bit down on her bottom lip. *Where did she even start?*

'He was drunk,' Hattie said quietly, a sense of betrayal flooding her despite everything her dad had subjected her to.

'I see,' the officer replied, nodding and writing down the comment in his notepad.

'When he came back, he was angry. He was threatening to . . .'

But Hattie couldn't finish her sentence. Saying the words would make everything real and she wasn't sure she was strong enough.

'Is there anything else you would like to tell me?' the policeman asked. His gaze had temporarily diverted to Diane and the nasty purple bruising that had appeared around her neck.

Hattie's eyes were wet, and the pools of tears escaped, as the horrors of the evening's events flashed before her. She had assumed their day couldn't get any worse after Vinny had attacked her and her mum. How little had she known.

'Nothing that matters now,' Diane interjected matter-of-factly. Her monotone statement was devoid of any emotion.

'I told him he couldn't come back in,' Hattie added, regret flooding her. 'I thought he would . . .' She took a deep breath. 'He was so angry . . .'

The officer looked at Hattie, his eyes silently quizzing her, quietly prompting her to reveal the secrets she and her mum didn't have the energy to share.

'He needed to sober up,' Diane explained stoically. 'He'd drunk too much.'

Chapter 18

Tuesday, 15 April 1941

'Hattie,' Patty said, gently wrapping her arms around her best friend. 'I'm so sorry. I came as quickly as I could. How are you?'

'I don't know. It was awful. I can't think straight,' Hattie replied, trying to stay composed.

'I'm sorry too, luv,' Dolly, who had accompanied Patty, added.

'Thank you,' Hattie replied gratefully, before leading her friends into the front room. She felt unable to stay in the kitchen for a moment longer than she needed to, awful flashbacks from the previous day terrorizing her thoughts.

'Where's your mum?' Patty asked, looking round at the tidy, but empty, room.

'I've sent her upstairs for a sleep. Neither of us got much last night.'

'I'm sure.'

'Did Mrs Wilson come and tell you?' Hattie asked Patty. 'I didn't know how else to let you all know.'

'She came late last night. I wanted to come straight away, but she said the police were with you.'

'They were.' Hattie nodded. 'It was horrible. I can't help thinking it was all my fault.'

'Oh, duck,' Dolly interjected. 'You can't be blaming yourself. Not after everything yer dad has put you through.'

'But I told him to go. If I hadn't maybe he would still be here.'

As soon as Hattie said the words, her body began to shake and her eyes filled with tears, which quickly flowed unbidden down her cheeks.

'I'm sorry,' Hattie said. 'I don't seem to be able to stop crying.'

'Oh, duck,' Dolly said, putting her arm around Hattie. 'There's nothing to apologize for,' she added, gently encouraging Hattie to sit down on the couch. 'You have a good cry. You can't keep it all in.'

'I know he hadn't been a good person of late but maybe I should have just let him stay in the house,' Hattie countered, then weakening, she added, 'I still loved him, though.'

'Of course you did,' Dolly said, putting her arms around Hattie. 'He was your dad. It's only natural you are so upset.'

'It's not just that,' Hattie replied. 'I just keep thinking it's all my fault.'

'What do you mean?' Patty asked as gently as possible.

In between sobs, Hattie retold the events of the night before.

'I forced him back out of the house. He must have walked away and stumbled into the road.'

With that, Hattie broke down again. Dolly pulled her close and for a minute or so, Hattie sobbed into Dolly's chest, her heavy tears soaking her friend's cardigan.

'You can't blame yourself,' Dolly said firmly. 'Your dad was drunk. You didn't make him try and cross the road.'

'That's what Mum keeps saying, but I just can't help thinking I could have prevented it.'

'Now, now,' Dolly soothed, deeply saddened by the sight of Hattie and the torment she was suffering.

'I just didn't want him to hurt Mum.'

'Of course you didn't,' Dolly reassured.

'He never used to be so mean,' Hattie explained. 'I remember as a little girl, he was so kind. He would read me bedtime stories and never raised his voice.'

'Maybe those are the memories you should try and remember,' Dolly suggested kindly. 'The things that make you smile.'

Hattie sighed as she dabbed her pink and puffy eyes.

'Why did he have to change?'

'Aw, luv. If we knew the answer to that, the world would be a better place. I can't answer your question, but the one thing I can confirm is that there's no pointing thinking about the ifs and maybes. You'll send yourself half crazy. Nothing good will come of you torturing yerself.'

'He was so horrible yesterday,' Hattie continued. 'And if I'm really honest, part of me didn't want him to come home. I was terrified he would come barging in the back door. I suppose you should never wish too hard for something.'

With that, Hattie dropped her head into her hands, her chest aching as she once again sobbed, her whole body shaking.

'Hattie,' Patty soothed, as she took a turn to put her arms around her friend's shoulders. 'It's okay.'

As Patty comforted her friend, Dolly nipped into the kitchen and made a pot of tea, memories of her own late husband's tragic demise flooding her mind. 'Vinny doesn't deserve all this sympathy,' she quietly retorted, but also recalled the same mixed emotions she'd felt when her husband had finally keeled over with a heart attack.

By the time Dolly went back into the front room, holding a tray adorned with a fresh pot of tea, three mugs and a little jug of milk, Hattie had managed to compose herself.

'Thank you,' she whispered, looking at Dolly.

'A cup of tea can't solve the world's problems, but it's always good for the soul.'

After accepting the freshly poured cuppa, Hattie said to Dolly, 'Mum's in a pretty bad way. Would you mind talking to her when she feels up to it?'

'Of course I will, duck. No matter what your dad

had put you both through, it's still very hard when you suddenly lose someone you love.'

'He was really awful yesterday,' Hattie confessed.

'In what way, duck?'

Hattie took a deep breath and explained what led up to Vinny's death. 'I really thought he was going to kill one of us,' she said after revealing how he had brutally attacked them both. 'Mum was gasping for breath, and her neck is black and blue where he tried to strangle her. I was praying he wouldn't come home as I knew he'd start again. And now he never will.'

'Oh, Hattie,' Patty gasped, swallowing back her own tears at the thought of what Hattie and her mum had suffered. 'You must have both been terrified.'

'We were. It's my fault, though. I should never have let Mum hide the money under the couch. He was bound to find it, and I knew once he did he would be furious. I just didn't think he would be as cruel as he was.'

'Now listen, luv,' Dolly interjected, 'you can't blame yerself for any of this. Drink drives people to do awful things. They don't think straight. None of this was your fault. You mustn't think like that.'

'I should have seen it coming. He was forever searching the house.'

'Did you tell the police?' Dolly asked.

Hattie shook her head. 'Not about the abuse, no. There was no point, and I could tell Mum didn't want to say too much. Besides which, it won't change anything. They just wanted to know how he . . . well, you know what I mean.'

'We do.' Patty and Dolly nodded in agreement.

'And now,' Hattie took a sharp intake of break. 'They could . . .' her voice now trembling, 'they might think I caused his death. By pushing him out of the house. That's what made him walk into the taxi.'

'No!' Dolly said firmly. 'You must never think like that. From what you said your dad had walked down the street before he stepped into the road. I know this is hard to try and accept, but like I've said – and I mean it in the kindest way – the only person that caused your dad's accident was himself.'

'What a horrible way for his life to end,' Hattie whispered, her voice faltering once again.

'I know, duck. But if it helps, your dad probably didn't even realize what was happening. It sounds like he'd had an awful lot to drink.'

'I think he had,' Hattie said, resigned. 'And he rarely could remember anything after a heavy drinking session.'

'Let that bring you some comfort, luv.'

Hattie nodded, but she knew in her heart of hearts she wouldn't just be able to accept that her dad's death was of his own doing.

'How's your mum coping today?' Dolly asked. 'Or is that a daft question?'

'In a state of shock. Neither of us could really comprehend what happened last night. After the policeman left, we sat at the table for hours. It felt like a bad dream. I kept thinking I would wake up at any minute and it would all be over.'

'Oh, Hatts,' Pattie said, squeezing her friend's hand. 'I'm so sorry.'

'Thank you. It all feels so surreal, and I can't even begin to imagine what tomorrow holds, let alone the next few months.'

'You don't need to think too far ahead, right now. Just take one day at a time,' Dolly offered. 'And we are all here for you. Whatever you need, we can help you both. You don't have to do this alone.'

'I appreciate that. We will have a funeral to sort quite soon, and then work out if Mum and I can stay in this house now that we won't have Dad's wages. And what if the police do blame me?'

'They won't,' Dolly assured firmly. 'I know it's hard for you to accept right now, but you are not responsible for your dad's death.'

'I didn't want him to die,' Hattie said.

'We know you didn't, duck,' Dolly replied. 'And on the money side of things. Maybe it won't be as tight as you think,' she added as tactfully as she could.

'Maybe,' Hattie replied, avoiding saying what they were both thinking. Bringing up how much her dad had spent on drinking somehow seemed in bad taste now.

'Is there anything we can do for you right now?' Patty asked.

'Could you speak to Frank and ask him to let the gaffers know that I will be back as soon as I can?'

'He's already done it. I thought you would want your boss to know, so after I told Frank what happened he went up to the office and spoke to the powers-that-be.'

'You don't think they will mind if I take a couple of days off, do you?'

'You need to take more than a couple of days,' Dolly insisted. 'No one would expect you back for a little while.'

'To be honest, I know I need to arrange everything, but once I know Mum is okay I want to get back to work.'

'You've had an awful shock, duck. Maybe you should take a bit of time.'

'I'll drive myself mad sat here all day. I can't even face being in the kitchen. All I can see is what Dad did. And I'm not sure how I can walk down the street again.'

Patty gripped Hattie's hand a little tighter. 'Did your dad hurt you?'

'Not really. Only my leg. Mum bore the brunt of it all.'

'I'm so glad you and the baby are okay,' Patty commented.

'We are,' Hattie confirmed, her free hand touching her tummy.

'Have you managed to get hold of John?'

'I sent a telegram today, but I've not heard back yet. I don't even know where he is. He may have already left for North Africa. I've just sent it to the last address I had.'

More than anything in the world, Hattie wished her

husband was here to try and help her through. She missed him now more than ever.

'I'm sure he will be in touch as soon as he can,' Patty assured her friend, as if reading Hattie's mind.

But before Patty or Dolly could answer, the front room door slowly opened.

'Mum, I'm sorry. Did we wake you?' Hattie asked, automatically standing up.

'No. I've dozed a bit, but I couldn't get to sleep. Then I heard voices, so I thought I'd come down.'

'Let me get you a cup of tea,' Hattie insisted. 'There's still plenty in the pot.'

'That would be grand, luv. Thank you.'

Then Diane turned to Dolly and Patty. 'Thank you so much for coming.'

Dolly was already on her feet.

'Oh, luv,' she said, enveloping Diane in her arms. 'Of course we came. I'm so sorry.'

'Thank you,' Diane whispered, tears already soaking the shoulder of Dolly's gingham apron.

'I don't know why I'm crying so much,' Diane said as she lifted her head. 'It's not like he was a good husband of late, but I still loved him. We had been together a long time, you know.'

'I understand,' Dolly said, leading Diane to the sofa. 'It's a terrible shock.'

'We were so scared of him coming home, but I didn't want him to die. Or maybe I did. I don't know.'

'There's no point overanalyzing it all,' Dolly comforted. 'You couldn't have changed anything.'

'I shouldn't have hidden the money in the first place. Our Hattie warned me it could end badly. I just never thought he would find it, and now look what's happened.'

'Like I've told Hattie, you can't blame yerself. Neither of you can,' Dolly insisted. 'No one forced Vinny to drink as much as he did.'

'He had so many demons in his head. I did try to help him.'

'We know you did, duck. That goes without saying. But sometimes, no matter how hard you try, you can't change someone.'

Diane nodded in resignation and then, just as her daughter had minutes earlier, buried her head in Dolly's chest.

'Oh, Mum,' Hattie said as she came back into the front room, holding a mug.

'I'm okay, luv,' Diane whispered, sitting up. 'I didn't mean to get myself in another tizz.'

'You don't have to apologize,' Hattie reassured her mum. 'It's me that should be saying sorry.'

'Let me pour that,' Patty said, retrieving the mug from Hattie, and letting her friend sit down next to her mum.

Hattie didn't protest. Instead, she placed her own hand over her mum's.

'I didn't mean for Dad to die,' Hattie said as she wept.

'Oh, luv,' Diane said, wrapping her daughter in her arms. 'I know you didn't. You can't blame yourself. If I'd have left him already, none of this would have happened. We'll get through this together. I promise.'

Chapter 19

Wednesday, 16 April 1941

'How were they both?' Betty asked as she sat down opposite Patty at the canteen table.

'Terrible, if I'm honest. They were so upset. It was horrible to see. I just wanted to do something to make it all better.'

'Of course,' Betty said, taking her pack-up from her cloth bag. 'It's such a terrible shock for them. I'm sure you both just being there and listening was a huge comfort.'

'Maybe. I hope so. They are in shock and they both feel so guilty. Not that they should. It sounds like Vinny was awful to them before he stormed off in a drunken temper. Diane's neck was a reyt mess. It was all bruised and swollen. I think he'd tried to strangle her.'

'Oh gosh. Really?' Daisy asked. 'That's awful.'

'I think he got nasty when he found the money Diane had been hiding.'

'Goodness,' Betty sighed. 'They have had it tough for a long time, but I don't think anyone could have imagined this happening.'

'Definitely not,' Patty agreed. 'I just feel so helpless. I don't know what I can do to help Hattie and her mum.'

'Just listening and being on hand with a hug is enough,' Betty repeated, reassuring her friend.

'Betty's right,' Daisy added. 'Seeing a friendly face and having someone to talk to counts for so much. I couldn't have got through the last few months without you all.'

'I'm sorry,' Patty interjected. 'I didn't mean to bring back painful memories.'

'Not at all. Losing my dad was very different, please don't worry. But I mean it, if it wasn't for all of you, I'm not sure Mum and I would have got through it.'

Betty gave Daisy a kind smile, knowing how much her friend had struggled since Alf had been killed. Daisy still woke up every few nights in tears or shouting out her dad's name in her sleep. All she could do was hold Daisy's hand, reassure her she was okay and stay close until she fell back to sleep.

'There must be something we can do to help,' Daisy said. 'Is there anything they need? Money will be tight, especially while they take some time off.'

'How about we send a food parcel? Maybe a pan of soup and a casserole,' Betty suggested. 'I bet neither of them are eating, and Hattie needs to keep her strength up right now. She should be eating more, not less.'

'You're right,' Patty confirmed. 'I don't think they've eaten a thing since the whole thing happened.'

'What's this?' Josie interjected as she approached the

table where the group were sat, giving the communal tea urn a little shake.

'We were just thinking of a way to help Hattie and Diane,' Daisy explained. 'Betty has suggested taking some meals round.'

'Dolly and I have just been saying the same thing. I think it's a good idea. Diane can't afford to lose any weight, and with Hattie being pregnant she needs to keep eating. That baby needs to keep growing.'

'I'm sure we could put together a food package,' Josie continued. 'It's the very least we can do. Diane has been such a tower of support to me since I lost Alf.'

'Let's organize it, then,' Betty encouraged.

'I could make some bread too,' Nancy offered. 'I could even do it tonight.'

'I'll make a big pan of soup,' Josie added. 'And Dolly has said she will whip up a casserole.'

'I could take it all tomorrow night,' Patty said. 'I know Hattie would insist we don't go to any trouble, but I'm sure she and her mum could do with it.'

'Yes, let's do that,' Betty rallied. 'I have no doubt Ivy will want to send something too. But it might actually be more useful if we set up a bit of a rota, otherwise they will end up with too much and it will go to waste.'

'You're right,' Josie agreed. 'I know I've only just got my appetite back.'

'Shall I make a bit of a list of who will make what?' Betty offered.

'That sounds like a good idea,' Nancy said, taking a bite of her sandwich. 'That way, we could take it in turns to visit too, and keep checking in on them both.'

'I think Hattie and Diane would appreciate that,' Patty commented.

'Everything will feel so odd for them,' Daisy interjected. 'They won't know if they are coming or going.'

'They will get there with the right support,' Josie assured the group, rubbing her daughter's shoulder, fully aware Daisy was still trying to come to terms with losing her dad. 'It feels tough right now, but as each day and week passes, they will find a way of coping.'

Patty nodded gratefully and turned towards Archie. She might have been worried sick about him every time he did an air raid patrol shift, but he was still there by her side. In the last few months, Daisy had lost her dad, and now Hattie was suffering the same unimaginable pain. They were living through the hardest of times, and Patty felt an overwhelming urge to wrap her arms around all her loved ones.

As if reading her mind, Archie affectionately winked back at his sweetheart. 'It will be okay,' he mouthed, sensing exactly what Patty was thinking.

Momentarily soothed, Patty told herself she would be the unfaltering friend Hattie needed and would do everything she could to help her. Somehow, they would get through this. *I just need to stay strong,* she thought, channelling Betty's hopeful optimism.

Chapter 20

Thursday, 17 April 1941

'Thank you for coming,' Hattie said as she invited Josie and Patty through the front door. Patty knew her friend had been steering clear of the kitchen, so she had deliberately avoided the back door, which led straight into the room where Vinny had attacked his wife and daughter.

'I hope this isn't too much, us both coming?' Josie asked as the women stepped into the hallway.

'Not at all,' Hattie replied. 'Mum will be pleased to see you. She's just in the front room. Go on through.'

'Have you eaten?' Patty asked, but seeing how gaunt and pale her friend looked, she suspected she already knew the answer.

'Not much, if I'm honest,' Hattie answered, confirming Patty's thoughts. 'I haven't got much of an appetite.'

'We've brought some fresh soup and bread,' Josie said, holding up the bag she was holding.

'You didn't need to do that,' Hattie protested.

'We know, luv, but we wanted to do.'

'Thank you. I'll take it into the kitchen,' Hattie responded gratefully.

'No, you go and sit down,' Patty intercepted, taking the bag from Josie. 'I can sort this lot out and I'll make a fresh pot of tea while I'm at it.'

'You really don't have to,' Hattie replied. 'I can do it.'

'It's no bother. Honestly, you go and sit down.'

Too wrung out to argue, Hattie led Josie into the front room.

'Mum,' Hattie started as she led Josie into the dimly lit front room. The blackout blinds were up, and the smallest amount of light was coming from a lamp in the corner. 'We have visitors. Josie and Patty are here.'

Diane, who was curled up on the corner of the couch, slowly opened her eyes.

'Sorry,' Josie whispered. 'I didn't mean to wake you.'

'No. No,' Diane murmured, readjusting herself into a sitting position, pulling the patchwork blanket around her to stop herself from shivering.

'Sorry, I don't seem to be able to get warm,' she added by way of explanation. 'It's lovely of you to come. Thank you.'

'I couldn't not,' Josie said, sitting down next to her friend. 'How are you, luv? Or is that a daft question?'

'I just can't believe it. I think I'm still in shock. I keep expecting him to walk through the door, ranting and raving. It's like a nightmare that I haven't woken up from.'

'I'm sure. It's only natural. I still have moments where I think our Alf will appear.'

'I just feel so guilty one minute and then angry the next, but mainly I'm just sad.'

'Of course, you are,' Josie empathized. 'Vinny was your husband. You had been together a long time.'

'I always hoped he would change. Right up to . . . Well, you know. Even after what he did to me on Monday.' Diane instinctively raised her hands to her badly bruised neck.

Josie tried to avert her gaze from the injuries Vinny had inflicted on Diane, one of the gentlest souls she'd ever met. But the deep purple bruising was a clear sign of how her husband had abused the kindness she had so freely offered.

'He wasn't in a good way,' Diane said by way of explanation.

'I don't doubt it,' Josie said gently, choosing her words carefully, appreciating how people never liked to hear an ill word said about the dead, no matter what type of life they led.

'I don't think he knew what he was doing. The drink had a hold of him. I promise he wasn't always like this.'

'You don't have to convince me.' Josie smiled supportively at her grief-stricken friend.

'When we first met, Vinny was such a kind man. He was a real romantic and ever so loving. He couldn't do enough for me. Bought me flowers and chocolates. He swept me off my feet in those early days. And when he found out I was pregnant, he couldn't stop pampering me. Treated me like a princess. And he adored Hattie when she came along.'

Diane looked across the room to where Hattie was sat in the old armchair with the sunken cushions. 'Do you remember, luv?'

Hattie nodded, her eyes glistening as she silently recalled the father who would pick her up when she fell over and gently wipe her tears away. Despite the police visiting earlier that day and insisting Hattie was not responsible for her dad's death, she still couldn't shake the guilt that was threatening to overwhelm her.

'Maybe these are the memories you should try and focus on,' Josie suggested.

'I'm trying,' Diane sighed. 'I don't think he ever meant to turn into such an awful man. It just came on gradually. Memories of the Great War started haunting him. It began with nightmares and him waking up in the night. He'd have the odd drink of a night, saying it helped him sleep, but then one drink wasn't enough.'

For a moment, just like Hattie, Diane seemed to drift into another world, her memories taking her to a time when she still believed there was a chance she could save Vinny.

'I tried to help him then, you know. I said he was relying too heavily on the booze, but he would get annoyed with me, saying I didn't understand. I suppose, if I'm honest, I didn't. I didn't really know what to do. I tried to talk to him. I thought if I could get the memories out of his head it would help, but Vinny refused to tell me about what he had seen in the war. He said he couldn't talk about it.'

'I think that's normal,' Josie sympathized. 'I don't think many blokes know how to explain what's going on in their heads. They're not like us women who like a natter.'

'If only he had,' Diane continued, her voice beginning to falter. 'Maybe that would have saved him. When this war broke out, his drinking got much worse. He'd get so agitated when he listened to the news or read the papers. That's when he really turned.'

'This war has a lot to answer for,' Josie confirmed.

'I'm sorry,' Diane said. 'You have had so much to cope with too.'

'We all have, but you and Hattie cannot blame yourselves.'

'I never thought Vinny would get as violent as he did or turn on our Hattie. He always loved the bones of her when she was a little one.'

Josie and Patty turned to look at their friend.

'Are you sure the baby is okay?' Patty asked.

Hattie nodded silently.

'That's the one saving grace,' Diane whispered, but she was once again filled with guilt for failing to protect her daughter.

Sensing how difficult this was for both Diane and Hattie, Josie interjected, 'I know it might be hard to imagine right now, but this baby is going to give you both something to focus on. You will eventually find a new normality, I promise.'

Hattie's hands went straight to her slightly protruding tummy, as she looked across the room to her mum. For the last few months, she had been terrified her dad could hurt her unborn baby. Hattie had spent endless hours thinking about how she and her mum could escape her dad's violent mood swings. She had hated him for what he had put them all through, but now... *Didn't they always say, be careful what you wish for? Have all my hateful thoughts*—Hattie shook her head in an attempt to dismiss the intrusive thoughts.

'Have this, luv,' Josie said, pouring Hattie a fresh mug of tea.

'Thank you.' Hattie willingly accepted the hot drink, even though she felt as though she hadn't done anything but drink tea since Monday night.

'I'm sorry,' Diane said, another surge of guilt coursing through her. 'You have only just lost your Alf, and here you are helping us. You already have so much to cope with. We should still be supporting you.'

'Don't be thinking like that,' Josie instructed, turning to her friend. It was true, she was still grieving. There wasn't a single hour of the day when she didn't miss her beloved Alf, and she still woke up most nights haunted by the fact her husband wasn't next to her, but she also knew how much Diane would need her friends to rally around her now to ensure she got through this in one piece.

'We all need to stick together at times like this. And you have done exactly the same for me. I couldn't have got to where I am today if it wasn't for you and everyone else. At times like this we all need our friends. Now it's my turn to help you.'

'Thank you,' Diane whispered gratefully. For years, Vinny's controlling and aggressive behaviour had pushed all her friends away. It was only when she started at the factory canteen that she'd begun to feel like she wasn't alone anymore.

'Now, tell me. What can we do, apart from being here, to help?'

'I'm not sure. The vicar came earlier to talk about a funeral. It doesn't seem real.'

'I know exactly what you mean,' Josie empathized. Alf's final goodbye had felt surreal – as though she was looking down on someone else's service.

'Have you got any thoughts on what you would like?'

'Not really. I just want a small quiet affair. Vinny didn't have any family apart from us and I can't imagine many of his workmates will turn out for it. He made a lot of enemies.'

'Well, we will be there,' Josie affirmed.

'You don't need to do that. I know you must have all thought Vinny was a terrible man.'

'None of that matters,' Josie assured Diane. 'We will be there for you. We won't let you do this by yourself.'

Diane felt an overwhelming sense of gratitude. The

idea of just herself and Hattie sat alone in a big, cold church filled her with dread. She hadn't imagined anyone else would be there. Vinny had even fallen out with the landlord and regulars at the pub he frequented, after too many pints of pale ale and bitter causing him to be argumentative and nasty. And Diane knew there was no love lost between Vinny and their neighbours, whom he'd regularly sworn and cursed at during his inebriated rants.

'I don't have to say anything at the church, do I?' Diane panicked.

'No,' Josie assured. 'No one would expect you to. The vicar will read the eulogy. You just need to tell him some things you would like said at the service.'

Thank goodness for that, Diane thought to herself. She would just have to try and remember the good man Vinny had once been. There was no point talking ill of the dead. Vinny was gone now; nothing could change that.

'How will I ever tell my baby about their grandad?' Hattie said, as if reading her mum's mind. The words left her lips before Hattie realized that she had said them out loud.

'Oh, luv,' Josie replied, her heart going out to Hattie. 'You don't have to think about that just now. You have lots of time before those conversations happen. Time will help you work out exactly what you tell your little one, as and when you need to.'

Hattie knew deep down Josie was right, but it still didn't take the piercing sting away. Her dad's behaviour over the last few years wasn't the legacy he should have left behind. Why couldn't he have been like Alf or Bill? Caring and kind. And why had she pushed him out the door?

'I have a feeling your baby is going to have lots of adopted grandads,' Patty said supportively, interrupting Hattie's thoughts. 'As well as John's dad, I can imagine my dad and Frank will want to be a big part of your baby's life.'

The thoughtful words caused tears to collect at the back of Hattie's eyes.

'What is it they say?' Patty said. 'It takes a village to raise a child.'

'Oh gosh,' Hattie whispered, her voice breaking.

'I'm sorry. I didn't mean to make you cry.'

'I'm just so grateful for how kind you all have been, especially with John being away too. Thank you.'

'Like Josie said, we are all here for both of you and your baby. You don't have to do this by yourselves. In fact, we would be offended if you tried.'

Hattie pressed her lips together and blinked back the ocean of tears that were threatening to overflow.

'I'm sure I'll be taking you up on that offer,' she managed.

'Good.' Patty smiled. 'Because you will have to fight me away from the door. I've asked Nancy to help me learn to knit again, so I can make some booties and maybe even a little hat and matching cardigan.'

The thought of Patty's normally quite questionable creations brought the smallest hint of a smile to Hattie's face.

'Thank you,' she said. 'We really are so lucky to have so many good friends.'

Chapter 21

Sunday, 20 April 1941

'John!' Hattie gasped as she came down the stairs to see her uniformed husband stood in the hallway.

'Come here,' he said, his arms wide open. 'I came as fast as I could. I'm sorry, I should have sent a telegram.'

'Please don't worry about that. I'm just so glad you are here,' she replied as she willingly fell into her husband's arms. 'I've missed you so much.'

'I've missed you too. I'm so sorry about your dad.'

'Oh, John.' And with that, the tears Hattie had been working so hard to keep at bay erupted, soaking John's khaki jacket, as she allowed the raw emotion of how she was feeling to pour out of her.

John enveloped his wife in his arms, gently rubbing her back, wishing he could hold her like this forever, and keep her safe.

'I'm sorry,' Hattie whispered when she finally lifted her head, her cheeks now puffy and pink and the rims of her eyes a deep red.

'Let's go and sit down,' John suggested.

'I've made you a pot of tea to share,' Diane interjected, appearing from the kitchen door with a tray in her hands. 'I'll pop it down and give you some space.'

'You don't have to do that,' John started. 'I've come to see you both.'

'That's very kind of you, but I'm sure you could both do with a bit of time to yourselves. I've got a few things to sort out before tomorrow. I'll come in and see you in a bit.'

Hattie gave her mum a grateful smile. 'Don't be by yourself for long. Come and sit with us soon.'

Diane nodded as she popped the tray on the front room coffee table and then quickly left the room, gently closing the door behind her.

'Tomorrow?' John asked as he ushered Hattie onto the couch.

'The funeral,' Hattie sighed, using a handkerchief to dab her tired eyes.

'Thank goodness I made it back in time. I wouldn't want you to do that without me.'

'I'm glad you are here too. I don't feel strong enough to look after me, let alone Mum. She's been a complete wreck. She keeps blaming herself. Not that she should. If anyone's to blame, it's me.'

'Do you feel strong enough to tell me what happened?'

'It feels like a bad dream,' Hattie whispered, as John carefully handed her a mug of steaming tea.

'Have this,' he encouraged. 'You look exhausted. Have you been eating?'

'A bit. The girls at work have been dropping off food for me and Mum.'

'I'm glad. It makes me feel a little better, knowing someone has been looking out for you both. You know you could both stay with my mum and dad.'

'I know. Your mum came to see us. She was kind, insisting she could look after us, but despite everything that has happened in this house we both want to be here. It's odd as it hasn't been a safe place for a long time, but it's where Mum and I feel most comfortable.'

'That's okay. I just wanted you to know you had options.'

'Thank you. I still don't like going in the kitchen, but I'm hoping that will pass with time.'

John gave his wife a quizzical look, his expression silently asking what on earth happened.

'You're not going to like it,' Hattie said by way of explanation.

'Do you feel strong enough to tell me?'

Hattie nodded as she nursed her hot mug, which was helping to steady her fluctuating emotions. For the next ten minutes, Hattie repeated the events that had led up to her dad's unfortunate death.

'He was in such a bad way. He was so angry with me and Mum. I thought he might kill one of us. That's when I slammed the door shut on him. Maybe if I hadn't . . .' Hattie's words trailed off.

John took Hattie's mug from her and placed it on the

table before pulling her close once again, his tender actions a sharp contrast to the internal anger he was doing his best to disguise. He knew Vinny had paid for his heinous actions with his life, but John felt so enraged by what he'd put his pregnant wife and Diane through. Holding Hattie tight, another emotion infiltrated the fury he felt. John swallowed back the guilt that he hadn't been there for his wife when she had needed him the most. And he had to also convince his grief-stricken wife she wasn't responsible for Vinny's death.

Hattie clenched her eyes shut for a second or two. No matter how many times she went over the fateful events, she still struggled to accept it was real or that she wasn't in some way responsible.

'I need you to listen to me,' John said.

Hattie looked at her husband, whose eyes betrayed the mix of upset and anger he was feeling.

'You are not responsible for your dad's death. He had drunk far too much. If you had let him in the house, I dread to think what he could have done to you and your mum, let alone our baby.' His eyes moved to Hattie's tummy.

'I know. You're right. It was just all so unnecessary.'

'It's over now,' John managed to say. Then, despite his own chagrin, he quickly added, 'He wasn't in control of his own mind,' desperately aware of Hattie's overwhelming loss and conflicting thoughts.

'No. I don't suppose he was. If only he'd talked about how he felt with Mum.'

'I think blokes find that a lot harder than women,' John replied, as his wife sat herself back up.

Hattie looked at John. 'Promise me, you will never close yourself off from me. I couldn't bear the thought of you having so many awful things in your head.'

'I promise,' John said, and silently hoped he would always be true to his word. But the truth was he had already seen fellow soldiers battling against the atrocities they had endured at Dunkirk. They were drinking more and their anger was rising at the mere mention of Hitler or the Luftwaffe.

'I couldn't cope with losing another man I love,' Hattie added.

'I know,' John testified. 'And I would never want to shut myself off from you. You aren't just my wife. You are my best friend. If I can't talk to you, then I can't talk to anyone.' But even as John said the words, another surge of guilt coursed through him. He would have to leave his wife again soon, in her greatest hour of need.

As Hattie looked at her husband, she silently prayed he would always stick by his words. She thought about Nancy's husband, Bert. Although he was a good man and had finally found a way to live again after Dunkirk, he'd still never told Nancy what he'd seen or had to cope with.

Sensing Hattie's fears, John steered the conversation in another direction.

'Our baby,' he said, tenderly placing his hand on Hattie's slightly protruding tummy. 'Is everything okay?'

'Yes,' Hattie assured. 'No harm done there.'

'Any movements?'

'I'm not sure.' Hattie was six months pregnant, but with everything else that had been going on, she'd barely had time to concentrate on her baby's movements. 'I've had a few flutters. I couldn't really say they were actual movements. They were more like bubbles in my tummy as opposed to kicks.'

'I'm sure this little one is jiggling around,' John commented, a pang of emotion threatening to paralyze him. 'You just need to allow yourself to relax, so you can feel them.'

'Yet again, I know you are right,' Hattie replied. 'I just hope I feel them.'

'What do you mean?' John asked.

'It's just, I feel so numb. I'm thinking about Dad so much, I'm scared I can't feel anything else.'

'Oh, Hattie' John gasped, instinctively feeling the sadness his wife was enduring. 'I can't profess to know much about these things, but my mum always told me that when she fell pregnant something inside her changed, that she immediately became aware of having a child growing inside her.'

'I know what she means,' Hattie agreed. 'This week has just been so hard. My emotions are all over the place.'

'I know. It's only natural, but I promise with time, things will start to feel a little easier. It won't happen overnight, but gradually you will find a way to get through this.'

'I wish you could be here all the time,' Hattie said, but then immediately regretted her words, knowing how hard John found it to be away too.

'I'm sorry,' she said. 'I know you don't like this any more than I do.'

'It's okay. I wish more than anything else in the world I could always be by your side, but I will be one day.'

'I can't wait.'

John squeezed his wife's delicate hand. 'Me neither.'

'How much leave have you been given?'

'I have to return the day after tomorrow.'

Hattie bit back the pain of knowing she would once again have to say goodbye to the man she loved.

'Then to North Africa?' It was a question more than a statement.

But before John could answer, the front room door slowly opened.

'Do you need a top-up?' Diane asked, her pale, drawn face appearing.

'No. We're okay for now, Mum. Why don't you come and sit down?' Hattie was aware her mum had made an excuse to leave her and John alone, even though she hated being by herself since Vinny's death.

'No. You two need time together.'

'I insist,' John interjected. 'Please join us.'

'We mean it, Mum,' Hattie reiterated.

'Only if you're sure?'

'We are,' Hattie affirmed kindly.

As Diane sat down on the armchair, she looked tiny, the frame almost engulfing her.

'Is there anything I can do tomorrow?' John asked, desperate to relieve his wife and mother-in-law from the huge weight they were carrying on their delicate shoulders.

'All the arrangements are done,' Hattie explained. 'But you just being there will help so much.'

'That I can do. Did your dad have any relatives?'

'Distant cousins maybe, but no one close by,' Diane replied. 'It will just be a small affair. It's probably for the best. He didn't endear himself to folk over the last few years.'

'Hopefully he's at peace now,' John said.

'I hope so, luv. He battled against too many demons for too long.'

Chapter 22

Monday, 21 April 1941

'Today, we have come here to remember the life of Vincent Thomas Johnson, husband to Diane and father to Hattie,' the vicar, dressed in his traditional attire, solemnly declared from the wooden pulpit.

Hattie squeezed her mum's hand. Diane looked as though she hadn't slept a wink in days. Her face was ashen grey with exhaustion, exaggerated by the redness of her eyes.

As the vicar continued, Hattie and her mum barely took in the words that were being delivered to the small congregation, but one sentence caused them both to shudder.

'Before Vinny, as he was known, started working in the local pit, he bravely served his country, fighting for peace in the Great War.'

'It ruined him,' Diane whispered.

Hattie held her mum's hand a little tighter, silently agreeing with her but desperate to try and keep her mum together. On the other side of Hattie was John, hoping he could do the same for his wife, who looked equally drained. He felt wretched that he would soon have to deliver more bad news, but for the moment he could do what Hattie needed.

'As Vinny passes from this life to the next—'

Diane audibly gasped. The words were so final. Her husband had really gone. There would never be another chance to try and find the man she had fallen in love with all those years ago.

Seeing her friend's shoulders shake, Josie placed a comforting hand on them from the pew directly behind Diane. It felt like yesterday since she too had been sat in church saying her final farewells to her beloved Alf. Just the thought of it caused Josie's eyes to swim with tears. Blinking them back, Josie did her best to force her own harrowing memories to a separate corner of her mind, knowing she could, and would, return to them later. For the time being she needed to support Diane, knowing today would be the hardest of days for her friend. The circumstances couldn't have been more polar opposite, but the pain was equally cruel. Daisy, who was sat next to her mum, was also desperately trying to be brave, despite cherished memories of her own dad flashing through her mind. She knew how much love Hattie would need to get through this.

After what felt like an eternity, but in reality was only twenty minutes, the poignant service came to an end. John protectively led his wife and mother-in-law out of the stone church to the graveyard for the private burial, which Diane had insisted just the three of them attended.

It was another half an hour before they entered the church hall, where Diane and Hattie's friends and colleagues had collected.

'Thank you all for coming,' Diane whispered as she approached the group. 'It was very kind of you.'

'How are you doing, duck?' Dolly asked.

'Yer know,' Diane managed, 'glad it's done with.'

'Here you go, luv,' Josie said, handing Diane a cup of tea. 'I've managed to scrounge sugar and popped some in.'

'Thank you.' Diane gave a weak but grateful smile. She'd only made one stipulation about the gathering – there shouldn't be a drop of alcohol consumed. The demon booze had, after all, killed her husband.

'You'll get through this. I promise,' Josie reassured.

'Ay. We will, won't we, luv?' Diane stated as she turned to look at Hattie.

'Yes,' Hattie confirmed, mustering up all her strength. It had been the hardest of days, but she knew they must find a way to move forward, despite how much there was to think about. Would they be able to afford to stay in the house? Could they pay their bills? Would her mum feel strong enough to go back to work?

'And, as I've said,' Patty interjected, 'we will be here to help, every step of the way.'

Despite the heavy pain in her heart, Hattie felt lucky to be surrounded by so much love. These women, not to mention Frank and Archie, had once again pulled together to ensure she and her mum would survive this terrible tragedy.

After an hour, sensing Diane and Hattie just wanted to go home, everyone said their goodbyes, each taking it in turn to wrap the two women in their arms.

'You must be exhausted,' John said when they finally returned to the house and he sat down on the couch next to Hattie.

'I am, but hopefully I'll be able to sleep a little bit better now today is over.'

Yet another overwhelming pang of guilt coursed through John at the thought of what he was about to tell Hattie, knowing it would cause her yet more sleepless nights.

'I've told my parents I'll be staying here tonight,' he said.

'Thank you. It's been so good having you here. I don't think I would have got through today without you.'

John pulled Hattie closer, until her head was perfectly nestled into the gap between his shoulder and neck.

'I wish we could stay like this forever,' Hattie sighed, her eyes ever so slightly beginning to close.

'I do too.'

'What time is your train back? And where have you got to go to?'

John knew he couldn't put the inevitable off forever.

Hattie felt John's chest rise and fall as he took a deep intake of breath.

'It's happening, isn't it?' she whispered, not daring to sit up and look at her husband, knowing she was on the verge of cracking yet again. She was also very conscious John would be feeling dreadful about the inevitable news he was about to break.

'You're going to Africa? Were you about to leave when my telegram arrived?'

'I am,' John confirmed, his voice ever so slightly faltering. 'And yes.'

Hattie didn't say a word for the next few seconds as she allowed the news to sink in, then finally asked, 'Are you going straight away?'

'Yes,' he replied guiltily. Although he knew this wasn't his fault, and he had warned Hattie where he would be sent to next, he hated himself for having to break this latest bombshell to her, especially today.

'Have they told you how long for yet?' But even as Hattie said the words, she knew John wouldn't be able to give her an answer. No one knew what was going to happen in this blasted war.

'I'm sorry. They haven't,' John responded, pulling his arm tighter around Hattie. 'I don't want to go, either.'

Hattie gulped back her feelings. As much as she wanted John to never leave her side again, let alone risk life and limb in whatever mission he was sent on, she knew John would have dreaded this moment.

'I know you don't,' she whispered. 'But you mustn't worry about me.'

'Oh, Hattie. I'll do nothing but worry. I should be here to support you and to be by your side as our baby grows, and when . . .' John took a deep breath, as the rest of the sentence hung heavily in the air. Was this what he'd signed up for? To miss the most important moments of his life?

'I'm going to be okay. I promise.' Hattie couldn't allow John to go away laden down with so much guilt.

'My mum and dad have said if there is anything you need, you just need to tell them. I can't bear the thought of you getting through the next few months without any support. You and your mum have already had to cope with so much. Promise me you will let them know if there's anything they can do to help.'

'I promise. That's very kind of them. I am very grateful.'

'You are part of their family. They see you as their own daughter.'

Hattie didn't say anything for a couple of minutes. Instead, as she nestled closer into John, she reminded herself she wouldn't be alone. She and her mum had made so many good friends at Vickers, each one of them had shown how much they cared. Although things seemed inconceivably difficult right now, she knew her friends wouldn't let her fall. They would be there to help shoulder the battles ahead and pick her up if she started to fall. And what was it one of the women had told her? *You are never alone while you are pregnant. Your baby will always be with you.* Hattie took comfort in the thought, placing her left hand on her tummy. And while she was carrying his baby, she had John with her too.

Then, just as Hattie let that thought offer her a blanket of hope, she felt a twinge. No, it was more than that. It was a sharp, but not wholly unpleasant, movement coming from inside her belly.

'Oh!' she gasped, sitting upright, her senses on full alert.

'What is it?' John asked, also alert.

'The baby.' Hattie smiled. 'I think I've just felt our baby move.'

'Really?' John's eyes flicked between Hattie's face and her belly.

'Yes. Quick, see if you can feel it.' Hattie placed her husband's hand on the lower part of her tummy, where she'd felt the internal nudge.

And just as she did, there was another movement; no doubt, a tiny hand or foot, or maybe an elbow, pushing outwards and causing a little but undeniable ripple on Hattie's lower tummy.

As John felt his unborn child wriggle for the first time, his frown vanished and a smile filled his face.

'Wow,' he gasped. 'Is that really our baby?'

'It better be!' Hattie laughed.

'I can't believe it,' John said. 'Our baby just moved.'

'They did.'

'Have you felt any movements like this before?' John's hand was still gently resting on his wife's belly. It felt perfect and for a few seconds it was as though nothing else mattered. Everything he wanted was right by his side.

'Nothing quite like this. I've had a few sensations but not as forceful. Our baby must have known you were here and was waiting to let their presence be known.'

With one hand still resting on his wife's tummy John lifted himself up slightly, repositioning himself on the couch, and leant down and tenderly kissed Hattie.

'That was nice,' Hattie said after they parted.

'I miss our kisses,' John replied affectionately.

'Me too, but it won't be forever.' Despite how much she longed for John to remain in Sheffield, she knew she had to be strong for her husband. Hattie knew John would understand if she faltered after what she and her mum had been through, but she didn't want her husband feeling any more wretched than he already did.

'I promise I'll be home as quick as I can,' John vowed.

'I know you will. Just promise me you won't take any risks and will do everything you can to stay safe.'

'I promise.'

'Good.' Hattie knew that was all she could hope for. Closing her eyes, exhausted by the day's events, she allowed herself to nestle back into John's arms, determined to cherish the last few hours they had together.

Chapter 23

Monday, 28 April 1941

'Are you sure you feel up for this, Mum?' Hattie asked as she forced herself to swallow the piece of toast Diane had made for her.

'Yes, luv. I can't stay at home all day. I know I'll end up spending the whole day in tears.'

'But do you feel strong enough to face a shift in the canteen? Dolly said you could take as much time as you needed.'

'And I have. Besides which, if you feel strong enough to go back, then I can too.'

Hattie looked at her mum. She was still pale and gaunt. The weight she'd lost since Vinny's death made her look more fragile than normal. Hattie also knew her mum had barely slept since the funeral a week earlier. She'd heard her crying through the nights and Hattie had gone into her room and climbed into bed next to her, holding her hand, until they had finally dropped off together.

'Okay,' Hattie conceded.

'Besides which,' Diane added, 'I'll feel better knowing I'm closer to you.'

'Me too.' Hattie knew she wouldn't be able to stop worrying if she was in work and her mum was at home. Although their neighbours, who had stayed away from the house for years due to her dad's vile tempers, had started popping in again, the thought of her mum spending hours by herself had left Hattie feeling uneasy.

'Me and you together,' Diane affirmed.

Hattie managed a small nod. In the days after John had left, despite how bereft she'd felt, Hattie had somehow found the resolve to sit down with a pen and paper and work out their finances. Although they were losing her dad's salary, Hattie had been grateful to discover they could just about scrape by on her and her mum's wages. She'd hated to think about it so coldly but had acknowledged that now that they didn't have to account for how much her dad had spent on booze, they weren't as badly off as she'd thought. John had also promised to send money home, but Hattie was determined to use that for anything they would need for their baby.

'Okay,' Hattie said, standing up. 'If we are going to do this, we better set off.'

'And you'll be okay?' Diane asked her daughter, her protective maternal instinct more heightened than ever.

'Yes. I'll feel better being back at work. I need to keep my mind busy.'

*

Half an hour later, Hattie kissed her mum on the cheek and hugged her goodbye, leaving Diane to make her way to the canteen.

'You're back,' Patty said, spotting her best friend in the queue to clock in.

'Yes. Mum and I decided we need to try and get back to some form of normality.'

'How are you feeling?' Patty asked.

'Oh, you know. A bit odd. It still doesn't feel real, and I wish John was here, but I can't let myself think like that, otherwise I'll never get through each day, and I need to be strong. Mum needs me more than ever, and I have this little one to look after too.' Hattie glanced down and placed her hand on her tummy.

'Yes, you do, and we are all here to support you.'

Then, right on cue, Hattie and Patty were joined by Betty and Daisy.

'It's lovely to see you,' Daisy said, wrapping her arms around Hattie. 'Mum and I thought we saw the back of your mum's head on the way up to the canteen just now. Mum sped up to catch her.'

'Thank you,' Hattie answered. 'I'm so glad my mum has your mum and Dolly to look after her. She's going to need it.'

'How are you both doing?' Betty asked, placing a hand on Hattie's arm.

'I guess as well as can be expected. I was worried Mum was coming back too early, but I think she's better off here than being by herself all day while I'm working.'

'I think you're probably very right,' Daisy agreed. 'It did my mum the power of good to get back to work.'

'And we can all look after you both,' Betty interjected, mirroring Patty's earlier comments.

'I'm very lucky to have you all,' Hattie responded, as she lifted her clocking-in card out of the metal rack and pushed it into the time machine.

'Just take it steady this morning,' Patty said, determined to make sure Hattie didn't overdo it. 'If it all gets too much, I'm sure your boss will understand.'

'I will,' Hattie promised. 'Besides which, how hard can it be typing up letters?'

Nobody argued, but they all knew it wasn't just the intensity of the work that might cause Hattie to crumble.

'Well, we will see you at dinner time,' Daisy said. 'I'll have a big mug of tea waiting.'

Ten minutes later, Hattie was sat at the long row of desks in front of her big metal typewriter.

'Do you think you can type up these invoices?' Mrs Hull, Hattie's superior, asked, placing a pile of papers on her desk.

'Of course.' Hattie nodded obligingly.

'And, Hattie,' Mrs Hull added.

Hattie immediately looked up.

'I was very sorry to hear about your father. It must have been a terrible shock. If there is anything you need or anything I can do to make life a little bit easier, please just say.'

Hattie was momentarily taken aback by the unexpected token of kindness. Until now, Mrs Hull had only ever been strictly professional, and quite often fairly officious.

'Thank you,' she finally managed.

'I mean it,' Mrs Hull said. 'I know how it feels to lose someone you love, so if there is anything you need, you just let me know.'

'I will,' Hattie replied.

'And if you need a minute to yourself, just nip off to the loo. I'll make sure no questions are asked.'

Hattie bit back the emotions that could easily consume her if she allowed them to.

Sensing Hattie was on the verge of tears, Mrs Hull squeezed her shoulder and discreetly left a small packet of tissues next to the pile of invoices.

'I'll let you get on,' she said with a kind smile. 'But I promise, you will find a way through this.'

Hattie didn't dare reply, fearful her voice would falter and she'd end up a gibbering wreck. She just about managed a grateful smile instead. Then, determined to remain focused, Hattie picked up the first invoice and wound a clean piece of paper into her typewriter. No good would come of getting herself in a state.

The next few hours passed in a blur. Hattie had no idea how many invoices she had typed up, or if she'd made any mistakes. But, when the clock on the office wall struck midday, she was simply grateful to have survived the morning.

Desperate to check how her mum had coped, Hattie left her desk quickly and walked as fast as her – now quite prominent – bump would allow. As soon as she entered the vast dining area, she spotted her mum behind the serving hatch. Hattie searched her face for clues. She looked tired, but her eyes weren't swollen or puffy – a good sign.

Hattie stood at the side of the serving hatch. 'Are you okay?' she mouthed.

Diane gave the faintest of nods, enough to indicate she was surviving.

At least she's here, surrounded by friends, Hattie reassured herself. She dreaded to think what sort of state her mum would be in if she was at home with only their four walls to keep her company.

'I'll send her over soon, duck,' Dolly said, catching Hattie's eyes.

'Thank you.'

'Hattie, there you are,' Patty said, coming up behind her friend. 'How's the morning been?'

'Not too bad,' she replied, allowing Patty to guide her over to the table their group had commandeered not long after they had started at Vickers.

Daisy had already poured several mugs of tea from the communal urn.

'I've got you a cuppa,' she said, indicating for Hattie to sit down next to her.

'Have you survived, luv?' Nancy asked.

'I have. To be honest, it wasn't as bad as I thought it would be, and Mrs Hull was lovely to me.'

'That's good,' Betty added. 'I'm sure everyone just wants to make sure you are okay.'

'I'm just glad to get back to some form of normality,' Hattie said, opening the pack-up that her mum had made for her. She didn't have much of an appetite, but Hattie knew she needed to eat properly, if not for her sake, then for her baby's.

'Hello, you lot,' Josie said as she approached the table.

'How's my mum coped?' Hattie instantly asked.

'Not s'bad, luv. Bit quiet but we're looking after her.'

'Thank you. I do appreciate it. She was nervous about coming back.'

'I'm sure. It's hard, but if your mum is anything like me, it will keep her mind busy and do her the world of good.'

'That's what I'm hoping for.'

'We will get her through. I know it's easier said than done but try not to worry. We won't let her fall to bits.'

Once again, Hattie felt an overwhelming sense of gratitude for this formidable group of women. Each of them had her own worries, but they had pulled together, wrapping her and her mum in a blanket of love and support.

'Anyway,' Hattie said, keen to take the focus away from herself, 'tell me what you have all been up to. Have you heard from your William, Betty? How's he getting on?'

'I have, actually. In fact, he is coming home this weekend. He's got forty-eight hours' leave.'

'Oh, that's lovely,' Hattie replied as enthusiastically as possible, pushing away any feelings of jealousy, knowing it could be months before she next saw her husband.

'I am looking forward to it. Did your John say when he might next get home?'

Hattie bit her lip. In the days after the funeral, she and her mum had hunkered down, and Hattie hadn't managed to tell her friends that John was now on his way to North Africa.

'It could be a while' is all she managed.

Although Hattie's reply wasn't any different to most answers from the thousands of wives whose partners were posted across Europe, and now even further afield, the anguish in her voice was undeniable.

'What is it?' Betty asked instinctively.

'Oh. Gosh,' Hattie started, a torrent of sadness soaring through her. 'Sorry,' she continued, biting back the wave of emotion that was threatening to crumble her resolve. 'I should have mentioned it earlier.'

'Mentioned what?' Patty quizzed, concerned.

'John is no longer in England. He's—'

Patty instantly wrapped her arm around her friend's shoulder.

'I vowed I wouldn't get upset again.'

'It's okay,' Patty reassured. 'You're allowed to, but what's happened?'

'John has finally gone to North Africa. We knew it was coming. I was just hoping that it might not.'

'Where's North Africa?' Patty asked, completely flummoxed. Geography had never been her forte.

'If you look at a map, it's south of Europe, and to the left of Asia,' Frank interjected.

'Why has he been sent there?' Patty asked, still utterly perplexed. 'I thought Hitler was only interested in Europe.'

'It's complicated,' Frank answered. 'But, in a nutshell, they are trying to prevent Italy and Germany taking over there as well.'

Although Hitler hadn't sent his aircrafts to Sheffield of late, his tirade in other parts of the world was progressing at a frightening rate. What Frank didn't say was that the battle in North Africa wasn't likely to end any time soon. Italy was doing their best to stamp their mark on this war.

'None of it makes any sense to me,' Patty admitted.

'It doesn't to most of us, duck. I'm afraid when it comes to greed and power, then any form of decency goes out of the window.'

'Did John say how long he would be away?' Patty asked, turning back to her friend.

'Sadly not,' Hattie replied, rubbing her eyes in a bid to stem the tears that were threatening to erupt.

'Ah, luv,' Nancy sympathized. 'I know how tough it is. I'm sure this must be the last thing you wanted to hear.'

'It is,' Hattie agreed, her voice ever so slightly faltering. 'But I knew it was coming. John had told me when he was last home that he would be getting a new posting. I'd just pushed it to the back of my mind.'

'That's understandable,' Nancy assured her crestfallen friend.

'I suppose I'd hoped John would still be in England when our baby arrived,' Hattie sighed, glancing down at her tummy. 'The thought of him not meeting our baby straight away is really hard.'

'Of course it is,' Josie empathized as she topped up Hattie's mug with steaming hot tea, understanding exactly how she felt. Her Alf might not have been away fighting, but losing him, especially while Polly and Annie were so young, felt inconceivably cruel. Taking a deep breath to bolster her courage, she added, 'This war will be over one day and you, John and your baby will be a family.'

Daisy glanced at her mum, knowing how hard it must have been for her to say those words when they were still coming to terms with their loss of her dad. Josie nodded, acknowledging the discreet message of love from her daughter.

'That's what I keep telling myself,' Hattie affirmed, taking a sip of her freshly poured tea.

'And as we keep telling you,' Patty said, 'we will all be here for you.'

'That we will,' Daisy confirmed, knowing more than ever how hard life felt for Hattie right now.

'I do appreciate it,' Hattie acknowledged, yet again grateful for the mountain of support.

'You know where we are,' Josie added, collecting up the empty mugs.

'I do,' Hattie replied. Then added, 'Is my mum really all right? I thought she might pop over.'

'She's doing as well as can be expected. I think she was worried if she stopped, she might get herself in a tizz.'

Hattie knew exactly how her mum felt. 'Okay.'

'Don't worry, luv. Dolly and I will keep a very close eye on her.'

Hattie thanked Josie once again, but it felt like such a small word in comparison to what everyone was doing to help her and her mum. As Hattie made her way back to the typists' office, she just hoped it would be enough.

Chapter 24

Friday, 25 April 1941

'William!' Betty grinned as she opened the door to her uniform-clad fiancé.

'Hello, my love,' came William's response as he affectionately lifted Betty into the air. 'It's so good to see you.'

'And you,' she said as her feet gently touched the ground again. 'And who is this?' Betty asked, suddenly aware of an identically dressed and very dapper pilot standing next to William.

'Sorry, this is my roommate, Oliver. He's come home for the weekend with me. You don't mind, do you?'

'Of course not,' Betty replied, ushering the two men into the hallway. 'Lovely to meet you, Oliver.'

'And you.' The blond man, who was just a little bit taller than William, smiled. 'I've heard so much about you. William never stops talking about you.'

Betty blushed. 'Well, as long as it's all good!'

'Every word,' Oliver assured.

'Well, come on in. You must both be so tired. Did it take long to get here?'

'A few hours,' William answered. 'But there were a few of us so it went fast.'

'Are you hungry?' Betty asked. 'Ivy has cooked a mini-feast. Well, as much as you can on rations and home-grown veggies. She and Frank are desperate to see you.'

'Does the day end in Y?' William chuckled, his infectious, cheery demeanour causing Betty to beam from ear to ear.

'Why am I not surprised?' She laughed.

'Do you think Ivy and Frank will mind if Oliver stays too?' William asked. 'If it's too much, my mum has offered to rustle us something up.'

'And risk offending Ivy? Rather you than me. I promise there's plenty,' Betty confidently assured her fiancé. Then turning to Oliver to make sure he knew he was welcome, she added, 'Ivy loves nothing more than feeding people. You are very welcome, and I promise you there will be more than enough to go round.'

'Thank you. I must admit I am rather looking forward to it. William hasn't stopped going on about what a great cook Ivy is.'

'She is that,' Betty agreed, feeling another surge of love for William at the thought of him being so complimentary about Ivy.

'Hello, hello,' came Frank's booming voice from down the hallway. 'I thought I heard a familiar voice,' he added, approaching the trio. 'How are you, son?'

'I'm grand, Frank. And can I introduce my good friend, Oliver Wright?'

'It's good to meet you, Oliver,' Frank said as the pair shook hands.

'Likewise,' Oliver replied. 'I believe congratulations are in order. William told me about yours and Ivy's recent wedding.'

'Ah, yes. It still feels like yesterday, even though it was four months ago now. I'm a lucky man, Oliver, but enough about me. Let me get you two a well-deserved drink. I should imagine it's been a long day.'

'Thanks, Frank,' William said as the group made their way into the dining room, which was already set for tea. As Frank poured three glasses of pale ale, Betty discreetly added another table setting to accommodate their unexpected guest.

'Ivy will be through in a minute. I've been shooed out of the kitchen while she finishes off. Apparently, I'm getting under her feet.' Frank laughed, rolling his eyes in mock jest.

'Does she need a hand?' Betty asked.

'No, duck. I've been told to tell you it's all in hand. Josie and Daisy are in there too. You are under firm instructions to stay with William.'

Betty couldn't help but smile. It was just like Ivy to be so thoughtful, knowing how scarce William's visits were.

'And what would you like, duck?' Frank asked Betty as he handed William and Oliver their drinks.

'Erm,' Betty mused, never one to normally have a drink with her dinner.

'We're celebrating,' Frank prompted.

'Maybe a small sherry, then.'

'I'll pour all you ladies one. I think you all deserve it.'

'Thanks, Frank.' Betty grinned, a tingle of excitement fizzing through her. Frank was right. This was a reason to feel jubilant. Her beloved William was home for a whole weekend. If she couldn't have a little drink to mark the occasion, then there was something very wrong.

Just as the glasses were poured, the kitchen door opened, and the clatter of dishes and buzz of lively chatter emanated through the house.

'Here they come,' Frank warned, more for Oliver's benefit than for anyone else.

A few seconds later, Annie and Polly burst into the room but ground to a halt, their lovely chitter-chatter silenced, at the sight of a stranger.

'It's okay, girls,' Betty quickly reassured them. 'This is Oliver. He is William's friend.'

'Hello.' Oliver smiled. 'William has been telling me all about you.'

The sisters simultaneously blushed, cautiously eyeing the unfamiliar figure.

But before Annie and Polly's shyness overtook them, Ivy, Josie and Daisy walked into the dining room, their arms laden with pots and trays of food.

'I could have helped,' Betty said at the sight of the three women.

'No need,' Ivy replied. 'It's all done.' Then turning to

William, she added, 'I thought I heard your voice. Let me pop this casserole down and I will say hello properly.'

The next few minutes passed in a flurry of introductions as Ivy, Josie and Daisy all welcomed William home and greeted Oliver with the same gleeful joy.

'This looks and smells amazing,' William enthused after he had obeyed Ivy's instructions and helped himself to a portion of chicken and vegetable stew.

'I'm sure you boys must be hungry after a day of travelling,' Ivy said.

'Always,' William replied, chuckling. 'You know me.'

'Indeed, I do. And how about you, Oliver? Do you have an equally healthy appetite?'

'I'm afraid so,' Oliver said, his Manchester accent revealing whereabouts he was from.

'And you're a trainee pilot too?' Josie enquired.

'I'm actually a navigator. I always wanted to follow in my late dad's footsteps.'

The word 'late' alerted Daisy, who had been quietly attending to her sisters, scooping a portion of cauliflower onto each of their plates.

'Was your dad in the Great War?' Frank asked, acknowledging Oliver's comment.

'He was. Unfortunately, I was only a toddler when he passed, but before my mum died she would always tell me that he was commended for his bravery.'

Daisy looked across the table where Oliver was sat diagonally opposite from her. There hadn't been an ounce of self-pity in his voice, despite the fact he'd lost both his parents. She couldn't be sure, but he didn't look much older than his mid-twenties. Was that why he'd come back with William? Daisy couldn't help but feel a wave of sympathy for the poor bloke.

'Well, I'm sure you are making him proud,' Frank asserted.

'I hope so,' Oliver said. 'It's all I've ever wanted.'

'He absolutely is,' William chirped up, patting his friend on the shoulder. 'Oliver here is tremendous at his job. I wouldn't want anyone else by my side.'

'How long have you two known each other?' Ivy asked, already forming a soft spot for this very courteous and well-spoken young man.

'We met when I first got to Harrogate,' William explained, dipping a slice of warm homemade bread into his stew. 'Then we shared a bunk in Scotland. Been pals ever since.'

'I hope William has been a good roommate?' Ivy asked.

'Most of the time,' Oliver said.

'Only most of the time?' Betty commented, now raising an eyebrow at her bemused fiancé.

'Well, he's become a bit of a dab hand at seven card rummy, so beats me hands down nine times out of ten.'

'What's seven card rummy?' Polly, the youngest of Daisy's sisters, asked.

'It's a card game,' Oliver replied. 'I could show you how to play later, if you like?'

Daisy felt a surge of warmth spread through her at Oliver's kindness, knowing how much Polly would love the attention.

'Yes, please,' she responded. 'Can Annie play too?'

'Of course,' Oliver answered. 'Hopefully one of you will give me a chance though, unlike this scoundrel.'

'Excuse me,' William retorted. 'You just need to pay more attention, then maybe you will improve. With a bit of luck, Annie and Polly will help enhance your game.'

With that, everyone around the table burst into a fit of giggles.

'You see what I have to put up with!' Oliver exclaimed, lifting his palms upwards. 'I deserve a medal.'

The rest of the meal passed in a haze of light-hearted chatter and laughter as William and Oliver entertained everyone with their stories. Although the tales often revolved around the pair sharing a room, and their competitiveness in the air and when it came to exams, they were told with such joy and boy-like mischievousness that Betty almost forgot William was serving as a trainee pilot and putting his life at risk to serve his country.

Daisy barely said a word, but she couldn't help but admire Oliver. For someone who been dealt such a difficult hand in life, he was certainly making the best of things.

Chapter 25

Saturday, 26 April 1941

'I wasn't expecting to see you two here.' Betty beamed as she, Daisy, Patty and Hattie exited the factory gates, only to be greeted by a delighted-looking William and an equally happy Oliver.

'We thought we'd surprise you,' William responded, pecking Betty on the cheek. 'It's not raining, and the sun is desperately trying to break through, so we thought we would treat you girls to an ice cream.'

Betty looked up at the sky. William might have been right about the welcome break from the incessant rain that had been ever present over the last few months, but she felt his chance of sunshine was a little optimistic to say the least.

'Maybe a hot cup of tea and a scone would be more fitting,' she suggested.

'We can do that, can't we, Oliver?'

'Absolutely,' Oliver affirmed, looking far more relaxed in a pair of navy slacks, a white polo shirt and a deep-blue bomber jacket.

'Can we treat you all?' William asked.

'I'd have loved to,' Patty replied, 'but I've promised my sisters I will take them out this afternoon.'

'Sorry,' Hattie added. 'I hope you don't mind but I need to go and help my mum with some jobs.'

Betty glanced at Hattie, knowing her reasoning was probably only a half truth, and what she'd avoided saying was that quite understandably she didn't feel much like socializing.

'Of course. Maybe next time,' William replied, as amiable as ever. Betty had told him all about Vinny and the accident in her letters. The last thing he wanted to do was put Hattie in an awkward situation.

'That would be lovely,' Hattie replied gratefully. 'I hope you all have fun.'

'Yes, have a great afternoon,' Patty added. 'I better dash. I promised my sisters I would get back as quick as I could.'

'See you next time we're home,' William replied, as Patty and Hattie headed off, leaving just himself, Oliver, Betty and Daisy.

'You'll join us, won't you, Daisy?' William asked.

'Erm. Don't you and Betty want some time alone?' Daisy was very conscious of the fact that by the time her sisters had finished playing cards with William and Oliver the previous evening, after several pleas for 'just one more game', it had been time for the two men to head back to William's parents. Poor Betty hadn't had a single moment by herself with her fiancé.

'Not much chance of that with this one joined at my hip.' William laughed, playfully nudging Oliver in the ribs.

'I can make myself scarce,' Oliver quickly jumped in.

'I'm joking,' William reiterated.

'Absolutely,' Betty quickly added. 'Don't you be listening to this one,' she said, tilting her head to William. 'It's lovely to have you here.'

'That's that then, Daisy,' William responded. 'You have to come with us.'

'Only if you're sure?'

'Of course I am,' William replied. What he didn't say was he was quite sure he'd seen Oliver discreetly glancing at Daisy over the dining room table the night before, and thought they would make a smashing couple. He'd not said a word to Oliver, though, knowing his pal would run a mile if he got the slightest inkling William was even thinking about setting him up.

'Yes, you must,' Betty insisted, convinced a little treat would do Daisy the world of good. She hadn't done anything for herself since her dad had died.

Twenty minutes later the foursome were sat around a table at Browns.

'This one is on me,' Oliver insisted. 'What would you all like?' he asked, glancing at the menu.

'You don't have to do that,' Betty quickly objected.

'I would like to,' Oliver insisted. 'You have all made me feel so welcome. It would be my way of saying thank you.'

'That's very kind,' Daisy replied gratefully, touched by

the gesture. 'But really, I should be thanking you after the hours of card games you played with my sisters last night. You know they will expect that every time they see you.'

'It would be my pleasure.' Oliver smiled. 'They are super girls. I always wanted a little sister.'

'Do you have brothers?' Daisy enquired.

'No. It's just me, I'm afraid.'

Daisy did her best to hide her sympathy, fairly sure Oliver wouldn't welcome a pitying response, but dear God, the poor man had lost both his parents and was an only child. Daisy knew you couldn't compare pain or situations, but at least she'd had her mum and sisters to help comfort her after losing her dad. Poor Oliver. Life had dealt him a cruel deal. No wonder he was so close to William. He must feel like a surrogate brother.

'Ahem,' William interjected, right on cue, indicating the menu he was holding.

'Sorry, buddy.' Oliver grinned.

Daisy and Betty swapped a knowing look. Just like they had been there for one another, it appeared William had been a rock for Oliver.

'Right, what shall we all have?' Oliver said, keen to ensure the atmosphere wasn't brought down.

'If it's okay with you, I'd love a scone and a pot of tea,' Betty replied.

'Of course. How about you, Daisy? Is there anything tempting you on the menu?'

'I think I'll have the same as Betty, but we could share?'

'Definitely not!' Oliver said, shaking his head. 'I think I can treat you both to a scone each. I should imagine you are both famished after a full morning in the factory. I know I always am after hours in a plane, practising an operation and making sure we stay on the designated route.'

Betty quickly gulped back the pang of worry Oliver's comment had prompted. She'd been trying her hardest not to envisage William high in the skies, facing goodness knows how many risks.

Daisy gently touched her friend's arm underneath the table, aware the innocent remark would send Betty's mind into overdrive, even if she didn't show it.

'It's definitely hungry work,' Daisy agreed, hoping to keep the subject away from flying. 'A scone will be perfect.'

After the orders had been taken by an immaculately dressed waitress, both William and Oliver opting for a beef sandwich, the boys entertained Daisy and Betty with yet more of their antics.

'This one,' Oliver started, a grin lighting up his face as he glanced at William, 'thought it would be funny one afternoon to run into our dorm and shout we all had to get into our flying kit because another practice drill had been called. We had only just wound down for the night after being up since the crack of dawn.'

'William!' Betty laughed, shaking her head in mock horror.

'Oliver is just as bad,' William retorted. 'Only last

week he claimed the canteen had been flooded and we had to all grab mops and buckets, otherwise there would be no chance of eating for the next two days.'

'It certainly sounds like you two have been having quite the time,' Betty said.

'I promise we do some hard work too,' Oliver assured.

'I have no doubt,' Betty replied, but she was happy to keep the conversation light-hearted, not wanting to dwell on what her beloved William and Oliver were having to do, knowing it would send her into a spiral of worry.

'It's important you have some fun too,' Daisy added, very conscious of how the awful atrocities of war could dominate and leave you feeling utterly desolate. If Betty and the rest of her friends at Vickers hadn't been there to keep her upright, Daisy had no doubt she would have drowned in a sea of grief and sadness.

'It is,' William responded. 'Now, talking of which, can we tempt you girls to come dancing tonight?'

Betty and Daisy glanced at each other.

'That sounds rather lovely,' Betty responded. 'It's been a little while since I've had an excuse to get dressed up.'

'What about you, Daisy?' William prompted.

'Oh. Erm, I don't know. Mum might need me.'

Betty discreetly grasped her friend's knee under the table, understanding exactly why Daisy was being hesitant. Apart from Frank and Ivy's wedding, it would be the first time since her dad had been killed that she would be going out and having some fun. Betty knew Daisy would feel guilty.

'We could do something a little lower key if you prefer?' Oliver suggested. William had told him all about the terrible loss Daisy and her family had suffered. After losing both his parents, he completely understood the complex emotions that came with grief.

Daisy's cheeks flushed as she realized that she had inadvertently made herself the focus of the conversation. She wasn't sure if she felt buoyant enough to go out dancing, and the last thing she wanted to do was be a misery guts and bring the atmosphere of the night down.

'There's no need to make a decision now,' Oliver added.

Daisy looked across the table at William's friend and smiled gratefully, touched by his empathy. He really did seem like a kind soul, so gently spoken and considerate. Daisy couldn't deny it would be nice to do something normal again, but could she bring herself to do something quite so jolly?

'Oliver's right,' Betty commented. 'Let's see how your mum is fixed when we get home,' she added, hoping it would give Daisy the breathing space she needed. 'You can make a decision then.'

'Thank you,' Daisy acknowledged appreciatively.

'A large pot of tea and two lemonades,' the waitress who had taken the group's order announced, helpfully giving them a distraction.

'This is just what I needed,' Betty said, as the white

porcelain teapot, matching milk jug, cups and saucers were carefully placed on the table. 'All the dust and the heat in the factory leave me parched.'

'You girls do a grand job,' Oliver said in praise as he took a sip of his lemonade. 'I can't imagine the works could run without you all.'

'No, they couldn't!' Betty confirmed.

William chuckled. 'Betty here is a real stalwart for her female workmates,' he said proudly. 'She won't take any messing and has done so much to help the other women.'

Betty blushed at William's compliment.

'The world needs more people like you,' Oliver responded. 'And how about you, Daisy? Do you enjoy your job at Vickers? William explained you're a turner, what does that entail exactly?'

'Yes, that's right. I basically help size and shape steel,' she answered, adding a drop of milk to Betty's then her own cup, grateful the conversation had moved on. 'I have to admit I was quite nervous at first. I'd only ever worked as a hairdresser, so it was quite the change, but despite the long hours and how filthy the shop floors are, I really do love my job. It feels worthwhile, if that makes sense, like I'm doing something useful.'

'You absolutely are,' Oliver affirmed. 'We've all got to do what we can.'

'And if that's not enough, both Betty and Daisy volunteer at the Women's Voluntary Service,' William boasted.

'Do you ever have any time off?' Oliver asked.

'I can't speak for Daisy,' William interjected, 'but Betty doesn't like to sit still for a moment, do you, my love?'

'You know what I'm like,' Betty replied. 'I don't like to sit around and do nothing if I can be of some use.'

'That's the understatement of the century, but all the more reason for me to take you out tonight. All work and no play is no good for anyone.'

'How could I refuse after that?' Betty smiled.

After a pleasant lunch, William and Oliver insisted on escorting Betty and Daisy home.

'Would you like to come in?' Betty asked as they reached the house.

'We best not,' William said. 'I've promised Mum and Dad I'll spend some time with them this afternoon. I think they might lynch me if I completely abandon them this weekend.'

'That's fair enough,' Betty replied. 'I can't blame them for wanting you to themselves for a while.'

'How about Oliver and I come back about six thirty and we can decide then how to spend the evening?'

'That sounds like a plan,' Betty agreed, as her fiancé kissed her on the cheek.

Once inside, Betty and Daisy made their way into the kitchen, where Ivy and Josie were peeling a pile of vegetables.

'Hello, you two,' Ivy said. 'Did you end up working over?'

'No. William and Oliver turned up and took us out for a bite to eat,' Betty explained.

'How wonderful!' Ivy exclaimed.

'That will have done you both good,' Josie reinforced.

'Yes, it was a nice surprise,' Betty agreed.

'Did they not come back with you?' Ivy enquired.

'They did, but William has promised his parents he will spend some time with them this afternoon.'

'Ah, I see.' Ivy nodded. 'I suspect if he was my son, I would be desperate to see him too. Have you got any more plans for the weekend?'

'We haven't spoken about tomorrow yet, but they are coming back later and want to take Daisy and me out somewhere.'

'Really? That sounds nice,' Josie commented.

'Would you be terribly upset if I didn't come out?' Daisy asked as she sat down at the table.

Before Betty could reply, Josie exchanged a quick glance with Ivy.

'Are you tired, luv?' Josie asked gently.

'No more than usual,' Daisy responded. 'It just doesn't feel right.'

Josie put down the small knife she had been using to peel the potatoes and came and sat down opposite her daughter.

'I'll just go and get changed,' Betty said, sensing Daisy and her mum needed some time alone.

'And I must check on how Frank and the girls are getting on in the garden,' Ivy said, also making her excuses.

Once mum and daughter were alone, Josie took Daisy's hand in her own.

'Your dad would want you to go out and enjoy yourself, luv.'

'Oh, Mum,' Daisy started, before a knotty lump in her throat constricted her from saying anything else.

'It's okay,' Josie soothed, moving around the table to sit next to Daisy. 'You don't have to be brave all the time.'

'I just miss him so much. I think about Dad every day.'

'Of course you do, luv. I do too. There are moments when I still expect him to walk through the door, or I go to tell him something, only to realize he's not there.'

'I'm sorry,' Daisy said, tears welling in her eyes. 'I didn't mean to upset you too.'

'I'm your mum, Daisy. If you can't talk to me, then I'm not doing my job right.'

'It's not that,' Daisy protested in a whisper. 'I just know how hard this is for you too.'

'Yes, it is, but it's hard for all of us. We are a team, remember?'

'I know we are.'

'Now, I know you think going out tonight would be some form of betrayal, when you believe you should still be grieving, but I don't agree with you. You and I both know your dad would be teasing you rotten right now for going on what appears to be a double date.'

'A date!' Daisy gasped.

'I'm not saying it is. I'm just saying your dad would be having great fun winding you up. Well, after he'd sussed out if Oliver was a decent young man or not.'

'Mum,' Daisy admonished again.

'What I'm trying to explain is that your dad would be ever so cross if he knew you had turned down the offer of a bit of fun. He would hate it, in fact. He would want us all to try and carry on. I've even decided to start doing some volunteering work with Betty at the WVS.'

'That's great, Mum.'

'What I'm trying to say is, your dad would want you to move on with your life.'

'Do you think so?'

'I know so,' Josie reiterated. 'He loved you and your sisters so much. He just wanted you all to be happy. And I know if he is looking down on us now, he will be willing you to go and have a night out.'

Chapter 26

'You look gorgeous!' William announced enthusiastically as Betty entered the front room, where her fiancé and Oliver were sat, both looking rather dapper in their smart slacks and polo shirts.

'Why, thank you,' Betty replied, doing a little twirl, her pale-blue skirt swirling. 'I must admit it's nice to get dressed up. It's been a while.'

'Do I assume by how fabulous you look that you would like to go dancing?' William asked.

'If the offer still stands, that would be wonderful.'

'Your wish is my command,' William affirmed, standing up and planting a kiss on Betty's cheek.

'And will Daisy be joining us?' Oliver asked.

Betty was sure she detected a hint of hope in his voice. She wasn't sure if it was down to the fact that he didn't want to feel like he was tagging along with her and William, or that he genuinely wanted to spend some time with Daisy. Betty hoped it was the latter. She too had noted how much attention Oliver had shown her friend, and Betty couldn't help but think a little bit of flattery and fun would do Daisy the world of good.

'She is,' Betty confirmed. Whatever Josie had said to her daughter in their heart-to-heart had convinced Daisy a night out was exactly the tonic she needed.

An undeniable smile appeared on Oliver's face. 'That is good news.'

'Speak of the devil,' William announced as Daisy appeared in the doorway in a sophisticated yellow-and-black swing dress, which flattered her slim, tall figure perfectly, the belt emphasizing her tiny waist.

Betty's eyes darted between Daisy, who was still looking rather apprehensive about her decision to come out, and Oliver, whose eyes had widened at the sight of her friend.

'I'm so glad you decided to join us,' William added. 'And can I say, you look quite the picture.'

'Thank you.' Daisy blushed, not used to receiving compliments.

'So, where are you two taking us?' Betty asked, aware of how self-conscious Daisy was feeling, especially as Oliver hadn't stopped gazing at her.

'How about the City Hall?' William suggested. 'I thought I could show Oliver part of the city that hadn't—' William quickly checked himself before he finished his sentence.

But Daisy knew exactly what William was referring to.

Apart from the steps leading up to the City Hall, it had miraculously escaped Hitler's destructive bombs.

'Do you think it will be okay?' she quickly asked, a shudder running down her spine as she thought back to that fateful weekend. The last time she had been out in the city the Luftwaffe had dominated the city skyline, obliterating the area around The Moor, leaving Daisy and her friends trapped in the vaults of the Yorkshire Bank. And then three nights later, one of those catastrophic explosives had killed her beloved dad.

'I'm sorry, Daisy. That was thoughtless of me,' William said. 'We can go somewhere else.'

Daisy rubbed her thumbs and index fingers together, as she tried to swallow back the overwhelming feeling that was threatening to consume her.

'Honestly, I am happy to do anything,' Oliver jumped in, feeling as though he had inadvertently caused Daisy to feel anxious.

'Why don't we just have a little drink here first and then make a decision,' Betty suggested.

'That sounds like a good idea,' William replied, inwardly kicking himself for being so stupid. He had been so desperate for this weekend to be special, and now he'd well and truly put a dampener on what should have been a wonderful evening.

A few minutes later, Betty played the perfect hostess and poured each one of them a drink. A port and lemon for herself and Daisy, and a pale ale for the boys.

'I meant to say,' Betty said, as they all sat around the coffee table, 'Ivy has invited you both for Sunday dinner tomorrow.'

'Thank you,' William answered. 'I've missed her Yorkshire puddings – don't tell my mum, though. She wouldn't be best impressed if she thought I favoured Ivy's over hers.'

'It must be the fresh eggs,' Betty said tactfully. 'The hens are still producing them in abundance.'

'God. Yes,' William exclaimed. 'Dry egg powder is the worst thing ever invented. It's even worse than the margarine we are given instead of butter.'

'Oh, William.' Betty laughed. 'You are a case. Always thinking about your stomach. Well, you will be pleased to know we have plenty of eggs, and Ivy has got ever so creative after listening to Marguerite Patten's cooking tips on the Home Service. She's even started making her own sausages, which Frank says are delicious.'

'I wish the cooks at our base would listen in,' William said, frowning. 'I really miss some good hearty Yorkshire fodder.'

As the conversation turned to William's voracious appetite, Daisy, with the help of her port and lemon, started to relax, her fears gradually abating. She recalled what her mum said. *Your dad would be ever so cross if he knew you had turned down the offer of a bit of fun. He would hate it, in fact.*

Come on, she quietly thought to herself, *you need to be strong*. What did her dad always tell her as a little girl when she fell off her bike and scraped her knees, leaving her in floods of tears? *You need to get back up again.* Besides which, Daisy knew Betty would be there if she had a wobble, not that she wanted to spoil her friend's special night with William.

'William told me your mum works at Vickers too,' Oliver said, bringing Daisy back to the present.

'Yes. Yes, she does,' Daisy replied. 'It's nice really. I like the fact we are together.'

'I bet. It must be a great comfort to you.'

Once again, Daisy felt touched by Oliver's empathy.

'It really is. And she has made some lovely friends.'

'We all need good friends, especially right now,' Oliver replied. 'I really don't know what I'd do without William, even if he never stops talking.'

'What's that?' William interjected. 'Did I hear you saying good things about me?'

'Obviously.' Oliver grinned, rolling his eyes as he took a mouthful of his drink.

With the tense atmosphere now dissipated and replaced by jovial banter, Daisy felt strong enough to announce her decision.

'Well, we better go for the bus, otherwise we will never get in the City Hall. The girls at work say it fills up pretty quickly.'

Betty turned to face her friend. Without saying a word, Daisy knew her friend was asking if she was sure, and she replied with a smile and a nod.

'Marvellous,' William responded, ensuring his tone didn't sound too excited.

An hour later, the four joined the throngs of people walking up the concrete steps of the City Hall.

'This is a beautiful building,' Oliver said in admiration.

'I brought Betty here for one of our first dates,' William announced, gripping his fiancée's hand a little tighter.

'You old romantic,' Oliver replied.

'Always.' William winked, and they made their way down the resplendent mahogany staircase to the cloakroom.

After handing over their jackets, the group zigzagged their way around the dance floor, where scores of girls dressed up to the nines were moving to 'Puttin' on the Ritz', to get to the bar.

'What can I get you all?' Oliver asked.

'Another pale ale would be perfect, pal,' William answered.

'Ladies?'

'May I have a port and lemon?' Betty asked.

'I'll have the same. Thank you,' Daisy added.

It didn't take long for Oliver to get served and for the quartet to find a table.

Daisy still felt slightly on edge, but the upbeat music and the sight of so many people enjoying themselves was helping to ease the angst she had felt earlier.

'Do you two come here often?' Oliver asked Betty and Daisy.

'Oliver!' William guffawed. 'That sounds like a corny chat-up line if I ever heard one.'

'Ah. I didn't mean it like that.' Oliver laughed.

'William,' Betty retorted. Even in the dim light, she could see Oliver's cheeks had reddened.

'I was only teasing,' William replied with a chuckle.

'I guess it did sound a bit cheesy,' Oliver responded, breaking the tension. Betty sensed poor Oliver probably did want to make a good impression on Daisy. 'But it is just such a beautiful dance hall. I can imagine it's quite popular.'

'It is,' Daisy agreed. 'I wouldn't say I come a lot, but it's always quite the treat.'

Then before Oliver could respond, 'Sing, Sing, Sing' by Benny Goodman burst through the speakers.

'Shall we dance?' William suggested, already standing up from his chair. 'I love this tune.'

'How can I refuse?' Betty laughed, amused by her fiancé's exuberant enthusiasm for the moment.

'How about you two?' William asked, looking at Oliver and then Daisy.

'I'm keen if you're keen,' Oliver said, smiling at Daisy. 'It's been quite a while since I had a good dance.'

Taking a deep breath, Daisy rose to her feet. She had come this far, and if the truth be known it had been nice to put all her worries and upset to the back of her mind.

'Okay,' she agreed.

The group made their way onto the busy dance floor

and found a space to commandeer. Within seconds they were all shaking their hips and tapping their feet as they moved from side to side to the bouncy beat.

One swing tune after another reverberated around the majestic hall, allowing everyone on the dance floor to escape the atrocities of the war and relax.

When Oliver took Daisy's hand and twirled her around, she didn't resist, letting herself be swept away in the moment. As she moved across the dance floor, Daisy couldn't help but smile. Oliver was gentle and put her at ease. And when she took in his features, Daisy noticed for the first time how handsome he was.

Chapter 27

Sunday, 27 April 1941

'That was wonderful, Ivy,' William sighed after he'd polished off his Sunday dinner. 'Perfect as always.'

'You are a charmer.' Ivy chuckled. 'But thank you. Team effort today. You have Josie to thank too.'

'Thank you, Josie,' William said. 'That really was a splendid roast.'

'We do our best.' Josie smiled.

'I'll second that,' Oliver commented. 'It's been a while since I had a homecooked roast.'

'Well, you are both welcome anytime.'

'Thank you,' Oliver said. 'That's very kind.'

Daisy couldn't help but smile. She had surprised herself by having a wonderful night at the City Hall. Not only was Oliver the perfect gentleman, but he had also made Daisy realize she could have fun again. They had danced the night away before he and William escorted herself and Betty home. Daisy and Oliver had deliberately slowed their pace as they got closer to Ivy's house, giving Betty and William some privacy to say their goodbyes.

'I've had a lovely night,' Oliver had said.

Daisy had mirrored the sentiments, and when Oliver had said he would like to do it again some time, she had found herself thinking the same.

'What else have you got planned before you head back, lads?' Frank said, interrupting Daisy's daydreaming.

'I'm going to take Betty to our favourite haunt,' William replied.

'Oooh,' Betty commented. 'I haven't been to the park for a while.'

'Oliver, you must stay here with us and put your feet up,' Frank quickly suggested, not wanting him to feel left out.

'I don't want to put anyone out,' Oliver said.

'You won't be doing anything of the sort,' Ivy insisted.

'Can we have another game of cards?' Annie asked excitedly.

'Of course.' Oliver laughed.

A surge of affection flooded Daisy at how accommodating Oliver was. She wasn't sure how many blokes of his age would be so happy to play cards with two little girls.

After everyone had enjoyed a bowl of rice pudding with the smallest dollop of blackberry jam on top – courtesy of Ivy's determination to make as much as possible when the hedge at the bottom of the garden had come into bloom – and the dishes had been washed, dried and put away, William insisted on whisking Betty out for a walk.

'Oliver, are you sure you will be okay surrounded by all these girls?' William winked.

'I think I'll survive. In fact, these two are teaching me a trick or two,' Oliver replied, nodding towards Daisy's younger sisters, who looked as happy as Larry as they regarded their hand of cards.

'We'll see about that when I beat you hands down,' William jested, chuckling.

'Come on,' Betty said, linking her arm through William's. 'You'll be lucky if Oliver plays you ever again with your relentless teasing.'

'Is he always like that?' Daisy asked, after the noise of the door shutting indicated William and Betty had left.

'He is, but it's all in good fun.' Oliver laughed.

For the next half an hour, Oliver and Daisy played round after round of rummy with Annie and Polly.

'You two are naturals,' Oliver said after he secretly let them win three games in a row.

'After you go, we can keep practising against Frank,' Annie exclaimed.

'He will love that,' Daisy encouraged.

'Did I hear my name being mentioned?' Frank said, appearing in the doorway of the dining room.

'Oliver says we are naturals at rummy,' Annie boasted proudly.

'You will have to show me what he's been teaching you,' Frank said with a smile.

'That's what Daisy said,' Polly commented.

'Well, after you have helped me in the garden, maybe we could have a couple of games? But first of all, there's a little bit of weeding that needs to be done.'

Full of smiles, the girls jumped down from the table, always keen to help Frank, whom they had grown particularly fond of since they had moved in.

'Thank you,' Daisy said, after her sisters had skipped out of the room.

'No need for thanks,' Oliver replied. 'Your sisters are a delight. It's been a joy spending time with them.'

'They are a delight,' Daisy admitted. 'The last few months have been very hard, but they have coped so well.'

'I was very sorry to hear about your dad,' Oliver responded, his eyes full of kindness.

'Thank you. And I was very sorry to hear about your parents too. Life certainly knows how to challenge us.'

'It does that, but we have to keep positive.'

'You're right,' Daisy agreed.

Then, Daisy could have sworn Oliver took a quick inhale of breath before he asked, 'Would you mind if I write to you after I get back to base?'

Daisy felt an unexpected feeling of something that resembled joy. It had been a long time since she'd received any male attention. The night before had been wonderful, and if Daisy was honest with herself, she had truly enjoyed how attentive Oliver had been.

'I'd like that,' Daisy replied.

'That's what I was hoping you would say,' Oliver

answered, his smile lighting up his face as he gently placed his hand on top of Daisy's.

A few streets away, William led Betty to their favourite park bench.

'Shall we?' he asked.

'Of course.' This bench that overlooked a patch of grass encircled by rows of bright yellow daffodils held special memories for the couple. It's where they had come when they first started dating, and where William had proposed.

'It's been so lovely to see you this weekend,' he said, keeping his fiancée's hand firmly encased in his own.

'Yes,' Betty agreed. 'It's been wonderful. I wish it didn't have to end.'

'Me too,' William sighed, squeezing Betty's hand a little tighter.

'I'm guessing you don't know when you will next get leave?'

'I don't, sorry. But I do need to talk to you about something.'

Instantly Betty froze, sensing what was coming wasn't going to be good news. Steeling herself, she took a discreet intake of breath, not wanting William to feel any worse about what he was about to say.

'What is it?' Betty gently urged, desperately trying to keep her tone neutral.

'Please try not to worry about what I tell you next,'

William said. But despite his own bravado, Betty could tell he was anxious about the yet untold revelation.

'I can't promise that, but I will try,' Betty responded.

William blinked, clasping his eyes shut for a second longer than usual, then turned to face Betty.

'I have passed all my courses,' he started.

Betty's heart lurched. She knew exactly what that meant, and had been dreading this day since William signed up to become 'the greatest pilot the RAF had ever seen'. Biting down on her bottom lip, Betty kept eye contact with William, willing away the tears that were threatening to burst their dams. Unable to speak, fearing she would falter, Betty simply nodded.

'I'm moving to North Luffenham,' William continued. 'It's in Rutland, in the Midlands.'

Again, Betty bravely nodded, acknowledging her sweetheart's comments.

'I don't know how to say this to make it any easier, but it means I'm now starting operational training.'

Betty gasped, unable to stop her audible expression of fear in time.

'I'm going to be okay,' William affirmed, doing his best to reassure Betty. 'I promise.'

Betty tried hard to smile, forcing her lips upward.

'It's just practice runs to begin with,' William added, hoping this would assist in putting Betty's mind at ease.

'How long does this last for?' she eventually asked, not even sure if she wanted to know the answer.

'I'm not sure exactly,' William confessed, 'but I think a few months.'

A few months. Betty let it sink in, the words whizzing around her head at a rate of knots. A few months before her dear, beloved William would then be on his way to patrol the skies, to fight off the Luftwaffe. It simply didn't bear thinking about.

'Okay,' Betty muttered as she digested the news.

'I'm sorry,' William said. 'I really don't want you to worry.'

'Oh, William. You have nothing to be sorry for,' Betty gasped. 'What you are doing is truly commendable.' And Betty meant it. She was so proud of her fiancé and his determination to do the right thing to defend King and Country. After all, wasn't that exactly the same reason she had started working at Vickers as soon as war broke out?

'I just don't like the idea of you fretting constantly.'

Betty allowed herself to fall into William's chest, the closeness a comfort.

'Just promise me you will do your best to stay safe,' Betty whispered.

'Of course,' William vowed. 'We have plans, remember? A wedding, a house full of children, holidays at the seaside.'

Betty managed the smallest hint of a grin at the thought of all the things she and William had talked about. Their hopes and dreams for when this godforsaken war was finally over and life could return to some form of normality. Wasn't this what got her through each day, especially when times were tough?

'That's the spirit,' William said at the sight of his fiancée smiling. 'What is it Archie's nannan says? *Turn that frown upside down*?'

Betty chuckled. Despite everything, William always had a way of cheering her up, but what Betty didn't voice, as if saying it out loud would cement the reality of the risk, was, *Please come home, William. Don't let anything happen to you.*

Chapter 28

Monday, 28 April 1941

'So!' Patty exclaimed, as she sat down at the canteen table and turned to Betty. 'How was your weekend? How's William? I bet it was lovely to see him, wasn't it? Was it all very romantic?' As always, Patty didn't stop for a breath in between her plethora of questions.

Despite how anxious she was feeling about William starting the next stage in his RAF career, Betty couldn't help but feel amused by Patty's well-meaning inquisition.

'It was really wonderful,' Betty admitted.

Nancy looked at her friend, the not-quite-joyous tone in Betty's voice alerting her to the fact her couple of days with William might not have all been as rosy as she was making out.

'Do I sense a but coming?' Nancy asked.

The women had all known one another long enough to be open and frank. They had all learnt in their own ways that there was no point trying to cope alone. The friendships they had formed were also the one thing that kept them all going when things got hard.

'Sorry,' Betty replied. 'I don't mean to sound like a misery guts. It was a wonderful weekend, and of course I loved seeing William. It's just, well, it's hard when you have to say goodbye and you don't know when you'll see them again.'

But as soon as the words had left Betty's mouth, she regretted them. Poor Hattie was sat directly opposite her, and the last thing Betty wanted to do was make her feel worse. Hattie had enough to deal with, and now John was off in North Africa. She too had no idea when she would see the man she loved with all her heart again.

'It really is,' Hattie empathized. 'But please don't apologize for that, especially on my account. I know exactly how you feel.'

'Thank you,' Betty acknowledged. 'And how are you feeling?'

'Good days and bad days,' Hattie replied. 'But tell us about your weekend. Besides which, Patty will burst with anticipation if you don't fill her in.'

Betty couldn't help but admire Hattie. No one would blame her for talking about her own heart-breaking situation, but instead she refused to take the attention away from Betty.

'Well,' Betty started, 'it was certainly eventful.'

'That sounds ominous,' Nancy replied.

'What do you mean?' Patty asked. 'What happened?'

'Sorry, I've made that sound more dramatic than it is,' Betty quickly responded. 'William arrived on Friday night with a friend. We went out dancing on Saturday night and all spent the day together on Sunday.'

'And how was that?' Patty enquired, her eyes widening. 'You must tell us everything!'

Daisy's cheeks instantly reddened, and she hoped with all the attention on Betty nobody had noticed, but her hopes were prematurely dashed.

'Daisy!' Patty gasped, not missing a trick. 'Is there something you want to tell us?'

'There's nothing really to tell.'

Patty glanced from Betty to Daisy, not believing a word.

'You're not fooling me,' she exclaimed. 'If nothing happened, why are your cheeks as red as those flaming furnaces?'

'Patty!' Archie admonished. 'Leave poor Daisy alone.'

'It's okay,' Daisy said, not wanting Patty to feel she had caused her any offence. 'But honestly nothing happened. William's friend was the perfect gentleman. He was lovely with the girls, and we just chatted.'

'While you were dancing?' Patty stated.

Incredulous, Archie shook his head. 'Patty!' he scolded.

'Okay!' Daisy surrendered, knowing Patty meant well. 'Oliver was lovely, and we have agreed to write to each other.'

'Ooh!' Patty enthused. 'This is exciting. He sounds like the perfect catch!'

'I am sat here,' Archie interjected, rolling his eyes in bemusement.

'I've only got eyes for you,' Patty replied, grinning at Archie. 'I just want to know more about this Oliver fella.'

The rest of the table were doing their best to stifle their giggles at Patty's enthusiasm.

'You don't have to succumb to Patty's constant interrogation,' Archie said, looking at Daisy.

'Hey!' Patty objected, gently nudging Archie in the ribs. 'What do you mean? Don't you tell me you aren't keen to hear about whether Daisy and Oliver, you know . . .'

'Stop!' Archie gasped, putting his hands in the air. 'You are too much.'

By now the rest of their friends couldn't hold back their amusement.

'You really are a case.' Nancy chuckled.

'That's one way of putting it.' Archie shrugged in mock despair.

'I promise there is no more to tell.' Daisy laughed. 'But to put you out of your misery, Patty, I did think Oliver was nice. I'll definitely write to him.'

'You see!' Patty exclaimed jubilantly. 'That's all I was trying to ask.' Turning to Daisy, she added, 'I am pleased for you. I hope you and Oliver get to see each other again soon.'

'Thank you,' Daisy replied. 'I do too.'

'You deserve it, luv,' Nancy commented, mirroring their friends' thoughts. The last four months had been hard for Daisy and her family. She deserved some happiness.

'And how about you, Betty?' Nancy added. 'It sounds like you and William had a lovely weekend?'

'We really did, thank you.' What Betty didn't say was she hardly slept a wink after she and William said their goodbyes. The thought of what lay in store for her dear, sweet William was too much to bear. When she'd sat up in bed to drink a glass of water, Daisy came and sat next to her. Oliver had told her too what the next stage of their flying training involved. 'We'll get through this together,' she'd comforted. 'I'm always here for you.'

Betty had been grateful for her friend's words, and genuinely terrified of what the future held, but right now the atmosphere around the canteen table was one of joy. She knew all her friends would rally around her if she voiced her worries, but they weren't going anywhere, and it could wait for another day. Right now, she was happy to see Daisy smiling again, and the sound of laughter was a welcome relief after all the sadness this war had caused.

Chapter 29

Friday, 9 May 1941

'Here we go,' Dolly said, placing the precariously full tray of drinks down on the table where her friends had collected in the corner of The Welly.

'Thanks, Dolly,' came the collective response of gratitude. It had been a long week at the factory. Nancy, Betty, Hattie, Patty, Archie and Daisy had all worked over every night, and the canteen had felt busier than ever.

'I reckon we all deserve this,' Dolly responded.

'I'll second that!' Patty exclaimed, bringing her glass of lemonade to her lips. 'I thought I'd never get down from that mucky crane.'

'From what I can tell by the invoices I'm typing, the orders are still coming in thick and fast,' Hattie explained.

'No sign of any let-up, then?' Nancy asked.

'It doesn't appear that way, I'm afraid,' Hattie replied.

'And how are you feeling, duck?' Dolly asked Hattie, whose much rounder tummy was a clear indicator her pregnancy was progressing well.

'Not so bad. I'm feeling a bit tired, but I'm not sure if that's due to the baby or just everyday life.' What Hattie didn't add was that she was sure part of her exhaustion was down to grief too, and how she still questioned if she could have prevented her dad's death.

'Well, I'm sure your little one is contributing,' Dolly empathized. 'My boys zapped every ounce of energy I had when I was carrying them. I could have fallen asleep stood up at any given moment. Are you sleeping okay?'

'Not especially but I think that's normal, isn't it? I don't seem to be able to get comfortable.'

'Afraid so.' Dolly nodded as she lifted her half glass of pale ale to her lips. 'I swear my two would start acrobatics every time my eyes closed. They were reyt little wrigglers.'

'I think this one is the same,' Hattie replied, giving her stomach a rub. 'I swear, every time I drop off, he or she gives me a little nudge. Don't get me wrong, it's lovely to feel them, I just wish they would do it in the day.'

'I think it's nature's way of getting you ready for what's coming,' Nancy added. 'Our Billy was a right little mover and shaker while I was pregnant, and he's never kept still since.'

'Ooh! Do you think you're having a boy, then?' Patty interjected.

'Maybe.' Hattie laughed. 'By the sounds of what everybody is saying, it's a distinct possibility.'

'I have to say our Linda wasn't as active as Billy,' Nancy said. 'But then again, it wouldn't take much beating.'

'How about you, Josie?' Hattie asked. 'Were all your girls wrigglers or were they calmer?'

'Do you know, each one of them was different.' Smiling at her eldest daughter, Josie added, 'Daisy was definitely the calmest. Too calm, if I'm honest. It would worry me sick when I couldn't feel her. I'd end up drinking ice-cold water, followed by the hottest cup of tea I could manage, to try and wake her up. I'd get myself in a right tizz until Alf calmed me down. And, of course, it was then that Daisy would give me a little nudge.'

'Sorry.' Daisy laughed.

'Nothing to apologize for,' Josie said. 'I just don't think you ever stop worrying from the second you find out you are pregnant.'

'You're right there,' Dolly commented. 'They are worth every second of it, though.'

'Maybe you *are* having a boy, then!' Patty exclaimed. 'I've been attempting to knit a white bonnet, but maybe I should start again in baby blue?'

'You're knitting a bonnet!' Hattie exclaimed. Patty wasn't exactly known for her knitting accomplishments. She'd spent the last two winters unpicking more than she'd produced.

'Oi!' Patty gasped in pretend shock to her best friend's reaction. 'I'll have you know I'm doing rather well.'

'Even if you do say so yourself,' Hattie jested.

'I am,' Patty protested. 'Aren't I, Nancy?'

'To be fair, you are, luv. I've been rather impressed.'

'Have you been giving Patty secret lessons?' Hattie asked, grinning.

'Maybe a few pointers,' Nancy replied kindly.

'Well, I'm very impressed,' Hattie said. 'I'm sure this baby will appreciate all your efforts.'

'Thank you!' Patty said proudly. 'But I still think we need to work out whether it's a boy or a girl.'

'And how do you think we can do that?' Hattie asked.

'The needle test, of course!'

'You don't really believe that, do you?' Betty chuckled. 'I thought it was just an old wives' tale.'

'I absolutely do,' Patty gasped incredulously.

'What on earth is the needle test?' Archie asked, completely bewildered.

Patty looked at her sweetheart in horror, as if he didn't know that B followed A in the alphabet.

Coming to poor Archie's defence, Nancy explained, 'You thread a needle, or a wedding ring for that matter, and someone holds it over the belly of a pregnant woman. If it starts making circles, then apparently the baby is a girl, but if it moves backwards and forwards, it's boy.'

'Did you do that with your two?' Archie asked, looking perplexed by what appeared to be a superstitious yarn.

'I'm afraid so,' Nancy concurred. 'It was just a bit of fun. I have to say, though, the predictions were true.'

'Really?' Archie gasped, shaking his head in disbelief.

'You see,' Patty chirped up. 'Just shows you. So can we do it on you, Hattie?'

'Oh, I don't know,' Hattie responded. 'I'd feel odd knowing without John. It doesn't seem right, somehow.'

'Have you heard from him?' Daisy asked.

'Just one letter so far. He didn't say exactly where he was, just in North Africa, but he seemed settled. I guess it takes a bit longer for the letters to arrive when they are coming from so far away.'

'It will do, duck,' Frank confirmed. 'But it's good to hear John is settled. Hopefully he'll not be out there too long.'

'I hope so.' Hattie nodded.

'I've got an idea,' Patty said, desperate to keep her friend buoyant after everything she had been through. 'How about I do the test, but you don't look. I can then write it down and we can see if it's right when the baby comes.'

Hattie knew Patty wouldn't stop going on about the idea until she'd conceded. 'Okay, but let's give it another week or so.' She secretly hoped Patty might end up being too busy or, by some miracle, forget.

'Perfect.' Patty beamed, delighted, in her own mind at least, that she would soon know the sex of her best friend's baby.

'Mind you,' she added, 'I'll have to keep what I knit afterwards a secret from you, otherwise you'll know by the colours!'

'But you can't even hold your own water!' Archie harrumphed.

'Oi!' Patty exclaimed once again, reproaching Archie. 'I'll have you know I'm very good at keeping secrets.'

As the pair playfully argued it out, Daisy, who was sat next to Hattie, discreetly asked, 'How are you and your mum doing?'

'It's tricky, but we are managing as best as we can. We have good days and bad days. I still don't really like being in the kitchen. I get awful flashbacks, and Mum still isn't sleeping very well either, but we are getting through. Knowing this little one is on his or her way gives us something to smile about,' Hattie said, rubbing her tummy. 'We have to stay positive, don't we?' she added, with more conviction than she felt. 'I just wish Dad hadn't been the way he was. I'd have liked him to have been a grandad. Obviously not the way he was, but like he was with me when I was a little girl, before the demons in his head took over and he started drinking as much as he did.'

'I'm sure,' Daisy sympathized, wishing she could say something that would alleviate Hattie's sadness, but she knew exactly how her friend felt. She'd always assumed her own dad would be a grandad to her children as and when the time came. 'Life doesn't half throw us some obstacles.'

Hattie apologized. 'You have enough to cope with without listening to me.'

'Not at all!' Daisy insisted. 'Isn't that what friends are for? You all listened to me after my dad died and I wouldn't have got through this year without you all.'

'I'm glad it helped a little,' Hattie replied.

'It really did, so you must let us help you too. No good comes of blocking things in our heads.'

'You're right there. I just wish my dad had realized that,' Hattie sighed.

'Oh, I'm sorry,' Daisy answered, silently admonishing herself. 'That was tactless of me.'

'It wasn't at all,' Hattie said. 'I knew exactly what you meant and I'm glad I can talk to you all about Dad. You have all helped me so much, and I know your mum and Dolly are doing the same for my mum. They really are keeping her upright. Coming into the canteen gives her something to get up for. That and becoming a nannan. We've got to keep focusing on the bright side. And we have all of you to thank for that.'

Daisy leant over and gave Hattie a hug. Both girls blinked back their emotions, but they knew when they needed to have a cry they would be surrounded by plenty of friends who would be on hand with a packet of tissues and as much love and support as they needed.

Chapter 30

Saturday, 17 May 1941

'Hello, luv,' Ivy said as Betty and Daisy walked through the back door and into the kitchen. 'How was work?'

'Busy!' both women replied in unison.

'Well, I have a nice crustless flan and freshly baked bread. Would that help?'

'That sounds delicious,' Daisy said.

'Sit yourselves down,' Ivy insisted. 'I'll bring it over. I've just made a fresh pot of tea too.'

'You are good,' Betty added gratefully. 'It's been another long week.'

'You're all doing a splendid job,' Ivy said, as she lifted the homemade vegetable flan out of the oven. 'It's the very least I can do.'

'Where's everyone else?' Daisy asked, noting how quiet the house was. 'Are my sisters in the garden?'

'Actually, no. Your mum came back and has taken them out for a little treat. They have gone into Sheffield.'

'Aw, they will enjoy that.' Daisy smiled. 'It's been a while since they have been out with Mum by themselves.'

'I'm sure they will all have a lovely afternoon,' Ivy agreed, placing the warm flan on the table.

'Yes, me too,' Daisy answered, pleased. In the weeks after her dad had died, it had taken every inch of willpower her mum possessed to just put one foot in front of the other. A look of sadness had shrouded Josie that Daisy thought would never fade, but slowly she had started to put a bit of weight back on, and her smile, no matter how weak, had gradually begun to make an appearance again. She had even started putting in the odd hour or two at the WVS with Ivy. Daisy had worried when Vinny died that it might bring back all her mum's own raw feelings of grief, and she suspected in some ways it did, but she had also seen her mum spring into action to help Diane cope with the pain she was enduring. Together they had been there for each other.

'This warmer weather makes you want to get out more too,' Ivy added, bringing Daisy back to the moment.

'It does,' Daisy agreed. 'I suspect that's half the reason Mum has taken the girls into town. I think they are in need of some lighter clothes.'

'Yes, she did mention that. She was trying to work out what she could get them on the new clothing rations. I told her I was happy to let her have mine too. I don't need anything, but she wouldn't hear of it.'

'That was kind of you,' Daisy replied appreciatively.

'I'm serious, dear. When you get to my age, you stop growing and I have a wardrobe full of clothes.'

Daisy had thought something similar herself. She mainly lived in her work overalls, so had told her mum, if the girls needed anything extra, they could use some of her quota. They were growing at a rate of knots and were bound to grow out of their dresses and shoes before their new annual rations were topped up.

'Right, let me get you some cutlery,' Ivy announced, the table now adorned with a hot meal, homemade bread and a fresh pot of tea.

'You really do spoil us,' Betty said gratefully, as Ivy handed her and Daisy a knife and fork.

'Oh, and I nearly forgot,' Ivy said, with a quick shake of her head.

'Forgot what?' Betty quizzed.

Ivy nipped into the hallway. When she came back a few seconds later, she had two envelopes in her hand. 'These came for you,' she said, handing Betty and Daisy a letter each. Betty immediately recognized the handwriting on the one addressed to her. It was from William.

Looking at Daisy, she said, 'Do you think that's from Oliver?'

'I don't know.'

'Are you expecting a letter from anyone else?'

'No!'

'It must be from Oliver, then.' Betty laughed. 'Are you going to open it?'

Daisy carefully fingered the white envelope, surprising herself at the flutter of excitement that was making her tummy feel like there were a million butterflies inside her.

'I don't know.'

'What do you mean you don't know?' Betty said. 'Of course you must open it.'

'I will. Maybe I'll just have my lunch first.'

Betty looked at her friend as though she had gone mad.

'Sorry! I know Oliver said he would write, but I suppose I wasn't sure if he really would.'

'He seemed like a nice fella,' Betty encouraged.

'I know. I've just had my fingers burnt before. Remember Tommy Hardcastle?'

'Don't! You can't compare Oliver with that ratbag.'

Daisy hoped Betty was right. Tommy Hardcastle had tried to cause untold trouble between herself and Patty before she had started at Vickers, and Daisy had vowed she would never let a man hurt her like that again.

'I hope so,' Daisy replied. In her heart of hearts, she was sure the two men were polar opposites. Tommy had acted like the cock of the north, whereas Oliver couldn't have been any kinder.

'Well, why don't you open your letter and see?'

'Shall we have lunch first?' Daisy suggested. She didn't want to admit it, but she was slightly anxious about what the letter might say. She had enjoyed spending time with Oliver and had hoped he would write, but what if he didn't feel the same way. *But why would he write?* Daisy was sending herself into a flummox.

'Okay,' Betty replied, amused by her friend's out-of-character reaction.

'Anyway,' Daisy said, 'it looks like you have a letter from William. Don't you want to rip it open and see what he's been up to?'

Betty hadn't mentioned to any of her friends how nervous she felt about the next stage of William's training, determined to try and stay positive, but she would be lying to herself if she didn't admit the very thought of what the future held had kept her awake at night.

'I think I'll wait too,' Betty replied. 'I quite like to take my time.'

Daisy nodded. It wasn't the first time she had seen Betty take William's letters up to their shared bedroom to savour them.

Twenty minutes later, after the two women had finished their dinner, they both did exactly that. As Daisy lay on her tummy, on top of her patchwork eiderdown, she carefully slipped the letter from the envelope and let her eyes roll over the words.

Dear Daisy,

I hope you have been keeping well since I visited and not working too hard, although I guess that's easier said than done.

I really did have the most wonderful weekend and enjoyed our time together. I'm keeping all my fingers crossed you did as well. It's a long time since

I've had that much fun, let alone gone dancing. Maybe next time I get some leave, I could visit you again? I would really like to take you back to the City Hall, or maybe even to see a picture? I'd love to see your sisters too. How are they getting on? Have they pinned Frank down to a card tournament yet?

Daisy couldn't stop herself from grinning if she tried. Oliver really did like her! She had been sure he had during his visit, but had got herself into a pickle thinking once he got back to his RAF base, that he might think differently. Out of sight, out of mind, and all that.

Everything here is moving on to the next stage. I'm still with William, in fact I'm part of his crew, but we have been moved to another base. I can't say where, but I am still in England.

If you get the chance, do let me know what you have been up to. Letters are few and far between here, so if you have a spare minute or two, it would be wonderful to hear from you.

In the meantime, stay safe and look after yourself.
Yours, Oliver

Daisy re-read the letter, digesting every word. She hadn't been sure about getting involved with anyone, especially so soon after losing her dad, but there was something about Oliver that she couldn't help feeling attracted to.

He seemed such a gentle soul and had endured so much. He'd be forgiven for being bitter and angry in life, but he was the complete opposite. And Daisy couldn't deny the fissure of electricity she'd felt when Oliver had spun her around the dance floor. There was no doubt in Daisy's mind, she would definitely be writing back.

As she indulged herself in a happy daydream, on the bed opposite, Betty was contemplating the words William had written in his missive.

My dearest, sweet Bet,

How are you, my love? I hope you are okay? I haven't stopped thinking about you since I saw you. I hated saying goodbye, but keep reminding myself that if I don't go away, I can't come back. Does that make sense? Hopefully you will understand what I mean. It helps me keep going when I'm missing you.

Our weekend together was wonderful. It was so good to have so much time together. And we must go dancing again next time I have some leave.

I think Oliver rather enjoyed it too, in fact, I know he did. He hasn't stopped talking about Daisy since. I know he has written to her, as we handed our letters in to be posted at the same time. He's had such a tough time, it's good to see him looking so happy. You must let me know what Daisy has said, so I can put the poor fella out of his misery. I know he's keen on Daisy, I'll keep everything crossed she is just as smitten.

And what have you been doing when you haven't been at the factory? Have you managed to put a few shifts in at the WVS? Daft question, I know. Of course you have. Please try and find some time to relax too. You always work so hard.

It's been all actions go here. Oliver and I have barely had time to stop. We have been finishing the last elements of our training.

Betty took a sharp intake of breath. Bolstering herself, she reminded herself what William was doing was truly admirable. But despite how praiseworthy his actions were, Betty couldn't help but feel anxious. Forcing herself to read on, she concentrated hard on the words that followed.

As part of this, I had to assemble a crew, which can feel a little daunting. It feels strange to now be classed as a Captain and pilot, but I suppose this is what I've been working towards for so long. Of course, Oliver is my navigator – I wouldn't trust anyone else. I've met some new chaps who have made up the rest of the crew. They are a good bunch, Betty. My wireless operator, Wally, is also from Sheffield, so we have all been talking about catching the train back together next time we get a few days off. The other fellas are from all over the place, some as far as East Lothian in Scotland. They are all a decent bunch. It goes without saying, I trust them all with my life.

Betty momentarily closed her eyes and tried not to think too deeply about the very real implication of those well-intended words.

Anyway, Bet, despite thinking we would be at North Luffenham for a while, we have been transferred again. I can't tell you exactly where we are or much about the place yet, as I haven't had time to explore. The digs are much of a muchness – not quite the standard of Harrogate, though! Not that I can complain. Your photo is next to my bed and seeing your smile morning and night keeps me going.

I'll write again soon and will look forward to your next letter. I know I keep saying it but try and have some fun in between Vickers and the WVS.
Sending all my love,
Yours forever,
William xx

Betty gripped the piece of paper between her fingers, not sure what to think. She was so unbelievably proud of William. He really was on his way to fulfilling his dream, but dear God, it hurt. She had no idea what the specifics meant of having his own crew, but she wasn't daft – he would soon be taking to the skies. No doubt the very skies the Luftwaffe had darkened with terrifying fury.

'Betty. Betty, what is it?' Daisy interrupted her friend's worries.

Betty looked up to see Daisy looking at her in alarm, and only then realized that silent tears were running down her cheeks, creating streaky rivulets in the dust that rested on her face after a morning operating a crane thirty feet in the air.

'Oh. Sorry.' Betty shifted herself into a sitting position on her bed and reached inside her overalls pocket for a handkerchief.

'Has something happened?' Daisy asked, coming to sit next to her friend. 'Is William okay?'

'Just ignore me. I'm being daft.'

'Don't be silly. You are not being daft, but what on earth was in William's letter to leave you so upset?'

'Nothing I didn't already know. It just . . . Well, you know, when I see it in writing, it just makes it all so real.'

'This war!' Daisy sighed, putting her arm around Betty.

Although Sheffield had escaped any more deathly raids, only a week earlier Hitler had sent the Luftwaffe across London again, causing a devastating amount of damage. Reports on the wireless and in Frank's *Daily Mirror* had stated the city had been ablaze, even Westminster Abbey and the House of Commons had been damaged, and thousands of homes destroyed. It was thought that the number of people who had been killed was over one thousand after hundreds of deadly bombs had been dropped across the capital.

'It's certainly been sent to test us,' Betty agreed, pulling herself back to the moment as she dabbed her cheeks, leaving a mucky smudge on her once pristine white handkerchief.

'I won't argue with you there. Is William all right?'

Despite being consumed in her own angst, Betty chose her next words carefully, unsure how much Oliver had told Daisy about his job.

'He explained that he had formed a crew for operations. I think it's still training, though.'

Daisy tried to recall what Oliver had explained to her about his job in the RAF. He worked closely with William, but he wasn't a pilot. He had mentioned something about memorizing routes.

'I know it must feel frightening,' Daisy empathized, putting her own thoughts away. 'But from what you have always said, and the bits I picked up from Oliver, he's excellent at his job.'

'Yes. I think he is.'

What Betty didn't say, though, was that it wasn't William's skill set she worried about. But she wouldn't dream of mentioning the Luftwaffe, knowing the pain it would cause her friend.

'Come on,' Daisy encouraged. 'I know it feels terrifying right now, but what have you always told the rest of us?'

Betty looked at Daisy, the hint of a small smile replacing

the angst that had consumed her. She knew Daisy was right. If the roles were reversed, she would be telling her friends to stay strong, to be positive. They had come this far; Hitler hadn't beaten them yet.

'I know. You're right,' Betty added, sitting up straight, her slumped shoulders now at right angles. 'I probably just needed to get it out of my system.'

'I'm sure. It's okay to get upset,' Daisy affirmed. 'You don't have to trap everything inside. It doesn't do anyone any good.'

Betty nodded in acceptance.

'But I tell you what does do some good,' Daisy added.

Betty glanced at her friend.

'A big hug and a hot cup of tea.'

And with that, Daisy wrapped her arms around her friend once more.

Chapter 31

Wednesday, 21 May 1941

'What do you fancy, potatoes or carrots?' Diane asked Josie, looking at the two giant sacks of vegetables that were sat on the factory kitchen floor, waiting to be peeled and cooked.

'Oh, I'm spoilt for choice.' Josie grinned. 'But I'll take the tatties. You did them yesterday.'

Grabbing a peeler each, and a bucket for the peelings, the two women set to work at one of the long wooden preparation tables.

'How's your Hattie getting on?' Josie asked. 'Every time I get a glimpse of her, her tummy seems to have grown a bit more.'

'Not too bad, not physically anyway. She never complains. I think she's getting a bit uncomfortable, and the baby seems to come to life at night, but she never moans.'

'She's a good girl. Like our Daisy in many ways.'

'They have both been through a lot.' Diane nodded in agreement. 'I don't know about Daisy, but our Hattie is far more resilient than me. There's been times over the last couple of months where I've just wanted to hide in my bed all day, but she keeps me going.'

'That sounds familiar,' Josie replied. 'After I lost Alf, there were days when I didn't want to be on this earth anymore, but I knew all three girls needed me. It wasn't easy, though. To be honest, it still isn't, it feels like a battle. I've lost count of the number of times our Daisy has come and found me in the kitchen in the middle of the night, and just sat with me until my eyes finally started to close. I don't know how she does it without falling to bits herself, but our Daisy has just got a way of reminding me that Alf would want us all to carry on and find a way to rebuild our lives.'

'It's not quite the same, but Hattie always seems to know what to say. She won't let me crumble. Even when I'm at my lowest, she finds a way to bolster me and get me through another day. I do feel guilty, though.'

'What do you mean?'

'I should be the one looking after Hattie, not the other way round. I'm the parent, after all.'

'I know what you mean. I've said the same to Ivy a few times. It doesn't feel right, does it?'

'No, and I'd never forgive myself if Hattie resented me for it.'

Josie turned to look at Diane. 'I'm sure she wouldn't. You are a team, you and your Hattie. You are there for each other in different ways.'

'She just has so much to cope with already, what with a baby on the way and her husband hundreds of miles away.'

'And you have always been there for Hattie. And I know I'm guilty of not taking my own advice in what I'm about to say, but remember, Hattie, like our Daisy, is an adult too. They want to help.'

'You're right. It just doesn't feel the way it should be, does it?'

'No. It definitely doesn't. It's the thing that I feel the guiltiest about. My girls, like your Hattie, have been through so much. I want to be the brave one, to shield them and make everything better, but I know, no matter how hard I try, I can't. Daisy has taken on more than her fair share of mothering Annie and Polly. Ivy and Frank have done so much too.'

'I know we are very lucky to have them,' Diane said, picking up another handful of carrots. 'I just wish I could make life better.'

'I reckon there's hardly a soul in the country who isn't feeling like that right now,' Josie concurred.

'You're probably right. Do you think things will ever feel normal again?' Diane asked, the hint of desperation in her voice not lost on Josie.

'Oh, luv. I hope so, but if I'm honest, I really don't know. I'm not sure if I'll ever feel normal again. People tell you that you'll find a new normality, but I miss our Alf so much. I don't want a new normality, I want the one I had, but I know that's not going to happen. There isn't an hour that goes by when I don't think about Alf. It's a struggle. As I say, I put on a brave face for the girls, especially the younger two, but inside,' Josie dropped the potato she was holding and brought her hand to the left-hand side of her chest, 'well, it still really hurts.'

'I'm sorry,' Diane offered. 'I didn't mean to make you feel worse. Your Alf sounded like a good man.'

'You have nothing to apologize for. None of this is your fault, but I'll not argue with you about Alf. He was a good 'un. One of the best. I still sometimes find myself going to tell him something and then realize he isn't there. I make do with having conversations with him in my head. I try and envisage his answers when I need to know something or want his opinion. I go down to the bottom of Ivy's garden and have a silent natter with him. I told him about starting at the WVS with Ivy, and I tell him what the girls have been doing, and what our Daisy is up to. I even told him about her going dancing with William's friend, Oliver, and asked him what he thought.'

'And what did he say?' Diane asked.

'Well. I imagined him saying, "As long as he's looking after our Daisy and he's a good lad, then it will be good for her."'

'I reckon he's right,' Diane said. 'Hattie was telling me all about them going dancing. She said Daisy couldn't stop grinning, so if that's what you think Alf has said, I don't think you can go far wrong.'

'I know it probably sounds a bit crackers, but it helps somehow. It's a comfort.'

'No, it doesn't. It's lovely. It's like your Alf is still with you,' Diane acknowledged. 'It's not quite the same but I find myself shouting at Vinny one minute, but then pleading to understand how he got to the way he did the next.'

Josie glanced at her friend. Although she was more than aware of the deep-rooted pain that grief brought, she knew Alf's death had been very different to Vinny's. It some ways it was more straightforward. She'd loved her husband with every fibre of her being, and Alf had never given her any reason to do anything but. But poor Diane had a myriad of complicated feelings to try and work through. Josie knew Diane had never stopped loving Vinny, but she was also aware of the pain he'd caused both her and Hattie.

'It must be so hard,' Josie said. 'Deep down, your Vinny was a good man. I know he put you and Hattie through a lot, more than anyone should ever have to endure, but from what you have said, he was fighting a lot of difficult battles in his own head.'

Diane nodded and blinked back the burning sensation of tears collecting behind her eyes.

'I'm sorry,' Josie quickly added, putting her peeler down, and placing a hand on her friend's arm. 'I didn't mean to upset you.'

'You haven't – not really. The same thing goes round

in my head over and over again. It's the one thing I can't make sense of. I tried so hard to get Vinny to talk, yer know. The memories of whatever he witnessed in the last war were haunting him, but no matter how much I tried to get him to tell me, he refused.'

'Male pride?' Josie suggested.

'I think that was part of it, but I also think he just didn't know how to articulate what he was feeling,' Diane explained. 'Men aren't typically talkers, and you're right about the pride thing. They aren't brought up to show signs of weakness. Being in the army doesn't help either. They are trained not to let their emotions overtake them. In some ways, I don't suppose he stood a chance, but I just can't help thinking maybe I should have tried harder.'

'Oh, luv. From what you've told me and Dolly, you couldn't have tried any harder. You can't force someone to talk if they don't want to, or more likely in Vinny's case, didn't know how to.'

'No. I suppose not. I just wished he hadn't turned to booze as the answer. He was always such a good man before all of this. This war made everything so much harder. His low moods became more and more frequent, but when he added liquor into the equation, I didn't recognize him anymore. He certainly wasn't the Vinny I'd fallen in love with. I guess he was just trying to drown out whatever was haunting him. No good comes of war, that's for sure.'

'You won't get any arguments from me on that one,'

Josie agreed. 'Far too many men have been lost because of it, and what for?'

'I wish I knew,' Diane said, shaking her head. 'They are all fighting someone else's war. But one thing's for sure, Hitler ain't suffering, is he? All he cares about is how many countries he can control. He doesn't give a flying monkey how many people are lost or damaged by his selfish actions. They are all just pawns in his game.'

'They are that,' Josie said. 'Neither of us should be sat here without our husbands.'

'No, we definitely shouldn't. The flaming shame of it is our Vinny survived the Great War, physically at least. But emotionally, it killed him, and your Alf wasn't even away fighting. He was just doing the right and decent thing.'

'I know, luv. It's not fair. Life is certainly cruel,' Josie conceded.

'I'm sorry,' Diane said. 'I didn't mean to get all maudlin on you. You have enough to cope with.'

'It's fine,' Josie assured. 'It's good we have each other.'

Josie meant it. She didn't want to stop talking about Alf and she knew Diane completely understood how she was feeling. Not only that, but Josie was also pleased Diane was opening up. She'd been like a fragile butterfly when she'd first started in the canteen. It may not have been the circumstances she wished for, but she was glad Diane felt she could trust her.

'Thank you,' Diane replied, truly grateful. Mirroring Josie's thoughts, she recalled how until she'd started at

Vickers, she hadn't dared air in public the secrets she'd kept behind closed doors. Not only had she feared what Vinny would do if he found out, but he'd made it impossible by driving all her friends away due to his volatile moods. There were days when she felt she had been going crazy trying to understand Vinny and constantly stepping on eggshells. As much as she wished she could change the past, Diane was grateful that after so many years of feeling isolated, she finally had people around her she could call her friends and confide in.

Chapter 32

Saturday, 24 May 1941

'Well, this is exciting,' Patty enthused as she, Hattie and Diane wandered around Banners.

'It is, luv,' Diane agreed, as the three women looked at the range of prams.

'I don't know where to start,' Hattie confessed, the inflection in her voice giving away how overwhelmed she felt.

'It's a good job you have got me and your mum to help you, then,' Patty said, linking her arm through her friend's.

Hattie smiled weakly. She knew she should be excited about picking out some essentials for her baby, but part of her had been dreading this shopping trip since Patty had suggested it.

'Thank you. I don't mean to sound like a misery guts.'

'You don't at all,' Patty assured her friend, determined to keep Hattie buoyant.

'It's just,' Hattie started, then took a deep breath, 'well, it feels a little odd without John being here.'

'I'm sure,' Patty said. She had been very conscious of the fact that Hattie would rather be shopping for the baby with her husband. 'I know it won't be the same, but maybe we could go for a cuppa and cake afterwards and make a bit of an afternoon of it.'

Hattie knew Patty was trying her best to make the day as special as possible. She had been so caring and attentive since Hattie had announced she was pregnant. Hattie was also very conscious that baby shopping would help her mum too. She knew how much the thought of becoming a nannan was giving her something to focus on, and stopping her from falling into a spiral of depression after Vinny's death.

'That would be lovely,' Hattie replied, hoping she hadn't come across as ungrateful. Despite how despondent she felt about the shopping trip, Hattie had known it was something she would have to do sooner or later. And if John couldn't be here, she knew there was no one else she would rather have by her side right now.

'Okay, so what would you like to look for first? A pram or a cot?' Patty asked.

'Gosh, I don't know.' Then turning to her mum, determined to ensure she felt involved, Hattie asked, 'What do you think?'

'Let's look at the prams,' Diane said, also aware her daughter was finding today hard. 'I used to love taking you for walks, watching you chatter away to yourself until you fell asleep. You were such a placid baby. It was always one of my favourite things to do with you. I cherished those moments.'

Hattie saw how her mum's eyes lit up as she reminisced. The words stirred something in her. She'd been so wrapped up in just being pregnant and worrying about John, she hadn't really thought about the magical moments ahead. But listening to her mum made her realize this was a special time and something to savour, even if John couldn't be by her side.

'What would you advise, Mum? You probably know better than Patty and me.' There weren't that many options to choose from, but Hattie knew her mum would love being involved.

'Well, I didn't have anything fancy,' Diane replied. 'A friend gave me her old one, and you loved falling asleep in it, swaddled in a blanket. You looked so snug. I could have watched you sleeping all day.'

'That's so lovely,' Patty cooed. 'And just think, you will be able to do it all again for Hattie's baby.'

At the thought of replicating the moment for her grandchild, Diane felt a smile spread across her face, and for the first time in months her eyes gleamed with happiness too.

'Oh, gosh. You will set me off,' she said.

'Happy tears, though,' Patty stated more than asked.

'Absolutely! I really can't wait to meet my first grandchild.'

'You will make the most perfect nannan,' Hattie said.

Then touching her tummy, she added, 'This baby is very lucky to have you.'

'Oh, luv. The thought of seeing you become a mum and being here to help with my first grandchild has made me feel like the luckiest woman alive.'

'Don't set me off,' Patty exclaimed. 'You will make me all broody!'

All three women grinned at one another, a mixture of amusement at Patty's comment and contentment about what this new life meant for them all. For a few precious moments, Hattie and Diane forgot about all their worries, so engrossed in the happiness this new baby was promising to deliver.

Maybe things will turn out okay after all, Hattie thought to herself. And Diane couldn't help but feel a tinge of excitement about the future either.

'My mom always says, every house needs a new baby to make you smile,' Patty interjected, as if reading Diane and Hattie's thoughts.

'She's absolutely right,' Diane agreed. 'You can't help but brim with happiness when you hold a baby in your arms and feel them all content. And the way they gaze up at you as if you are the only person in the world. It's just magical.'

'I assume that's why she and Dad had five of us, then!' Patty half gasped, half laughed. 'She must really love those moments. I'm not sure I could cope with more than two.'

'Well, none of us really know how we are going to feel,' Diane explained. 'I reckon nature has a way of making us forget the harder moments, so those who want to don't hesitate to have more.'

'Would you have liked more than one?' Patty asked, but then instantly regretted her question, realizing a second too late how intrusive it was. 'Sorry, that was rather thoughtless of me.'

'Not at all,' Diane said, waving off Patty's apology with a kind smile, knowing her daughter's best friend would never intentionally mean to cause any upset. The truth of the matter was, Diane would have liked more children. She had always imagined having a house full of little ones, but after Hattie came along money was tight, so she and Vinny had decided to wait a little while. Then by the time they could have afforded another baby, his bad moods had started, and Diane had worried about bringing another baby into that environment. To begin with, she'd told herself he just needed time, but instead things only got worse.

'I didn't mean to speak out of turn,' Patty added, bringing Diane back to the moment, cursing herself for opening her mouth before she thought about what she was saying.

'You didn't,' Diane insisted, refusing to allow the special day to be ruined. It had been a long time since she'd had such a wonderful shopping trip and she was keen to ensure Hattie enjoyed it, knowing how hard her daughter was finding things without John, on top of losing her dad. Then, just to ensure the joyous atmosphere wasn't destroyed, Diane added, 'Our Hattie was all I ever wanted. She was the most perfect little girl. In a way, when there was just the two of us at home, it was like we were in our little world. It was as if we were in a bubble that no one could burst. I enjoyed being able to give her all my attention.'

'Thanks, Mum,' Hattie said, touched by her mum's poignant recollections.

'You'll know exactly what I mean when your baby comes along,' Diane said. 'It's hard to put it all into words, but it really is very special.'

'I am looking forward to it,' Hattie replied, confirming to herself that she really was. The last few months had been the hardest of her life, and she wished with all her heart things could be different, but no amount of hoping would change things or the way her dad had died. Instead, Hattie knew she had to focus on the things she could control, and ensuring her baby was loved and cared for was something she could definitely do.

'Good!' Patty proclaimed. 'Because I am certainly looking forward to being the best surrogate auntie your little one could hope for. I've even started knitting another pair of booties.'

With that, Hattie and her mum started giggling, both very aware of the disasters Patty had made when it came to knitting in the past.

'Can I help?' a sales assistant in a neat navy dress asked, interrupting the women's laughter.

'Yes!' Patty exclaimed, happy to divert the attention away from her failed escapades with a pair of knitting needles. 'My friend here is expecting her first baby, and she needs to buy a pram.'

'Well, you have definitely come to the right place,' the woman said. 'We don't have the biggest of selections, but I'm sure you can find something suitable.'

For the next twenty minutes, the enthusiastic and helpful assistant talked Hattie through the prams they had in stock.

'Do you have a price in mind?'

Hattie blushed. She had never been comfortable talking about money, after years of saving every penny she could. But John's parents had been to see her and insisted on paying for a pram. 'Our treat,' his mum had said. 'We want to help.'

'No, not really,' Hattie answered the assistant. 'Just something reasonable.' Even though John's mum and dad had insisted she choose whatever Hattie wanted, she couldn't bring herself to be overly extravagant.

'This one is very functional,' the assistant started, pointing out a navy-and-cream pram with large rubber wheels. 'It has plenty of space for your baby to grow, and it's quite deep too, so as your little one gets a bit more mobile, he or she won't be able to easily climb out. And, because it's one of the newer models, it even has brakes.'

'You chuffin' need 'em in Sheffield,' Patty interjected. 'You don't want yer baby to go flying down a hill.'

'Only you,' Hattie said, amused, as the group of women laughed at Patty's remark.

'To be fair,' the assistant smiled, 'your friend has a point. Sheffield is built on seven hills, and I've seen many a woman struggling to control her pram on some of the steeper streets.'

'You see, I'm just being practical,' Patty said. 'And another thing, my mom would have killed for a pram that was a bit deeper. Our Tom Tom was forever trying to climb out of his. We were all convinced he would do himself an injury. We had to watch him like a hawk.'

'Now, why doesn't that surprise me?' Hattie grinned, secretly hoping her baby wasn't quite as much of a handful.

'I know,' Patty replied, rolling her eyes in mock horror at her little brother's antics. 'He's still a climber now. My dad caught him the other night trying to jump off the back of the sofa in a cardboard box. He thought he could fly.'

'Don't worry,' Diane stepped in. 'There's every chance your baby won't be quite as active. You were always a quiet little soul.'

'Thank goodness. I'll keep everything crossed that this one is the same,' Hattie said, looking down at her tummy.

'So, what do you think?' the very patient assistant prompted.

'I do like it,' Hattie admitted, already envisaging herself pushing her baby around High Hazels Park.

'We can store it here until closer to the time, if it helps? I know some people get a bit superstitious about taking things home too early.'

'It's okay,' Hattie insisted. 'I'd quite like to take it home with me and get used to having baby things around.' What Hattie didn't add was that it would be nice to fill the house with things that made her and her mum smile. She still struggled to go into the kitchen without getting flashbacks of the night her dad attacked her and nearly strangled her mum. If she could replace those awful memories with something new, Hattie was sure it could stop those dreadful flashbacks.

'That's absolutely fine,' the assistant said. 'So, is this the one you would like to buy?'

'Yes,' Hattie affirmed, an obvious tinge of excitement in her voice. She only had eight weeks left before her baby was due. Hattie knew the months ahead would still be difficult at times, and she would constantly worry about John, as well as wish things had turned out very differently with her dad. But Hattie also knew she had a lot to look forward to, and for today at least, she was going to enjoy thinking about all the special moments becoming a mum would deliver.

Chapter 33

Sunday, 8 June 1941

Sitting down at Ivy's dining room table, Daisy took out the new pad of paper she had bought especially to write to Oliver. Over the last three weeks, the pair had exchanged a couple of missives, and Daisy had started to look forward to each letter that arrived addressed to her. So much so that it had now become habit to always look on the hall stand as soon as she got home from work, to see if any mail addressed to her was waiting.

Oliver had explained how pleased he was that he and William had been teamed up as part of the same crew. They had been allocated a screen pilot who had more experience to start off with, but apparently he had a terrible stammer. *You know William, though,* he'd written, *he's very polite but had started pre-empting the instructions. He had to – we'd never get off the ground, otherwise.*

In his last letter Oliver had explained that during one of their night operations they had flown dangerously close to a barrage balloon, somewhere near Hull. *William did this pretty amazing manoeuvre. It's called a climbing spin.*

It's a good job he knows what he's doing, as those balloon cables can cut through aircraft wings.

In each letter that had arrived, Oliver had mentioned one escapade or another. Night flights over Oxfordshire where they had realized they were low on fuel. *I had to use all my navigation skills to find us an airfield.* It was as Daisy had read these notes, detailing what sounded like near misses, making her audibly gasp, that she realized her feelings for Oliver had begun to develop in a way she hadn't really expected.

So, as she started her letter, she felt compelled to write:

Dearest Oliver,
   I do hope you are keeping yourself safe. No more scary flights, I hope?

It had gradually become common knowledge through news reports that taking a position with Bomber Command, which Oliver and William were part of, was one of the riskier roles. Daisy and Betty deliberately hadn't looked too hard at how many crews had lost their lives battling against the Luftwaffe or the Axis forces. Daisy had been cautious about falling too hard for Oliver, not sure she could cope with losing someone else to this awful war, but she'd found herself thinking more and more about him. Not only that, but she also caught herself smiling as the time she and Oliver had spent together crept into her thoughts.

Things are much the same here. We are as busy as ever at work and staying on for a couple of hours every night. Not that I can complain, we get paid for it, and it feels good knowing I am doing my bit. And Ivy is so kind. Betty and I get home every night to a cooked meal.

My sisters wanted you to know they have now beaten Frank several times at cards. I think he lets them win, but I'm not going to ruin their excitement. He's ever so good with them. If he's not outside in the garden with them, he's playing games. He really has become a surrogate grandad to the girls. They absolutely adore him.

I've decided to do a bit more at the WVS in the next couple of weeks. I struggled to go after we lost dad. I wasn't in any fit state, and I needed to spend what free time I had with Mum, Annie and Polly, but I think it's the right time to go back. They are such a nice bunch of women and I like helping out. Mum has started going too.

What Daisy didn't say was it also helped keep her mind busy. If she had too much free time on her hands, she would find herself in floods of tears thinking about her dad, or about how much more destruction this war would cause. On more than one occasion, she had found herself quietly praying Oliver and William would survive this war in one piece. But determined to keep her letter light-hearted and upbeat, she wrote:

Our friend Hattie is really beginning to show now. Her bump is getting much bigger. It's not long until her baby is due. Patty is fussing around her like a little Mother Hen. She's even attempted to knit booties. Her first attempt was a complete disaster. They had more holes in them than sense, but she's getting better with each attempt.

Anyway, I have promised the girls I will also help out in Frank and Ivy's garden this afternoon. There's plenty to keep us all busy out there. The carrots and beans need picking, and more seedlings need popping into smaller pots.

I hope you are managing to get some downtime to relax. Please say hello to William for me.

Stay safe and I hope to see you again soon.

Daisy hesitated for a second about how to sign off, then before she could think about it any further, penned:

Much love,

And, to her own surprise, she even added a couple of kisses.

Daisy xx

'Hiya, luv,' Josie said, interrupting Daisy's thoughts as she sealed the envelope. 'Is that to who I think it is?'

Daisy's cheeks coloured as she looked up at her mum.

'I didn't mean to sound like I was teasing you,' Josie quickly added. 'I'm pleased for you, luv. I really am.'

'Are you sure?' Daisy asked, suddenly worrying that people would think she was jumping into a relationship too quickly after losing her dad.

'What do you mean?'

'Just. It's not too soon after Dad, is it?'

'Oh, luv,' Josie said gently, her voice soft. 'Of course it isn't. Like I've told you before, your dad would want you to be happy. He'd be cross if he thought you had stopped having fun on his account.'

'I just don't want people thinking I've forgotten about Dad, because I really haven't.'

Josie sat down next to her daughter at the table. 'No one would ever think that,' she reassured her concerned-looking daughter. 'Everybody knows how much you loved your dad.'

'I didn't think I had any love left to share with anyone else,' Daisy replied. 'Does that make sense?'

'It does.' Josie nodded.

'Oh sorry, Mum. That was insensitive of me.'

'Now stop that,' Josie said firmly. 'You aren't offending me. I'm your mum and you can say anything to me.'

And Josie meant it. Of course, there wasn't a single hour of the day that passed without her thinking about

Alf. She missed him with all her heart. If anybody had told Josie she would have survived the last six months back in December, she would never have believed them. But with the help of her friends at Vickers, as well as the constant support from Ivy and Frank, Josie had survived. She couldn't imagine ever feeling completely normal again, but that didn't mean she didn't want Daisy to find someone to make her happy. Quite the opposite, in fact. She desperately wanted all three of her daughters to find a way to feel as though there was a reason to smile.

'You are young, Daisy,' Josie added. 'You have the rest of your life ahead of you. You can't allow the grief and pain you have endured to stop you finding happiness.'

'Really?'

'Yes,' Josie affirmed. 'It doesn't have to be one or the other. Emotions are complicated, and never black and white.'

'Thanks, Mum.' Daisy smiled. 'I think I needed to hear that.'

'Your dad would be absolutely thrilled for you, and you know he would be pulling your leg and teasing you about falling in love.'

Tears suddenly besieged Daisy. 'I wish he was still here, Mum,' she cried. 'I'd give anything to have him teasing me.'

Josie moved a little closer to her daughter, pulling her in for a hug. 'I know, luv. We all do.'

Josie's maternal instinct kicked in. Despite how much her whole body still ached with grief, she knew, in this moment, she had to be strong for her daughter.

As the tears flowed down Daisy's cheeks, soaking her mum's apron, Josie gently rubbed her daughter's back, just like she used to when Daisy was a little girl and had fallen over and scraped her knee or woken up from a bad dream. For months, Daisy had tried to remain strong, barely breaking down. Josie had suspected she had saved her tears until she crawled into bed in a bid to protect her, but she knew it would do her daughter good to have a good cry.

'I'm sorry,' Daisy said after a couple of minutes, lifting her head from her mum's chest. 'I didn't mean to get myself into such a state.'

'As I keep telling you, you have nothing to be sorry for,' Josie comforted. 'No good comes from blocking your emotions up inside you.'

'Thanks, Mum.' Daisy rubbed her cheeks, patting away the remainder of her tears.

'You don't have to thank me, luv. I'm your mum. That's what I'm here for.'

'I know, but you have had to cope with so much,' Daisy replied, hoping her own emotional breakdown wouldn't cause her mum to fall into a similar state.

'This life feels far from kind at times, but we have to find a way through,' Josie said. 'There have been times when I thought I couldn't face the day ahead, but you girls gave me a reason to carry on. You all make me smile so much, and I know your dad would want you all to be happy. He would be cross at me if I let his death consume us. That would be the last thing he wanted. So, I guess what I'm trying to tell you is, you must allow yourself to be happy.'

Daisy squeezed her mum's hand, grateful for the words of encouragement. Although she knew her mum, or her dad for that matter, would never begrudge her for being happy, she hadn't really appreciated how much she'd needed the pep talk. Daisy had been happily writing to Oliver, attracted to his sensitive side, but there had been a part of her that worried if it was too soon after losing her dad to feel happy again.

'Now,' Josie added, trying to lift the mood, 'tell me. What do you think of Oliver? Judging by the way you react after receiving a letter, I assume he is making you happy?'

'I suppose he is,' Daisy confessed. 'He's just very kind and caring. He's interested in what I'm up to, and always asks about you, Annie and Polly. I don't think I've ever had a—' Daisy hesitated.

'Boyfriend?' Josie encouraged.

'Well, I suppose.' Daisy even managed a small chuckle. 'But we have only spent a couple of days together.'

'It's got to start somewhere.'

'I suppose you're right.'

'That's wonderful, luv. You deserve it.'

'Do you think Oliver might feel the same way about me?' Daisy asked.

Josie discreetly smiled to herself, remembering all too well those first feelings of angst and insecurity after meeting a man you really like. She'd been the same with Alf. And although remembering those cherished moments had been too painful, it now felt right. A comfort. Something she wanted to hold on to.

But before Josie could allow herself to be transported back to that special time in her past, she looked at Daisy, who was waiting for her reply.

'Judging by how quickly he replied to your last letter, and how he looked at you the weekend he was here, I have absolutely no doubt!'

And it was true. Although she wouldn't allow her own memories to overtake her conversation with Daisy, it was embedded in Josie's memory how Alf had wooed her with offers of nights out and walks around High Hazels Park, and always showered her with an abundance of compliments.

Josie's comment made Daisy visibly grin, confirming not only her own thoughts, but that of her mum's – she really had well and truly started to fall for Oliver.

'This is a nice thing,' Josie added, reassuring her daughter. 'Enjoy it, luv. It's very special.'

Daisy's smile stretched further up her face. She hadn't

gone looking for romance. It had been the last thing on her mind, but she had to admit there was something about Oliver that had sparked something inside her and made her feel alive again. She couldn't help but feel excited by what it all meant.

Chapter 34

Saturday, 14 June 1941

'What do you think?' Hattie asked Patty as she showed her how she had rearranged her bedroom to accommodate her new arrival. She was now nearly eight months pregnant, and her neat but prominent bump revealed that Hattie didn't have long to go.

'It's lovely.' Patty beamed as she looked around the room.

The subtle changes had turned it from a room that had been that of a young woman, containing a dressing table full of make-up, perfume and hairclips, and a wardrobe dominated by skirts and dresses, to one of a mother. Now, next to Hattie's single bed, there was a beautiful wooden cot, which had been John's when he was a baby. It had been dressed in a cream fitted sheet and a gorgeous patchwork blanket that had been Hattie's as a baby. In Hattie's wardrobe were wooden boxes full of essentials. There was a pile of neatly folded cloth nappies, another full of little white-and-lemon sleepsuits, and another where a collection of hand-knitted cardigans, jumpers, booties and beautiful little hats was accumulating.

'I have something to add to your collection,' Patty announced, holding up a brown paper bag. 'Actually, it's two things, but one of them may not quite be as lovely as the other.'

'You didn't have to get me anything,' Hattie protested.

'They aren't for you.' Patty laughed. 'And of course, I did! What sort of auntie would I be if I didn't spoil your baby?'

'Thank you.' Hattie smiled, accepting the bag, which had been tied with a thin white ribbon.

'Open it,' Patty insisted, her eyes gleaming with excitement.

'Okay.' Hattie carefully undid the ribbon. Lifting off the top layer of tissue paper, she picked up a pair of dainty pink booties.

'Pink?' Hattie quizzed.

'I have a gut feeling,' Patty pronounced confidently.

'That's quite the instinct.' Hattie grinned, bemused. 'I just hope you are right, because these are beautiful.'

'You are just being kind,' Patty said. 'My knitting skills still aren't up to much.'

'No! I mean it,' Hattie exclaimed as she examined the perfectly created gift in awe. There wasn't a single stitch missing, each bootie was exactly the same size, and they had even been finished with a strip of white broderie around the top.

'Did you really do these yourself?' Hattie asked in astonishment. After all, she had witnessed Patty's previous attempts at knitting – scarves that had so many holes, they would be of no use nor could they be ornamental, socks that looked as though they would fit a giant, let alone all the garments that had to be unpicked as they didn't resemble anything like what the pattern had suggested.

'Well . . .' Patty started, a guilty expression appearing across her face.

'Oh!' Hattie laughed. 'Go on.'

'I may have got a bit of help.'

'Never!' Hattie replied in mock horror.

'Nancy helped,' Patty confessed.

'Well, they are beautiful,' Hattie said. 'And I'm sure you must have had some input into them.'

'I did, but I can't lie, Nancy was forever repairing my mistakes.'

'It doesn't matter. I love them and I'm sure this little bean will look lovely in them,' Hattie said, gently patting her rounded stomach. 'We just better hope I am having a girl!'

'You are!' Patty reiterated with even more gusto.

Hattie threw her friend a bemused glance.

'Right, let's do the needle test, then,' Patty suggested.

'I'm not sure that's a fool-proof method.'

'You won't know until you try,' Patty insisted.

Hattie knew she wouldn't get any peace until she gave in to her friend's challenge.

'Okay,' she conceded. 'We can do it now if you really want to?'

'No!' Patty admonished.

'Why?' Hattie laughed in response to Patty's stern reaction.

'We need to involve everyone at work. We should take bets.'

'Bets?'

'Yes. A little wager. It will be fun.'

'You're not going to let me say no to this, are you?'

'Absolutely not!' Patty confirmed.

Hattie couldn't help but grin, knowing her friend was doing everything she could to make her pregnancy as enjoyable as possible, in a bid to stop her getting upset about John not being around.

'When do you propose we do this, then?'

'How about Friday lunchtime?' Patty proposed. 'In the canteen! We can lay you down on a few chairs. It will only take a minute.'

'No!' Hattie exclaimed vehemently. She was willing to go along with Patty's crazy idea, but she wasn't prepared to make a spectacle of herself in front of scores of her co-workers. This was one point she wasn't prepared to back down on.

'Really?' Patty asked, genuinely perplexed.

'Yes,' Hattie said firmly. 'I will do it, but it needs to be somewhere a little more private.'

Patty considered her friend's wishes. 'Okay, let me have

a think, but you're not getting out of it. Then you will see – you are definitely having a girl.'

'You are a one,' Hattie responded, raising her eyebrows. She really didn't mind whether she had a boy or a girl. If she was blessed with a son, Hattie hoped he would be just like John, and inherit his sensitive, but protective, traits. She could also envisage the pair of them kicking a ball around High Hazels Park, and John teaching their son how to make paper aeroplanes or building dens. But if she had a girl, Hattie couldn't help but think about the pretty outfits she would dress her in, and how much her own mum would adore spending hours making paper crafts and teaching her how to bake – not that she couldn't do that with a boy. Maybe a boy would be better, though – men certainly seemed to have it easier in so many ways. Okay, they were being sent off to fight someone else's war, but in general, they were paid more, could pursue a career even after becoming a parent and were unlikely to ever become a punchbag. Hattie shook her head in a bid to shake away the intrusive thoughts.

'What is it?' Patty asked.

'Nothing,' Hattie quickly answered. 'Just ignore me. I'm just overthinking things again. You know what I'm like.'

'Tell me,' Patty gently pushed. 'Problem halved and all that.'

Hattie sighed as she sat down on her neatly made bed.

'I just worry about bringing a girl into this world sometimes. They have to fight so much harder than boys.'

Patty sat down next to Hattie. If she was honest, she had never really questioned how men and women were treated differently, instead she had just taken it as a given.

'I suppose you're right,' Patty conceded.

Hattie turned to look at her friend, all the joy she had felt minutes earlier now overridden by a sudden feeling of despair. 'I would just hate it if my daughter, if I have a girl that is, ended up being as downtrodden as my mum,' she said. 'My dad controlled her life and there was nothing she could do about it. He pulled all the strings. We live in such a male-dominated society.'

Again, Patty felt slightly stumped. She knew everything Hattie was saying was true, but she had genuinely never questioned the status quo before.

'Oh, I'm sorry,' Hattie said. 'I didn't mean to get all philosophical. I just worry, that's all.'

'You have nothing to be sorry for. It's not your fault women aren't treated fairly.' Patty surprised herself by her comment. Then, as she thought more about what Hattie had said, 'It's just plain wrong.'

'I guess we should at least be grateful for Emmeline Pankhurst,' Hattie sighed. 'But look at how hard the suffragettes had to fight, and how badly they were treated, just so women were given the right to vote.'

'I wish we could vote to stop this blasted war!' Patty proclaimed with gusto.

'Absolutely. Me too. I can't see Winston Churchill backing down any time soon, though.'

Patty thought hard about what she said next, determined not to let what started off as a lovely afternoon end on such a down note.

'I think we women are stronger than you think,' she began.

Hattie looked at her friend again, with a quizzical look in her eye.

'Well, we are,' Patty bolstered. 'Look at how we keep Vickers going. And we aren't the only ones. There are women across Sheffield working in factories, making sure soldiers have what they need. And not just in Sheffield either. Betty said there are women all over the country employed in different factories, like the shipworkers in Sunderland, and others going off to be nurses in the army. And what about all those women ambulance drivers? Maybe after this horrible war is over, men will start to treat us differently and realize we aren't just good for washing-up and cooking dinners.'

Hattie couldn't help but smile at her friend's proclamation.

'So,' Patty added, clearly on a roll, 'I reckon your little girl, because she *will* be a girl, is going to be okay. Not only because we have started to show those old fuddy-duddy men how brilliant we are, but also because she will be surrounded by strong women.'

At this, Hattie's grin spread from her face up to her eyes.

'Maybe, you're right,' she answered, buoyed by Patty's enthusiasm.

'I am,' Patty responded authoritatively. 'And do you really think any of us are going to let anyone mess with her? We will all be like her guardian angels.'

'Oh, Patty,' Hattie gasped. 'That's so kind. I couldn't wish for a better group of women to surround my baby girl, or boy, with.'

'Girl,' Patty insisted.

'If you insist. But seriously, thank you. I needed that chat.'

'Nothing to thank me for. In fact, I think I surprised myself.'

With that, the two women burst into a fit of giggles, before giving each other a hug.

'Ooh, I nearly forgot,' Patty said when the pair pulled apart.

'What?' Hattie asked.

'Your other gift! You haven't seen what else I bought the baby.'

Hattie picked the brown paper bag up out of the cot where she had placed it while she had admired the booties.

'Gosh, I didn't mean to be rude.'

'You weren't.' Patty rolled her eyes. 'But open it or I will take offence,' she jested.

Hattie opened the bag and carefully pulled out the little package wrapped in pink tissue paper. She gently opened the parcel to reveal a little rag doll dressed as an angel, in a beautiful ivory silk dress, complete with its own delicate halo created from white wool and silver thread.

'My goodness, Patty. It's beautiful. Thank you.'

'I'm glad you like it. As soon as I saw it, I knew I had to get it. And now it really does feel perfect.'

'It does,' Hattie said, her voice ever so slightly faltering. 'My baby will always have their own guardian angel looking over them.'

Chapter 35

Thursday, 19 June 1941

'Ouch,' Hattie gasped, a sharp pain rippling across the bottom of her tummy and causing her to drop into a kitchen chair.

'What is it, luv?' Diane asked.

'I'm not sure.' Hattie winced between gritted teeth, holding her stomach.

'Is it a kick?'

'I don't think so. It went right across my tummy. Everything went tight.'

'Is it still hurting now?'

'Mmm,' Hattie hummed. Then, 'Yes. It's happening again.'

Diane looked at her daughter, whose face was scrunched up in pain. Hattie was now eight months pregnant, and although she still had three or four weeks to go, in reality the baby could come at any time now.

'Do you need me to go and call for Mrs Taylor down the road?'

Mrs Taylor had been delivering babies for decades and

was any expectant mum's first point of call when labour started.

'I'm not sure.' Hattie grimaced, the colour draining from her cheeks. 'It does hurt, but it's not agonizing.'

'Let me make you a hot cup of tea and see if that eases it. If it doesn't, I'll go and ask Mrs Taylor to come.'

'Do you really think this could be it?' Hattie asked, unable to hide how uncomfortable she felt.

'I don't know,' Diane confessed, filling the kettle with water. 'It could just be tightening.'

Hattie nodded, concentrating on her breathing as she endeavoured to manage the pain.

'In,' she whispered, then slowly counted to three in her head, before saying, 'Out.'

For the next few minutes, as Diane kept a firm eye on her daughter, Hattie managed to keep herself calm by taking deep breaths.

Then, just as the kettle screeched, indicating the water had reached boiling point, another high-pitched siren reverberated around the room.

'Not now,' Diane said, inhaling, horrified by the timing of the air raid. They hadn't been as frequent over the last few months, as Hitler had concentrated his tirade on Russia and the Mediterranean, but it was sod's law one would happen as her daughter was paralyzed with what could be contractions.

Equally as incredulous, Hattie shot her mum a frightened look.

For years, Diane had been so run-down she had allowed her daughter to take charge in these situations, but she knew it was time for her to look after Hattie.

'Okay,' she started, grabbing the flask from one of the kitchen cupboards. 'We have two choices.'

Hattie looked up at her mum, not used to her sounding so authoritative.

'We do?' she asked, feeling increasingly anxious about how the evening would unfold.

'Yes,' Diane affirmed. 'We can stay here, take shelter under the stairs and wait it out. At least that way if the baby comes, you will be at home.'

What Diane didn't say was she had no idea how she would deliver a baby, let alone during an air raid, but she couldn't allow that worry to overtake her mind right now. What her daughter needed was for her to stay calm.

'And the second choice?' Hattie whispered, the pain in her tummy making her feel slightly faint.

'We go to the communal shelter and deal with whatever happens.' Again, she didn't reveal what was going through her mind. Giving birth in an Anderson-style shelter was far from ideal, but at least there would be other women there who might be able to help, including Mrs Taylor.

Hattie tried to think through her options. She hated staying at home during a raid. It reminded her of all the times her dad refused to leave the house so she and her mum had been left with no choice but to take cover in the small cupboard that wasn't big enough to swing a cat in. But Hattie wasn't even sure she could walk to the shelter, the sharp pains taking her breath away.

Seeing how undecided her daughter was, Diane poured the boiling water over the tea strainer into the flask.

'Let's go,' she said affirmatively. 'I'd rather know we are safe. If you really can't walk, we will come back.'

'Okay,' Hattie agreed, happy for her mum to take the lead.

'Right,' Diane said authoritatively. 'I'm just going to grab a few things and then we'll get going.'

As Diane dashed out of the kitchen, Hattie pushed both hands down firmly on the chair to lift herself up and make her way over to the coat hooks by the back door. Although the weather had been kind to them lately, the shelters could be cool.

A couple of minutes later, Diane was back, holding a bag that contained a few towels and cushions. It wasn't exactly ideal, but it might make Hattie a little more comfortable if her grandchild decided to arrive.

'Do you think you can walk?' Diane asked.

Hattie concentrated on her tummy. The surges of pain were still there. Hattie couldn't work out if the agony was easing or she was just getting used to it.

'I'll try,' she said.

'Okay,' Diane said, opening the back door.

As the two emerged from the ginnel between their house and their neighbour's, the siren reminding them of the urgency of the situation, Diane put her free arm around Hattie's back.

'You can do this, luv,' she reassured her, as they joined the throng of workers making their way towards the communal shelter.

Hattie's neighbour came alongside them. 'Are you all right?' Mrs Wilson asked, concern etched across her face as she took in how uncomfortable Hattie looked.

'Actually,' Hattie replied, 'the walking is helping a little.'

'You're not in labour, are you?' Mrs Wilson asked.

'I'm not exactly sure,' Hattie admitted.

'She's having some tightenings,' Diane explained.

'Chuffin' 'eck!' Mrs Wilson exclaimed. 'Let's hope this raid is another false alarm.' There had been a fair few of them lately.

'And that this baby decides to stay put, for tonight at least,' Diane added.

A few minutes later, the neighbours joined the orderly queue to enter the public shelter.

'How are you feeling, luv?' Diane asked.

'Just a bit weak.'

'I'll pour you a hot cup of tea as soon as we are sat down,' Diane said.

Hattie nodded as she let her mum guide her down the steps into the dimly lit, cavernous chamber.

Seeing how fragile Hattie looked, their friends and neighbours made room for her to sit down on one of the wooden benches.

'Concentrate on your breathing,' Diane reiterated. 'It will help.'

'Well, this will be a first for this shelter,' someone piped up, as more and more people realized the state Hattie was in. 'A baby being delivered.'

'It might make the evening go a bit quicker,' another woman chuckled. 'Is Mrs Taylor in here? We might need her tonight.'

'I'm here,' came the chirpy reply.

Shuffling over to Hattie, Mrs Taylor sat down beside her on the wooden bench.

'How are you feeling, duck?'

'Actually,' Hattie started, as she made herself comfortable and sipped on the steaming tea her mum had poured her, 'I think the cramps are beginning to ease.'

'Did they last long?' Mrs Taylor asked, as she endeavoured to take in Hattie's appearance in the limited light.

'Maybe twenty or thirty minutes. I think the walk here helped. I don't feel in as much pain now.'

'That's a good thing then, duck. How many weeks have you got left?'

'Three or four. Is it normal for this to happen?'

'It is. It's yer baby's way of letting you know that he or she is getting ready to make their entrance into the world.'

Hattie felt a mixture of excitement and nerves course through her. In one sense she felt as though she had been pregnant forever, but at the same time it only felt like two minutes ago that she discovered she and John were having a baby.

'Do you think I'll go into labour quite soon?'

'I couldn't say for sure, duck, but tightenings are usually a good indicator.'

'Maybe you should think about stopping work now, luv?' Diane gently suggested.

Hattie hadn't given much thought to when she would give up her role at Vickers. If anything, she was hoping to be able to return when her baby was old enough.

'Maybe. I'll just give it a few more days and see how I feel,' she replied.

If the truth beknown, the money was handy, and it wasn't exactly arduous sitting behind a desk typing away all day.

'Okay, luv.' Diane nodded. 'But please don't overdo it.'

'I won't, Mum.' Hattie smiled, knowing how much Diane worried about her. But at the same time, Hattie preferred to be at work. The idea of her real contractions starting when she was at home alone, while her mum and friends were all at work, was terrifying. What if she was too weak, or in too much pain, to go and get Mrs Taylor? Would she end up giving birth by herself on the front room floor? Hattie quickly shook her head in a bid to dismiss the thought that was too daunting to even consider.

'Are you okay, luv?' Diane quietly prompted.

'Sorry. Yes,' Hattie said, endeavouring to sound as

positive as possible. 'I suppose it's all just getting a bit real now.'

Diane squeezed her daughter's free hand. 'I'll be there for you every step of the way,' she assured her daughter.

'Thanks, Mum.'

'Listen, duck,' Mrs Taylor interjected. 'If I had a h'penny for every woman I'd seen looking as anxious as you before they gave birth, I'd be living the life of riley right now, but I promise yer, the thought of it is far more terrifying than the real thing.'

'I hope so,' Hattie whispered vulnerably.

'Now listen here, duck. Having a baby ain't pain free, but it is the most natural thing in the world. And as night follows day, I can say with my hand on m' heart that most lassies get through it without any problems.'

Of course, Mrs Taylor had seen her fair share of difficult births, and had delivered a few babies who had entered this world without a breath left in them, but this wasn't the time to bring up such matters. What Hattie needed now was reassurance, and she had become a dab hand at that over the years.

'That's good to hear,' Hattie replied, taking another sip of her tea, the warm liquid a comfort.

'Aye, but have you ever delivered a baby in one of these chuffin' shelters?' a voice asked.

'I can't say I have,' Mrs Taylor admitted. 'But it came a bit close in December. Those raids seemed to act as a catalyst for a few pregnant women. There was one woman who only just made it through until the all-clear chimed out. Thankfully, she didn't live far away, and her house was still in one piece. We managed to carry her home before her little 'un made his debut into the world.'

'My goodness,' Hattie gasped, placing a hand on her now very rotund tummy. 'I really hope this baby stays put for the time being at least.'

'Well, just you let me know if those cramps start up again. But I reckon yer going to be all right, for tonight at least, duck. From what I can see, you've got a bit of colour back in yer cheeks. That's always a good sign.'

'Thank you again,' Hattie said, relieved that she wasn't about to give birth in a cramped air raid shelter, full of people she had never clasped eyes on before. That certainly wasn't how she'd envisaged her baby arriving.

With all the talk of babies and labour, Hattie and Diane had barely thought of what might be going on outside, but as they tuned into the other conversations they soon discovered it was beginning to sound like another false alarm.

'I reckon Hitler has realized he don't stand a chance of taking Britain,' one bloke piped up.

'Yer might be reyt there, pal,' someone else responded. 'Despite all the bloody harm and destruction he's caused, we ain't surrendered, have we? Not even London surrendered, unlike France.'

'He didn't know who he was messing with, that's why.'

'He chuffin' didn't,' another voice, this time of a

woman, commented. 'He didn't account for the British bulldog spirit.'

'That's right, luv. He might have guns and planes, but we aren't just going to roll over and give up our country. He thought he could break our morale, but he was wrong.'

Despite how weak and frightened she'd been just an hour earlier, Hattie felt buoyed by the determined banter around the semi-underground shelter. Hitler had tried to break the British spirit, as he destroyed their towns and cities, but the country hadn't succumbed to his relentless tirade. Quite the opposite, they had pulled together and fought back. England had refused to buckle or give up hope, and that's exactly what Hattie was doing too. She might be about to bring a baby into the world while her husband was hundreds of miles away, but she knew whole-heartedly they were together in spirit. Times might still be tough, but Hattie was not going to allow this never-ending war to take away the joy of becoming a parent. If anything, she felt more determined than ever to remain strong for her baby, and to be a mum, as well as a dad, to her little one until John came home and they could become a family.

Chapter 36

Friday, 20 June 1941

'Well, we could have done without that.' Patty yawned as she plonked herself down at the canteen table. 'I'm chuffin' shattered now.'

'At least it didn't go on too long,' Betty said. 'Were you all okay?'

'Our Tom Tom took an age to get to sleep once we got home, so I feel like I need matches to hold my eyes open today.'

'Billy was the same,' Nancy sighed as she unwrapped her pack-up. 'You would think they would be exhausted, wouldn't you?'

'Yes,' Patty attested, 'but that brother of mine is a ball of energy at the best of times, so there was no hope after the excitement of a nighttime outing. I suppose I should just be relieved he doesn't understand what it's all about.'

'How was your Bert?' Betty asked Nancy. Her husband had really struggled during the air raids, each one causing him to have flashbacks from his time trying to escape Dunkirk.

'Not as bad as he has been, but he still struggles, I'm afraid. Just being in the shelter puts him on edge. Thankfully there were no bombs, so he managed to stay a bit calmer. I just keep our Linda and Billy busy, so they don't see how unsettled he is. It helps that Doris's kids were there, so they all kept themselves entertained.'

'That's good. Is he still enjoying being at the Home Guard?'

'He is. It keeps his mind busy and gives him a purpose.'

'I am pleased,' Frank, who had first encouraged Bert to join the service, interjected.

'And how were you all?' Nancy asked, understanding how Daisy, her mum and her sisters must find the raids, even when they are false alarms.

Daisy took a deep breath as the memories of the night before flooded back. The Anderson shelter in Frank and Ivy's garden wasn't big enough to hold them all, so they had made their way to the public communal shelter. 'My sisters got quite upset,' she explained. 'I think they worry they will lose me or Mum.'

'I'm sorry,' Nancy empathized. 'That's understandable. It's very hard.'

'I think it just brought everything back,' Daisy said, desperately trying to stop her voice from faltering. Her sisters had been so upset when they got home that Daisy had slept with Annie, and her mum had got into bed with Polly. They had both woken up in the night crying, and only after lots of cuddles and a mug of cocoa each did they eventually fall back to sleep.

Instinctively, Betty touched her friend's arm.

'How were the girls this morning?' Nancy gently asked, her heart going out to Daisy.

'A little bit emotional, but I think a lot of that was tiredness. We encouraged them to go to school, though.'

'Hopefully that will distract them,' Nancy said.

'I'm sure it will,' Daisy agreed, more in a bid to convince herself.

'It will, luv.' Nancy remembered how school would stop Linda fretting so much while Bert was missing in France.

'I know you're right,' Daisy conceded. The girls had started a new school not long after they had moved in with Frank and Ivy. Despite initially missing their old friends, they had settled in well. 'I guess we're all just a bit tired this morning.'

'I'm sure,' Nancy said. 'You did well to get yourself here. I'm sure the gaffers would have understood if you hadn't come in.'

'I know. Mum looked utterly drained this morning. I told her Dolly wouldn't mind if she took the day off, but I think she was like me and would rather keep herself busy.'

'I understand,' Nancy responded. 'Now, would you like another tea?'

Daisy looked down at her empty mug. She'd drunk the first one in a couple of minutes, the warm liquid acting as a balm to the soul.

'Actually, that would be lovely.'

Nancy immediately stood up, taking Daisy's mug to the stainless-steel tea urn on the nearby table.

When she returned, Daisy was nibbling at her sandwich as she and Betty quietly talked. A bit further down the rectangular table, attention had turned to Hattie.

'I can't believe you thought you could be in labour,' Patty gasped, suddenly alert at the idea that her best friend could have had her baby.

'Apparently it's quite common,' Hattie explained.

'Did you ever have these tightening things?' Patty asked Nancy as she placed Daisy's mug of tea down.

'Not with Linda, but I did with Billy. Saying that, he never kept still while he was in the womb. I think he was desperate to make his grand appearance. Our Linda was much calmer. And, to be fair, nothing's changed since.'

'Did they happen more than once?' Hattie asked, curious to learn more.

'I hate to say it,' Nancy admitted, 'but they did.'

'Oh,' Hattie groaned. 'I was hoping last night would be it. It was such an odd feeling.'

'Sorry,' Nancy said. 'But just because it happened to me, that's not to say it will happen to you. Everyone's different. I really don't think two pregnancies are ever the same.'

'That's what I'll keep telling myself.' Hattie grinned, looking down at her tummy.

'It's exciting!' Patty trilled. 'You are going to have a baby!'

'There's no denying that,' Hattie agreed, amused by her friend's enthusiasm.

'And I can't wait to prove to everyone how accurate my prediction is that you are having a girl,' Patty added.

'I don't think we'll get any peace until then!' Frank chuckled.

'Oi!' Patty scowled. 'I seem to remember you placed a bet too.'

'Frank!' Hattie exclaimed in mock horror.

Frank put his palms in the air in defeat. 'I promise I had no choice. There was no way Patty was going to let me off making a prediction. She would have nagged me until I surrendered.'

'I have no doubt,' Hattie responded, very aware of how persuasive Patty could be.

'I don't remember twisting your arm up your back,' Patty protested.

'I'm a wise man,' Frank said by way of explanation. 'I've been on this earth a long time and know the best route to a quiet life.'

'You won't be complaining if you make a few bob,' Patty light-heartedly retaliated.

Frank rolled his eyes in jest, knowing he would never win when he was up against Patty, even if it was just a bit of fun.

'Anyway,' Nancy interjected, turning back to Hattie, 'last night's cramps could mean your baby is nearly ready to join the world.'

'That's exactly what Mrs Taylor said.'

'Should you still be here? In the factory, I mean?' Patty quizzed, suddenly concerned.

'How did I know you would say that?' Hattie responded.

'Well, I am your best friend. It's my job.'

'I think I'm just going to see how I get on for the next week or so. Apart from feeling huge, I feel absolutely fine today. Not even a twinge, just the odd little kick.'

'But you do need to take it easy,' Patty insisted.

'I promise you, my job in the office isn't exactly strenuous. It's nothing like being on the factory floor. In some ways, it's actually quite relaxing.'

'But you're still working,' Patty said incredulously.

'I am, but I know if I was at home I wouldn't be able to sit still and would end up washing or cleaning. While I'm here, I'm just typing. It's really not that hard.'

'But what if you go into labour?'

'Well, at least I will be surrounded by people. If I was at home there's a good chance I would be by myself, and I'm not sure I fancy that.'

'I hadn't thought of that,' Patty confessed. 'But your neighbours. They would help you.'

'Yes, I'm sure they would. But I would still rather be surrounded by friends and know Mum was nearby.'

'I can understand that,' Nancy empathized. 'Try not to worry, though, luv. Your baby will arrive as and when he or she is ready.'

'She!' Patty interjected.

'Of course.' Nancy laughed, then turning back to Hattie, added, 'I guess what I'm saying is, you can't really plan these things so don't overthink it.'

'Thank you.' Hattie smiled. 'I know it sounds off, looking at the size of my rather round tummy, but it still doesn't feel entirely real yet. Even last night when those cramps started, I still couldn't imagine holding my baby in my arms.'

'That's very normal,' Nancy reassured her. 'Even after I had our Billy, I couldn't envisage having a second. It's a strange old thing, but I promise it's also the most magical thing in the world. As soon as you set eyes on your baby and hold them for the first time, all these worries and concerns will become a distant memory.'

'That's lovely,' Hattie replied. 'And thank you. I think I needed to hear that today.'

'You're welcome, luv,' Nancy said, reaching across the table and squeezing her friend's hand. 'You really do have exciting times ahead.'

Chapter 37

Saturday, 28 June 1941

'Come in. Come in,' Ivy said, opening her front door. 'It's so lovely to see you all. Betty, Daisy and Dolly are all in the kitchen.'

'Thank you for having us,' Hattie said as she stepped into the hall followed by Diane, Patty and Patty's mum, Angie.

'It's my pleasure,' Ivy said, taking jackets. 'It's always wonderful to see you all. And Hattie, you really are looking lovely.'

'Thank you. I have to say, despite how big my tummy is getting, I do feel well.'

'That's good, dear. I am pleased. Now come on in. I've made a few snacks for us all.'

After Hattie's false alarm, and the fact she had conceded to carrying out the needle test, Betty had spoken to Ivy, who had suggested a girls' night at her house. Patty had been beside herself with excitement when Betty had told them all in the canteen on Tuesday. In her eyes they couldn't leave it any longer and risk Hattie's baby arriving without predicting the sex.

Betty led the group of women into the kitchen, which was already a flurry of activity. Dolly was cutting homemade scones in half, Daisy was making a pot of tea and Frank was offering those who wanted it something a little stronger.

'Just in time,' Frank said, as Diane, Hattie, Patty and Angie joined the group. 'Who would like a little port and lemon?'

'That would be lovely,' Angie replied. 'Our Tom Tom has run me ragged today, and that sounds like just the tonic.'

'Consider it done,' Frank obliged. 'And how about you, Diane? Can I also tempt you?'

Diane quickly glanced at her daughter.

'Enjoy it, Mum,' Hattie encouraged. 'Despite how enormous I am, I don't think this baby will be arriving tonight.'

'In that case, that would be lovely,' Diane replied.

'And you, Patty?' Frank offered.

'No!' she said firmly. 'I need to be on full alert. I have a rather important task ahead.'

The kitchen filled with laughter at Patty's statement.

'What?' she demanded, hands on hips. 'I can't get this wrong. People have placed their hard-earned cash on this.'

'Really?' Hattie gasped. 'I thought it was just a bit of fun. I didn't think you had taken money off people.'

'No point having a wager if there isn't a bit of cash involved.'

'You are a case!' Hattie exclaimed. 'Please tell me you aren't telling people the answer for definite based on tonight's little experiment?'

'No! I'm not that daft. They will have to wait until your little girl is born to see if my prediction is right.'

'I'll give you one thing, duck,' Frank chuckled as he handed Angie and Diane their drinks, 'you're certainly persistent.'

'I can feel it in my bones,' Patty said, her face poker straight.

'You are like an old woman.' Hattie laughed.

'You will all be laughing when you see I'm right,' responded Patty, who refused to budge.

'Can she really tell?' Polly, who was sat at their table with Annie, asked their mum.

'No,' Josie whispered. 'But we are happy to entertain her.'

Annie and Polly put their hands to their mouths to stifle their giggles, as Josie threw them a conspiratorial wink.

'Okay, cup of tea, then?' Daisy interjected, looking at Patty and Hattie.

'That would be lovely,' Hattie responded. Then turning to Ivy, she said, 'These are for you,' carefully lifting out a bunch of pink and white chrysanthemums from her cloth bag.

'Thank you. They are lovely, but you didn't have to do that, dear.'

'It's just a little something to say thank you for having us all here tonight.'

'It's always my pleasure. I love having you all here. Now, shall we go into the front room, where there is more space?'

'Enjoy yourselves, ladies. I think I shall make myself scarce,' Frank said as the group made their way out of the kitchen, cups and glasses in hand.

'He's a good 'un,' Nancy said as she and Ivy made their way down the hallway.

'I won't argue with you there, dear. I really got very lucky with Frank.'

Then, as Hattie was ushered into the front room, she suddenly froze to the spot at the sight in front of her.

'My goodness,' she gasped, 'have you done all of this for me?'

As Hattie glanced around the room, she took in the handmade blue and pink paper chains hanging from the ceiling, and a somewhat scrumptious-looking Victoria sponge standing tall and resplendent on the coffee table, surrounded by an array of neatly wrapped little parcels.

'You can thank Annie and Polly for the decorations,' Ivy said, praising Daisy's sisters. 'It was their idea and they have been scouring my house for off-cuts of paper all week to make them.'

'How lovely of you both. That was very kind,' Hattie said, smiling at Annie and Polly, who looked delighted not only to be included in the little soiree but to be thanked for their efforts.

'Why don't you have a seat, and I'll cut us all a slice of cake?' Ivy suggested.

'Thank you,' Hattie replied. 'I must admit that cake does look rather tempting, and my appetite has definitely returned.'

'Good!' Patty chirped up. 'You are eating for two, after all.'

'I wish I had that excuse,' Dolly chuckled, tapping her slightly rounded tummy. 'I swear I only have to look at a biscuit and my apron feels an inch tighter.'

'Well, we all need a little treat every now and again,' Nancy countered as the women all found a seat and Daisy's younger sisters sat on the floor in front of the fireplace, where Ivy had thoughtfully placed two cushions so their bottoms wouldn't go numb.

'We do that, ladies,' Ivy agreed. 'So, now you are all sitting comfortably, I insist you all have a little slice of cake each.'

As Ivy cut into the perfectly moist cake, revealing a slim but luxurious layer of ruby-red strawberry jam, the room audibly purred over the decadent treat.

'You really are a marvellous baker,' Nancy said after swallowing her first bite. 'This is delicious.'

'You can say that again,' Patty added, her words slightly muffled as she popped another forkful into her mouth. 'This is heaven.'

As everyone enjoyed their cake, Ivy, the perfect hostess, topped up their glasses from the port decanter and bottle of pale ale on the sideboard.

'That really was heavenly,' Josie confirmed after she

had finished, while she automatically collected up the china side plates.

'You are all too kind,' Ivy replied modestly, waving off the compliments with a little shake of her hand. Then turning to Hattie, she added, 'We have a few little treats for you.'

Hattie blushed. 'You really didn't have to. You have all been so kind already.'

'And as I said earlier, a baby is very special. Now, if you are ready, Annie and Polly would like to hand you them.'

'Of course,' Hattie replied graciously, still a little overwhelmed by the effort everyone had gone to for her.

'Here you go,' Annie said, handing her a flat square parcel. The co-ordinating brown paper tag, which revealed who it was from, read: *Dear Hattie, I hope this fits, Lots of Love, Nancy xxxx*

Hattie carefully opened the beautifully wrapped package, which had been finished off with a swirl of white ribbon. Inside was the daintiest hand-knitted white matinee jacket, with tiny, circular mother-of-pearl buttons.

'Oh, Nancy. This is gorgeous,' Hattie exclaimed, marvelling at the exquisite handiwork.

'You are very welcome, luv. It was a pleasure.'

As Hattie held the little cardigan, the fact she was only a few weeks away from becoming a mum suddenly hit her.

'It's all getting very real now,' she said, vocalizing her thoughts, a mixture of nerves and excitement coursing through her.

'Yes. Not long now.' Nancy smiled. 'And it's very normal to feel a little anxious.'

'Thank you,' Hattie replied. Then, determined to enjoy the evening, she added, 'I can't wait to see my baby in this. You really have done a truly wonderful job.'

'And here is your next gift,' Polly said, giving her an oval package. 'The tag says from Ivy and Frank.'

When Hattie opened it, in her hands was the most elegant silver photo frame.

'I thought you could pop a picture of your baby in, when he or she arrives,' Ivy explained.

'How thoughtful. That's very kind and, yes, I will.'

Over the next ten minutes, Hattie opened one present after another. Josie had knitted a lemon bonnet with matching mitts, Dolly had bought a set of cot sheets, and Angie had bought a giraffe-shaped teddy. Betty had bought a patchwork blanket, while Annie and Polly had made a little booklet from different-coloured pieces of paper for Hattie to fill in with details about her new baby, from his or her weight, the colour of their eyes, to what their favourite toy was.

Hattie looked at the pile of gifts she had placed next to her feet.

'I really didn't expect all of this,' Hattie said gratefully, looking at her friends, her eyes ever so slightly glistening. 'You have all been so generous and kind. I am so touched and very thankful.'

'Well, we couldn't let an occasion like this go unmarked,' Ivy commented.

'Even so,' Hattie added, as she looked around the room at all her friends, gently touching her tummy, 'you have spoilt me and this little one.'

'It's been a while since we have had a new baby to celebrate,' Dolly said.

'And a baby girl at that,' Patty reiterated, still firmly adamant her prediction was correct.

'Of course!' Hattie laughed, the tears that were threatening to erupt now abating. 'I'm not sure how you are going to cope if I have a boy!'

'I won't need to because that is not going to happen. In fact, now you have opened all your gifts, it seems like the perfect opportunity to prove to everyone that my hunch is right. Hattie, would you like to lie down on the couch? I have my needle and thread ready.'

'Do I have any choice?' Hattie teased.

'No!' Patty said firmly, ushering her friend to lie back on Betty's long brown Chesterfield couch where she had been sitting.

'Come on. You need to lie flat, and I'll get my needle and thread out.'

'Looks like you've been given your orders,' said Patty's mum, Angie, laughing.

Hattie rolled her eyes in bemusement and did as she was told, repositioning herself, shuffling down the couch until she was flat on her back.

'I hope this won't take long,' she announced. 'This baby takes quite a strong objection to my lying in this position.'

Patty raised her eyebrow in mock impatience as she fiddled inside her handbag to find the necessary tools.

'I remember that well,' Josie said. 'I had to lie on my left side with all the girls. It was the only way I could get any sleep.'

'I was exactly the same,' Nancy added. 'But even then, our Billy would have at least an hour a night jiggling about like a jack-in-the-box.'

'Right,' Patty said, once again commandeering the conversation, determined not to let the group get distracted from the job in hand.

With her sewing needle dangling from a good twelve inches of navy thread, she stepped closer to Hattie.

'Just remind me how this works again,' Hattie said, taking a deep breath and trying her hardest to stifle her laughter at the very serious look on her friend's face.

'I will remind you,' Patty said authoritatively. 'When I hover it over your tummy, if it starts going round in a circle, it means you are having a girl, so obviously that's what it will do. But if it goes back and forth, it means you are having a boy, but that's not going to happen. I have a strong feeling that my instinct is right about this.'

Annie and Polly looked at each other with anticipation, their faces lighting up at the thought of finding out whether Hattie was having a baby boy or girl.

'Medically proven, then?' Hattie giggled.

'You may tease, but I guarantee it, you will see,' Patty affirmed. 'Right, is everyone ready?'

'Yes!' Annie and Polly replied in unison, struggling to contain their excitement.

'Go on, then,' Dolly said, chortling. 'Let's see if this old wives' tale will come true.'

With a look of pure concentration on her face that none of the women had ever seen before, Patty lifted the thread with one hand above Hattie's tummy and held the stainless-steel needle perfectly still with the other.

'When I let go of the needle, no one move, I don't want anyone saying a draught affected the result.'

'We wouldn't dare,' Angie mocked.

Patty threw her mum a stern look. 'I'm serious,' she asserted. Then, when she was sure everybody had obeyed her orders to stay perfectly still, Patty let go of the needle.

The room fell perfectly silent, and all eyes were on the narrow, shiny instrument. For what felt like an eternity, but was only a fraction of a second, the needle stayed perfectly still. Then, gradually, it started to move, and there was an audible intake of breath from around the room.

'Oh,' Annie gasped, as the needle started to move around in the smallest of circles.

'A girl?' Polly asked more than stated. The pointy instrument seemed to pick up momentum, moving round and round a little bit faster, leaving the group in no doubt whatsoever to the shape it had formed.

'Well, I'll be damned.' Dolly laughed. 'It would appear your prediction could be right.'

Patty's eyes lit up with pride. 'I told you so,' she said, without a single ounce of modesty.

'What do you reckon, luv?' Diane asked, looking at her daughter, who still appeared a little perplexed by the whole episode.

'Am I allowed to get up?' she tentatively asked Patty, not daring to move a muscle until she had been officially granted permission.

'Yes!' Patty grinned, looking rather pleased with herself. 'My job here is done.'

Hattie used her elbows to lift herself back into a sitting position.

'A girl, then?' Diane prompted, looking quite excited by the prospect of having a granddaughter.

Despite the reservations about becoming a mum that Hattie had shared with Patty nearly a week earlier, she couldn't help feeling a tinge of excitement, even though she knew there was no scientific evidence behind Patty's test.

'A girl would be lovely,' Hattie said, the thought of being able to dress a daughter in pretty little outfits once again warming her.

'Girls are the best!' Annie squealed, no longer able to hold back her absolute delight by the news.

'Yes, they are,' Patty enthused.

'A granddaughter would be rather nice,' Diane

marvelled, stepping across the room to give her daughter a hug, as she remembered how much she had loved playing with dolls and colouring with Hattie when she had been little.

'And I can say, from my own experience, granddaughters really are delightful.' Dolly smiled, thinking of her own two.

As Diane sat down next to Hattie on the leather couch, mum and daughter shared a tight hug. They had suffered so much pain, but as they sat enveloped in each other's arms, they both hoped this baby would mark a new beginning.

The rest of the room fell silent, not wanting to spoil the special moment. In silent agreement, the women accepted it didn't matter whether Hattie had a girl or a boy, her baby would be so loved, and each and every one of them would be on hand to help out with anything she and her little one needed.

Chapter 38

Sunday, 6 July 1941

'Well done, girls!' Frank said, applauding while Annie and Polly gently lifted a spring cabbage from the ground, being extra careful not to rip any of the outside leaves. They had spent the whole afternoon weeding and harvesting the vegetables that were ready.

'Ivy will be pleased,' Frank added, looking at his wife's wicker basket, which he had appropriated from the kitchen solely to collect their latest harvest. Alongside the cabbages, there was a huge bunch of bright pink rhubarb, at least a dozen spring onions, more radishes than sense and a couple of heads of green lettuce.

'And we managed to find eight eggs this morning,' Annie announced proudly.

'You are good little finders,' Frank said. 'A couple of those hens are good at hiding their eggs, but they forget I have the two best hunters on the case.'

Annie and Polly giggled at the compliment.

'They taste too good not to find,' Polly exclaimed. 'The yolks are always so orange.'

'Well, I suspect we will be having an egg salad for tea,' Frank said.

'Can we have it outside?' Annie pleaded. 'It's too sunny to be indoors.'

'You are girls after my own heart,' Frank enthused. 'I'm sure we could give the wooden table a bit of a wipe-down and it will look as good as new. Ivy might even have a tablecloth we can pop over it.'

'I'll go and get a cloth,' Polly offered. And before Frank could say another word, she had run back into the house, and a minute later was back outside with an old rag and a bowl of water.

From the kitchen window, Josie smiled as she watched her two daughters busy themselves with Frank.

Josie turned to Ivy. 'You found a gem in Frank. He reminds me a lot of our Alf.'

'Just a few years older,' Ivy replied, chuckling.

'Yes, but the same big heart and caring ways.'

'He has that,' Ivy said. She could have said so much more about never thinking she would ever find someone like Frank, but the last thing she wanted to do was upset Josie, knowing how much she missed Alf.

'He's been so good with the girls. I know he looks out for Daisy at work and he's such a treasure with our Annie and Polly.'

'He enjoys being around them,' Ivy assured Josie. 'He often tells me they are like the daughters, or granddaughters, that he never had. He really does love all three of them. As do I.'

'Thank you,' Josie said. 'That means a lot. I know I keep saying it, but you and Frank have been ever so good to us. We really would have been lost without you, and I'm sure none of us would have coped half as well as we have.'

'Well, we all need to stick together,' Ivy replied. 'This war is testing the bones of most of us. Besides which, we really do love having you here with us.'

'About that,' Josie said. She had been thinking about the next chapter of her life over recent weeks and wondered if it was time for her and the girls to start looking for a new house to rent.

Ivy popped the tea towel on the kitchen side and turned to face Josie. She didn't say anything, but steeled herself, dreading what Josie might say next. Ivy hadn't been exaggerating when she'd said they had loved having Josie and her daughters with them. Despite the utterly harrowing circumstances, the house finally felt full. Annie and Polly, with their cheery personas, had helped it come to life again. Besides which, it was too big for just herself, Frank and Betty, and Ivy couldn't envisage ever taking in any lodgers again like she had before the war. It finally felt like a family home, and that's how she really hoped it would remain.

'Why don't I pour us a cup of tea each first?' Ivy said, partially for courage, partially to delay hearing what Josie had to say.

'Okay,' Josie said. 'That would be lovely. I'll get the milk from the pantry.'

Five minutes later the two women were sat at the kitchen table, each with a fresh cup of tea in front of them. For a few seconds neither of them said a word, the silence creating an unusual tension.

'I just—' Josie started, at exactly the same time Ivy said, 'Was there something you wanted to chat about?'

'Sorry,' Ivy added. 'I didn't mean to interrupt you.'

'No. No. You didn't,' Josie insisted. 'But I have been meaning to talk to you about—' Then she stopped, not sure how to phrase the next sentence.

Ivy took an intake of breath. 'Yes?' she gently prompted.

Josie took a sip of her steaming tea, before replacing the china cup, decorated with pink roses, back down on the matching saucer.

'Well, I just wondered if it was time for me and the girls to find somewhere more permanent to live.'

'Oh,' Ivy gasped, unable to stop the word passing her lips, her face ever so slightly crumpling despite suspecting this was what Josie was going to say.

'You and Frank have been so kind to us all, and I would hate to outstay our welcome.'

'You couldn't possibly do that,' Ivy exclaimed.

'But surely you and Frank would like your house back? I'm sure having a house full wasn't the romantic start to the married life you had expected.'

'Josie, dear,' Ivy began, nursing her own cup, 'Frank

and I didn't even know we were getting married seven months ago. We had absolutely no preconceptions about what the start of our marriage would be like. And as for romance, well, I won't say we are too old, but by the time you get to my age, there's a few things that come first.'

Josie looked at Ivy, her eyes asking the question she didn't need to voice.

'What I'm trying to say is having you all here has made Frank and me very happy. You have made our lives full, and we couldn't imagine you not being here.'

'Are you sure?' Josie asked. 'I would feel terrible if—'

'No ifs,' Ivy gently interrupted. 'If I'm truly honest, Frank and I would be incredibly sad if you decided to leave. And I'm fairly confident I speak for Betty too. She and Daisy are so close and it's clear they have been a great comfort to one another.'

Josie couldn't argue with that. She knew Daisy had confided in Betty, who had been a huge support to her eldest daughter. Josie had no doubt Daisy had opened her heart to her best friend multiple times, and Betty had been there to wipe her tears and listen. She also knew Daisy had turned to Betty to try and shield Josie from the pain she was feeling, determined to help her through what had been the worst time of their lives.

'You're right.' Josie smiled. 'Betty has been a godsend. We all need good friends at times like this.'

'We do,' Ivy agreed. 'If it wasn't for my old friend, Winnie, I'm not sure I would have got through after Lewin didn't come home in the Great War. She was the one who eventually made me get out of bed and face the world again. She really was a rock and has been ever since.'

'Those friendships are very special.' Josie nodded. 'I have never valued friends as much as since this war started.'

'Well, I hope in that case you will accept our long-term offer of friendship and a home to call your own here.'

Despite thinking she couldn't possibly have any tears left, Josie blinked back the little ducts of water that were welling behind her eyes.

'That really is so kind of you,' she whispered, the words catching in her throat.

Ivy extended her hand across the table.

'You will be making Frank and me very happy by accepting, but we will fully understand, too, if you and your girls would prefer your own space and home.'

Josie considered Ivy's words. She had thought about what it would be like to move into a house of their own. But every time her mind drifted to what it would be like for herself and her three daughters to find a small house that they could call their own again, she got herself into a state. Josie was frightened that without Alf, a new house would be a constant reminder he was no longer with them. Alf had always been the rock of their family, the backbone that kept them together when things went wrong. Josie had no idea how she would cope by herself. Being a good mum had been hard enough over the last six months, knowing she had to be even stronger than usual. Josie didn't want to feel weak or incapable, but if the truth be known, she didn't feel quite ready to take the next step without her Alf.

'Josie, are you okay?' Ivy prompted, sensing her friend had drifted off into her own mind.

'Sorry. Yes,' Josie replied, coming back to the present moment. 'I have been trying to work out how I would manage moving into a new house without Alf, but it just felt so daunting. Every time I try and think about how I will cope without him by my side, I start to panic. It's not just being able to emotionally support the girls, which feels hard enough, it's the idea of the house feeling empty. What if that adds to the pain the girls are already feeling? I don't want to set them back. They have been through so much already. And I can't even imagine having to do all the fixing and mending Alf did. Does that make me sound a little pathetic?'

'No,' Ivy said kindly. 'I know how hard it is to run a house by yourself. It's not easy. And you're right, your girls have come so far, as have you. I would hate to see any of you struggling when you don't have to.'

'Thank you,' Josie responded, once again overwhelmed by the kindness Ivy and Frank had bestowed on her family.

'You are very welcome,' Ivy replied. 'So, can I take that as decided? You would like to stay here with us?'

'Yes please, as long as you are sure.'

'I am,' Ivy confirmed. 'And I know Frank will be very happy too.'

A sense of relief flooded Josie. The extra tension she

had been feeling for weeks, which she had attributed to grief, evaporated.

'I am too, and I know the girls will be. You have made us all feel so welcome.'

'That's settled then. Please class our house as your home for as long as you would like it to be.'

For the first time since Alf had died, something that resembled contentment warmed Josie. Of course, she still desperately missed him, but she was happy here. Her youngest daughters were settled, and Daisy was surrounded by the love and support she needed. Josie would never have imagined back in December that life would take a positive turn again, and that the help she had so desperately needed would come from this house. Life threw some awful curveballs, but it also sent angels in disguise when you most desperately needed it. Ivy and Frank were definitely hers.

'Just one more thing,' Josie said.

'Yes?' Ivy asked.

'Can we come to a more permanent arrangement about rent and shopping?'

'There's plenty of time to talk about that, but if it makes you feel better then we can. Let's chat about it later.'

Before Josie could argue, determined not to take advantage of Ivy's generosity, the back door swung open.

'It's really sunny and Frank said we can have dinner outside,' Polly announced, beaming. 'Have you got a tablecloth we can put on the table?'

Ivy was more than happy to oblige. Giving Josie's hand one last affirming squeeze, she stood up from the table.

'I certainly have,' she replied. 'Dinner outside sounds like a perfect idea. It's about time we enjoyed some sunshine. And the little jam tarts you helped me make yesterday will be the perfect dessert to celebrate some happy news.'

'What happy news?' Annie instantly asked.

'I will let your mum tell you,' Ivy answered. 'But let's get that table set and then we can all get ready for dinner.'

Ivy turned back to look at Josie, who was just finishing her cup of tea with a smile that spread to her eyes.

Chapter 39

Thursday, 10 July 1941

'Hello, you two.' Ivy smiled as Betty and Daisy dropped their bags and gas masks by the back door and walked into the kitchen. 'I was just about to send out a search party. Frank got home well over an hour ago.'

Daisy instantly looked apologetic. 'Oh, sorry, it's my fault, I dragged Betty into Banners after work for a quick look round.'

'I'm teasing,' Ivy said. 'It's good to see you having a break. You girls work far too hard. I've deliberately not popped dinner out yet, as Frank said you might be a bit late. Now tell me, did you treat yourselves to anything nice?'

'Only a new lipstick each,' Betty said.

'Is that it?' Ivy asked. 'You are allowed to push the boat out every now and again. You deserve it, all the hours you put in at that factory.'

'We ended up wandering into the baby section and picked up an extra little something for Hattie.'

'Did I hear something about babies?' Josie asked, coming into the kitchen from the hallway.

'These girls have been shopping for Hattie's little one again, when he or she finally arrives,' Ivy explained.

'It can't be long now, surely,' Josie stated.

'She is looking very tired,' Daisy affirmed. 'Hattie won't say anything. You know what she's like – always determined to stay cheerful, but she looks worn-out and I get the impression just walking about is getting harder.'

'She does seem to be trundling.' Josie nodded. 'Poor luv. It takes me back. By the time you three were due,' she said, turning to Daisy, 'I was waddling around like a duck!'

'Sorry,' Daisy said, grinning.

'You were all worth every minute of the discomfort, and I'm sure Hattie will feel exactly the same way too when her little one comes along.'

'I hope so,' Daisy said. 'I think she's really missing John too.'

'I'm sure,' Josie replied, fighting back her own feelings. There wasn't a day that went by when she didn't miss her Alf. The world still seemed a very different place without him. But this conversation wasn't about Alf, and as much as Josie knew Ivy, Betty and Daisy wouldn't mind her talking about her husband, she didn't want to bring the mood down.

'So,' Josie added, genuinely intrigued, and determined to keep the conversation upbeat, 'what did you buy for Hattie's little one?'

'You'll love it, Mum,' Daisy said, picking her bag up. 'Betty and I chose it together.'

The four women sat down around the kitchen table as Daisy carefully lifted the gift from her bag. Gently removing the tissue paper, Daisy held up a beautiful lemon-coloured cotton romper, with a Broderie anglaise collar and a matching bonnet.

'Oh, isn't that beautiful,' Ivy said in awe.

'We couldn't resist,' Betty said. 'It was just too cute.'

'It really is,' Josie agreed, touching the gorgeous little outfit. 'It's so tiny too.'

'Do you think it's too small?' Daisy asked, suddenly worried.

'No. Not at all. It will be perfect. And I'm sure Hattie will be over the moon with the outfit. It really is quite lovely.'

'I know we all bought her little gifts at our get-together, but I suspect money might be a bit tight,' Betty said.

'I think you're probably right,' Josie replied.

'Diane was telling me that Hattie has already said she will come back to work as soon as she can, so she can earn some money again. She said John's parents have offered to help out financially, but I don't think she's comfortable taking money off them.'

'They are family, though,' Ivy commented. 'I know we are a proud bunch, but I suspect John's parents will want to help. Am I right in thinking this will their first grandchild?'

'Yes,' Daisy said. 'John has been sending money home too. Hopefully when the baby comes along, Hattie won't overthink it as much. I think she's always been independent, but maybe the baby will help her see things differently.'

'I'm sure it will,' Ivy said. 'I do hope she can take a bit of time off to enjoy her baby and not rush back to work too quickly.'

'Me too.' Josie nodded. 'You don't get those first few months back and it goes so quickly. It's hard work at times, but it's very special too.'

'Fingers crossed Hattie won't make any rash decisions,' Daisy said. 'I know we can't help much in the day, but we could give her a hand of a weekend and of an evening. I'm sure Patty will spend more time there than at home.'

'Hattie won't be able to keep her away,' Betty professed. 'She's been excited for months. If this baby doesn't come soon, it wouldn't surprise me if she thinks up some convoluted way to induce the labour!'

'And God help us all if Hattie doesn't have a girl. We will never hear the end of it,' Daisy affirmed.

'Saying that,' Betty interjected, 'if it's a boy, I dread to think what excuses Patty will come up with for getting her prediction wrong.'

'It doesn't bear thinking about,' Josie said, laughing.

'Right,' Ivy said. 'On that note, I'll get this chicken pie out of the oven. I'm sure everyone must be ready for their dinner.'

'Before you do,' Daisy said, 'I've got a little something for you too.'

'Me?' Ivy asked, perplexed.

'Yes.' Daisy lifted a tall, rectangular box out of her bag.

'What on earth is this for?'

'It's just a little thank you for everything you have done for us.'

Ivy glanced between Daisy and Josie, and then to Betty who was smiling, knowing how touched she would be.

'Please open it,' Daisy prompted, passing the neatly wrapped gift to Ivy.

'Okay.' Still feeling a little overwhelmed by the unexpected gesture, Ivy untied the white ribbon and matching paper, careful not to tear it, knowing it could be used again. Then from the cardboard box, she lifted out a tall milk-jug-style vase decorated with delicate pink roses.

'My goodness,' Ivy exclaimed. 'This is truly lovely.'

Popping the vase down on the table, Ivy walked round to Daisy and hugged her.

'My dear girl,' she said when she let go. 'There was absolutely no need to buy me anything, but it really is very nice. I shall always treasure it.'

'I thought you could put some of your roses from the garden in it.'

'That's a splendid idea. I shall get Frank to cut me some after tea. But again, you didn't have to spend your money on me.'

'I wanted to,' Daisy protested. 'You have been so kind to me, my mum and sisters. I just wanted you to know how much I – sorry, we – all appreciate you giving us a home.'

'Oh,' Ivy whispered, taking a white handkerchief from the cuff of her blouse and dabbing her eyes. 'You have made my eyes leak.'

'Sorry,' Daisy replied. 'I didn't mean to.'

'Don't be listening to me. I'm an emotional nitwit at times. I'm just so glad I could welcome you all into this big old house. It needs a family to fill it with joy.'

'And we love being here, don't we, Mum?'

'We do indeed,' Josie confirmed, proud of the thoughtful young woman Daisy was.

As Betty watched the emotional scene unfold, she was once again struck by how lucky they all were to have one another. In times of need, they really had pulled together. And she was sure when Hattie's baby came along, they would do exactly the same for her.

'And I'm very happy to have the best roommate a girl could ask for,' Betty added, bringing herself back to the moment.

'Me too,' Daisy replied, returning the compliment. 'Although I'm sure I have disturbed your sleep far too often.'

'Not at all. Besides which, you would do the same for me.'

Before Daisy could reiterate how grateful she had been to Betty for all the nights she had held her hand or wiped away her tears in the dead of night, the kitchen door swung open again. This time Annie and Polly burst into the room, followed by Frank.

'I think we have two very hungry little girls,' Frank announced.

Ivy looked at Annie and Polly. 'Bless you both,' she said. 'What have you been up to out there?'

'Picked some more beans, and some of the tomatoes are ready too,' Polly replied, looking very pleased with herself.

'And I found three eggs!' Annie added, holding her hands out to reveal the latest delivery from the hens.

'I must have missed them this morning,' Ivy said. 'But we shall have them for breakfast tomorrow.'

'Yummy.' Annie grinned. 'With soldiers?'

'Of course,' Ivy confirmed, happy to accommodate chucky eggs and toast, sliced into rectangles. 'Now why don't you girls go and wash your hands and I'll get dinner out of the oven.'

Carefully handing over the eggs, Annie, followed by Polly, gave their hands a scrub under the kitchen tap.

'And you,' Ivy said, turning to Frank and nodding towards the sink.

'Your wish is my command.' He chuckled.

Ten minutes later, everyone was sat down at the kitchen table as Ivy and Josie served out chicken pie, boiled potatoes and spring greens.

'This is grand, my love,' Frank said, congratulating his wife as the delicious aromas spread through the kitchen.

'You are very welcome,' Ivy replied, convinced she would never tire of being able to serve up a meal for her husband and extended family.

'Tomorrow evening, you must let me make tea,' Josie insisted. 'You do so much for us all in the week, you deserve a rest.'

'That's very kind, but I really don't mind. I'm not the one working in a mucky factory all day.'

'Even so,' Josie insisted. 'I'd like to.'

'In that case, I won't argue,' Ivy replied. 'Maybe the girls and I could make an apple pie for dessert. I collected a basketful that had fallen early from the tree today.'

'Yes please,' Annie said.

'That's that, then,' Ivy affirmed.

After everyone had finished, Betty and Daisy cleared the plates, and Josie instantly started washing up.

'Oh girls, I nearly forget,' Ivy gasped as she stood up and walked into the hall.

'Forgot what?' Betty asked.

'These,' Ivy replied as she came back into the kitchen with two letters in her hand. 'I'm so sorry. They came this morning. It completely slipped my mind when you came in.'

Betty and Daisy looked at each other, delighted smiles spreading across their faces.

'Go on,' Ivy said, handing over the mail. 'You two go and read them. Josie and I can take care of the dishes.'

'But—' Daisy started, feeling guilty that she wouldn't be helping out.

'No buts,' Ivy instructed. 'It won't take us ten minutes. Now go.'

'Thank you,' Betty said.

It didn't take any more convincing. Betty and Daisy quickly ran upstairs to their bedroom, and just as they had got into the habit of doing when letters arrived, got comfortable on their own beds before opening the missives.

For a few minutes the women fell into a companiable silence as they absorbed the latest notes they had been sent, digesting every word.

Betty opened her letter. As she had come to expect, it started with

My dearest, sweet Bet,

As always, I am missing you so much and hoping it won't be long before we see each other again.

I hope you haven't been too busy between the factory and helping out at the WVS? Please tell me you have been taking a couple of breaks to relax too, or maybe been to see a picture with Daisy?

While I remember, I should tell you Oliver still seems to be completely smitten by Daisy. You should see his face when a letter arrives from her. I've never seen him smile so much. I literally can't stop him grinning. You must tell me, are Oliver's letters having the same effect on Daisy? I do hope so. As soon as we both get some leave, I will bring him back to Sheffield with me, if Daisy would like me to.

Now, Betty, I know no matter how many times I say this to you, I strongly suspect you will worry, but try not to if you can. As you know, I can't say much as all our letters are censored, but I'm pretty

much fully operational now. I promise I will always do my best to stay safe. I will come home to you, Betty, don't ever doubt that. I've already been on one mission. I can't say where, as they will only delete it, but it went okay. I did it, Betty. I really did it. Didn't I tell you that I would be the greatest pilot the RAF has ever seen? We all got back in one piece, and I handled the plane without any problems at all. What was quite unexpected was after we landed, we were bombarded with questions by some of the trainees. We were made to feel like veterans, which seemed quite strange after our debut operation.

But as I say, I am here to tell the tale, Betty, so you mustn't worry. I'm not sure how long we will remain at this base, but I will let you know if we are posted on.

In the meantime, please do take care. I hope Hattie is doing well. It can't be long until her baby is due now. I hope everything goes well. I have no doubt you will all be looking after her, and I bet Patty is chomping at the bit to find out if the baby really is a little girl. You must write and tell me as soon as he or she is born.

In the meantime, I will be thinking of you, Betty. Your photo remains in my breast pocket close to my heart, so you are always with me.

I love you, now and forever.
William xxxx

Betty held the letter to her chest as she fought back the tears that were threatening to erupt from behind her eyes. So, this was it. Her precious William really was a fully qualified pilot at what felt like one of the most dangerous moments of their lifetime.

'Oh dear,' she whispered.

'Are you okay?' Daisy asked.

'Sorry,' Betty responded, not realizing she had expressed her concern out loud and trying to shake herself out of the entanglement of worry she had so quickly found herself in.

'What did William say?' Daisy asked gently.

'Erm,' Betty muttered, still trying to absorb what was in his letter.

'Betty,' Daisy prompted, seeing how worried her friend now looked. 'Is everything okay?'

'Well, yes, I suppose it is. I'm guessing Oliver may have told you the same?'

'Go on,' Daisy urged, not wanting to guess what William had said.

'I knew it was coming, especially after his last letter,' Betty began, holding the piece of paper with one hand, anxiously rubbing her thumb against her fingers. 'I just suppose I didn't want to think about it.'

Daisy slid down off her own bed and came to sit next to her friend.

'William's now fully operational?' Daisy asked.

Betty nodded, just about managing to remain composed. 'Has Oliver told you the same?'

'He has.'

'Ignore me. I'm just being a bit of a ninny. I guess it was just hard seeing it written down.'

'Of course it is,' Daisy affirmed, wrapping one of her arms around Betty's shoulders. 'He's your fiancé. It's only natural. You wouldn't be human if you didn't feel frightened.'

'I just wish this rotten war was over and all the people we love and care about were home.'

'I know,' Daisy comforted. 'I'm sure it will be soon. It can't last forever.'

Betty looked at Daisy, and quickly checked herself. Her William might be in a dangerous role, but he was alive, unlike Daisy's dad. But despite that, Daisy was being the brave one.

'I'm sorry. I didn't mean to get so het up.'

'You have nothing to apologize for. It's okay to be angry and upset, or just worried.'

'Thank you. There are times when I just get scared. I do worry about William, but you don't need to hear me getting myself in a tizz.'

'Nonsense. You are hardly getting yourself in a tizz. And even if you were, it would be okay.'

'Thank you,' Betty said gratefully. 'You have had to cope with so much, though.'

'I have,' Daisy admitted. 'But that doesn't make your fears any less important. You have always been there for me, and no matter what happens I will be there for you.'

'Oh Daisy,' Betty said, letting her head rest on her friend's shoulder. 'You really are quite remarkable and such a good friend. I do have a lot to be grateful for.'

'We both do. And we will get through this. I promise you.'

With that, the two women embraced, tightly wrapping their arms around one another, each knowing the other would be there to carry her through whatever lay ahead, no matter how difficult it might be.

Chapter 40

Tuesday, 15 July 1941

'Are you all right, luv?' Diane asked as she popped a couple of slices of toast on a plate in front of Hattie.

'I'm just a bit tired. I didn't sleep well,' Hattie replied.

'Hopefully the day will pass quickly,' Diane said, her maternal instinct on high alert. 'Are you in any discomfort?'

'A few niggles, but no worse than normal.'

'Do you think you should be going to work today?'

'Absolutely. Besides which, I'd be bored at home,' Hattie replied, not really acknowledging the pains in her lower abdomen.

'Please make sure you take it steady, luv,' Diane said, not sure if her daughter was putting on a brave face or if she really did just feel a little uncomfortable.

'I will,' Hattie promised. 'But to be honest, it's really not very hard when I'm sat behind a desk all day. And honestly, I don't feel any different to how I've felt the last couple of weeks.'

'Okay,' Diane conceded. What she didn't say, though, was that Hattie might look back, after her baby came along and she didn't have a minute to herself, and wish she'd enjoyed the chance to be bored. But Diane also knew that most new mums only realized this with hindsight too, so she kept her thoughts locked away. She knew Hattie was determined to work as long as she could, and nothing Diane said would persuade her otherwise.

Even so, minutes later, as the pair walked to work, Diane couldn't help but worry.

'Have you had any more twinges or tightenings?' Diane gently probed.

'No,' Hattie replied with a small shake of her head. 'I think the baby is just lying at the bottom of my tummy now.'

'Are you in any pain?'

'I'm not actually. I'm just a bit tired, that's all. I'm sure if I get an early night tonight, I'll feel better.'

'We can slow down,' Diane suggested, trying to hide her concern.

'If we go any slower, I'll be crawling.' Hattie laughed. 'I promise I'm okay. You don't need to worry.'

But it was impossible for Diane to do anything but. She felt more protective than ever of her daughter.

'She's not daft,' Dolly tried to reassure her friend later, after Diane had explained how drained Hattie had looked. 'And I'm sure Mrs Hull will keep a close eye on her.'

'I know you're right. I would just rather—' Diane sighed but then cut herself short. She had said the same thing to Dolly countless times and was beginning to sound like a stuck record. 'Oh, I don't know. I just want her to be okay.'

'And she will be, duck,' Dolly said, passing Diane a freshly brewed cuppa. 'Here. Have this. You will feel better afterwards. And I promise you if anything does happen, you will be the first to know. Someone will come and fetch you straight away.'

Diane knew Dolly was right, but for the entire morning she was on high alert. Every time someone walked up to the canteen counter, she was convinced they were going to tell her Hattie was either in labour or had collapsed in pain. Only when she saw Hattie enter the dining hall just after midday did she take a breath of relief.

'I'm all right,' Hattie mouthed across the busy canteen, reading her mum's mind.

'Okay,' Diane said out loud, but more to placate her daughter. In her eyes, Hattie still looked pale as she hobbled across the canteen, slower than a snail.

'I have to say, Hattie looks incredibly well for how far gone she is,' Dolly, who was stood next to her also serving out hot meals, commented.

'Yes. I suppose she does,' Diane said, not sure who she was trying to convince more.

Hattie waddled her way over to the table she and her friends shared and plonked herself down.

'I saw you coming,' Patty said, putting a mug of tea in front of Hattie.

'Thank you. I might get some water too. It's been warm and stuffy in the office all morning.'

Before she could attempt to get a glass, Patty was already on her feet again.

'I'll get it,' she insisted. 'You need to rest.'

'Not you as well.' Hattie half laughed, rolling her eyes in mock frustration. 'My mum must have said the very same thing one hundred times.'

'Well, it's true,' Patty protested vehemently. 'And what sort of best friend would I be if I wasn't looking after you.'

'I'm guessing I don't have any say in the matter?'

'I don't think there's any point arguing, duck.' Frank chuckled. 'You'll not stop Patty fussing.'

'I'm not fussing!' Patty protested. 'I'm just looking after Hattie.'

'I promise I'm okay,' Hattie insisted, despite feeling a little woozy. 'I'm pregnant, not ill,' she added as if to remind herself more than anyone else.

'It doesn't matter,' Patty exclaimed. 'I'm your best friend, so I have the right to look after you.'

'Thank you.' Hattie smiled. 'I know I look a bit worn-out, but I promise I'm okay.' She had convinced herself that the tiredness and slight nausea she was feeling were typical of anyone so late in their pregnancy.

'I can assure you,' Nancy interjected, 'I looked a right state when I was heavily pregnant with both of mine, Billy in particular. His constant wriggling meant I barely got a wink of sleep and looked as though I'd been dragged through a hedge backwards.'

'The mornings are getting harder,' Hattie confessed. 'It takes me a while to get going. Mum was fretting this morning. I seem to improve as the day goes along, so hopefully today won't be any different.' But even as Hattie said the words, she felt a strange tugging sensation from the depths of her tummy. Not wanting to cause a fuss, she blinked away the dull ache, sure it was just another tightening.

'Fingers crossed, luv,' Nancy replied. 'I think I was in a state of complete exhaustion for the last few weeks.'

'Not long to go now,' Betty commented.

'It does feel rather imminent,' Hattie confessed, endeavouring to keep her voice level.

'I can't wait! I am going to be the best aunty,' Patty announced, causing everyone around the table to smile, aware of how excited Patty was about the new arrival.

'I have no doubt,' Hattie said, pleased the conversation had moved on slightly. Despite how bemused she was by Patty's exuberant enthusiasm, she also knew she was very lucky to have such a loyal friend.

'You will never get rid of her.' Archie laughed.

'Just think,' Frank added, turning to Archie, 'you will get a break.'

'Oi!' Patty gasped. 'I'm here, you know.'

'We are only teasing, duck,' Frank responded. 'You know that.'

'And I will be grateful for the company and a helping hand,' Hattie added, smiling at her friend.

'Thank you,' Patty said fervently.

'So, what are you all up to this weekend?' Hattie asked, thinking it was probably wise to change the subject before Patty took offence at the light-hearted banter.

Patty beamed. 'Archie is taking me to see a picture.'

'That will be lovely,' Hattie said. 'What are you going to see?'

'*The Philadelphia Story*,' Patty replied. 'Cary Grant is in it.'

'Oh, you are in for a treat, then.' Hattie smiled.

'I know.'

'Erm,' Archie interrupted, bemused.

'You know I only have eyes for you really,' Patty insisted.

'How about you, Nancy?' Hattie asked as the table laughed at Patty, who was quickly trying to dig herself out of the hole she had got herself into.

'Bert has got a shift with the Home Guard, so I think Doris and I are going to take the kids to High Hazels Park. The funfair is back, so that should be fun.'

'Ooh, maybe we could go too, Archie?' Patty suggested, pleased the conversation had moved on.

'You would be very welcome,' Nancy replied.

'I'm sorry to spoil your plans, ladies, but I'm afraid we need to get back to it,' Frank said, rising from his chair.

'It always goes too quick,' Patty groaned, taking the final slurp of her now tepid tea.

'Ah well,' Frank chuckled, 'the sooner we get going, the sooner we get finished.'

'I suppose,' Patty conceded.

As they all stood up, Hattie felt a piercing pain ripple across her stomach.

'Ouch!' she gasped.

'What is it? Are you okay?' Patty asked instantly.

'I don't know,' Hattie whimpered. Suddenly overcome with pain, she gripped her stomach with one hand and grabbed the back of the chair with her other.

Within seconds Patty was by her side.

'Hattie,' Patty repeated. 'Is something wrong?'

'Erm—' But before she could finish, Hattie felt something warm seep down the inside of her legs.

Chapter 41

'Hattie!' Nancy exclaimed. 'Your waters have broken. You need to sit down.' Then turning to the rest of the group, she added, 'Someone go and see if they have got any towels in the kitchen.'

'Am I in labour?' Hattie asked, panic-stricken. 'Or is it another false alarm?'

'I think you probably are,' Nancy confirmed, keeping her voice calm. 'But that's not to say anything is going to happen straight away. These babies have a tendency to take their time in making their first appearance.'

But no sooner had the words passed Nancy's lips, than Hattie gasped in agony again.

'Ow!' she cried, her eyes watering. These pains were on a different level to what she had felt before.

'Okay, Hattie,' Nancy said, taking control. 'We need to get you somewhere a bit quieter.'

'Where can we take her?' Patty asked, looking as frightened as Hattie.

'Do you think you can walk?' Nancy asked.

'I don't know. It really hurts.' *Why hadn't she listened to her mum this morning, or her own body for that matter?* Hattie silently admonished herself.

Nancy looked at Betty, who would normally have a plan for any emergency, but even she looked slightly out of her depth. Thinking on her feet, Nancy turned towards the canteen counter and the kitchen. Dolly, Josie and Diane would be there. And there was bound to be somewhere clean to lay Hattie down if it came to it, let alone an abundance of towels and hot water.

'Right,' Nancy said authoritatively. 'We are going to help you walk to the kitchen. Do you think you can manage that?'

'The kitchen?' Patty chirped, the high-pitched inflection in her voice betraying the horror she felt.

'It will be better than the workshops,' Nancy reasoned.

'Okay, ladies, I don't think you will want me by your side, but is there anything I can do?' Frank asked pragmatically.

'I guess you could ask if there is anyone who has ever delivered a baby?' Nancy suggested.

'Am I really going to have my baby here?' Hattie whimpered as she tried to control the sharp stabbing pains that were searing through the bottom of her abdomen.

'There's a chance you are,' Nancy said gently. 'But let's just see what happens. Now, do you think you could walk, with a bit of help?'

'I'll try.'

Instantly Betty and Daisy went to either side of Hattie in a bid to be useful, while Patty still looked in a state of shock.

'I'll clear the way,' Archie offered, already moving chairs to ensure Hattie had a path to the kitchen.

As the group slowly zigzagged their way through the maze of tables, they looked quite the sight, attracting the attention of the workers they passed.

'Is she all right?' one woman asked.

'Poor luv, she looks like she's about to faint,' said another.

'Bleedin' 'eck, the poor lass doesn't look s' grand.'

'She's in labour,' Patty announced, perturbed by the comments.

But if she was trying to stop the remarks, Patty's outburst had the opposite effect.

'By 'eck. Is the poor lass going to have a bairn 'ere?' one woman quizzed. 'Poor luv.'

'Good luck, duck,' someone else called.

But Hattie was oblivious to the heckles as she tried her best to concentrate on putting one foot in front of the other. Hattie now realized all the discomfort she had been feeling was her body's way of telling her that the time had arrived for her baby to make his or her appearance.

'Dolly!' Patty shouted as the party approached. 'We need help. Quick.'

The canteen manager looked up from the counter where she had been dishing out another portion of today's speciality and gasped as she took in the sight before her. 'Oh, Lord, is this what I think it is?'

'It is,' Nancy confirmed calmly. 'I think Hattie is in labour.'

'Chuff me. Right, take her around the back. Diane is through there. She was just getting the next pie out of the oven.'

Archie stepped aside as the group of women passed him and ushered Hattie past the till, behind the serving counter, and into the depths of the kitchen.

'Let me know if you need anything,' he said as Dolly gave him a final glance.

'Actually,' Dolly said, 'can you take over from me? This queue ain't going anywhere and I think I'm going to be needed back there.' Dolly glanced from the line of workers waiting for their snap to over her shoulder where Hattie had been led.

'Erm,' Archie hesitated, more comfortable at manoeuvring a crane than tending to a haul of hungry workers.

'Come on, Archie,' Josie encouraged. 'I'll show yer what to do.' Then turning to Dolly, she added, 'You go. Archie and I will hold the fort here.'

'Okay.' Dolly nodded, indicating to Archie to take over quick sharp.

Within seconds, seeing he had no choice, Archie was behind the counter with a ladle in hand, and Dolly dashed to the emergency that was unfolding behind her.

By the time Dolly had appeared by Hattie's side, Diane was already holding her daughter's hand.

'You're going to be okay, luv,' she said to her daughter, who was sat on a chair gritting her teeth and trying to breathe through a piercing contraction.

'It really hurts, Mum,' Hattie whispered, her eyes misty with tears.

'I know, luv. Just squeeze my hand every time it starts to hurt.'

As Diane tried to soothe her daughter, Betty and Daisy flew around the kitchen, scooping up as many clean tea towels as they could.

'We will need boiling water, too,' Nancy said.

'We have plenty of that, duck,' Dolly affirmed. 'I'll get a couple of pans of water boiling.'

'Am I really going to give birth here?' Hattie repeated in between the crippling pains that had overtaken her body at a speed she hadn't been prepared for.

'We can try and get you to a hospital,' Betty said. 'Frank can arrange a car to take you.'

'Okay.' Hattie nodded, but as she attempted to stand up, the searing spasms ripping across the bottom of her tummy forced her back down.

'I can't,' she cried, her face crumpling in agony.

'Okay, luv,' Diane said in as reassuring a tone as she could muster. 'You're going to be all right.'

Diane desperately looked to Dolly, who was already pulling out a few blankets and cushions from a cupboard.

'I kept these here in case we ever got stuck in an air raid overnight and couldn't get to the shelter.'

Then looking at Hattie, Dolly added, 'This might not be where you imagined having your baby, but we are going to make you as comfy as possible. Frank will have raised the alarm and will be trying to get a doctor here, but in the meantime let's make sure you are ready if this baby is about to make an appearance.'

Hattie's eyes betrayed the fear she was feeling. It was hard enough not having John nearby, but she had assumed when the time came for her to give birth it would be in the comfort of her home, and Mrs Taylor would be by her side. *Why had she ignored all the warnings her body had given her?*

'Will my baby be okay?' Hattie managed to murmur in between winces.

'Absolutely,' Dolly confirmed without an ounce of doubt in her voice. 'You are surrounded by a team of brilliant women, three of whom have brought babies of their own into this world. We aren't about to let anything happen to yours.'

Dolly wasn't sure who she was trying to convince. It was one thing giving birth, it was another delivering a baby, but now wasn't the time to dwell on the matter. What Hattie needed now was reassurance, and Dolly wasn't going to fail her friend at the first hurdle.

'Right, let's get you comfortable,' Dolly said, taking charge. She laid the thick woollen blankets on the floor and put the cushions at one end. 'Let's ease you down,' she said kindly.

With Diane on one side and Dolly on the other, they gently helped a now frightened and anxious Hattie onto the floor.

'Mum,' Hattie whimpered. 'You'll stay with me, won't you?'

'Of course,' Diane said, kneeling down next to her daughter and taking hold of one of her hands. 'I will be here every step of the way.'

'Okay, Hattie,' Dolly gently interjected. 'I'm no midwife, but I was on hand when both my granddaughters were born, so I'm going to do my best to help you until Frank gets us someone else.'

Hattie looked down her body at Dolly, who was positioned at her knees, which were bridged into an arch, and took comfort in her friend's calming tone.

'What do I need to do?' Hattie's voice quivered, her face contorted with pain.

'Just take deep breaths,' Dolly gently instructed. 'Concentrate on your breathing.'

Hattie closed her eyes, bit down on her bottom lip and tried to focus on what Dolly had asked her to do. For a few moments a feeling of calm came over her. She could sense her mum on one side of her, and on the other Patty was placing a cool cloth on her forehead. And for those few seconds, everything felt serene. But then, just as quickly as the moment of tranquillity had started, a fierce pain shot through her.

'Arrrgh,' Hattie gasped, a deep guttural moan coming from deep inside her.

'Hattie,' Dolly said, going into full midwifery, 'I think your baby is on its way. I can see the head.'

'What? Really?' Patty responded, looking utterly stunned at Dolly's proclamation.

'Yes. I think so. It would appear this little one didn't want to hang around.'

'I can't do it.' Hattie grimaced through the searing agony that was draining her of all her energy.

'Come on, luv,' Diane encouraged. 'I know it hurts, but you can do this. I promise you.'

'Muuuum,' Hattie cried in response, unable to further articulate how dreadful she felt.

'Just a couple of big pushes and your baby should be here,' Dolly reassured Hattie.

Betty, Daisy and Nancy, who were also still in the kitchen, all took a collective intake of breath. They were a few steps away from Hattie, providing Patty with fresh cloths and ready with the spare towels.

'You can do it, luv,' Nancy whispered, willing her friend through the next few minutes.

'It hurts so much,' Hattie trembled.

'I know, but you're nearly there,' Diane said as Hattie's grip on her own hand tightened, indicating another contraction was taking hold. She could have kicked herself for not realizing that morning that her daughter was probably in the early stages of labour.

'Push now,' Dolly said, mustering all the enthusiasm she could in a bid to hide how terrified she was by the fact she really didn't know how to deliver a baby. She was acting on instinct and memory alone, while simultaneously praying she wouldn't let Hattie down.

Hattie squeezed her eyes shut. And as she tried to follow Dolly's orders, Hattie felt as if she was on a different plane, the red-hot pain dispersing as she concentrated on pushing as hard as she could.

'That's it,' she heard her mum say.

'You can do it, Hattie,' Patty encouraged.

But it was as though she was no longer in her own body. Everything was happening around her; Hattie's senses had been numbed.

Then suddenly, an excruciating tearing sensation coursed through her, catapulting Hattie back to the moment. The violent scream she emitted bounced off the kitchen walls, her whole body overtaken with a pain she had never experienced before.

'That's it, duck,' Dolly encouraged. 'One more little push.'

With an inner strength Hattie didn't even know she possessed, she concentrated on pushing with everything she had left to force her baby from her own body, gripping her mum's hand as tightly as she could.

Then the pain that had consumed Hattie vanished as quickly as it had arrived, and a feeling of relief flooded her, a new noise filled the room. The sound of a baby's first cry.

'You've done it, duck,' Dolly cheered as she held the tiny baby in her arms.

Hattie opened her eyes and looked to Dolly, a surge of emotions soaring through her.

'My baby,' she whispered.

Dolly quickly indicated to Diane to cut the umbilical cord with the sterilized scissors that Betty had retrieved from the kitchen. As soon as the task was done, Dolly carefully placed the now squealing newborn on Hattie's chest.

Propping herself up slightly with the aid of some extra towels, Hattie gazed down at her baby. 'A girl,' she whispered. 'I've got a little girl.'

'You have that, duck,' Dolly confirmed. 'And a real beauty she is too.'

As Hattie gazed down at her daughter, an overwhelming feeling of love flooded her. Her baby's little body was still wrinkly and blotchy, but Hattie didn't care. The pain she had endured had vanished and all she could focus on was how utterly beautiful her little girl was, and the fact this tiny little dot of a child was actually hers. Hattie counted her daughter's tiny fingers and toes, and marvelled at her perfect cherry lips as she held her in her arms.

'Hello,' Hattie whispered, placing the most gentle of kisses on her baby's soft head, which was already covered in a mass of dark hair.

As if in reply, her little girl let out a tiny mew of a cry.

'Oh.' Hattie smiled, astonished by the bird-like squeak coming from her daughter.

'She might be hungry, luv,' Diane suggested, the sight of her own daughter becoming a mum causing her eyes to tear up.

'Shall we try and get you a bit more comfortable first?' Dolly said.

Hattie looked round at her surroundings for the first time since her contractions had started, taking in the spot on which she had just given birth. She was at the back of the kitchen, sat on a pile of now very bloody towels, only metres away from the hustle and bustle of the canteen.

'I've got more blankets,' Josie said, fortuitously appearing from the serving hatch, then stopped in her tracks as she took in the sight before her. 'Oh wow! Congratulations, luv,' she said with a huge smile.

'And she's a girl!' Patty announced.

'You won the bet,' Hattie replied, managing a small giggle and causing Patty's face to light up even further.

'Aww,' Josie continued. 'You have a little friend for life there.'

'I hope so.' Then turning to her mum, Hattie squeezed Diane's hand. 'Thank you,' she mouthed, the words barely audible. Those two small words said so much more that neither Hattie nor Diane needed to expand on right now, both knowing how grateful they were for one another, and now a wonderful new addition to their small but perfect family.

Hattie's friends helped her get more comfortable, using the blankets and cushions to create a makeshift bed. Then they quietly stood back and watched in awe as the new mum and her baby spent their first precious moments together. For the time being, at least, the worries of the world were put to one side. The look of absolute love on Hattie's face revealed how much she already adored her daughter. The bond was instant. And the tiny little dot of a baby seemed to be gazing back at her mum in bewildered adoration. Already they were a unit. Diane was sat next to her daughter and granddaughter, her eyes glistening, but this time the tears were borne from gratification and joy. Their healing may be far from over, but as Diane and Hattie beamed down at the newest member of their family, their delighted smiles revealed the fulfilment they had waited so long for.

Epilogue

Dearest John,

Thank you for your last letter. As always, I cherished every word and count down the days until your next note arrives. Reading your words, and knowing you are safe, makes my day.

I have started reading your missives to Tilly. That way she can hear about you too, not that I ever stop talking about you. We point at your photo next to my bed every morning as soon as we wake up and again as I put Tilly to bed of an evening. I'm convinced 'Dada' will be the first word she says, the amount I say it to her. She really is an absolute delight. I still have to pinch myself that she is really ours. She makes me smile so much. I can't wait for you to meet her. Like me, you will be completely smitten. She is such a happy little thing, always grinning, and her giggle is so infectious. Although we have had a few grizzles over the last few days – I think her first tooth might make an appearance soon. She's got ever so rosy cheeks, keeps putting her fist in her mouth and needs a few extra cuddles – not that I mind. I could sit and snuggle her all day long, given half the chance.

I feel ever so lucky that I have been able to take these past six months off work. I can't thank your mum and dad enough for all the help, it has meant I've had the loveliest of times with Tilly, and for that I'm forever grateful.

The time has flown by, and I go back to work on Monday. I am feeling a little nervous about leaving Tilly. I'm sure it will be an absolute wrench, but she will be in safe hands. It's all finalized, your mum and Patty's mum, Angie, are going to take it in turns to look after Tilly. I have no doubt she will be spoilt rotten! And as you can imagine, Patty is beside herself with excitement at the thought of our little girl being at her house two or three days a week. There's no risk of Tilly being in want of any cuddles.

Everyone at work is doing as well as can be. In between shifts, Betty and Daisy are still busy volunteering at the WVS. Ivy and Josie go along too. They are all doing more than their bit to help. To be honest, I think it helps them all in different ways. Daisy feels like it's her way of paying tribute to her dad and Josie likes to keep herself busy. Understandably, Betty constantly worries about William.

On a lighter note, Daisy is still gushing about Oliver. Every time she visits, she tells me about every letter he writes. It seems to have really given her a boost. It's lovely to see her smiling again. She's hoping Oliver will be able to squeeze in another visit to Sheffield with William when they next get some leave. I hope so, Daisy deserves some happiness after all the heartache she, her mum and sisters have suffered.

Please let me know how you are getting on. I know you can't tell me much, but I hope that the battles over there are over soon.

Anyway, my love, I best come to a close as it's getting late, and no doubt Tilly will have me up at the crack of dawn tomorrow. She's still an early riser! I know whatever I say, you will, but please try not to worry about me. I promise I am taking care. One day all this will be over, and we will be together as a family.

Sending all my love,
Your wife,
Hattie xxx

Author's Note

I started the Steel Girls series after spending two years researching the true life stories of the women who worked in the factories that lined the River Don during World War Two. Their tales of hardship, strength and resilience left me humbled and in complete admiration of what this tremendous generation endured.

Many were mums or young girls, with no experience of what it was like to be employed in one of the ginormous windowless factories, which were described on more than one occasion as entering 'hell on earth'. The deafening, ear-splitting cacophony of noise mixed with the perilously dangerous but accepted working conditions, alongside the relentless and exhaustingly long shifts, was a huge culture shock for so many of the women who walked through those factory doors for the first time.

Those who had young children had no choice but to hand their precious sons and daughters over to grandparents or leave them in the care of older siblings, some of them only just out of school themselves, but expected to grow up fast and to do their bit to help.

What struck me in the course of my research, though, was how little resistance was offered to this new arduous, strangely unfamiliar, and frequently quite terrifying way of life. 'We were just doing what was needed' was an all-too-common answer when I asked the women I had the pleasure of talking to why they so eagerly took on the somewhat risky roles they volunteered for. 'We had no choice. It was what was needed to keep the factories going.' This is true, the foundries desperately needed workers, with so many of the opposite sex signing up to begin a 'new adventure'.

It soon became clear to me that this band of formidable, proud and hardworking Yorkshire women were not going to just stand by and let Hitler and his troops wreak havoc across Europe and beyond, without them doing what they could to aid their husbands, brothers, sons and uncles, who were off fighting someone else's war.

Over and over again, I was left in complete awe of how much the women of Sheffield sacrificed, day in and day out, for six long years. It's hard for most of us to comprehend now what a difficult and seemingly never-ending length of time this was. As well as working night and day as crane drivers, turners, making camouflage netting, or working next to a red-hot and at times fatal Bessemer Converter, they were also terrified by the very realistic fear they may never see their loved ones ever again.

One lady, Kathleen Roberts, told me that whenever a shooting star was seen going over a factory, it was a sign another soldier had fallen and a telegram bearing the bad news would be delivered soon afterwards. To live with that level of sheer terror, let alone cope with the ominous air raid sirens that indicated the Luftwaffe could be on their way, is truly unimaginable. But this is the harsh and constant reality that thousands of women lived with across Sheffield.

It wasn't all doom and gloom, though. The one thing that struck a chord with me while talking to the women and their families was the way in which they counteracted the harshness life had thrown at them. They created unbreakable bonds with their new fellow workmates and a camaraderie that even Hitler himself couldn't break. In a determined bid to 'keep up morale', our feisty factory sisters focused on safeguarding a warm community spirit to keep them all going when times got hard. Friendships were created in the most unlikely of circumstances, often amongst women who would never normally mix, lipsticks were snapped in half and divided between colleagues, and a single wedding dress could be worn a dozen times to ensure a Sheffield bride didn't walk down the aisle without looking her absolute best. It really was the era of sharing what you had with your neighbour and never letting someone in need go without.

Of course, it would be easy to romanticize this period, or hail it as 'the good old days', but the reality is it wasn't that either. It was simply a case of facing head on the atrocities and getting on with it as best you could. Some had it easier than others, but no matter what, all these women woke up in September 1939 to a new life and somehow managed to take it in their stride. But they really didn't have much choice with no savings to fall back on to tide them over, or a welfare state to lighten the load; it was a case of 'cracking on' and doing what was needed.

In 2009, Kathleen Roberts rang the *Sheffield Star* and asked why she and others like her, who had sacrificed so much of their lives, had never been thanked, after watching a TV show on the Land Girls. What started as a frustrated phone call, developed into a campaign by the local paper to ensure that the women of the city, who had worked day and night in the steel works, were finally recognized. Kathleen, alongside Kit Sollitt, Dorothy Slingsby, and Ruby Gascoigne, representing this whole generation of women, were whisked down to London to be personally thanked by the then Prime Minister, Gordon Brown. Afterwards, a grassroots campaign was launched by the *Sheffield Star* to fundraise for a statue representing the female steelworkers to be commissioned and erected in Barker's Pool, in the city centre, directly outside the dance they would often visit on a Saturday to escape the drudgery of their lives.

In June 2016, the larger-than-life bronze statue, paid for entirely by the people of Sheffield, was unveiled to the sheer and rapturous delight of the still surviving women of steel, their contribution to the war effort now immortalized.

Although the characters in this book are entirely fictional, their experiences a result of my creative imagination having a bit of fun with itself, the truth is that every page is based on the interviews I conducted, factual books I've read from the period, and the ongoing research I'm still undertaking. Any factual errors made are my own.

I hope within my books that I can also help keep this generation's memory alive. I interviewed women who flew up crane ladders, others who were scared witless, and many who remember only too clearly what it was like to live in absolute poverty. So, despite the poetic creation of Betty, Nancy and Patty, I can envisage their real-life counterparts, hear their voices and recall their experiences – the reality of it is, I simply couldn't make the raw bones of some of these stories up. Only after hearing first-hand how terrifying it was to live through the Sheffield Blitz could I put pen to paper and serve our real women of steel the justice they rightfully deserve.

I truly hope, as a Sheffielder (well, just about – I've been here 28 years), I have served the women of this hard-working industrious city well and you have enjoyed reading this book as much as I have writing it.

Acknowledgments

Firstly, I would like to thank every female steelworker of the First and Second World War and their family members, who over the course of the last seven years have so generously given up their time to talk to me, recalled memories and answered my endless questions. Without these women, the Steel Girls series would not be possible. Although the characters are fictional, they are created from the true life stories that have been shared with me. I am also so grateful to the women and their relatives for their ongoing and tremendous support, which means so much. At every step of the way they have been my biggest cheerleaders, and for that I will be forever grateful.

I am indebted to every author, historian, journalist and social commentator who enabled me to look at this period of time in extra detail, allowing me to understand the wider issues and feelings of the women who lived and worked through World War Two, creating a new way of life in the most troubled and hardest of times.

I must say a huge thank you to the fabulous Sylvia Jones, whose own 'little nannan', Ada Clarke, was a Woman of Steel. Sylvia has become my 'go to' expert on anything Attercliffe or Darnall based. Sylvia has taken me on several walking tours of the area, pointing out all the old shops, picture houses and pubs so I could envisage all these landmarks, which was utterly invaluable. I'd like to add my thanks to the late Dick Starkey, who recorded his wartime RAF memories in his book *A Lancaster Pilot's Impression on Germany*, which I have read from cover to cover, after another reader, Sandra Kay, pointed me to it.

I must also say how grateful I am to every book blogger who has been kind enough to support me, continually shouting about the books and offering immense support.

Enormous thanks must be given to the extremely dedicated Elizabeth Counsell at Northbank Talent Management, who is always on hand to offer reassurance, encouragement, and invaluable advice.

I must also offer the greatest of thanks to my extremely conscientious and talented editor, Priyal Agrawal, who has shown so much enthusiasm and passion for this book, for which I am eternally grateful.

I must offer my sincere thanks to my magician-like copyeditor, Eldes Tran. A huge thanks to Anna Sikorska for designing the most fitting and beautiful of covers. I'd also like to extend my gratitude to Georgia Hester for helping create the publicity for The Steel Girls and to

Emily Scorer and Brogan Furey in sales, for getting this book on actual shelves.

I am so grateful to each and every one of my family members and truly amazing friends, who have offered unfaltering support in writing the book. As always, I can't fail to mention my good friend and long-suffering running mate, Leanne Hawkes, who has very patiently lived every one of my books with me, listening to me three times a week as we pound the hills of Millhouse Green, and kept me sane throughout. I think at least two of my characters are named after members of her family, including Ivy (Leanne's lovely mum and now Betty's landlady), which we decided on during one particularly rainy and windy run. I must also thank Ann Cusack for offering relentless support and being the greatest friend anyone could ever wish for.

I would also like to say the biggest thank you to the truly amazing, and quite frankly fabulous, group of people I work with at the University of Sheffield, who have always been my greatest cheerleaders.

I cannot end this passage of gratitude without acknowledging my two amazing children, Archie and Tilly. They are simply the best, even if my now teenage son rolls his eyes when I mention anything that isn't gaming or ice hockey focused. I sincerely hope I have instilled into them that if you work hard enough for something, you can achieve your dreams, no matter how big or insurmountable they might feel.

Go back to the beginning of the Steel Girls series

With war declared, these brave women will step up and do their bit for their country . . .

The Steel Girls start off as strangers but quickly forge an unbreakable bond of friendship as these feisty factory sisters vow to keep the foundry fires burning during wartime.

Don't miss this festive tale of courage and friendship on the Home Front

As the Steel Girls face their first Christmas at war, can they come together this winter?

In the harsh winter of 1939, our feisty factory sisters must rally around each other to find hope and comfort this Christmas season.

Catch up with the third heartwarming book in the Steel Girls series

As the war rages on, can they be there for each other?

In spring 1940, the war is raging on but the Steel Girls find themselves fighting battles closer to home . . .

Be swept away by the next gripping tale of bravery in the Steel Girls series

In their darkest days, they'll find the courage to carry on . . .

As the Steel Girls come together to be there in Nancy's hour of need, will life ever be the same again?

Make sure you've read all the books in the heartwarming Steel Girls series!

With their city under fire, can they find hope in each other?

As the bombs begin to fall, with heartbreak on the horizon, will the Steel Girls find shelter together?

ONE PLACE. MANY STORIES

Bold, innovative and empowering publishing.

FOLLOW US ON:

@HQStories